# ANOTHER
## *Man's*
# WIFE

OTHER BOOKS BY SHONDA CHEEKES
*In the Midst of it All*

# ANOTHER Man's WIFE

## SHONDA CHEEKES

**SBI**

**STREBOR BOOKS**
NEW YORK LONDON TORONTO SYDNEY

Published by

SBI

Strebor Books
P.O. Box 6505
Largo, MD 20792
http://www.streborbooks.com

This book is a work of fiction. Names, characters, places and incidents
are products of the author's imagination or are used fictitiously. Any
resemblance to actual events or locales or persons, living or dead, is
entirely coincidental.

Cover Design: www.mariondesigns.com

ISBN  0-7432-9611-7
LCCN 2003111334

First Strebor Books mass market paperback edition August 2006

10  9  8  7  6  5  4  3  2  1

Manufactured in the United States of America

For information regarding special discounts for bulk purchases,
please contact Simon & Schuster Special Sales at 1-800-456-6798
or business@simonandschuster.com

# DEDICATION

*"Friends are precious gifts that we give to ourselves."*

To Zane…
for always knowing that I could
and never letting me forget it.
Thanks for being a precious gift.

# ACKNOWLEDGMENTS

Like most people who are blessed with something extraordinary, I would like to thank my creator first. Without Him, nothing would be.

**Very Special Peeps:** Calina and Ramzey—the greatest works I will ever create. Thank you for being patient when Mommy needed it most. I love you both very much! Mama, for teaching me about strength and faith and that nothing is too big to overcome as long as you believe. Zane—what can I say? You have definitely been a big factor in making my dream into a reality. I just hope I can reach the heights with my work that you have with yours. Michelle V., you will eternally be my sisterfriend who owns a big space in my heart. Thanks for being a part of my life. Eric Jerome Dickey, thanks for announcing my book to the world via your acknowledgements in *The Other Woman*. You have definitely been a good friend and a great mentor.

(It's all about the Altoids, man...LOL) Pamela Crockett, you are the greatest! Like you've told me time and time again, it's my time to shine!

**Family:** my sister, Sheri (Lynette), for pushing *Blackgentlemen.com* as if it were your own, and my brothers, Lance, (we'll get those pictures straight next time...lol) Brian, and Mario—I know I may have been a pest and at times bossy (Mario), but thanks for loving me. *Nephews:* Brandon, Travon, & Montell; *Nieces;* Tiara, Kantrell, Shy, Destiny, Morgan A. (Cookie), and Morgan R.,; all my aunts and uncles; Auntie Jo—for always being open and for the little tips that I have definitely put to use in my adult life. *Cousins:* The Robinson clan—you were more like siblings than cousins. Tammy, thanks cuz for running out and buying every copy of *Blackgentlemen.com* that you could get your hands on and making sure everyone in the family had one; the rest of my cousins by way of the Rothwell, Walker, Monroe, and Cheek, we're a huge family and I don't think I have enough space to mention you all by name, but you know I love all of you! & the Cheekes family.

**Sistah-girls** *(new and old):* Sonja Kennedy, my sisters-in-law Denise Thomas-Rathwell, & Chiquita Thomas, Camille Jenkins (my Carmen), Marlina Williams, Della Mayo, Jilma (Mima) Pinate, Xiomara

(Puchi) Lobo, Tefonee Graves, Kiki Jewel, Onita Sanders, Camille Hartley, Denise Shorter, Haydee Osario, and Robbyne Kaamil. Wow! Can you believe that the majority of you have known me for more than 20 years?

**Friends:** J.C. Gibson & family, Kirk & Cheryl Duggan; Joe & Maddy Calascibetta (for the offer of a little piece of heaven to write in), Perry & Luetta Bell, Gladys Nesbitt & family, Dorthea McKinney, Joyce Ousley (Mama Gert), Anita Bryant, Andrea Shaw—for reading *Another Man's Wife* in its rawest form, Otie Daniels (the Book Lady), your enthusiasm for books has been contagious.

**Industry Peeps:** the entire Strebor family, from those who run things to the writers, Tracy Cloyd (Hot-105), Jill Tracy (99 JAMZ), Broward County Library System (Sharon Morris), Lolita Files and family, Eric Brackett and family, Leslie Esdaile, Kim Roby, J.D. Mason, Eileen M. Johnson, and every author I have had the pleasure of meeting and developing friendships with over the years; and Janet Mosely—(Tenaj is very missed.)

**Book Clubs:** Voices of Essence, Euphoria, (Ms. Pat), Onyx (Jackie Chew), Sister Chat, Sistah Girl, and all the book clubs I've yet to meet—thank you for making this all possible due to your love of words.

**Forget-me-nots:** This is for anyone that I have forgotten to mention, (because I know I have somehow) forgive me; my mind is in overdrive right now.

**The Husband:** Warren, (you're always my wrap up) thanks for the kids, all the talks, and the years of memories. You will always be a force in my life that springs from love.

# Yani

## CHAPTER 1

My grandmother used to always say, "One man's trash is another man's treasure."

"Well, maybe someone will find some treasure in all of this trash that I'm putting out," I thought out loud as I taped closed the box that contained the last of Jarrin's belongings.

Yesterday was the five-year mark of the unexplained disappearance of my husband. The man I had been happily married to for ten years, up until that point. I know I promised for better or worse, but it's pretty hard to be in a relationship when your mate is MIA.

Being the devoted wife and mother that I am, or rather was, I just knew he was coming back. So I waited through the birthdays, the anniversaries, and every other holiday that came and went during the five-year time span. I turned a deaf ear to those who would comment amongst themselves how crazy I was for wasting my time beyond the second month. If it had been them, they would've declared him dead after six months and lived fat off the insurance money I stood to gain.

Jarrin had been a part of my life for so long that I didn't know how to let him go; even though he'd obviously let go of me.

I guess the main thing that kept me going all these years are those nagging thoughts that were always in my mind. The ones that made me feel that he was in some type of danger. I kept having a recurring dream of him being tied up and held in a dark room. After the first year, I expected the police to knock on my door and tell me that they'd found his body in a desolate field, bound and gagged. No matter how gruesome the dreams, after the third year, I had to draw the line somewhere. How long was I willing to sit around waiting?

I pushed the box out of the walk-in closet into the hallway.

"That's it?"

"That's it," I said to my best friend Carmen, as I straightened up from the stooping position I was in.

"I don't know why you don't have one of those yard sales like your girl did in *Waiting to Exhale?* You'd easily make enough to pay off your mortgage with all this stuff."

Carmen and I bent down and lifted the box to carry it in the living room.

"You mean a *Love Hangover* sale? Remember, she sold his stuff in an attempt to hurt him. I, on the other hand, doubt if Jarrin would remember half of this shit if he were to come back."

"If you're not suffering from a love hangover, I don't know who is."

We dropped the box near the front door.

"I'm not hung over. I'm just *over* it."

"You'd still be over it, but with a few more dollars in your bank account."

"I'd rather give this stuff to the people at Camillus House and let needy people have it than deal with trying to sell it. Besides, throwing it in the boxes was much easier than going through each piece trying to figure out what it's worth."

"If you say so."

"And I absolutely say so."

I took my foot and pushed the box with the other fifteen that were stacked and waiting near the door.

"Bryce should be here any minute. He had to run to the airport to pick up a friend of his." She stretched her back and looked down at her watch.

"You mean the frat brother you've been talking about non-stop? What's his name? Umm…"

"Alex."

"How could I forget? You've only said his name what? About a hundred times within the last hour?"

"All I can say is, when you see him, you'll know why."

"Know why what?"

"Well…"

"Carmen, don't start. I just made the decision to put one man out of my life and you've already got me hooked up with another one. I don't know if I'm ready…"

"Ready? Woman, please. Your ass should be in that oversized room you call a closet picking out something to wear tonight so you can make up for lost time. You don't know if you're ready to date?" She rolled her eyes and sucked her teeth for added emphasis. "Hell, my godchildren have been without a male figure in their lives long enough."

"They have male figures in their lives. What do you call Bryce…"

"Not their daddy."

"He's their goddaddy."

"But he's not in an intimate relationship with their mother. Hopefully they won't have a problem with intimacy when they get older."

"What am I supposed to do, bring home the first man I meet?"

"Look, crazy girl, you need to get over your fears and get up running. If you're going to be truly over Jarrin, you've got to get back into the dating game. You've had five years to prepare yourself."

"What would I do on a date? Think about it, I haven't dated anyone but Jarrin. I've been with him since I was fourteen and I'm damn near thirty-six now."

"So what? The only way you'll ever know is if you try it."

"You have no idea what the dating scene is like today…"

"And neither do you. But if Bryce were to pull the shit Jarrin did, Girl, my ass would be hanging out Monday through Saturday."

"What would Sunday be? Your day to repent for being a hoe all week?"

"Hell, no. It would be the day I would need to recuperate from the mind-blowing sex I'd had the night before with the fine ass man I'd met that week." We both laughed.

"Let's finish before your *husband*, who I might add is madly in love with you, gets here."

"Mommy, what do you want me to do with these?" Jay stood in the doorway clutching three large photo albums.

"Bring them to Goddy, baby." Carmen held out

her hands to him.

"I was thumbing through them last night," I said as I took a seat on the steps near the door.

"While you were waiting for that call that never came?"

"That would be correct." A sudden sense of loneliness seemed to come over me as I looked at the books again.

Each book was a documented photo tribute to my life with Jarrin. From the first date, to the first kiss, to the first house we shared together. Everything that had ever happened was captured on a photo in those books.

"Oh, this is the apartment y'all lived in when you were in Atlanta."

"Umm hmm."

"Remember how your mama went ballistic when you told her y'all were moving in together?"

"Do I? I remember that conversation I had with Mama like it was yesterday."

❤❤❤

"Yaniece Fenton, I didn't raise you to be shacking up with no man!" By the tone of her voice and the fact that she'd called me by my first and last name, I knew she was fuming. I could just picture my mother with her hand on her hip and her eyes slightly bulging out of her head. I even imagined a slight waft of smoke smoldering from the center of her auburn dye job.

"Ma, we're not shacking up. We're doing what you would call…" I paused, trying to find just the right words. Delivery was everything in this one-shot deal. "A trial-run marriage." Hey, it sounded good to me. Too bad she didn't agree.

"*A trial-run marriage?!!* What the hell kinda shit is that?" She was an octave away from shattering glass.

At that very moment, I was glad that I'd decided to have this talk with her by way of Ma Bell. A face-to-face would've had me enduring some type of bodily harm.

"Put it this way," I said, still trying my best to sell her on the idea. "When you go to the shoe store to purchase a pair of shoes, don't you at least try them on to make sure they fit?" Not giving her a chance to respond, I quickly added, "Well, I want to try on marriage before I buy it, get it home and find out that it just doesn't fit."

I'd overheard this chick on campus tell this to her friend as an explanation for why she slept with every guy she went out with. I smiled and made it a mental memory to put away for a rainy day, and this conversation was close to becoming a category five storm.

After a few minutes of terrifying silence, Mama sighed. "You know, it's your choice, Yani, but I'm letting you know right now, I'll never agree with it. I know you've got to make your own mistakes in life though. I just thought you were smarter than this."

Smarter? Why this was better than smart—it was brilliant. At least, that's what I thought then.

Mama's voice resounded that of defeat, which made me feel bad, but not bad enough to change my mind. I was determined to be with Jarrin, and no one was going to prevent that. Not even Mama.

❤❤❤

"I remember when you called me. You were so excited." Carmen turned the page.

"It took some getting used to, but things worked out fine."

"You basically turned the man into everything that you thought he was supposed to be, so of course they did."

"I did not."

"Girl, please. Did you not have to teach his ass how to make a bed?"

"Well, yeah."

"And did you not have to teach him how to wash dishes?"

"Yes."

"Did you not teach him how to cook?"

"Okay, okay. So I did have to do a lil' retouching here and there."

"Retouching? Huh, you built a new model." Carmen flipped through a few more pages of the book. "Oh, look…this is when I came down to visit you."

"Look at you, showing off your engagement ring." I smiled as we stared at the picture of Carmen with her hands splayed out in front of her.

"Bryce really surprised me."

"Surprised you? I knew you were going to marry Bryce from the first moment I met him. You talked about me with Jarrin, but you were just as stuck on Bryce. At least he's still stuck on you though."

"O-kay, then. I'll just put these in the closet in the spare bedroom." Carmen closed the books and walked off through the kitchen and down the short hall that led to the guest bedroom.

I grabbed the back of my neck and gently began to massage it.

"Can I interest you in a chocolate shake?" Carmen asked.

"Mmm, that sounds good, but Bryce is on his way? If he gets here and we're not here…"

"I'll call him from the car and tell him that you're

going to bring me home. He'd much rather play catch-up with Alex without me in the way."

"Then just let me grab my purse."

I made my way through the living room to the other side of the house. I peeked into the office where Natalia and Jay were tapping away on their computers.

"Hey, guys, Goddy and I are going to get shakes from Checkers. We'll be back in a few."

"Okay," they both called out in unison, never taking their eyes from the screens.

"Mommy, am I still going over to Travis' house?" Jay asked.

"Oh, yeah. I almost forgot. Go get your stuff now and we can drop you off while we're out."

"Woo hoo!" he shouted with his hand in the air. He sprang from the chair and ran down the hall to his room.

"So what are you going to do, Ms. Lady?" I asked Natalia.

"I guess I'll be here. If something comes up, I'll call you on your cell," she nonchalantly said without moving her hands away from the keyboard.

"No, you call me to make sure it's okay with me for you to do anything. If something comes up? I keep telling you that I'm the mother and you're the child. Understand me?"

"Yes, Mommy," she said with a hint of an attitude.

Since she'd turned fourteen, I found myself having to remind her of our roles every now and then. I'd already warned her that it's not in the plans for us to do the talk- show circuit. I will not sit on stage crying that I can't control a child that I have to clothe, feed, and give shelter to. Huh, she'll find herself on the porch or in the backyard somewhere.

I left her and walked down the hall to my room. I grabbed my purse from the dresser and returned to the kitchen where Carmen sat at the bar patiently waiting.

"Ready?"

"As soon as Jay gets his things we can roll."

I grabbed my keys from the rack on the wall.

"I still say you should sell some of this stuff."

"Carmen, if you see something you want to sell, go right ahead and take it, but think about the good it will do somebody that's in need." I looked at her solemnly.

"Damn, you sure know how to make a sistah feel bad. Let's go before I make you swing by my house and grab some of Bryce's things." We both laughed.

Bryce was known for being a pack rat. Carmen had been plotting for years on how to get rid of some of his "insignificant crap," as she called it. He held on to stuff so long that he still had his uniform from Burger King; his part-time gig in high school. The burgundy sort of brown-colored ones that looked more like a clown suit than anything else. I couldn't think of anyone who would want that.

"Girl, you should reconsider throwing that uniform away. Maybe one day it'll be a collector's item and be worth some good money," I said to her one day as we did a Goodwill cleaning.

"You think so?" she said.

I knew that would get her off his back; for a little while at least.

Bryce is such a good guy. He's everything most women claim they're looking for. He's kind and gentle, tall and extremely handsome, and to top it off, he worships Carmen and loves their three kids more than anything else in the world. Plus, he's very supportive of his wife.

He's not one of those men who's hung up on things. He doesn't see a problem with showing affection in public like some men. They're always touching and feeling on each other—it's enough to make a love-deprived person sick.

"Are you going to open the door?" Carmen asked as she stood behind me with her arms wrapped around a box. I shook off the daydream and looked at her.

"Yeah. Sorry about that."

"Another visit to La-La Land?"

"Just thinking. Jay!" I yelled.

*Alex*

CHAPTER 2

I leaned back in the leather seat as the plane lifted into the air. I'd brought my laptop along so that I could get a little bit of work done, but after the flight attendant informed me that I'd have to shut if off until we were in the air, I decided that I was officially on vacation and put it away for the rest of the trip.

This would be the first time in ages that I would spend any part of the holidays away from home. There's nothing like New York at Christmastime, but I was close to a meltdown and needed to get away. After the invitation came that arrived like clockwork yearly, I took it as a sign and called Bryce to let him know that I'd definitely be there.

Bryce and I have been boys since our college days and every year his wife throws him a birthday/New Year's party. It's been a long time since I've attended, but, for some reason, I got an unexplainable urge to make it my business to be there this year. Besides, it will be a well-deserved break, especially after the hectic week I've had.

My company just took on a huge project and I'd finally found the courage to break it off with Taylor—the woman I've been seeing for two years. She's more like a barracuda though. The typical class-A gold digger. I think Taylor's first words as a baby were "I want." I know I'd heard it one time too many and couldn't stand to hear it again.

I'd reached the point in my life where I wanted to settle down. All that party over here, party over there stuff had gotten tired. I realized that what I wanted most was to go home to a woman who's at least bringing something to the table. While I'm not referring to food, it doesn't necessarily have to be money.

Taylor does her little decorating thing, but she's not serious about it. She blows off business and would rather try and spend up my money than make her own.

The scene a few days ago was the straw that broke the camel's back.

❤❤❤

"Mr. Chance?"

"Excuse me," I said to the room as I picked up the

phone to chastise my assistant. I'd given her strict instructions not to interrupt this meeting for anything.

"Constance," I forcefully whispered into the receiver.

"I know, Mr. Chance, but she's out here and she's ready to perform."

"She who?"

"Taylor." *Not today*, I thought as I glanced around the room at the waiting faces.

"I told her…"

"Okay, okay." I could hear the frustration in Constance's tone. It was no secret that she had no love for Taylor.

"Tell her to wait in my office."

"No problem." Twenty minutes later, I emerged from the conference room to find Taylor sitting in my chair, feet up on the desk, gabbing away on the phone to one of her girls.

"Look, I'll get back with you later. Umm hmm. You know I am. All right, Girl. Bye." I took a deep breath as I walked into the room.

"You mind?" I asked as I spun the chair around.

"Well, hello to you, too."

"Taylor, believe me, this is neither the time nor the place for this."

"Seems to me that it is since it's the *only* time I've

been able to see you in the past few weeks. I feel like I'm having an affair with your voice mail and that bitchy middle-aged secretary of yours." I rolled my eyes toward the ceiling and began the count. I'd started using this technique from the first time Taylor had me at the point of boiling over. I figured if it worked for parents with children it had to work for spoiled-ass adults, too.

"Taylor." I said her name as if she was a five-year-old instead of twenty-eight. "I'm in the middle of closing a very big deal. I really don't have time for this. Now, when I finish tying everything up, I'll call you."

"A big deal, huh? Can we finally take that trip to Jamaica then?" Her eyes lit up with excitement.

"I can't promise that right now. Right now I need to call my team together for a meeting so we can put the finishing touches on..."

"Your team? Is that all you can think about? Look, if you can't give me what I want, maybe I need to move on and find someone who will."

"You know what, that sounds like a good idea to me."

She stared at me with eyes stretched wide. "What do you mean that sounds like a good idea?"

I tried to think of a good way to handle this. I've never been one for airing my dirty laundry in public. If this thing got ugly, it would be talked about around the office for years.

"Look, I should be finished up here soon. Why don't you meet me at the coffee shop across the street. Then we can talk." I put my hand out to help her out of the chair.

"All right, one hour. If you're not there by then, I *will* be back. And this time, everyone will know that I'm here."

I opened the door for her and followed her out.

"Constance, can you tell everyone to meet me in the conference room in five minutes?"

She glared at Taylor disgustingly as she strutted by her desk. "Right away, Mr. Chance."

I walked behind Taylor as she headed for the elevator.

"Remember, one hour. Don't disappoint me, 'cause I won't disappoint you."

I looked at her and shook my head. I kept walking to the conference room; not acknowledging her threat.

Twenty minutes later, I sat in an empty conference room with Ed. I'd informed everyone of what would be expected of them and Ed let us know what the projected figures would be.

"So, are you going across the street to meet her?"

"I don't want to, but I can't keep doing this. It's

like I'm dealing with a spoiled child." I shook my head and massaged my temples.

"Damn, I can't believe she had the nerve to come up in here acting ghettofied."

"You?! Man, I'm tired of this whole situation. My image is too important for me to be dealing with this high school mess. You'd think a woman damn near in her thirties would be on a different level than that."

"You knew she was a hood rat when you met her."

"No I didn't, man. When I met her, she was all business. I didn't find out about the rat in her until after I'd been there a few times."

"See, that's what you get for thinking with the wrong head."

"Man, don't I know it. I should've just hired the gay dude to decorate and saved myself the misery."

"And some cash." Ed let out a hearty laugh. His slightly overgrown belly, from the beer he consumed on a daily basis, jiggled around.

"Man, this is one of those times that if I could have a 'do over' I'd throw her ass back so quick and keep moving."

"Too bad you can't. So, what's your next move?"

"I'm going to go over there and tell her it's over."

"And then what?"

"Then tomorrow I'm jumping on a plane to Florida

for at least two weeks. Hopefully by then, she'll have grasped the concept."

"Then leave your cell and pager. 'Cause you and I both know that Taylor is not going to just let you dump her like that."

"Maybe I'll come back with a wife," I jokingly stated.

"Now something like that might do it, but when did you become interested in marriage?"

"Things change. You just get to that point in your life I guess."

"I feel you. I felt that way when I asked Jen to marry me. It was just time."

"You're right about it being time. Jen had put up with your ass for four or five years. She deserved a ring and more."

"Yeah, keep talking shit. That's exactly what Taylor's girls are telling her. Matter fact, you need to get your ass cross that street before she comes up in here and does a song and dance number that you'll never live down."

As much as I was dreading it, I knew it had to be done. I ran my fingers through my hair and scratched my scalp as I stood up.

"I know."

"You need me to come with you?"

"Damn, man. None of the letters in my name are

in the word punk. Leave your cell on, just in case."

"In case what?"

"I have to call the police on her ass. You know they're quick to take the man away in those situations. Then I'll need you to come and bail me out."

"Okay, punk." We both laughed.

"Check you later." I gave him a brotherly hug and a dap and walked to my office. Constance was shutting down her computer and gathering her things to go home.

"So you're on your way across the street to deal with that she-devil?"

"Yeah. Look, I'm sorry about what Taylor said earlier. You know…"

"You don't have to apologize just because she doesn't have any home training. You just remember to tell her that she's not the only one that grew up in the hood. I'll give her a BBD that she'll never forget. Then we'll see who's middle-aged."

"A BBD?"

"A Brooklyn Beat Down."

I shook my head and smiled as I thought of Constance's thicker frame against Taylor's thin one.

"I'll be sure to tell her. I'll see you in two weeks."

"Oh, that's right, you leave tomorrow."

"I most certainly do."

"Well, happy holidays, boss." She came around her desk and gave me a hug.

"Same to you, Constance. Hold down the fort for me. Oh, and check your top left drawer. Just a little something to express my appreciation for you and all that you do for me." I winked and walked into my office. I slid some papers in my briefcase and closed my laptop. I slipped on my leather jacket and glanced around the office one last time to make sure everything was in place and I wasn't forgetting anything.

"Okay, I'm out," I said to Constance as she inspected the envelope I'd left for her.

"Good luck with dealing with your lil' problem and if you need me, just holler. I catch the train from there and I'll be in the vicinity."

"I'll remember that. A BBD, right?"

"A real good one."

I laughed and headed toward the glass doors. As the elevator arrived I heard someone let out a yelp. I smiled, knowing it was Constance's uncontrollable, joyous response to the five-thousand dollar bonus check she'd found stuffed in the card.

She deserved it and more. She's the reason Chance Productions runs like a well-oiled machine. I don't know what I would do without her some days.

I stepped off the elevator and made my way around the corner and through the lobby area. As soon as I looked up I saw Taylor spinning her way through the revolving doors.

"Damn." I prayed she wasn't going to show out. If she did, they'd really be calling the police after I yoked her ass out.

"I was beginning to think you weren't coming."

"I told you it was an important meeting."

"Oh, well. I got tired of sitting there, people watching. I want something to eat. Run me uptown to…"

"Taylor, we need to talk."

She folded her arms across her chest like the spoiled brat she was as she tapped her foot on the marble floor.

"I'll be a better listener after I get some food in my system." Her hand was now placed firmly on her hip as she stared at me.

I took a deep breath and without any words, I walked out the same way she had just come in. I stepped out on Park Avenue and walked a short ways up the block and crossed over in the direction of Grand Central Station as she followed close behind me. For exercise, I made it a habit to walk to work. That was one of the benefits of living in the city. Parking was definitely a bitch in New York, which is why most people who live outside the city limits opt to park their cars somewhere uptown where it was free and catch the bus or the train from there to work.

I pushed open the glass door and held it open for

her. She strutted in like the diva she was, being careful not to let anyone bump into her. Something that's almost an impossible feat this time of day due to all the commuters trying to catch the trains that took them back to suburbia or the other four boroughs that make up the metropolis of New York.

"Are we going up to Michael's place?"

"I thought we'd just grab a quick pastry and a cup of coffee from the little bakery around the corner from here." She shot me a nasty look. "It's either that or a slice of pizza? Make a choice."

"Pizza? I'm not eating any greasy ass pizza in this." She gestured to her overpriced outfit: a red leather pantsuit, the matching red leather bag on her shoulder, and a pair of red leather boots with a good three-inch heel. All of it bearing the name of a designer; something that was a must with Taylor.

"Then the coffee shop it is." I walked ahead of her; not giving her time to protest, as I knew she would.

"I thought you had something you wanted to talk to me about? How can we talk in here?"

I stood at the counter waiting to order. "Easy. There are only two other people in here besides us and they're too busy working to be interested in what you and I are talking about."

"Why can't we go somewhere else? Somewhere we can sit down and have a decent meal at least."

SHONDA CHEEKES

"Because, I don't have that kind of time."

"Where are you rushing off to?"

"That's not for you to worry about."

She screwed her face up and I knew she was about to show her ass so I cut her off before she could get a word in edgewise.

"Look, this thing between us isn't working. You know it as well as I do. I say we cut our losses and walk away as friends."

"Friends? What are you talking about, Alex? You're definitely on a different page than me."

"I don't think so, Taylor. I think we're both on the last page of the final chapter."

A look of panic registered on her face. I was her lifeline to a life she felt she deserved. Exotic trips, shopping sprees, endless parties—I couldn't understand, for the life of me, when my money became her money.

"Maybe we should talk about this, baby. This is something that you need to think about with your head..."

"That's just it, Taylor, I have thought about it. Hell, I even made a list about it and I'm sorry to tell you that the cons clearly outweigh the pros. I couldn't think of one good reason for us to stay together. You said so yourself that we barely see each other anymore. I'm going to be extremely busy

24

with the projects we've just acquired and you...
well, you should take this time and concentrate on
getting your business really rolling. Stop pussy-
footing around and go for it," I said as encouraging
as I could muster up.

She took a deep breath and then a long sip of the
liquid contents in the cup the lady had handed to
her.

"Look, I'm not trying to put you down or anything like that, I just know that you have much
more potential than you're putting out now. Ever
since you and I got together, it's like you stopped
doing your own thing."

"You know what? You're absolutely right. I mean,
I had a flourishing business when I first met you.
Hey, that's the reason we met."

❤❤❤

I thought back to the day she first walked into
my office. She'd been recommended by a mutual
friend. She walked in my office looking like she'd
just stepped off a runway in Paris. Her butter-tan
skin looked as if she'd sat in the sun a few hours to
get that perfect glow. Donned in one of her signa-
ture designer business suits, her "I-workout-at-
least-five-days-a-week" figure was enough to com-

mand the attention of any man. To think that I could have all her beauty to myself caused me to make an unwise choice. After a few minutes of talking to her about the ideas she had, I hired her on the spot. I also asked her out to dinner that night. A decision a year and a half later I'm desperately trying to undo.

She flung her hair over her shoulder in a seductive way. If only her inside was as beautiful as the outside, she'd be okay, but you know what they say about a person who's ugly on the inside. It makes them ugly period.

"So I guess you're telling me that you need space? Okay, no problem. Go and have your—space," she spat. "But you remember that Taylor Vincent waits for no one."

"I'm not asking you to wait."

She pulled her compact out of her bag, making sure her makeup was fresh. After applying a fresh coat of lipstick she closed her bag and pulled it up tighter on her shoulder. She grabbed the bag of pastries that I'd just paid for and walked out as I followed behind her.

Her head held high, she swung around and looked at me. "Can you give me cab fare uptown?"

I laughed at the irony. It was like I had to pay her to be free.

"How much?" I asked, testing the depth of her greed.

"Fifty would be enough to cover the ride and the tip." She smiled coyly.

"I'll do you one better, here's a buck fifty."

"What am I supposed to do with that?"

"Catch the train. That way you don't have to worry about tipping the driver."

I placed the money in the palm of her hand and walked right past her. I knew she was fuming but I never looked back to find out how much.

# *Asia*

## CHAPTER 3

I stepped out the elevator into the lobby dragging my luggage.

"Looks like someone is going on a trip," Carl at the main security desk said as I slid my hands into my black leather gloves.

"You got me. What gave it away?" I smiled and winked at him.

"Headed home?"

"Yeah, thought I'd spend the holidays with my family this year." That was better than spending them alone like last year.

"It's good to be with family. You just make sure to bring back some of that Florida sunshine. It's going to be mighty cold here."

"So I heard. That's why I'm trying to get out of here on the next thing smoking." I pulled the belt of my coat tight as I prepared to step out on the street.

"Let me help you with those." Carl grabbed the largest piece of luggage and rolled it out the revolving door.

"You don't have to do that," I said as I jumped in the slot behind him.

"It's not a problem." He signaled for a taxi and opened the door after the driver stopped on the curb. The driver jumped out and loaded my bags in the trunk.

"Well, you have a Happy New Year, Ms. Fenton."

"You too, Carl." I slipped an envelope in his hand and closed the door.

"What's this for?"

"Just my way of saying thank you for doing what you do."

"You don't have to give me anything. It's my job."

"Go buy Mary something with it then. Bye." I waved as the driver pulled away from the curb, leaving Carl standing there with the envelope in his hand.

"Where to, lady?"

"Kennedy." I sat back in the seat and thought about the conversation I'd had with Linda earlier.

I'd called her to make last-minute arrangements to fly out that same day. As usual she'd come through for me. First-class, no doubt. She'd said I'd been in luck; one of her clients had an extra ticket that he'd purchased for his colleague, but he wasn't going to be able to go after coming down with the flu overnight.

❤❤❤

"Is it a first-class seat?"

"I know you don't like to fly any other way now."

We laughed at the inside joke. Ever since she'd hooked me up with first-class accommodations by accident, I'd ask for nothing else since.

"How much is it going to cost me?" Since it was a last-minute thing, I knew she was going to be talking a grip.

"Believe it or not, you don't have to pay anything. Being that it's a business trip they're going to write it off and were willing to let you have it to keep it from going to waste."

"Really?!" I couldn't believe my luck.

"What company is this?"

"Don't worry about it. You can ask him all about his company since you'll be sitting next to him."

"Girl, sitting next to him…For a free first-class ticket, I'll think about sitting in his lap if that's what he wanted."

We both laughed.

"You do know that I'm joking though?"

I may be many a thing, but trifling isn't one of them.

"Funny you should say that."

"Why?"

"'Cause you have sat in this man's lap before."

31

"What are you talking about? It's someone I know?"

"Of course it is."

"Who?"

Just then her phone beeped. "Hold on for a second."

She clicked over. I tried to think of who I knew that was generous enough to give me an expensive plane ticket.

"Asia, it's one of my clients. I'll talk to you later. Call me when you get to Yani's and tell her I said to keep her head up."

"Okay, but…"

Before I could form the question, she had clicked over. I sat there and wondered who this mystery man was and when did I sit in his lap. Since I wasn't a heavy drinker that got drunk enough to forget what I'd done, it had to be someone I knew well. And I know Linda wasn't talking about Santa.

❤❤❤

I walked into the American Airlines terminal to check-in. I gave the lady at the counter the information Linda had given me and waited as she changed the ticket over to my name and information. It was an open ticket, so I would need to call them and let them know a day in advance when I was returning.

After receiving the ticket in hand, I walked down

to the gate area and found a seat. I found myself scanning the room for any familiar male faces, but found none.

"I wonder who it is," I mumbled under my breath.

With twenty minutes left before departure, I was still scanning the faces of everyone who passed by me on the way to their seats. Maybe Linda was just messing with me. Or maybe the mystery man was somewhere caught in traffic and wouldn't make the flight. An urge to release myself of all the water I'd taken in earlier began to overwhelm me. I slipped into the bathroom near the back of first-class. You know, the place where the curtain separates the supposedly haves from the have-nots? Whatever. Yes, I love the amenities of sitting in first-class over coach—bigger seats, more leg room, nice meals, but for the price difference some of these airlines charge, they should have a door that separates the two. Not some flimsy ass curtain.

A few minutes before takeoff, I returned to my seat. Just as I was about to sit down, I heard a familiar voice coming from the muscular body that stood in front of me blocking the entrance to my seat.

"I thought you were going to disappoint me and not show."

I slowly raised my eyes from the chest area until I reached his face.

Oh, I'd definitely sat in this man's lap before. Sat

in it, bounced around on it, and a whole lot more.

"Hayden Miles? Oh, my God. How long has it been?"

"Too long. Much too long." He placed his hand on my lower back and kissed me on the cheek. I was paralyzed for a moment. Being that close to him had all my senses on alert.

"I think we should sit down before the flight attendant comes over here." He waved his hand toward our seats.

"Oh—yeah…we should." I slid in and he followed.

I couldn't get over it. Here I sat with the man I had almost married two years earlier. It had been just that long since we'd seen each other.

❤❤❤

We'd met at an art gallery in SoHo. Jilley, a mutual friend, was having her first showing. Jilley had talked non-stop about this friend of hers she wanted me to meet.

"You will love him. He's successful, extremely good-looking, and has his own place. The three things most women look for in a man."

Aside from good credit and whether or not he had a decent ride.

"Am I that desperate that you need to set me up on a blind date?"

"Of course not, Girl. I just know that you two would be perfect for each other."

She hooked her arm around mine and led me over to where a crowd of people had gathered around one of her favorite pieces. As she stopped to explain the particular work to everyone, I took the opportunity to slip off to the bar.

"A white wine, please."

I looked down at the black jersey, matte dress I wore. The mesh-covered slingbacks were a perfect match with the sheer mesh material that covered the back of the dress.

After handing me the drink, I asked the bartender how much.

"Allow me," I heard a sexy male voice say.

I turned around to address the owner of the outstretched hand that was paying for my drink to inform him that there was no need to put himself through the trouble. I wasn't one of those women willing to put up with a man all night for a couple of free drinks. I'd rather pay for it myself and enjoy the rest of my evening without the stalker from hell.

"Excuse me," I said to the Adonis of a man standing closely behind me.

He smiled. "I couldn't think of any other way to get you to notice me, so I thought this would do the trick."

As fine and good looking as he was, I would've definitely noticed him. "Thank you, but…"

"No buts about it. If you don't want to talk to me any further than this, I'm fine with that, but I'm still buying you the drink."

"You know, normally I wouldn't do this, but okay. Thank you."

The bartender handed him his change.

"And just to set the record straight, this isn't something that I normally do either," he said.

I smiled at his tack of evening the score. Honestly, if his ass wasn't so damn good-looking, I would've flipped on him.

As I sipped on the drink, I scanned the room in hopes that Jilley and the faceless man wouldn't appear and ruin my chance at getting to know this fine specimen of a man a little better. At least give us a chance to exchange numbers.

"So what brings you here tonight?" he asked as we began to stroll through the gallery at a gingerly pace.

"The artist is a good friend of mine."

"Really? Now I know that we have something in common."

"What's that?"

"We're both friends of Jilley's."

We stopped in front of a beautiful painting of a little black boy and girl hugging as they sat on a stoop smiling at each other.

"Isn't her work wonderful?" I asked.

"Oh, she's definitely on the right track. I own five of her originals. Earlier pieces back when she was selling them much cheaper."

"I have three. Free of charge."

"Oh, I guess I have to talk to Jilley about that."

"Well, just think of what your small investment is worth now."

"That's true."

We looked at the painting quietly for a moment.

"So, since Jilley is our friend, that sort of makes us friends," he said.

"Well, friends should know each other's names," I said with my hand extended to him. "I'm Asia Fenton."

"It's a pleasure to finally meet you, Asia."

I gave him a puzzled look. Then it dawned on me. "Hayden?"

"Not bad for a blind date?"

"Not bad at all," I said as he held my hand in his. *Thank you, Jilley,* I thought as I stood there looking at his beaming smile.

For the next two and a half years, Hayden and I would date each other exclusively, six months of it being engaged. Sitting here with him for the first time in two years, I couldn't for the life of me remember the exact reason for our breakup.

♥♥♥

"We're prepared for takeoff. Please make sure that all seatbelts are fastened and trays are in the upright and locked position," the flight attendant informed us.

As the plane made its way down the runway, I grabbed Hayden's hand tightly. There's something about takeoff that doesn't sit well with me.

"I see you're still not that crazy about flying." He squeezed my hand. I gave him a weak smile.

I'd already made plans to get reacquainted after the plane reached cruising altitude and leveled off. 'Cause if Hayden looked good that night all those years ago, he looked even better now.

*Lord, please deliver us safely in Miami, and Lord, please make Hayden still be single,* I asked with my eyes closed and my head leaned back into the headrest.

# *Yani*

## CHAPTER 4

After making the rounds, I dropped Carmen off at her home and promised to give her a call later. I had one hour before Asia would arrive.

This would be the first New Year's in about five years that she would be spending at home with us.

She'd been in New York for about fifteen years now, which was long enough to classify her as a New Yorker. She was the full package. The attitude, the ambition, and the accent. I think she'd been working on that accent from the very first trip she'd ever taken there as a child.

We'd both been captivated by all the buildings and lights, but I never found the courage to tackle living in the big city. Miami was city enough for me.

I used to visit her on a regular basis, but Jarrin complained so about me going there as much as I did, until I stopped going altogether. Another regret that I harbored about my life with him. I finally realized that I was to blame for that, so I've moved on. Right now I'm just glad that she called and said she was coming home this year. It's been a year since I've seen my sister.

I pulled into the parking garage at Fort Lauderdale International Airport. That's the one thing that I request if I have to pick you up; you've got to fly into Fort Lauderdale as opposed to Miami. The traffic isn't as congested, parking is much cheaper, and it isn't as confusing as Miami.

I hit the button on my key to activate my car alarm and walked toward the terminal. I was decked out in a pair of khaki capris and a white cardigan twin set with a pair of mule platform sneakers from Victoria's Secret.

I hurried across the walkway in front of the waiting cars. Once inside the terminal, I checked the monitor to see if her flight was on time. It informed me that it was landing. I ran upstairs so that I could meet her at the gate.

After being scanned and cleared through security, I stood at the American Airlines gate anxiously waiting for the passengers to disembark the plane.

Asia was the fourth person to walk up the jet way. In my excitement to see her, I didn't notice the man that followed close behind her. I ran up to her and grabbed her in a tight embrace.

"Hey!" we sung as we spun around in our happy dance.

"I'm so glad to see you. Don't you ever stay away this long again."

"And what's wrong with you making a trip up to see me?"

"I have children that are always doing something."

"They're old enough to stay home by themselves."

"Whatever, Asia. You just got here so behave." I hugged her tight again and stood back to give her a once-over.

"I love your hair." She wore it in a short cut.

"Thanks, I wanted to wear my natural curls for a little while."

"Yani, you remember him, right?" My attention went to the man who had been invisible up until that point.

"Hayden?! Oh my God!" I hugged him. "What are you doing here? I haven't seen you in eons? Are you the reason why I haven't seen my sister?"

"Unfortunately I can't take the blame for that. I think you've seen her more recently than I have."

Asia smiled when we focused our attention on her. "Yeah, yeah. Can we go get the bags? I'm in no mood to stand here while you two try and figure out who was the last to see me."

I shook my head. "Nice to see that the absence

hasn't put a damper on that winning personality of yours."

Asia had always been one to speak her mind. Even as a child. If there was something that she thought about you, you best believe she was going to tell you. So she was destined to live in New York.

Hayden grabbed her hand as I walked slightly ahead of them toward the escalator down to baggage claim.

"So, how long are you going to be here, Hayden?" I asked as we stood waiting for the carousel to spit out the luggage.

"Maybe a week or two. It depends on when I can wrap things up."

"Oh, so you're here on business?"

"Yeah."

"If you say you haven't seen her in a long time, how is it that you two ended up on the same flight?"

"I see you're still your nosey self," Asia responded.

"Curious is more of what I am." I turned my attention back to Hayden.

"Umm…"

"It's a long story. I'll tell you later," Asia said, coming to Hayden's rescue.

"Are we going to drop you off somewhere?"

"No, no. I've got reservations for a rental car."

"Where are you staying?"

"What's with you and the fifty questions?" Asia looked at me with a questioning smile.

"I just told you that I'm curious, and besides, you know I'm a very hospitable person. If he wants, he can stay in the spare room…"

"That's been taken care of, too. I've got reservations at a hotel on South Beach."

"South Beach? Why so far?"

"Well, the business that I'll be handling while I'm here will be in an office in the downtown area of Miami."

"Oh, okay. You do know how busy South Beach is now?"

"Yani, sweetie, you really need to get out more. That's one of the reasons he chose to stay there." Asia shook her head and smiled.

"Contrary to what you may think, little sister, I do hang out down there."

"Then you have to come down while I'm here so we can all hang out and go to dinner or something."

"That sounds good."

"We need to take her to a club," Asia added.

I rolled my eyes at her. The buzzer sounded off letting us know that the bags were coming.

I sat in the car listening to Chico Debarge sing about love having no guarantees as Asia stood talking to Hayden. I'd taken him to the Budget lot, off Perimeter Road, to pick up his vehicle.

"Don't I know it," I said aloud, agreeing with Chico.

Asia walked over and tapped on my window. "I'm going to ride with Hayden to check into his hotel and then we're going to grab something to eat. Wanna come?"

"Yeah right. I'll relieve you of your guilt and I'll see you when you get to the house. You will be coming there tonight or will Hayden be buying a lobster dinner as well?"

"I'm not going to make any promises. But I think I might see lobster in my future." She winked.

Buying lobster meant she would be obliged to have sex with him since he'd allowed her to eat from that side of the menu.

"I guess I'll see you when I see you then."

"You're not upset, are you?"

"Hell no! Girl, if I had a man that looked that good wanting to spend time with me, I'd ditch your ass, too."

We both laughed.

She reached in and hugged me. "Maybe we'll work on that while I'm here."

"Bye, Asia." I rolled the window up and then down again before she walked off. "Do you want to get your bags?"

"No, take them with you."

"At least get your bag with personal stuff in it. Can't have you being funky."

"Don't worry. I'll pick something up if I need to."

"Have a good time." I stuck my hand out the window and waved at Hayden, then drove off the lot. Just then my cell phone rang. "Hello?"

"Where are you?" Carmen asked.

"Leaving the airport. Why?"

"Just wondering. What are you doing tomorrow?"

"I'm not sure. Why?"

"You and this why. I wanted you to go with me to pick out something to wear to the party."

"You still don't have anything to wear?"

"I know exactly what I want. All I have to do is run in the store and pick it up, but I wanted your opinion."

"My opinion? Girl, you're the one that used to be a model. Still could be if you really wanted to."

"That's in the past. I'm perfectly happy being a businesswoman, wife and mommy."

"Where are we going and what time are we leaving?"

"Over to Aventura. We can go after you finish

your running around."

"Any time tomorrow afternoon is good for me."

"So, about one then?"

"That'll work."

"Where's Asia?"

"Check this, Chica gets off the plane holding hands with a man."

"She brought a man with her?"

"Not exactly."

"She met a man on the plane and left with him?"

"You remember Hayden?"

"The guy she was engaged to?"

"Yep."

"They're back together?!!"

"From what he said, they just happened to run into each other on the plane."

"So, she's gone to get some long time no see sex."

"You are so bad."

"Hey, I ain't mad at her. Speaking of a long time and sex…"

"I'll see you tomorrow."

"Yani…"

"Bye, Carmen." I clicked off my phone before she could start. I knew exactly where that conversation was going and right now, I'm in no mood for it.

Opting to take the scenic route, I rode down US 1 to S.R. 84 and jumped on 595 heading west as Chico asked if the love was still good. My 328 sailed down the highway. The speedometer registered that I was doing seventy-five so I was on the lookout for the troopers that liked to sit off in the cut.

A little more than half an hour later I pulled into the semi-circular driveway of the beige and white rancher I'd called home for more than fourteen years. Not in the mood to look for the garage door opener that had fallen earlier, I parked and walked around to the front. I unlocked the frosted glass door and stepped into the foyer.

"Auntie!" Natalia yelled as she ran into the living room from the family room area. Her eyes questioned my lone stance.

"She'll be here later. She went out with a friend." I dropped my keys in the crystal bowl on the foyer table.

"A friend? Who?" Natalia asked.

"None of your business. Did you finish what I told you to do?"

She quickly turned and headed back to where she came from. "Yes, Mommy. Everything is washed and put away."

"Good. I'm surprised you haven't found anything to get into. You've only got a few more days of Christmas break left."

"Dania and Kemisha called about going to the movies earlier, but I thought Auntie was going to be here, so I told them no."

"Sorry 'bout that, sweetie. Auntie happened to run into an old friend and they decided to go get something to eat." I looked at my watch. It was almost eight o'clock. She slumped down on the beige leather sofa, hugging a pillow to her chest. "Want to go grab something to eat?"

"From where?"

"It doesn't matter. Shells, the Alehouse. Whatever you want."

She closed one eye and looked toward the ceiling with the other one as she contemplated her answer. "Can we go to Chili's and split a fajita?"

"That sounds good. Come on." I grabbed my leather bag from the counter and walked over to the phone on the wall near the fridge. I picked it up and listened to the dial tone that indicated someone had left a message. I dialed up the service while I waited for Natalia to come back. My heart raced as the computer-generated voice told me that I had four new messages waiting for me. The first one was from my mom asking me what time Asia's flight got in. I made a mental note to call her later and went on to the next one. Two were hang-ups and the last one was from Carmen asking if Asia was here yet.

Disappointed that the message I'd wanted wasn't there, I hung up and called for Natalia to hurry. I could hear her shoes slapping against the marble tile as she walked into the living room.

"Ready, Mommy."

I looked at my beautiful daughter who had turned into a young lady since her father had last seen her. Her sparkling hazel eyes, beautiful golden brown skin, and hair that fell a few inches past her shoulders down her back, made her a perfect candidate for a beauty queen. She had been a mini replica of Jarrin as a child.

"As ready as I'm ever going to be."

I took a deep breath and clutched my purse tightly on my shoulder. I slowly exhaled and walked out the front door. That hopeless wish I'd carried for the past five years was over and done. There would be no call nor would he ever walk through the door proclaiming his love for us. As of this moment I'd made up my mind that Jarrin Thomas Miller was dead.

# *Alex*

## CHAPTER 5

"Well, good morning, sleepyhead. I guess that flight wore you out?" Carmen stood at the stove cooking breakfast. The mouth-watering aroma wafted through the room.

"It's only nine o'clock."

"Leave the man alone, woman. Not everyone gets up with the chickens like you do." Bryce kissed her on the back of her neck.

"Is there any coffee ready?" I asked.

"All the time," Bryce said as he reached in the cabinet and pulled down a mug for me.

"Turn that TV down!" Carmen yelled to the older kids. The Rugrats theme song blared from that direction.

"I know you heard Mommy," Bryce bellowed in support of Carmen. Finally Sean, the ten-year-old, aimed the remote at the intended target obediently.

"Thank you," Carmen said to the pot she stood over.

"See what you're missing, man?" Bryce teased.

I smiled and took a sip of the piping hot coffee that I'd loaded up with sugar and cream.

"So what are you guys planning on doing today?" Carmen asked as she removed the pan from the stove.

"I was thinking that we'd take the kids over to Game Works out at Sawgrass. Later on we're going to go shoot some hoops. It's been a while since I've kicked his butt." Bryce looked at me smiling.

"If I remember correctly, you've never kicked my butt," I said as I sat down at the table in the breakfast nook area. Carmen walked over with a dish of bacon and sausage and set it in the middle of the table.

"Are you taking Mya with you?"

"Mya? She's a baby, Mommy. She's just going to get in the way." Sean had walked over to the kitchen area in search of something to put in his mouth.

"Was I talking to you? I don't think so. Honey, are you?" They both looked at Bryce who'd just lifted baby Mya into her high chair.

"Well, Sean does have a point, baby, but if you want me to, I will."

"No, it's not a problem. I'll see if Mama will watch her for a couple of hours."

"Why can't you watch her?"

"Uh, hello. I have to finish planning for a party that's slated to happen in two days. I need to finish picking up a few things for the menu and the party favors. Then Yani and I are going to run to the mall so I can pick up my dress."

"I thought you had something to wear already."

"I changed my mind. I saw something else that I like better."

"So that means you're going to take the other one back, right?"

"Of course, dear." She winked at me as she sat the omelet in front of me.

"So you stopped modeling all together, Carmen?"

"Yep. Right before we decided to have Mya, I quit. I've always loved putting together events, so I decided to go into business with my girlfriend."

"And how's that going?"

"Ask Bryce who brings home the biggest piece of bacon around here."

"My baby brings home the whole pig," Bryce said as he walked up behind her and wrapped his arms around her slender waist and kissed her neck.

"Mathew, let's eat," she called over to the six-year-old, who was glued to the television screen. He slowly lifted himself from his spot and joined us; looking back at the screen the entire way.

I sat back and admired the way they all seemed to

move in rhythm. This one passed as another one opened. I knew that this was something that I wanted to have in my lifetime. A shared harmony with another person.

❤❤❤

"I'm going to run upstairs and change."

"Don't get too pretty now. 'Cause it doesn't matter what you're wearing, I'm still going to kick your butt royally today."

"You sure are talking a lot of smack for a man who's never really had much game to begin with."

"That should tell you something then."

"Tell him what? You going outside to play with the boys a little doesn't enhance your playing skills, baby," Carmen said.

"So much for my wife having my back. Confidence, baby. You're supposed to be my cheering squad."

"I am. I just know your limits." She kissed him and walked upstairs with me on her heels.

I pulled out an AND 1 outfit. Black jersey shorts and white T-shirt with the faceless ball player in a dunk pose. I looked in the closet for the shoes that matched it perfectly and sat them on the side of the bed as I slipped the shirt I was wearing over my head.

After gearing up, I checked myself out in the full-length closet mirror and laughed. I knew Bryce was going to try and clown me for this outfit, but I wore it for the comfort. The fact that it looked good was just an added bonus.

I came downstairs and made my way toward the kitchen where I heard an unfamiliar female voice.

"Where's your wife? I know she's ready. I told her I was on my way and to meet me at the door."

"Yani, you know Carmen almost as good as I do. She's as slow as molasses. So I know you were expecting to wait."

"I told her I don't have all day. What's there to drink in this place? I'm thirsty." I rounded the corner into the kitchen and stopped short of bumping into the owner of the voice.

"O-oh. I'm sorry," she said slow and softly.

"No problem." And it really wasn't. She was gorgeous. Her hair was pulled back into a tight ponytail with loose curls on the end that grazed her back. I got caught up in her beautiful brown eyes topped with perfectly arched brows. Her sultry lips were lined with a darker brownish red color and filled in with gold. Her makeup-free, smooth caramel skin glowed under the recessed lighting.

"Hello," she said. Embarrassed for openly staring, I pep-talked my brain into working.

"Hey?" was the best thing it could come up with.

"This is Carmen's oldest and dearest girlfriend, Yani," Bryce said.

She extended her small hand, which I noticed was adorned with a natural length of nicely manicured nails. Not those gaudy long acrylics most women sport.

"Yani, this is my frat brother…"

"Alex. It's nice to finally meet you."

"It's a pleasure to meet you too, Yani." The most beautiful smile beamed back at me. While still holding her hand in mine, my eyes traveled over her petite frame, which was proportioned just right. She looked like one of those sistahs who had the entire Tae-Bo and Donna Richardson collections at home.

"Hey, Girl, you ready?" Carmen asked as she rounded the corner.

"I was ready when I pulled into the driveway, just like I said I'd be." She looked down at her hand and back up at me. I quickly released it.

"Well damn, I had to use the bathroom. Is that a crime?" Carmen looked at us. "I see you've met, Alex," she said without missing a beat.

"Yes. Bryce, introduced us," Yani quickly replied.

"You're late as usual," Bryce piped in.

Yani pulled her tan, leather bag higher on her shoulder. It must have been a signal that she was ready, because Carmen grabbed her bag and keys off the counter and gave Bryce a kiss.

"Don't be out too late, you two. I'm making a nice dinner tonight," Carmen called out as she and Yani walked toward the front door.

"I hope you're not going through all that trouble for me. We can order a pizza or something for all I care," I said. Bryce and I trailed behind them to the door.

"Don't even try it. I'm cooking and that's that."

"So what time should I expect your return?" Bryce asked.

"You know me and your wife in a mall... there's no telling."

"No, babes, we'll be back in a couple of hours. I've got to get dinner going." Carmen gave Bryce a long kiss on the lips as Yani and I exchanged glances.

"Don't they just make you sick?" she said in a joking manner.

"If you're going to get back here in enough time to cook, you better come on then." Yani walked out the door to her car. "Alex, it was nice to finally meet you. Maybe I'll get a chance to see you again before you leave. Adios, Bryce." She turned and saluted him.

"Same here," I finally said. She turned back to me and gave me a smile that would be burned into my memory until I saw her again. This time I was staring openly as she and Carmen walked away. She was definitely someone I would want to see again.

"Stop drooling, man. Have you no shame?" Bryce slapped me against my back.

"Some things can't be helped."

"Ready to get your butt whooped?"

"Not by you? At least not in this lifetime."

"We'll see. Let me put on my shoes." Bryce walked back into the house as I stood on the porch until the dark blue BMW pulled out of the yard.

*Just maybe…*

# *Yani*

## CHAPTER 6

"Want me to drive?" Carmen asked as we headed down the driveway to the car.

"Now why would I put myself through that torture? You know your ass drives too slow for me." We reached my car and I slid in. Before I could get my key in the ignition good, she started up.

"Okay. So what did you think of Alex? Isn't he gorgeous and fine as hell? And I thought I'd let you know that he's very, *very* single." Her eyes glazed over with that "I'm-the-matchmaker" look that I knew all too well.

"He's okay, I guess. I didn't really look at him that hard," I lied. "Besides, you know I'm not trying to meet anyone." I backed out the driveway into the street and placed the car in first gear.

"Girl, please. Did you not notice the way that he was looking at you? Hell-ooo... and you might as well be trying to meet somebody." She slid her purse under the front seat and pulled the seatbelt firmly across her front. "It's not like you've got someone at home waiting for you. And your ass isn't getting any younger. The older you get, the slimmer the pickings."

"Whatever. I'm not sure if I'm ready for all that yet." I continued to lie. I had definitely checked out Alex and took notice of how fine and extremely handsome he was. His buttery brown complexion and those gray eyes were enough to demand the attention of every woman he came across.

While being grilled every which way from Sunday, I got us to the mall in no time flat. We walked around until we reached the specialty shop that carried designer dresses at a fraction of the cost. Carmen had spotted a dress she really wanted during our last weekend outing. It did look good on her.

"Have you got your dress for the party yet?" She paused briefly before adding, "I don't know why I asked that question."

"Neither do I. I think you're confusing me with you and Asia with that last-minute shit."

We passed by a shoe store. I can honestly say that I'm a shoe fanatic. I've got two closets full of them to prove it.

"I know you're not going in there looking for another pair of shoes. Girl, keep it up and you're gonna have to build another *house* just to have room for them."

"I'm just looking, so hush." I put the shoe in my hand back on the round table. I was going to ask the salesperson for my size, but I wouldn't hear the end of it. I decided that I'd come back for them later when I was alone.

"Oh, I want you to see this dress at Caché I've had my eye on," I said.

"Caché? I didn't know you liked their clothes," she said, surprised.

"Girl, don't even try me like that. I buy what I like no matter where it is or how much it costs. Anyway, I thought I'd get your opinion on it since you do have some kind of fashion style." We continued walking.

"I hope it's something sexy. You should really get something that shows off your figure. You've worked so hard to get it and always keep it covered up. Girl, you better flaunt it before it fades away with the years."

"If you don't sound like my sister."

"I thought I was your sister?" Carmen asked.

"You know you are, but I'm starting to think you and Asia are twins. Your minds are always in the gutter and you've always got some kind of advice for me about what I should and shouldn't do." We passed by another shoe store. I inched as close as I could to peek through the window.

"We're looking for a dress, not shoes."

I glanced at her from the corner of my eye. "I wasn't going in."

She grabbed me by the elbow. "Come on. Caché is down here and we've got to get out of here so I can get back home and get dinner started." I noticed that all-too-familiar, "I have a great idea look" settle on her face. Next was the devious smile that always followed. "I just had a wonderful idea." Told you.

"And what would that be?" I asked sarcastically.

"You're going to have dinner with us tonight," she stated.

"What?!"

"I think Alex would like to get to know you better. You heard him say that he wanted to see you again." Boy, could she stretch and twist things into what she wanted them to mean.

"Here you go. That is not what he said."

"Yes, it is."

"No, it's not. He acknowledged my statement about seeing him again before he leaves. How did that turn into, 'I want to see you again'?" I folded my arms across my chest as I waited for her response.

"You know how men are. He may not have said it that way, but that's exactly what he meant. Without a doubt." She pulled my arm so we could resume walking.

"I don't think I should impose on you guys. He's

here to spend time with Bryce and you. I'd be a third wheel."

"I think it would make you the fourth wheel, which will balance out the ride. You know?"

"Okay, Ms. Matchmaker." I nudged her with the side of my arm.

"I'll take that as you're coming."

"Do I really have a choice?"

"I'm glad you realized that. Now, let's get to Caché so we can get back and get dinner started."

"Wait a minute. How did I go from not being there at all to cooking?"

"Say whatever you want, you and I both know that you're going to help me cook. Then you're going to go home, wash your ass, get dressed, and come back and enjoy dinner. Girl, the torch has been put out in Jarrin's case and it's time for you to light another one with someone else." She looped her arm in mine. "Now let's go. We're going to have two very handsome men that are going to be extremely hungry when they get back from playing basketball."

I rolled my eyes at her and shook my head.

"Yeah, and we've still got a million things to do, so stop running your mouth and let's get a move-on."

# *Asia*

## CHAPTER 7

"So what time should I expect you? All right then. I'll be ready and waiting." I heard keys in the door. The alarm gave off a double chime indicating the door had been opened.

"Don't worry about what I'm wearing. I know how to dress." I laughed seductively.

"I miss you, too. Okay. Bye." Yani came in the family room with bags in her hands.

"Looks like you've hit a shoe store again."

"Some habits are hard to break. You and Hayden going out again tonight?" She placed the bags on the breakfast counter and walked over and sat on the sofa next to me.

"Nope."

"Then who were you just talking to?"

"Hayden." She looked at me like I had lost it. "He's going to this dinner party with some friends, but tomorrow night. Although, he did invite me to hang out on South Beach, I thought I'd pass. I want to spend some time with you and the kids. Are you tired?"

"Not really. Just thinking about the night ahead."

I continued to flip through the channels. I ended up settling for music videos.

"Now that's the jam there." Jay-Z's song "Can I Get A..." was on. I got up and started bouncing like the girls in the video. I was jammin'. I love dancing.

"Come on, Yani, bounce with me?" I walked over and started bouncing in front of her.

She looked up at me and shooed me away with a flip of her hand. "Girl, get your coochie out my face. You know I don't get down like that."

"Oh, so you got jokes now? You know I'm strictly dickly." I turned the volume up on the TV and went back to doing my thing. Yani sat there smiling at me. I grabbed her by the arm and made her get up.

"Now watch me." I demonstrated the moves to her and threw in a few extras of my own; bouncing down to the floor and back up in one fluid move. Straight up Miami-style is what they called it. "Now you try it."

I stood across from her so I could see her good. I don't know what caused me to have a lapse in memory and forget that it was my big sister who'd taught me how to dance. Girlfriend started bouncing better than the chicks in the video. Blew me away when she dropped down on her haunches and popped back up as smoothly as I did. She was bouncing like she'd choreographed the video herself. She stood in front of me and made her ass cheeks jump up and down.

"Damn, Girl. You been working as a booty dancer and keeping it on the DL?" By now, I'd stopped bouncing myself so I could check her out.

Paying me no mind, she continued to work it. Then, she really blew me away when she started saying the chick's part of the rap. Word for word. I had to pick my bottom jaw up from the floor. She was all into it.

"Wait a minute. Where have you been hanging out that you know this song?" I was blocking her view of the TV. She kept on dancing and rapping, as she turned and patted her butt in a familiar gesture. She turned back around to find me still staring at her.

"Now what's wrong with me knowing this song? Damn, I do consider myself to be a connoisseur of music. Meaning I like all kinds of music. I have a copy of this CD in my car and this song happens to be my favorite cut off that one. Now, if you don't mind, could you move your ass out the way so I can finish enjoying my song? I haven't seen this video in a while."

All I could do was laugh. For some reason, I realized that I had been seeing my sister as this home-body that doesn't enjoy anything.

What the hell? I thought. I walked over and started bouncing with her and tried my best to outdo her. When the song finally finished, I turned the volume back down and we fell back on the sofa laughing.

"So… what do you want to do tonight? Wanna catch a movie or something? Maybe we can find you a man while we're there. I should get Hayden to hook you up with one of the guys from his office here…"

"Why is everybody trying to *hook* me up? No, thank you." She grabbed the copy of *Black Enterprise* off the coffee table and started flipping through the pages.

"Everybody like who? What are you talking about?"

"Carmen has been riding my back all day about a man. She even invited me over to have dinner with her, Bryce, and Bryce's frat brother who's visiting them from New York."

"A blind date or something?"

She continued to flip through the book with an uninterested look on her face. "No. I met him today."

"And…" I asked impatiently. She knew the suspense was killing me.

"And what?" she responded with her eyes still glued on the pages of the magazine.

"Is he good-looking?!!" I wanted details.

"Umm, hmm," she said as she pulled the magazine closer to her face in an attempt to appear as if she was really into the article.

"Umm, hmm? Umm, hmm he looks okay? Or, Umm, hmm, his ass looks good as hell and you can't wait to rip his clothes off?"

She never looked up from the magazine. "Oh, he's very good looking." She placed the magazine in her lap.

"Ah ha, so you were feeling him. I see that smile. So I guess he's fine, too, and you've already pictured him on top of you breaking in the virginal thang you've got now."

She threw the pillow at me. "Your ass is so nasty. You've got sex on the brain."

"Whatever. I take it that you're going then?"

"Going where?"

"Don't play stupid with me. To Carmen and Bryce's to have dinner with this good-looking... He is single, right?"

"Carmen claims he's *very* single."

"Good-looking, fine, single man." I nudged her with my shoulder. The smirk turned into an all out smile. "Yeah, your ass is going. Trying to sit up here and act like you're not interested. Bitch, please. I know your ass is horny as hell."

"No I'm not."

"Shit, well I'm horny for you. When I think about

you not having any dick in five years. *Five* years! Damn, that's a long ass time."

She nudged me in the back of my head playfully. "Some of us have other things to occupy our time than sex. Okay?"

"Don't even try that shit. I'm not saying that I sit around all day thinking about who and when I'm going to fuck. But, I can't see me going five years without it either."

"You never know what you can do until you try it," she said.

"What-the-fuck-ever. Anyway, that's not what I was asking you."

"Anyway, what was it that you were asking me then?" she said in a mocking tone.

"Are you going to Carmen's tonight?" I softened my tone and draped my arm across her shoulder. "I think you should, big sis. It's time to start living again."

She laid her head on my shoulder. "I know, I know. I guess I'm going. 'Cause brother is sho-nuff fine as hell!" She jumped up and sexily sauntered off to her room.

"Aww suki suki now!" I yelled as I jumped up to follow behind her. "I'll help you find something to wear. We want you to blow his mind. No need to be covering things up."

"You really do think I'm old, don't you? I'm what, barely three years older than you?" She stopped in front of the mirrored closet door and slid it open.

"Did I say you were old? Did, damn Yani, your ass is old, come out of my mouth? Huh?"

"No. Because you know if you said it that way, I'd kick your scrawny, anorexic ass." She playfully pushed my shoulder.

"Okay now. You think that if you want. I don't care how many years older you are, the fact is that you're the *oldest*. You could be only one day older than me. You're still going to become a senior citizen before I do." I flipped the switch to turn on the light in the closet. We had to get her ready for her first date in probably twenty years.

"Now, you just go and take your shower while I find you something to wear."

"Don't have me looking like a hoochie mama. It's a friendly, casual dinner among friends. Okay?" she called out as she made her way into the bathroom.

"Just get in the shower." I stepped inside the closet. "Now you know there is no reason for anyone to have this many pairs of damn shoes."

Her closet is the bomb, though. Being the neat freak that she is, it was organized like something you see in the decorating magazines.

"Now, this is nice." I pulled out a sexy burgundy

dress. It fell just above the knee with straps that crisscrossed the back area. It showed just enough skin. The front had a wide, square neckline and mesh cap sleeves. Hugging in all the right places, this would show off her curves in a subtle kind of way.

"This is so perfect. Now, to find the shoes." I knew she had a pair that went with it perfectly. I went to the shelf where she kept her burgundy/red-colored shoes. Didn't I say she was a neat freak? I came across a sexy strappy pair with a nice four-inch, stiletto heel. I took my findings and laid them out on the bed for a better inspection.

"Yes, big sis, you're going to blow his mind with this little number."

"Who are you talking to?" She was in her terry bathrobe, vigorously rubbing a towel through her wet hair.

"You know how I like to think out loud. So, what do you think?" I did a Kiki Shepard move, waving my hands to show her the ensemble.

"Well, I must say that I'm impressed. Where'd you find this?" She picked the dress up and held it up for inspection.

"In your closet. Where else? I take it that you do approve? Especially since you obviously bought it."

"Yes, baby sister, ya done well. Now all we have to do is find the right accessories to complement it and then tackle this hair."

"Girl, don't even worry about it. I've got just the right hairstyle. Now come on so you can get going." I pushed her back into the bathroom in front of her vanity. She pulled out her jewelry box and picked out a simple diamond necklace that had the matching bracelet and earrings. Then I hooked her hair up.

We blow-dried it straight and then pulled it into a tight neat bun at the nape of her neck. I put a little makeup on her.

After I finished, she checked herself out in the mirrored closet doors. "Do I look good or what?" She spun around to face me.

"He's not going to be able to take his eyes off you."

"Where'd you learn to do makeup like this?" She was closely inspecting her makeup in the mirror.

"I've paid enough money to get mine done. I just paid attention to what they were doing and realized it wasn't anything miraculous. Then I practiced on a few of my girlfriends."

"Wow, Mommy! You look good!" Natalia said as she stood in the doorway. "Where are you going?" She walked in sporting the FUBU gear I bought her for Christmas.

"Over to Carmen's for dinner."

"Are you sure you're only going to Goddy's house?"

"Of course I'm sure."

"Why don't you go find us something to watch on TV?" I asked. She rolled her eyes at me on the sly.

"I saw that. Don't make me have to drop kick you."

"Don't start, Auntie." She sucked her teeth and rolled her eyes.

"Don't start, Auntie, nothing." I playfully pushed her out the door. "Now we need to get you out of here." I grabbed the matching bag from the bed and handed it to Yani. I checked her out one last time to make sure everything was in place. "Damn, Girl, you look good!" I had an overwhelming feeling to cry.

"Thanks to you." She winked at me.

We walked to the front door. I flipped the foyer light on. Yani grabbed her keys from the porcelain bowl she kept on the table against the wall.

"Can you drive the car so the kids and I can ride in the truck?"

"Okay. You know where the extra keys are?"

"I sure do."

She hugged me lightly and pecked me softly on the cheek in an attempt not to mess up her makeup. "See you when I get in tonight."

"I hope not," I shot back.

"Shut up. Bye."

"Bye."

I walked to the window and watched her until she pulled out into the street and her rear lights disappeared down the block. I smiled as I realized she was on the road to healing. I'd prayed for years that she would find someone that would realize the treasure Jarrin had thrown away.

Natalia came up behind me. "Auntie, you did a good job hooking Mommy up. She looked like a real dime piece."

I draped my arm over her shoulder. "What do you know about someone being a dime piece?"

"Come on, now. I do know the lingo. The real question is…what do you know about being a dime piece?" she said as she pointed her finger at me.

"Never underestimate your auntie, baby. As Tupac once said, '*I get around.*'" I winked at her. "Now, how would you like to get out of this house? Maybe go to a movie or get something to eat?"

"Or both? I wanna see this movie that just came out." Her eyes lit up with excitement.

"If it's rated R, you can forget it. Your mom is already trippin' when I say a few four-letter words around you guys. If I took you to a movie she didn't approve of, I'd never hear the end of it. And besides, your brother is going with us."

"Dang. Can't we send him to one of his friends' houses?" She sulked.

"Now is that fair? I want to spend time with both of you."

"We might as well look in the kiddy section then.

We wouldn't want to take Jay to anything that would corrupt his little mind."

"Or yours either, Ms. Thang." She rolled her eyes at me. "And I advise you to adjust your lil' attitude or we can just stay home. I don't want to have to tap that ass. I don't care how old you are." I grabbed the cordless phone from the coffee table and dialed the number to Hayden's hotel. The operator put the call through.

"Hello?"

"Hey. Whatcha doing?" I sang out in my sexiest voice.

"Sitting here wishing you were with me."

"In that case, I was thinking that maybe we could catch a movie? Then go somewhere for a quick bite to eat."

"Sounds like a plan to me. Should I pick you up?"

"No, that's okay. I'll drive. Let's see…we should be there in about thirty minutes or so."

"We? Is this a double date?"

"Not exactly. I decided to treat the kids to a night out. Still down to go?" I was hoping the idea of having the kids with us wouldn't be a turn-off.

"Of course. I'll see you guys in forty-five minutes then."

"Okay. Don't take all night getting dressed. Just throw on some jeans or something."

"I know how to dress. You just get here and I'll be ready. Bye, sexy."

"Bye."

"Thought you wanted to spend time with us? Auntie got a booty call…"

"Shut up, lil' girl." I playfully tossed a pillow at her. As long as I had them with me, there would be no calling of the booty.

# Alex

## CHAPTER 8

"I'm not going to say anything about how you cheated," Bryce said as I held out my hand.

"Yeah, okay. Just pay up."

"All right, all right. Just don't say anything around Carmen. I'll never hear the end of it."

He reached into the glove compartment to retrieve his wallet and pulled out the twenty spot he owed me. I swept him six games. I've heard that marriage and fatherhood would mess up your game, but he was almost pathetic.

"Man, I'm hungry! I sure hope Carmen has finished cooking." I looked out the window at the houses we passed as we drove toward home.

"Ahh, I think it's only fair that I warn you about this dinner my wife has planned for you."

"What's that?"

"Well, since she's cooking a gourmet meal and not just a meal, that means she's expecting us to get spiffy. You know, shower, shave, and put on some decent attire."

"That's a given. I wouldn't show up to dinner funky and you and I both know I've got the wardrobe covered. I never go anywhere unprepared where that is concerned."

"What I'm trying to let you know is that Carmen loves to play match-maker."

"And…"

"You can expect to see Yani at dinner tonight."

"What?" I tried to act a little thrown off when I was actually pleased to know that I was getting another chance to see her again so soon.

"Usually when they go shopping, Carmen drives over to Yani's since she lives closer to the mall. So when Yani came to pick her up today, I knew Carmen had staged the whole thing so you two could meet."

"So you're saying they're both in on it?"

"Naw, Man. Yani probably had no idea. I think my wife orchestrated the whole thing. I bet Carmen worked Yani over from the moment her butt hit the seat in the car."

I laughed. "So you're telling me that I should put on my most expensive cologne tonight?"

"If I know Carmen, and I do know Carmen, things are going to go down just like I explained. So bring out your arsenal."

"What makes you think she had to talk Yani into having dinner?"

"Yani wouldn't voluntarily invite herself. She probably didn't have one thought of you two being anything at all."

"Oh, so you saying there's something's wrong with me?"

"You all right. Not that I'm interested in you, but …" We both laughed.

"So what's the deal with Yani? Is she married? Children?"

Bryce seemed to stiffen slightly. "Look, you'll have your chance tonight to ask all the questions you want. I just wanted to give you a heads up. Can't let my boy go in without any preparation. Besides, I remember how hard you were staring at her earlier. My hunch is that you definitely want to holler at her."

I laughed. "I'll admit she's a very attractive lady. Any man in his right mind would want to holler at her; especially when she clearly didn't have any rings on her fingers. While I do appreciate you looking out for your bruh, I think I can handle a simple dinner date."

"Well, consider yourself warned," he said as we pulled into the three-car garage next to Carmen's silver Mercedes truck.

As we opened the door to the house, a delicious aroma dominated the air. Following the smell into the kitchen, we found Carmen hovering over the stove. Her hair was tied down with a scarf and she was wrapped in her white terrycloth robe.

"Hey, you two. How was the game?" Carmen asked Bryce before he kissed her.

"Umm, Baby. Damn, that smells good." She shoved the wooden spoon toward his mouth so he could taste.

"How bad did you beat him, Alex?"

I looked at Bryce and chuckled. "Let's just say that you're doing your job with him."

"What does that mean?" she asked, obviously confused.

"Inside male joke, Baby." He smacked her teasingly on the butt. "I'm going up to get ready for dinner. What time should we expect Yani?" he said as he headed out.

She clumsily dropped the pot top as she held the spoon in midair en route to her mouth. "How'd you know she was coming for dinner?"

"I noticed you set the table for four and it's only three of us," he lied.

The table was hooked up real nice. Candles in elegant holders, fresh flowers, and a set of what had to be her good china adorned it.

"Carmen," I called.

"Yes?" she said in a sweet voice as she came around the corner drying her hands on a towel.

"You didn't have to go through all this trouble for me. I could sit in the family room and eat off a TV table," I said, messing with her.

"Negro, don't make me act ugly in here with you. This was no trouble at all. I didn't even break a sweat. Speaking of sweat," she said as she grabbed her nose. "Y'all need to hurry up and get in the shower."

"Come here, Baby," Bryce said as he playfully grabbed at her.

"Stop now! I just got out the shower!" She ran past us and up the stairs as he gave chase.

❤❤❤❤

Decked out in my all-black ensemble—linen slacks, pullover, and shoes, I gave myself the once-over before going downstairs. There was a soft tap on the door.

"You dressed yet?" Carmen asked.

"I'll be out in a minute."

"Okay. We're downstairs waiting."

"All right." I looked in the mirror again and ran my hand through my short, thick curls. Before leaving the room, I put everything back in its place.

As I made my way down the stairs, I could hear two female voices. I was tempted to take the stairs two at a time, but calmed myself. Couldn't come off as too eager. As I got to the bottom step, the voices got louder as Carmen and Yani walked out of the kitchen with platters in their hands.

"Can I help with anything?" I asked.

They both looked up.

"That's okay. These were the last two platters to bring out and Bryce is getting the wine. So, you can have a seat," Carmen replied.

Yani still hadn't said anything as she sat the platter she was carrying on the table.

"Yani, you can stay here with Alex. I'm going to run in the kitchen and help Bryce. He always has a hard time getting the cork out. We'll be right out," Carmen said.

Yani gave her a knowing look. "You sure there's nothing else I can help you with?"

"I've got it all under control from here." Carmen gave Yani a slight nudge in the direction of her seat. The one directly across from mine.

I decided to break the ice. "Don't worry, I promise not to bite."

She laughed nervously. "I'm glad to hear that. Even though you don't look like that type, it's always reassuring to know."

"Umm, a sense of humor. I like that."

"You do?"

"Of course. You don't?"

"But of course."

I held out her chair for her. She smelled divine. A soft but fresh scent.

"Issey Miaki."

"Excuse me?"

"Your perfume. Is it Issey Miaki?"

"How'd you know?"

"I'm wearing the same thing. The men's version of course."

She laughed. "I hope so."

"Tell me something."

"What's that?"

"How is it that you know these two characters?"

She looked down in her lap and smiled and brought her gaze back up to meet mine. "I've known Carmen since high school. We've actually been friends for, oh, quite some time now. She and Bryce are the Godparents of my children."

I shifted in my seat at the plural mention of children. "If you don't mind me asking, how many children do you have?"

"Only two. I'm not housing the Brady Bunch. My daughter is fourteen and my son is ten."

Okay, two kids, and they're not babies either. "I hope I'm not prying. I tend to be blunt sometimes. It comes with my business territory," I said as I set her up for the bigger question; even though I knew she wasn't. If she was, there was no way Carmen would go all out to set us up, but I wanted to hear it from her.

"It doesn't bother me. I'm the same way. I feel if you want to know something the best thing to do is ask the source." She smiled shyly.

"Well I'm glad to hear that. Since it's not bothering you, would you mind if I asked you another personal question?"

"Go ahead."

"Are you married?"

# *Yani*

## CHAPTER 9

**W**hoa. He wasn't lying about being blunt. He'd just slapped me with the million-dollar question. The one question I had no idea how to answer any more. My mind began to race a mile a minute. I shifted around in my seat a little.

"Umm," I cleared my throat. Just as I was about to open my mouth, Carmen and Bryce walked in.

"I hope you guys are starving, because I've prepared a four-course meal and I expect everyone to eat," Carmen said.

I knew Carmen was talking because I could see her mouth moving, but my hearing was muted as I mused over the question. Was I still married? I'd already called the insurance people to begin the process to declare Jarrin dead. I guess that would make me a widow and single again. Death had done us part.

I looked up at Alex, who was talking with Bryce

and Carmen. This time I really checked him out. His golden honey-colored skin was a tad bit darker than mine. His grayish eyes were downright dreamy. A girl could definitely get lost in them. He parted his lips and exposed a smile that was nothing less than perfect. As Asia would say, he was eye candy. She'd also probably say that it was typical of me to be attracted to a pretty boy. He looked as if a sculptor had gone through great lengths to chisel out perfect muscles on his arms, chest, and abs. Damn, his...

"Did you hear me?" I looked over to find Carmen was talking to me. At that moment I wanted to slide under the table and disappear as it was blatantly obvious that I'd gotten caught staring at Alex as everyone at the table looked in my direction.

"I'm sorry, Carmen, what did you say?" I pulled my chair a little closer to the table.

"I asked if you could pass the salt. That's all."

She smiled that irritating smile she had when things were going the way she wanted them to go. I found the salt on my left and passed it to her. I had to think of something to say to ease myself through this uncomfortable moment.

"Everything looks delicious, Carmen."

"I can tell that you noticed," she replied.

Just like her ass to take things a little further. God, I hope my cheeks aren't a blazing red.

"It's hard not to," I said. I wasn't about to let her have one up on me.

We started dinner with the appetizers. A nice shrimp roll. The shell was made from scratch and stuffed with shredded vegetables, topped with a delicious cheese sauce.

The dinner went by smoothly. It was filled with good conversation as we devoured the excellent feast of seafood gumbo. We finished up our dessert, a delicious peach cobbler, topped off with a scoop of Edy's French Vanilla ice-cream. After we ate our fill we went into the living room for drinks.

"How about a little music?" Bryce asked.

"That sounds good to me. Ladies?" Alex looked at Carmen and me.

"Sure," we both said.

Thirty minutes into our little gathering of the minds, Carmen suddenly remembered that she needed Bryce to help her find this particular photo album that we just *had* to see. I knew she'd find a reason to get us alone sooner or later.

At first Bryce was reluctant to go. Asked her all kinds of questions. Looking at her flustered face, he realized that he was getting pretty close to having to sleep on the couch, so he reluctantly followed her.

During dinner I'd learned a few things about Alex. He has a great sense of humor, is very knowl-edgeable about many different subjects, which makes it enjoyable to have a conversation with him, and most importantly, he's very down-to-earth.

"Is she always that obvious?" he asked.

"Well, you know...she has a tendency...to umm..." Unable to think of any nicer way to put it, I went with the truth. "Yes." We laughed. "Being discreet is not one of Carmen's finer points."

With his left arm draped across the back of the sofa, he swirled the ice in his drink around with the right.

"I'll be honest with you," he said.

I looked at him. "What's that?"

"I was hoping they would get tired or something and excuse themselves." I took a sip of my drink of coconut rum and Coke. "I hope I didn't make you uncomfortable with that statement. It's just that..."

"Believe me, you didn't. I'm actually flattered that you're enjoying my company, because I'm definitely enjoying yours. It's nice to talk to another adult."

"So I'm not making you uncomfortable?"

"I would've made a beeline for the door as soon as dinner was over if that were the case." We chuckled.

"You know, you never answered my question."

Damn, I was hoping he'd forgotten about that. I nervously took another sip of my drink.

"What question is that?"

"That's cute. I think you know what question I'm talking about."

"Would it hurt for you to remind me?" I gave him a flirtatious smile.

"Are you married?" he asked in a non-condescending tone.

My shoulders stiffened a little and my breathing slowed a bit. Why was such a harmless question putting me on the defense?

"I'm getting the feeling that this is a difficult subject for you."

I leaned back into the soft comfort of the sofa. "I don't know if I should bore you with details."

"I couldn't imagine you boring anyone, let alone me," he crooned in a sexy tone that sent chills up my spine.

I took a deep breath and stared down at the glass I held cupped in my hands as I began to speak. "I guess you can say as of a few days ago, I'm now considered to be a widow."

"Oh, I'm sorry to hear that. How did he die?"

"I'm not absolutely sure that he's dead. I haven't seen or heard from him in five years."

"That's definitely a sign of death. Or he wanted out..."

"I was nothing short of the perfect wife," I quickly added in my defense.

"Another clear reason that he was either unreasonable or just plain stupid."

"Is there any other reason for a man to want out of what seemed to be a perfect marriage?"

"Look, from the short time that I've spent talking with you tonight, I can't imagine anyone wanting to disassociate themselves with you, let alone lose you as their wife. You seem to be a beautiful woman—inside and out."

I could feel myself begin to blush. I looked up at him, trying my best not to smile too hard. It had been quite some time since I'd had some welcomed male attention. I thought I'd melt as he stared back at me with those sexy gray eyes that seemed to sparkle when he smiled.

The subject sparked a conversation that went from relationships, to world views, to politics. You name it, we discussed it.

I told him all about my business. How after Jarrin disappeared I went back into the workforce and worked for an advertising agency for two years handling their special events department. After much nudging from my boss, I decided to approach Carmen about starting a business together. She had been talking about doing something that would allow her to be at home with the kids. After a huge success, we branched out to New York when my sister, who'd been working in the field of PR for umpteen years, started to tell us how lucrative the market was there.

He in turn told me all about living in New York. He vaguely brushed the subject of the work he did at a production company. It was as if neither of us wanted the night to end. Finally, I glanced at my watch.

"Wow, I didn't realize it was this late. I really need to get going."

"How far are you from here?"

"About twenty minutes or so. A quick ride on I-75."

"I guess that's not that long. I'm not real familiar with the area so, I don't really know where I-75 is."

"More than likely it's the expressway you guys took to get here from the airport. I'm a speed demon so I'll be home in no time."

He laughed. "Now, *that* I find hard to believe."

"That I like to drive fast? Why not?" I cocked my head to the side and looked at him teasingly.

"I don't know. I just wouldn't take you as the type that drives fast. Then again, you never know a person until you live with them."

He had this devilish grin on his face. I decided to just drop that one. That was a can of worms I wasn't ready to open up yet.

"Well, believe it. I love to drive fast. There's nothing like a five-speed."

"And you drive a stick shift, too?"

"What's so big about driving a stick? I learned to

drive in a stick-shift car. That was the only car my father would buy me. He said it was much cheaper and better on gas. So, if I wanted to drive my brand-new car, I had to learn how."

We cracked up off that one.

I looked at the staircase. "You know something?"

"What's that?"

"Have you noticed that our gracious host and hostess never came back down? I think I smell the stench of a conspiracy floating in the air. How about you?"

He followed my gaze and smiled; running his finger underneath his chin. "I think you have something." He smiled.

We were so wrapped up into talking that we never really missed them. I smiled at him and slid to the edge of the sofa to stand.

"I really need to get going. It's almost one-thirty in the morning. I can't remember the last time I stayed out this late."

"I don't know if I should feel honored or like a schmuck for being the reason then."

"Oh, it's definitely an honor." I stood and walked back to the family room to grab my purse. I fished around for my keys and checked my cell phone to see if Asia and the kids had called. When I returned to the living room Alex was standing.

"Since this was an honor, why don't we do it again? I'll be here for at least another week. What do you say?"

"I say I'd like that. Why don't you give me a call and this time we'll go out or something. Drive down to South Beach and hang out with the 'Beautiful People.'" We laughed at the familiar saying.

"We can definitely do that. So be on the lookout for that call."

Oh, I would. *With binoculars and all*, I thought as he walked me to the door.

"Make sure to tell the other two that I said good night."

"Let me walk you to your car."

"You don't have to do that. It's a little chilly out here and you don't have on a jacket."

He began to laugh. "You Floridians kill me with your fear of cold weather. We wish for nights like this in New York in December. Come on." He opened the door and placed his hand near the small of my back and guided me out the door. "Nice ride," he said as I disarmed the alarm and door locks.

"Thanks. One of the few pleasures in life I allow myself."

"What is it? '98 or '99?" He stuck his head inside and checked out the inside.

"It's a 2000. They called me before the first one hit the lot."

He laughed. "I take it that you're a serious BMW lover."

"I get a new one every two to three years. I wanted to be one of the first with a 2000. Does that sound shallow or what?"

"No, not at all. You work hard, why not reward yourself."

"Thank you."

"Maybe one day I'll be able to get one."

"Hey, you work hard, why not reward yourself?" We laughed.

"I'm just a poor city boy trying to survive."

"I'm thinking about graduating to the big one next time."

"The 740. That's nice and *expensive*. What is it that you said you did again? I think I need to quit my job and come work for you."

"It's a tax write-off for me."

"You are a smart businesswoman."

"Have to be."

We stood there silent for a moment. I was partially in the car while he stood guard in front of me. He stared down at his feet as I pretended to search through my purse for something. Sensing that the moment was starting to get a little awkward, I slid into my seat and started the car.

"Thanks for making sure I got to my car. I think I better get going before my kids file a missing persons report." If I didn't make a run for it, we would probably end up spending another hour talking.

"I'm serious about seeing you again."

"Give me a call tomorrow." I pulled one of my business cards from my case and scribbled my cell number on the back.

He bent down and leaned his head into the car. I got nervous at the thought of him kissing me. Was I ready for this? Would he think that I was easy?

He pulled something off my dress and then smoothly said close to my face, "See you tomorrow." He closed my door, stood back and waited for me to drive off. He'd faked me out.

I put my car in reverse and pulled out the driveway. I waved before putting it into first gear and zooming off down the street.

As I got on the ramp of the expressway I began to wonder what kind of kisser he was. Was he the type that gave soft irresistible kisses? Or was he one of those, wet, sloppy, face swallowers?

*Maybe I'll find out soon*, I thought as I cranked up the volume of Chico and sped toward home. I realized I was doing something that I hadn't done in a long time where a man was concerned. I was actually smiling.

# *Alex*

## CHAPTER 10

It seemed as though I was making it a habit of watching her drive off. After her taillights disappeared down the street I walked back toward the house. I looked up and saw a thin ray of light coming from an upstairs window.

"Carmen." I waved up to her. Busted, all she could do was wave back. If she was half as nosey as Bryce and Yani say she was, she'd probably been watching us since we'd opened the door to come outside.

As I walked into the house, I could hear the television in the family room on what sounded like ESPN. I walked in and sat next to Bryce.

"So?"

"So what?" I countered.

"You know I've been sent down here to get as much info as you'll give up. And give me something worth talking about. I'd like to get some sleep tonight."

I laughed. "Carmen can't possibly be that bad."

He slowly rolled his head toward me with a look of disbelief on his face. "All right man. My bad," I said. My hands raised in defense.

"Thank you."

Feeling that I had nothing really exciting to tell, I told him how much I enjoyed talking with Yani. That I was very interested in seeing her again.

"We discussed her marital situation."

"Yeah?" he asked, surprised.

"Told you we talked about some of everything."

"So?"

"So, what?"

"What do you think about it?

"I don't know. I mean, what am I supposed to think? If a man doesn't make any kind of communication with his family and that's not his normal way of handling things, he has to be dead."

"Everyone else has felt that way for years, but Yani took the 'keep a candle burning' thing to another level."

"She admitted that, but she also admitted that she was over it and ready to move on."

"Bottom line, Man, do you think you guys hit it off? You know that'll be the main question I get asked."

We laughed.

"I can only speak for myself, but I think so. She

gave me her number." Him being my boy and all, I decided to 'fess up and told him how I'd really wanted to kiss her when we were at her car.

"So why didn't you?"

"I don't know. Didn't want to scare her away. Besides, we have plenty of time for that."

"So what did you tell her about you?"

"The basics."

"What's the basics?"

"My name, where I live, you know. The basics."

"Look, we've known Yani for a long time and I can honestly say..."

"That she's not like that. Yeah, I've heard that before. Man, you and Carmen have dated since college, so you know your wife loves you because of you. Not because you have money or these great connections and you can help her out. No disrespect, but I'd rather do things my way."

"I just hope this doesn't blow up in your face. You'd be missing out on one special lady."

"I'll second that, baby." Carmen had walked into the family room.

"You just couldn't wait for me to come back up?"

She flipped her hand up to him to stop his ranting. "Alex, I respect you, but Yani is like my sister. Don't do anything to hurt her. And this is not a request. Take it as the warning it is." She gave me an unrelenting stare. One that said she meant business.

"I think we're jumping the gun here. I haven't gone on the first date with her and you're threatening me already? She must be as special as Bryce says then."

"And some."

"Well, I'm looking forward to finding out just how much."

"I want you to know that my friend is a good woman. She's not one to depend on a man to get what she wants or needs. She's been through quite an ordeal and still managed to come out on top." She went into the kitchen. "Would you guys like something to drink?" she called out to us. It was as if she hadn't uttered those last words.

"Bring me a little green bottle, Baby. What about you, Alex?"

"Think I'm going to pass and head upstairs to get some rest." I stood up and slapped him firmly on the shoulder. Carmen came out with an open Heineken bottle in her hand. I gave her a tight hug. "Dinner was excellent, lady. So was the company."

"See you in the morning," she said as she hugged me back with her free hand.

"Okay. Goodnight, you two." I walked away and turned around as she handed the bottle to Bryce and slipped into his lap and snuggled close to him. He kissed her lightly on the lips and wrapped his arm around her.

*All I have to do is find my perfect fit*, I thought as I headed toward the stairs.

My head was filled with thoughts of Yani as her fresh-scented perfume still danced in my nostrils. I knew tonight my dreams would also be filled with her as the sight of her face and the sound of her voice would dance in my head.

# Asia

## CHAPTER 11

"So, did you enjoy yourself?" I asked Hayden as we stood in the lobby embracing.

"Very much. The kids are wonderful."

"My sister is very blessed."

"What do you have planned for New Year's?"

"I'm going to a party."

"A party, huh?"

"My sister's best friend has one every year."

"Sounds interesting."

"Hayden…"

"Yes?" He looked down at me with those sexy ass eyes.

"Would you like to accompany me to the party?"

"Only if you promise me that we can ring in the New Year in a very special way first. You know, the way we used to do it." He kissed me full on the mouth; teasing me with his tongue.

"Umm, that sounds reasonable enough."

"So what's the agenda for tomorrow?"

"I was planning to spend the day with Yani, but I'll see you tomorrow night."

"All night?"

"That'll work."

He bent down and kissed me again. Knowing the kids were in the car waiting and it was getting late, I pushed the button to summon the elevator. The ding announcing its arrival brought Hayden up for air.

"I guess this is my cue."

"Yes, it is."

He kissed me one last time before stepping into the elevator. "Call me when you get in."

"I'll try."

He smiled and winked at me as the doors slid closed.

I looked around the lobby to make sure we hadn't caused a scene worthy of an audience. It was as deserted as it was when we'd walked in ten minutes before. I quickly made my way out to the truck where the kids were waiting. Nat popped the locks for me.

"Had to give him a good-night kiss?"

"Stay out of grown folks' business." I pulled away from the curb into the never-ending traffic creeping up and down Ocean Drive.

"Is that your boyfriend?"

"He's my friend. Why?"

"Friends don't act the way you two acted tonight."

"And what way would that be?"

"Auntie, he was all over you. Rubbing your back, kissing the back of your neck. I know you think that I'm just a little girl, but I do know that when someone likes you, they can't keep their hands off you." She smiled at me as I tried to ignore her.

"Is your brother still sleeping?"

"Can't you hear him? The boy can outsnore a grown man."

"I can't hear anything over this radio." I pressed the button to turn it down a few notches.

"You still haven't answered my question."

I jumped on 395 heading away from the beach back to the mainland. The opposite direction was packed with cars full of people in search of a good time in one of the many clubs on the beach side. Boy, things had changed since I'd left. I remember when this place was like a ghost town. The neighborhood was made up of the 55 and older crowd.

"I guess that means it's none of my business then."

"Nat, not that it *is* any of your business, Hayden used to be very special to me. Once upon a time, yes, he was my man. I think I would be jumping the gun to give him that title again, so soon. Why am I telling this to you? You're right. It's none of your business."

"Sorry for asking. You and Mommy—boy…" She

rolled her eyes and reached for the knob to turn the radio volume up.

"Me and Mommy what?"

"Nothing." She turned her head and looked out the window.

"Nothing hell. What were you about to say?"

"Noth…"

"Don't tell me nothing again."

"All right then. You two need to realize that I'm not a baby anymore. I'm so sick of saying it." She sucked her teeth.

"Girl, it's not that deep. Believe me. What I wouldn't give to be your age again."

"We can switch anytime you're ready."

"All right now. Don't let your mouth get your behind in trouble. You need to enjoy being a child while you can. No worries or headaches."

"What's so hard about being an adult? You come and go as you please. No one telling you what to do."

"Yeah, and let's not forget working to pay your bills. Lights, water, rent, car payment, gas, money for food. Shall I continue?"

"I get the picture." She turned her head toward the window again. A massive jet flew over the car as we passed Miami International.

"Look, take my word for it, being an adult is not all it's cracked up to be. It's definitely overrated at times."

"Wonder if Mommy had a good time."

"Me, too."

"So Goddy hooked her up with someone?"

"Boy, I've definitely got to get used to you and your slang."

"You do know what it means?"

"Girl, I was saying that word before you were a thought in your mama's head or a twinkle in your daddy's eye. Do I know what it means? Why do you feel that we're so old? Never mind. Don't answer that." We both laughed.

"Did you like my daddy?" She looked at me out the corner of her eye.

"I liked him. I'm not crazy about him now, but Jarrin was cool with me."

"Oh," she said and began to bounce her head to the reggae tune on the radio.

"Wanna talk about it?"

"What?"

"About how you feel about your daddy."

"I don't know. I mean, he's dead, right?"

"There's nothing set in stone saying he is, but we believe he is."

"How do we find out how he died or if he is or not?"

"Maybe we'll find out one day, but there's the possibility that we may never find out. Have you talked with your mom about how you feel?"

"No. I try not to bring him up at all. When we

used to ask about him when we were younger, she would always cry. So Jay and I stopped asking."

"Does she ever talk about him with you guys?"

"Not really. She did talk to us when she decided not to wait anymore. We'd already stopped hoping that he'd come back. I know one thing, if he is alive, I hope he dies."

"That's harsh, Nat."

"No, it's not. He doesn't want us. We never did anything to him. And the way Mommy has suffered, I wish he would try to show his face."

"Believe me, nothing would keep him away from you guys except death. So don't think he abandoned you. If I know one thing, I know your daddy loved you, your brother, and your mom. Okay?"

"Okay," she mumbled.

"If you ever need to talk about it, or anything else— and I mean n-e-thing, I'm just a phone call away."

"Thanks, Auntie." She smiled as I clasped her hand tight.

I pulled up to the house and parked in the garage since it was inevitable that I would have to carry Jay in the house. Better yet, drag him since he's more than half my size.

After getting the kids settled in, I checked to see if Yani had made it in yet. Finding no sign of her I went into the kitchen and checked the clock on the microwave, which said it was after one in the morning. I settled in front of the TV and waited for her to come.

Staying out this late, I know that heifer has got some juice to talk about when she gets in.

# *Yani*

## CHAPTER 12

I smiled the entire ride home. I'd just had a wonderful time talking to a very intelligent, delightful, fine-ass, good-looking man.

I pulled into the driveway and hit the opener. I pulled beside the 4Runner. *Wonder why she parked it here*, I thought as I closed the garage door. I noticed a few lights on inside the house and knew before I hit the corner that my sister would be up waiting for a play-by-play of the evening. Especially since I've missed curfew. Good thing she is still up though, 'cause I'd planned to wake her up if she was sleeping.

I grabbed my purse off the floor on the passenger side and leaned back against the headrest and closed my eyes in an effort to conjure up a picture of Alex in my head. My lips curled up into a pleasing smile.

"Tap, tap, tap." My eyes flew open.

"How long are you going to sit your ass in this

car and keep me waiting?" Asia was standing with her face close to the widow. Her breath blew against the glass causing it to fog in the spot near her nose. Her hand was planted firmly on her hip. I flung the door open in an attempt to hit her.

"What the hell is wrong with you? You scared the shit out of me. Damn near made me piss in my clothes." I jumped out the car and snatched my purse up on my shoulder.

"Whatever."

"Why didn't you put the truck back in its place?"

"Because I had to drag your big, heavy ass son in the house. He fell asleep and I couldn't get him to wake up. Since this side is closer to the door, I parked here."

"Where did you guys go?"

"Dave & Busters in Hollywood. They said you didn't mind."

"We've gone there before. It's been a while though." I hit my alarm. We went into the house and I pulled off my jacket and hung it in the coat closet. "So you guys had a good time?"

"We'll talk about that later. Come on." She dragged me by the arm into the family room.

"What?" I sang innocently as I reluctantly followed her.

"Your ass comes rolling up in here after two and

wants to talk about what me and the kids did? I think you have more to tell than I do." She pulled me down on the couch.

"What is there to tell? He's a very nice man who I enjoyed talking to. Were there sparks flying in the air? Sort of. We promised to hook up again so I can show him around." I tried to rise up to my feet. She stopped me.

"Where does he live? What does he do for a living? Is he married? Or has he ever been married before? How many children does he have? Those are the type of questions that you should've been getting answers to. I know it's been a while since you've been on a date, but damn."

I attempted to stand again without success. "I see that I'm not going to get any sleep unless you get some satisfaction."

"Yep. So start talking."

"Look, I'm tired. All I can remember is that he said something about working at a production company in New York. Which one, I don't know. He's originally from New York and loves living in Manhattan. He's never been married and doesn't have any children. Now, if it is okay with you, Warden Fenton, I'm going to go get undressed and climb into my bed for some well-deserved sleep."

She leaned back into the sofa. "So you're telling me that you just found a diamond in the ruff and on your first try? He's fine, good looking, and has a good job? You just seem to have all the luck, don't you?"

I grabbed her hand to help her to her feet. "You've already got me married off to him when we haven't gone on our first date." I walked into my room and into the closet and slipped off my shoes. "I'm not looking for a husband. I have…" I paused at the flash of reality. An intense pain filled my heart.

"Say it in the right tense. You *had* a husband. So if you want to get another one, there's nothing stopping you." She helped me pull the pins from my hair. It cascaded down and danced around my shoulders. Asia grabbed the hairbrush off the vanity and made me sit on the stool and gently brushed my hair.

I sat staring at my reflection in the mirror. I noticed a slight change in the expression staring back at me. It was completely different from the one that stared at me for the past five years. The involuntary scowl that had become a semi-permanent resident on my face had been replaced by a welcoming smile. The delightful feel of the brush making contact with my scalp was another reason that I was smiling. But I knew the main reasons were the wonderful thoughts about tonight and Alex.

"Remember the time when we were kids and we'd sneak out the house after Mama and Daddy went to sleep? It was so easy since they went to bed with the chickens."

"How could I forget? I think that's one of the reasons I stay up as late as I do. I go into Nat's room and check on her in the middle of the night. There's nothing she can pull that I haven't already done. Remember how I used to sneak Jarrin in the house?"

"Remember that time you guys overslept and Daddy was up?"

Boy, had she hit a memory chord. I would never forget that Sunday morning that seemed like an eternity ago.

❤❤❤

We were able to get away with murder during our teen years. After a certain time of night, Janice and Albert Fenton went to bed. We didn't have to worry about seeing them until the next morning. We would watch TV and wait. Once we heard the familiar faint sound of their singsong snoring, we were out of there. Sometimes I would sneak Jarrin in. He would stay with me all night and leave right before it was time for Daddy to get up for work.

This one particular morning, we'd overslept. I woke up to my daddy playing his Sunday morning special. A little gospel, blues, and a few oldies but goldies mixed in. I jumped up so hard and fast that Jarrin nearly fell out of the bed.

"Oh shit! Get up!! Get up!!" I was up running around the bed looking for my clothes.

"What's wrong?" Then it registered in his brain what was wrong. "What time is it?" he asked.

"I don't care what time it is. He's up and we've got to get you out of here!" I had slipped my gown on and threw him his shirt. He was hopping around on one foot trying to get his pants on.

"Hurry up!" I said in an excited whisper. As soon as he got his last shoe on, there was a knock on my door. We both froze.

"Think. Think," I said to myself. I turned to him and motioned for him to get under the bed. He dropped and rolled so fast under the bed, it was like he was auditioning for a fire drill commercial. I looked around the room to make sure nothing was on the floor, bed, or any other surrounding areas that would give away that someone else was in my room with me.

Daddy knocked again. "Yani? You up, Baby?"

"Hmm?" I put on my best sleepy voice.

"Open the door. I got something I wanna ask

you." I took my time, checking under the bed one more time. I placed my finger over my lips to make sure that he knew not to make a sound, then opened the door.

"Hey, Daddy. What time is it?" I said groggily, pretending to rub sleep out of my eyes.

"Put some clothes on and come go to breakfast with your old man."

"You're not going to work today?" I said as I tried to suppress the panicky feelings that threatened to give me away.

"Nope. I decided to take the day off and spend the morning with my girls. After breakfast we can go to the Thunderbird Flea Market up in Fort Lauderdale."

"Okay." I had to think of something and fast. How was I going to get him out before we left?

"I'm going to wake up my sugar britches. So, get dressed now." He kissed me on my head and went to Asia's room. I quickly closed the door and locked it. I plopped down on the floor. Jarrin had fear written all over his face.

"What are we going to do?! I can't stay up under here all day!"

"Let me go check on something right quick. When I tell you to, you get up and make a bee line to the front door." I pulled my housecoat out of the closet and went to check Daddy's whereabouts. He was just coming out of Asia's room when I walked up and gave him a hug.

"You gon' get ready or not?" His words were occasionally laced with his North Carolina accent.

"In a minute. I realized I forgot to give you a hug good morning. I was so sleepy when you came in." At that moment, I came up with an idea that I hoped would work. I began sniffing the air. Frowning up my face, I looked at Daddy. "What's that smell?"

"What smell?" he said as he sniffed the air.

"Daddy, I think you need to jump in the shower."

He lifted his arm. "You tellin' me I'm funky?"

"I don't know what it is exactly, but you're not smelling your freshest right now. If I can smell you, you know as the day goes on, especially with us going to the flea market walking around in the heat, after thirty minutes everyone will be able to smell you." Asia came to her bedroom door scratching her head. We both looked at her. She paused and looked at us.

"What?"

Daddy walked over to her. "Sugar, do you think I smell?" I gave her a nod and she registered the look in my eyes. She knew the drill.

"Let me see." She sniffed him. She looked back at me. I gave her a slight nod.

"Eww, Daddy. Maybe you should go and take a

shower before we go. Yani and I will wash up and be ready by the time you finish." We pushed him off in the direction of his room.

"I told your momma to take it easy last night." He gave me a wink and laughed as he went into his room. I stood there for a moment trying to figure out if that comment was made more for him or me. Asia walked over and pushed me.

"Girl, you better get that nigga out of here. You know Mama will be back from church soon."

Immediately I snapped back to my senses and ran in my room. Before I could say anything, Jarrin rolled from under the bed. I peeked out the door and Asia gave me the okay signal. We ran to the front door. I pecked him quickly on the lips good-bye, then pushed him out the door.

"I owe you one, Girl," I said to Asia as I slumped against the door.

"Hey, what are sisters for?" I hugged her as we walked back to our rooms to get dressed.

That day turned out to be one of the best days we'd ever spent with Daddy. He took us everywhere and bought us almost everything we wanted. It was sometime before I pulled that stunt again. At least not on a Saturday night.

If Asia and I had been rivaling siblings, she would've had me with that one.

❤❤❤

"I really miss Daddy."

"Me, too. He's been gone for more then ten years now, but I can still hear his voice."

"At least we got the time we had with him."

"Well, I'm off to bed before I get too sentimental. Thanks for the trip down memory lane."

"Anytime, little sister. See you in the morning."

She walked out, closing the door slightly behind her. I pulled the bottoms of my pjs on and pulled the covers back. Still hyped a bit from the eventful evening, I located the remote and turned on the TV and channel-surfed until I found something that piqued my interest. My phone rang. I glanced at the clock and slowly clicked the talk button.

"Hello?" I said sort of hesitantly.

"Hey, it's Alex. I just wanted to make sure that you got in safe."

My heart raced. "I've been home for over thirty minutes. I told you it wouldn't take me long. Thanks for calling though."

"I wouldn't have been able to sleep tonight if I hadn't."

I smiled as I felt my cheeks flush. "I'm channel-surfing myself."

He laughed. We talked for a good half an hour

before bidding each other a good night. Promising that we'd definitely talk later.

I smiled as I placed the phone on the nightstand and lay back into the mountain of pillows that surrounded me. Sleep came fast as I thought about seeing him again and the possibilities of what lay ahead.

# Asia

## CHAPTER 13

There's nothing like the smell of bacon cooking in the morning to wake you from a deep sleep. I blinked my eyes a few times and stared at the ceiling as I gave thanks for waking another morning. After my ten minutes were up, I slowly sat up and took a few deep breaths. I know Iyanla said to do the breathing first, but this has worked for me for the past year. I dragged my tired body out of bed and headed to the bathroom to perform the daily musts.

I grabbed my robe from the back of the door and let my nose lead me down to the prize that awaited me in the kitchen.

Yani had thrown down. She'd made omelets, pancakes, biscuits, grits, bacon, of course, breakfast potatoes, and she even had a pitcher of freshly squeezed orange juice.

"Damn, you're in a good mood this morning," I said as I continued my inspection. She playfully bumped me with her hip.

"What are you talking about? I always cook breakfast on the weekends."

"Yani, this much breakfast? You'd think you were expecting a local branch of the armed forces to drop in."

"Okay, so I got a little carried away."

"A little? Whatever you say." I grabbed a plate from the counter and began to stack my plate full of things that I probably would only taste. Once there was no room left for anything else, I went and sat at the breakfast bar with the kids who looked as if they were inhaling their food. Their heads were close to their plates. You would've thought it was the first meal they'd had in weeks.

Yani walked over with a glass of orange juice.

"Here ya go. You sure you don't want anything else?" I gave her a look of disbelief.

"I'll do good if I finish half of this. No, I think I'm okay. Are you eating?"

"Oh, no. I had my cup of coffee and a bagel earlier."

She pulled the pan from the glowing red eye on the stove. I stopped my fork in midair. "Wait a minute. You mean to tell me that you cooked all of this food and you're not going to eat any?"

"I'm just not that hungry this morning, for some reason."

"Oh really? Would that reason happen to be named uh…what's his name again? Oh yeah, Alex?"

I popped the eggs into my mouth followed by a generous scoop of buttered grits. "Don't you think you're rushing things? I mean, goodness, I just met him last night."

She began to move things around in a nervous manner. "Oh please. Save me the drama. I don't even know the man. I just know it's exciting when you meet someone new. It makes you happy and jittery." She stopped rearranging and looked at me. "There's nothing wrong with it, Yani. Matter fact, I'm getting a kick out of seeing you like this."

I shoveled another fork full of food into my mouth.

"So, what are you doing today?"

I chewed my food and swallowed enough to answer. "I don't know. Why? You have something in mind?"

"Not really. Did you get your dress for the party tomorrow night?"

"I have something, but you know me, I'll change my mind at the last minute and run to the mall for something else."

I dragged the cinnamon-covered slice of French toast through the syrup.

Yani perked up at the mere mention of the word

mall. "So, you want to go today and look? I mean, maybe I can find something a little more, you know…"

"Sexy?" I sputtered out through a packed mouth.

"What's wrong with that?"

I grabbed the glass of orange juice to stop myself from choking. "Nothing. I guess I'm a little shocked. You know, you've played the role of good lil' wife so long that that's how I see you."

She was about to respond as the phone rang. She smirked at me as she grabbed it.

"Hello?" she sang out. "Hey, woman. So what happened to you and your husband last night? Did you find whatever it was you were looking for?" She walked off laughing and talking.

I looked at my half-empty plate and couldn't believe that I had been able to put that much food away.

"So, what are you guys doing today?"

Natalia, who had finished and went in the family room, pulled her attention away from the TV. "Umm, I think I'm going to go over to Kelly's for a little while. We have a project that we're working on."

"Is it a school project or a personal project?" I never knew she could turn so bright red. A sign that I'd hit the target.

"It's for school," she whined.

"Umm hmm. Auntie, she likes the boy that lives next to Kelly." Jay added his two cents in.

"Boy, mind your business. You don't know what you talking about," Natalia said.

"All right now. No need for an argument." I got up and threw the few scraps remaining on my plate into the garbage disposal and placed the plate in the dishwasher. "If your mother comes back out, tell her I'm in the room getting dressed."

"Okay," they sang. Their attention was already glued back to the cartoon that was playing on the tube. I laughed at the sight and remembered when Yani and I used to do the same thing.

I called Hayden to make sure that he was all set for the party.

In the short time that we'd been here we'd spent most of the time together. I'll admit that I'm enjoying every moment of it. Thinking about our reasons for ending our relationship in the first place became questionable. Maybe the old saying about absence making the heart fonder was true after all. Or maybe it's the Florida heat and humidity that was making us act this way. Whatever it was, I decided that I'd just go with the flow and enjoy it for as long as it lasted.

# *Alex*

## CHAPTER 14

Istarted the day off with what I thought would be a quick run. The development was so large I damn near got lost. It seemed the street wound all the way round into another city. Thank God a brother knows to turn around and head back the way he came. I could just see Bryce laughing if I'd called him to come get me. That would've been one I'd never live down.

I slid back into the house and showered before anyone else was up. I sat on the bed and glanced at the clock. It was just after eight. I spotted the card with her number on it and picked it up. I'd already committed the numbers to memory in that short time. I laughed as I placed it back on the nightstand. How many times had a woman walked up and slipped me their number only for me to throw it out in the nearest trash can.

I stared at the paper and then at the phone. I wondered if she was up yet. Whether or not she and I had shared the same dreams. Had thoughts of last night plagued her sleep like they had mine? I decided it was too early to call.

I opened up my laptop for the first time since I'd arrived. It was custom to close the office down for the holidays, so there'd been no need to use it. Hard as I'd worked before coming here, my mind had shut down the work department. It was the only way I was going to enjoy myself.

I plugged in the phone line and opened up Outlook to check my emails. As usual my mailbox was full. I had an outgoing message that informed everyone that I was on vacation and wouldn't be back for at least two weeks. I scrolled down and spotted something from Taylor. I was in too good of a mood to open it. I'd read it once I got back.

There was a light tap on the door. I tightened my robe around me and went to the door.

"Yeah?"

"Just wondering if you were up. I'm about to make breakfast. Anything special you want?" I cracked the door and looked out at Carmen. She had the baby over her shoulder patting her back. Her hair was still wrapped around her head secured in place by a colorful silk scarf.

"Whatever you cook is okay with me. You know you don't have to go through any extra trouble for me."

"Nonsense. You're a guest in our home."

"Now here I was thinking that I was like family."

"You know you are. But…"

"Then treat me like it."

"All right now. Watch what you ask for." We both laughed.

"Bryce and the kids are downstairs, so whenever you're ready."

"I'll be down in a sec." She walked away as I closed the door.

I threw on something quick and shut my laptop down. I glanced at the phone one last time before deciding against calling her. After breakfast, I thought as I walked out the room and down the stairs.

# Yani

## CHAPTER 15

I pulled my cell from my purse and punched in Carmen's number. "Let me see if she needs anything while we're out." I knew she was probably stretched three ways from Sunday trying to make sure everything was ready for tonight.

Asia and I had just left the salon at the spa where we'd had the royal treatment. Manicures, pedicures, facials, massages, and hairdos that would knock 'em dead. The only thing we had to do was get dressed and touch up our makeup. Even the kids were taken care of. They'd left for their destinations earlier, wishing us a happy New Year before leaving.

"All right, you better keep your eyes on the road before you kill us!" Asia grabbed the door handle tightly. "I didn't get beautiful to go to the E.R. Give me the damn phone." She grabbed for the earpiece I was struggling with.

"I got this now. If I can't do anything else I can drive." I found the ear part and stuffed it in my ear as I pushed the send button. Carmen picked up on the second ring.

"Where are you?"

"In the car. We should be home in ten minutes."

"I'm here helping to set up. The DJ and the staff are here as well. You *will* be here early? Asia, too. I need my divas at my side to greet everyone." She gave me a sly laugh. "Not to mention that someone else is hoping that you get here so…"

"Anyway," I said, cutting her off. I was trying to get Alex off the brain. Especially since we hadn't talked since the night of the dinner. I guess after he had a chance to sleep on what we talked about he had a change of heart. "Let me get off the phone so I can get there in time to help you greet your guests. Bye."

"Okay. Oh and don't forget to bring an overnight bag. I've got four rooms reserved."

"I'll think about it."

"Think about it?! Don't start any shit now. It's our tradition."

"Then why do you feel the need to remind me? You'd think by now that it would be like second nature for me."

"Are we PMSing?"

"Not at all. I'm doing more than seventy in a fifty-five zone so that I can get home and get dressed and talking to you is messing with my concentration."

"So hang up before she kills us!" Asia called out.

"All right then. I guess I'll see you when you get here, in what…two hours?"

"Love you."

"You, too."

"Me, too, Carmen!" Asia yelled.

"Tell her, her, too." Carmen laughed.

"Bye." I flipped the phone closed and placed it on my lap.

"Why do you have to drive so damn fast?"

I looked over at her as I dodged from behind a car and sped up to pass him. "Please, your ass is a New York City cab patron. This should be a walk in the park for you."

"Whatever. They get paid to drive."

"That right there should let you know that you're safer with me behind the wheel. I don't have the prospect of making a dollar pushing me."

"You also don't have anything to lose if you get a ticket or have an accident." I rolled my eyes at her as I slid back over in front of the car. "So, have you talked to what's his name since the other night?"

"What time is Hayden going to meet us? Is he coming here or does he plan on just meeting us at the hotel?"

"Nope. He's coming to the house. He should be there around ten."

"Why doesn't he just meet us at the hotel? Doesn't make sense for him to drive way out here when he's already on the beach."

"Maybe I want him to."

"Figures." I got over in the far-right lane as I neared the exit. "Well, it's almost seven now, so that gives us almost three hours to get ready and be at the hotel. So I suggest you tell Hayden to get to the house by nine. No later than nine-thirty. You know how much I hate to be late."

"Yes, Mother."

"Whatever. Like I said before, I don't like being late."

"Yani, everything is under control. You need to relax. Damn, you're acting like it's that time of the month. Want some chocolate?"

"Hell, no. I eat some chocolate now and I'll be in the bathroom for an hour." We both laughed as I turned on my block.

I ran through the front door and headed straight to my bedroom. Strolling in behind me as if she didn't have a care in the world, Asia went into the family room and searched through my collection of CDs. A few minutes later the classic party anthem blared through the speakers. I smiled as she walked into the room with her hand out in a gesture for me to join her. As Luther sang about sneaking out to a party, Asia and I dipped and swerved to the song that was a representation of childhood memories of the house parties our parents had. The ones where we would be confined to the room with our cousins having our own rendition of a party as we danced and sang to the music that blared through the walls.

"Every-body's sing- ging... Dancing to the music..." we sang.

Once the song was done she skipped the player forward to the *Love Jones* CD to use it as a backdrop while we got dressed.

I hummed as I stood in the mirror to remove my diamond studs. I was still humming having a party with a smile plastered on my face.

"See, I knew that's what you needed." She draped her arm on my shoulder.

"Thanks, Girl." I gave her a playful bump with my hip.

"Now let's get you into this bad ass dress! I can't wait to see the heads turn when you walk in." She walked over to the chaise where I'd place the last dress I would wear in the year of 1999.

I removed the plastic covering from the dress Asia had talked me into buying. The cream-colored, beaded, sleeveless dress came up high in the front and crossed high up in the back giving it a bareback look. The high slits on the sides would give an ample amount of exposure to my legs that would definitely look sexy in the strappy, four-inch heels that were a perfect match in color.

"Don't even think about changing your mind. You're wearing it."

"I..."

"I nothing. I see that look on your face and I know you. You're wearing the damn dress. Even if I have to dress you myself, you're wearing that dress," she said to me in a matter-of-fact tone.

I grabbed my perfume and cream from the dresser and placed it on the bed next to the invisible thong I'd bought to wear. Asia looked at me from the corner of her eye.

"So I guess you're gonna sit there and watch me?"

"Do I have to?"

"Go get dressed."

'Remember what I said."

"Damn, I'm wearing it!" I smiled and licked out my tongue as she walked out.

I pulled the dress up next to me and danced around in the mirror. I thought about Alex. Wondered why he hadn't called like he'd promised. Then I thought about Jarrin and decided it wasn't worth worrying over. I'd done my share of worrying about a man and I wasn't about to do it over a man I barely knew.

The phone rang. I reached over and grabbed it off the nightstand.

"Hello?"

"Hi, Yani, is Asia there?"

"Hey, Hayden. She's here. Are you on your way?"

"Yeah, umm, I just needed to ask her something before I leave." He cleared his throat in a nervous gesture.

"Hold on a minute." I walked over to the intercom on the wall near the door. "Hey."

"What's up?"

"Your man's on the phone."

"Okay. Let me see what he wants and I'll be in there in a minute to help you out."

I hung up after she'd picked up. I sat on the bed and opened the cream and squeezed an ample amount in my hand. I started with my feet and worked my way up to my shoulders. After I sprayed my erotic zones with the perfume—my neck, wrists, and cleavage—I dabbed a little behind my ears and sprayed behind my knees. I put on enough that you'd smell it long after I'd walked by, but not enough to make you sick.

A few minutes later Asia walked in. She had her satin wrap on. "Ready?"

"Yeah, give me one second." I wrapped my robe around me and sat at the vanity. I needed her to do a few touchups here and there to my makeup.

"Let's get your dress on." She grabbed the dress and prepared it for me to step into.

"Was Hayden getting ready to leave?"

"He said he would be here within the hour. Question…" I looked at her. "Would you be upset if I didn't ride with you? I mean, we were planning to go somewhere else. Ya know?" She gyrated her hips in a suggestive motion as she gave me a wicked grin.

"Of course not. I probably would do the same if I had somebody to do it with."

We laughed.

"Never know. You just might find someone that'll hook you up tonight." Her left brow was raised slightly, an indication that her mind was taking a dip in the gutter.

"Yeah right. Fasten me up."

She zipped and snapped everything into place and stepped back. I slid the shoes on and walked over to the mirrored closet door.

"Yani, you look beautiful! Hmm, if Alex wasn't impressed the other night, he's going to be drooling all over himself when you strut in there tonight." She was beaming.

"I'm not worried about what he thinks. He didn't call so his loss. Been there done that. I'm not losing sleep over another man."

"We're feeling the part, are we?" She came up behind me and made sure the straps and everything was straight and stepped away from me.

I turned from side to side in an attempt to check and make sure the low dip wasn't too low. I had to make sure the crack of my ass wasn't showing. Got to admit it though, I looked and felt sexy as hell. I looked at Asia with a big smile on my face.

"I told you that was the one. Look at my sister!" Her hands sat on her hips as the corners of her mouth moved upward forming a smile. "Damn, you look good!"

"You're the one that's going to be turning heads," I said as she walked out to put on her dress.

Halfway out the door she called over her shoulder, "I know." She laughed a sweet laugh as she walked off.

Twenty minutes later, as if on cue, the doorbell rang and Asia stood in the hallway. I opened the door for an Armani-clad Hayden. His black slacks and jacket were accented just right with a crisp, white collarless shirt.

"You look absolutely stunning, lady."

I felt myself blushing. "I bet you say that to all the girls," I playfully replied. "At least you will in this house tonight." I opened the door wide enough for him to enter where Asia stood waiting in the living room. He slowly walked down the steps toward her.

Her silver dress shimmered from the light in the foyer. She looked just as he'd said a minute ago to me, absolutely stunning. The jersey knit dress hugged her well-toned body in all the right places. The peek-a-boo look sides, which were held together by silver links, gave a view of her golden skin. We laughed when she tried it on because we knew everyone would think she didn't have on any panties. Although it wasn't quite J-Loish, it was definitely a daring dress that had my sister's name written all over it.

Hayden slid his hand around her waist and gave her a soft kiss on the lips. They whispered to each other in between pecks. I took that as my cue to do a last minute check before we left.

I grabbed the cream-colored handbag from the dresser and checked inside to make sure all of my "must haves" were in there. "Let me see… my cell, lipstick. Can't forget the lipstick. American Express card, driver's license, and keys." I zipped the bag closed and walked over to the full-length mirror for one last glance. "You are going to knock 'em dead tonight, Ms. Miller," I said to myself before I walked back into the living room.

"Are we ready to bring in the new millennium?" Asia turned around to flash me a beautiful smile.

"Ready when you are."

# *Alex*

## CHAPTER 16

Carmen had left for the hotel earlier, leaving instructions for us to be there by nine, no later than ten o'clock.

I came down in my midnight blue, Shaka King ensemble. A silver shirt with large lapels fell over the collar of the jacket, which added a nice contrast. My diamond cufflinks, a gift from another ex, were fastened in place.

I found Bryce in the kitchen rummaging through the fridge.

"Ready, man?" he asked as I walked in. I strolled over to the middle of the room and struck a pose. He finally looked up after I didn't respond.

"No wonder it takes your ass as long as a woman to get dressed. You're sharp as shit, man."

"Whatever. Now back up off me." I brushed my hands across my sleeves and pretended to pop my collar.

"Give me one minute," he said as he turned his

attention back to the fridge. "I was looking for something Carmen asked for." After locating it, he closed the door and straightened his frame. He did a cool pimp over to me and popped his collar. "Well?"

"Man, you know you're together. Your wife makes sure of that."

We both laughed.

"Fuck you, man. How do you know I didn't pick this out?" He grabbed his keys off the counter.

"Sinbad gave that secret away."

"Whatever. Let's roll before Carmen starts killing my cell."

"Wouldn't want you to spend your birthday in the dog house."

"Rest assured that I won't be there alone. Company or not, Carmen doesn't have a problem dishing it out."

"I'm at your mercy, so she'd know it's your fault."

"Just like a niggah to throw you under the bus."

"Man, to keep from feeling the wrath of a black woman, this niggah will throw your ass under a train."

We both laughed as we jumped in the truck and left.

❤❤❤

"All right, it's showtime," he called over to me. We both straightened out our gear before stepping out of the Navigator under the overhang in front of the hotel. I walked toward the door held open by a bellhop who was greeting everyone.

"Welcome to the Eden Rock Hotel."

I stepped inside as Bryce retrieved the valet ticket from the young Hispanic man dressed in khaki shorts and a white polo shirt. Once he joined me, we made our way through the lobby over to the stairs near a sign that read "Grand Ballroom: Douglas Party." The music was cranked up and people seemed to fill the room by the dozens. After greeting a few people, we finally made it in the room.

The room was decorated in shimmering shades of silver, blue and gold. 01-01-00 hung from the ceiling and graced the walls. As centerpieces, she had huge balloons with 01-01-00 filled with surprises. Each table was set for at least ten people.

Bryce spotted Carmen on the dance floor with a group of women who were working it out. He walked up behind her and wrapped his arm around her waist.

"I hope you saved one for me," he said close in her ear to be heard over the music.

She spun around, still moving to the beat. "Oh,

and this you know." She kissed him and grabbed his other hand so that she was completely encircled in his arms. I cleared my throat.

"All right now, maybe you two need to go upstairs and get a room."

She pulled away from him and turned her attention on me. "That's already been taken care of. Now let me check you out."

I took a step back and did a Mack pose; slowly turning from one side to the next so that she could get the full range of things.

"Baby, can you believe he took longer than you to get dressed? I was downstairs almost an hour waiting on him." Bryce was grinning.

"Well, it was well worth the wait. You look marvelous," she said in her best Billy Crystal imitation.

I nodded toward the ladies Carmen was dancing with when we walked up. I'd scanned to see if Yani was one of them. Carmen's radar was on.

"She's here. I'm not sure where, but she got here about thirty minutes ago." She winked at me and pulled Bryce so they could resume their dance.

"I'm gonna go to the bar for a drink. Catch you later." Uncomfortable being the third wheel, I strolled over to the bar as I scanned the room in hopes of finding Yani.

I felt bad because I hadn't had a chance to give

her a call since the night we met. Bryce had asked me to help him out with something and I couldn't tell him no. He was the reason I was here.

I caught a glimpse of someone that looked like Yani. She was with a guy that was holding on to her so tight he seemed to be an extension of her. I was relieved once I got close enough and realized it wasn't her.

"Umm, umm, umm. Who are you?" the female voice demanded.

I glanced slowly to my left in the direction of the voice to find a woman in a dress that was *two* sizes *too* small approaching me. Her hair, done up in a gaudy, plastic "look-at-me" style, was the same color as her dress—fire-red.

Not wanting to straight up diss her, I kept going as if I hadn't heard her, trying my best to walk a little faster. When I reached the bar I placed my order and felt a tap on my shoulder. Determined to be polite I turned around.

"Excuse me?" She reeled back a bit. "I'm Y'vetta and you are?" She extended her hand up close to my mouth. I quickly grabbed it and brought it down for a firm handshake instead.

"Oh, I'm Alex, a friend of Bryce and Carmen." My mind raced as I tried to figure out an escape. I had to practically pry my hand from hers.

"I'm Carmen's cousin. So wuz up witch'you? You here witch'yo lady?" She smiled, showing her two front teeth that were clad in gold armor. I reeled back slightly.

"As a matter of fact, I am. I came over here to get us something to drink. It was nice talking to you, umm…Y'vetta," I said as I tried to make a quick getaway.

Before I could take another step, she'd latched on to my arm.

"Well, if she ain't ackin' right, all you have to do is holler and a bitch like me will come runnin." She let go and strutted away like a cat on the prowl.

I shook my head in disbelief. I definitely needed a drink after that.

"Yeah, let me get a scotch and water on the rocks." The neatly dressed bartender came back and handed me the drink.

"Thanks," I replied. I grabbed my drink and crossed the room back to where I'd left Carmen and Bryce who were no longer there. I looked around for a familiar face and decided to grab an empty table near the back of the room that would give me a bird's-eye view.

I glanced down at my watch, which read 11:45.

It's almost showtime, I thought as I emptied the remaining contents of my glass. I looked over to my left and caught sight of Carmen giving instructions to the serving staff. They were setting the table up with flutes to be filled with chilled champagne.

The sight of that made me feel a sense of urgency to find Yani. I wanted to bring in the New Year with her at my side. You know they say who you bring in the year with is usually who you spend it with.

"Hey, Man." Bryce slapped me on the shoulders. "What are you doing? Hiding out? I saw Y'vetta up in your face." He laughed.

"Man, I can't believe she and Carmen are related."

"You know we all have those family members that we'd rather not talk about. Did you see Yani?" His expression of humor was quickly replaced with one of mild seriousness.

In an attempt to keep my cool and not seem pressed, I answered him nonchalantly.

"Naw, Man. Why?"

"Aw, Man! She's got on this dress…"

"Wait a minute, aren't you a married man?"

"What's that got to do with it? Matter fact, my wife and I were discussing how good she looked. When you see her, you'll see why."

I glanced at my watch again. The staff had begun

to hand out party favors and flutes filled with the expensive champagne.

"Five more minutes." I had to find her soon. Unable to keep up the façade of Mr. Cool, I asked Bryce if he knew where he'd seen her last.

"She's over at the table with Carmen." He gestured with a quick nod of his head. I craned my neck in an attempt to see if I could spot her.

"Come on, man. By the time we push our way through, it'll be time to start counting." I could see him smile as he led me through the crowd of people who stood staring at the large projector screen that hung from the ceiling, waiting for the ball in Times Square to make its descent down the pole indicating that another year had come and gone.

As the timer showed the two-minute mark, I nudged Bryce to make him hurry. I had to see her before the clock struck midnight.

# *Yani*

## CHAPTER 17

"**G**irl, this place is packed! I didn't expect to see this many people here. Let the media tell it, most people were opting to stay home." I yelled near Carmen's ear to be heard over the loud music. Her elegant black halter dress, draping the top of her shoes, made her look like a movie star.

"You know people were looking for something to do."

"And what could be better than a spectacular Douglas New Year's bash?"

"Ya know? Here, grab yourself a glass of bubbly. We've got less than a minute left now." The server handed each of us a glass and continued making her rounds.

"Now where in the hell is my husband?" She glanced around the room. I'd wanted to ask her about Alex, but that would be out of character for me. Besides, if he wanted to talk, he'd have to come to me.

"Oh, here he comes now." I turned and looked in the direction where her attention was. Following close behind him, looking astonishingly handsome, was Alex. I couldn't pull my eyes away from him.

*Get yourself together, Girl*, I said in my mind as I tried to look unaffected. *I hope my mouth isn't hanging open*, I thought.

"Yani...did you hear me?"

"What? I couldn't hear you over the music," I lied.

"Yeah right. Come on." She grabbed my hand and dragged me closely behind her.

"Honey!" she called out waving her hand to get Bryce's attention. We forged our way toward them through the throng of people. The closer we got, the faster my heart began to beat. As we finally reached each other, the countdown to midnight began.

"Ten, nine..."

"I was wondering where you guys had disappeared to," she said to Bryce.

"Had to save pretty boy here from Y'vetta."

"Oh, God." Bryce pulled Carmen into a loving embrace.

"Six, five..." Alex stepped from behind Bryce and walked closer to me. He quickly seized a glass of champagne from the tray of the server as she whisked by him.

"Three, two..." He now stood directly in front of me.

"One! HAPPY NEW YEAR!" The whole room came alive with cheering as confetti fell from the ceiling. I glanced over at Carmen and Bryce as they shared a passionate kiss.

Alex bent down.

"Happy New Year, Yani," he breathed into my ear. A warm feeling vibrated through my body. As I parted my lips to wish him the same, he'd covered my mouth with his and smothered the words deep inside my mouth as his tongue softly invaded my unsuspecting, but receiving mouth. He held on to me at the small of my back.

*Get your head back, Girl*…I advised myself. The kindling sparks building in the pit of my stomach made me feel as if I would melt. His lips were oh so soft.

"You can come up for air now," Bryce said, jolting us back to the realization that we were in a room of more than two-hundred people.

Alex continued to place soft kisses on my lips before he pulled away completely. Carmen gave me a soft bump with her hip as she mouthed, "All right, girlfriend."

I could feel my golden face turning red as I noticed a few others looking on with approving smiles and a few envy-filled female faces.

Alex held my hand. "Can I have the honor of being the first person you dance with in the new millennium?"

"Might as well since you decided you'd be the first one to get a kiss," Carmen blurted out.

"I'm taking her away. You kids enjoy yourself." Bryce pulled her out onto the dance floor that was starting to fill with couples. Alex stood waiting for an answer.

"Of course," I replied. We made our way to the middle of the dance floor a few inches away from Carmen and Bryce. The DJ played Eric Benet's duet with Tamia, "Spend My Life with You." He wrapped me close in his arms and tilted my chin so I could look up at him.

"You really look beautiful tonight," he said. I blushed.

"Thank you. You're lookin' pretty sharp yourself."

He smiled and pulled me a little closer. His cologne was driving me wild. "You know I've been looking for you since I hit the door?" he said.

"Really?" I replied as I tried my best not to break into a Miss Celie from *The Color Purple* smile.

"You say that as if you're surprised."

"Well, I do have a reason to be. I haven't talked to you since our initial meeting. So, I took that as a hint that you weren't interested." I moved my face closer to his shoulder so I didn't have to make eye contact at that point. I fought the urge to run my fingers through the soft curls of hair at the nape of his neck.

"I want to apologize for that. I had sort of an emergency at work that had to be taken care of. Then Bryce and I hung out a little and by the time we got in I thought it was too late to call."

"You don't have to explain anything to me," I said to his shoulder.

"But, if you'd let me, I'd like to make it up to you."

"I'm listening."

"I'd love to take you up on that tour you offered me. Maybe you can take me to one of your favorite restaurants while we're out. I mean, that is if you'd like to have dinner with me." He tightened his grip around my waist slightly.

My head rested against his shoulder as I relished the feel of being in his arms. He waited patiently for my answer. He ran his hand softly over my exposed back.

"I think I can do that," I said as he pulled me in a little closer.

The song went off and the DJ immediately went into Marvin's party song, "Got to Give It Up." It seemed like people were running to the dance floor. Next thing we knew, we were in the middle of a Soul Train line.

"Would you like to get some fresh air?" he asked.

"That's a good idea."

He grabbed my hand and led us through the crowd and out the door.

Out in the lobby people were gathered in various spots. A group of five or more women were huddled over in a corner talking about how wrong the predictions for the night had been.

"You know that's why I'm standing out here. I thought the lights were going to go out and there would be a stampede or something," one woman said. The others laughed out loud.

"Well, since everything is okay, let's make our way back to the party, 'cause Girl, they're playing my jam," another one said as she snapped her fingers and headed toward the door.

Alex guided me toward an empty sofa and had a seat. By the amount of stragglers hanging around, there had to be quite a few other functions going on there that night. Alex pulled me close to him, my hand still in his grasp. We sat there like that for a little while, not saying a word.

"You know they have one of the most beautiful boardwalks behind here?"

"I've never been on this part of the beach."

"Wanna have a peak? It's really nice."

He stood and handed me his hand. It was my turn to lead. We exited through the doors near the restaurant and made our way out to the pool area.

A cool breeze reminded me that I wasn't quite dressed for any outside activities. Alex noticed my quick shiver and took off his jacket and draped it over my shoulders.

"Better?"

"Much better."

We continued to walk and talk before deciding to go back to the party. I felt like a teenager as we walked and talked hand in hand. When we got back to the ballroom, the party was in full swing. It seemed like everyone in the room was on the dance floor jamming to the funky sounds of "Let's Dance to the Drummer's Beat." I mean, people who were standing around acting as if they were too cute to smile earlier were now sweating like they'd been doing two hours of advance aerobics.

Curiosity getting the best of me, I pulled Alex out to the dance floor to see if he had any skills. I walked through the crowd parting people like the Red Sea until I reached the very middle where he would be unable to escape. He smiled at me.

"I didn't know you wanted to dance."

"Well, I didn't think a *Woo* moment was appropriate." He looked confused.

"A *Woo* moment?" I laughed.

"You know the movie with Jada Pinkett Smith and Tommy Davidson?"

"What does that have to do with us dancing?"

"Have you ever seen the movie?"

"I kind of remember it."

"Remember the part where she yelled out, 'That's my song,'" I said imitating the same attitude she'd put into it. He nodded.

"It was her cue that she wanted to dance, remember?"

He laughed. "Oh yeah, I do remember that, and probably would've caught on if you would've given me the same hint."

Before he could say anything else, I threw my hand in the air like Woo and shouted, "That's my song." I started rocking from side to side as I wanted to get my groove on before the song went off. Alex stood back and stared at me for a brief moment as if I'd caught him off guard, then proceeded to join me and hit it step for step.

We danced for what seemed like hours. We did everything from the Electric Slide to a grind out, high school, slow drag. And I must say not only were his moves on point, but the bulge was pretty impressive, too. Had to catch myself a few times. You know how those naughty little thoughts can cloud your otherwise good judgment.

Around 4:30 I decided to call it a night. The crowd had started to thin out and Carmen and Bryce looked as if they were ready to crash themselves.

"Oh my God!" I said placing my hand over my mouth.

"What's wrong?"

"I just remembered that my sister was here. I didn't even tell her Happy New Year." Then it hit me that I'd seen Asia and Hayden slip away right before the counting started. At least that's what I think I saw. After I laid eyes on Alex, I can't remember seeing much of anything or anyone else for that matter.

"I guess I'm to blame for that. I dominated your time the whole evening. Or should I say morning? I hope she's not mad with you."

"Mad? Please. Believe me she was definitely tied up with someone she'd rather be with than me." All of a sudden a vision of Asia being willingly tied to a bed flashed before my eyes and I shook my head.

"Do you think she's still here?" He turned to scan the room.

"No, she's long gone by now. She'd informed me of her early departure before we left the house."

"So how'd you get here?" A look of concern flashed across his face.

"I drove."

"Alone?"

"Yeah," I said as I gave him a "duh" look.

"You're not going to drive all the way home now?"

"Oh no. It's tradition that we all stay overnight at the hotel and get up and have breakfast together."

"So, you're going to stay overnight?" His gray eyes twinkled as he smiled at me.

"Just how much did you have to drink tonight, buddy?"

"I'm just making sure that I'll definitely see you in the morning. Well, later this morning. Would you mind an escort to your room? I promise I'll be nothing but a gentleman." He feigned a look of innocence as he held his hands up to indicate that his intentions were on the up and up.

"Can't see any trouble in that, but for future reference, thought I'd let you know that I'm more than capable of handling any *trouble* that comes my way." I smiled as I sashayed away to find Carmen and Bryce.

"Then maybe I'll change my name to Trouble," he said as he followed me. We spotted Carmen and Bryce as they told a group of partygoers goodnight.

"Well, Mr. and Mrs. Douglas, I must say, this has been one of the best parties I've been to in years."

"We's aim to please," Bryce said as he bowed slightly.

"And since I didn't get a chance to tell you earlier, Happy Birthday." I hugged his neck.

"I thanks you very much."

"I think I need to get my husband upstairs and in the bed. All the liquor he's consumed tonight is affecting his ability to speak."

"Alex is having a problem comprehending questions and Bryce thinks he's back on the plantation somewhere." I laughed. Carmen looked at Alex.

"She's joking." He pulled me back into him and wrapped his arm around my waist and placed a soft kiss on my neck.

"We're on our way upstairs."

"We?" Carmen's antenna went up. She'd been paying close attention to our interaction as much as she possibly could.

"Yes, Alex is going to walk me up to *my* room and then go to *his*. Is that okay with you?"

"Not really. Now if you were going to same room, I'd be happier than a…"

"Good night, Carmen. Bryce, see you at breakfast, sweetie." I pecked him on the cheek and gave him a tight hug. I shot Carmen a look, then hugged her.

"Can I get the key to my room?" She reached inside her bag and handed the card to me.

"I guess I should also get my room key now?" Alex said playfully to Carmen.

"What would you do if I told you that I didn't have any more?" she said playfully.

"I guess I would have to go up to the front desk and get my own room then."

"And what would you do if they're all booked up for the night?" She taunted him some more.

"Then I guess I'd have to sleep in the room with you and Bryce and I know that's not what you want." He smiled at her and held out his hand for the key he and I both knew she had.

Once she handed him the key, my naughty side came out.

"Damn, I was just about to say that you could sleep in the room with me, but since you have your key, that offer's off the table." I turned and headed for the door knowing I'd left three stunned faces behind me. When I reached the door I turned back toward them.

"Does the offer still stand, Alex?" He looked at me confused.

"Which offer is that?"

"The escort to my room. What other offer is there?"

"Of course." He stumbled over his words as he walked toward me.

"We'll see you two in the morning," Bryce called out.

"Oh, and by the way, your rooms are right next to each other, so all you have to do is open up the connecting door and it'll be just like you're sleeping in the same room." Carmen blew me a kiss and winked, an indication that she'd ended up being one up on me.

*Right next to each other?* I thought as I walked toward the elevator holding Alex's hand.

# *Asia*

## CHAPTER 18

**B**efore the clock struck midnight good, Hayden and I had made our way out to the valet area. Five minutes into the New Year we were on our way down to the south part of the beach where the non-stop parties were taking place.

I thought about looking for Yani to let her know that we were out, but I'd just see her some time tomorrow.

"Maybe I'll just give her a call in the morning," I said to Hayden.

"You think she'll be okay getting home?"

"She's got a room at the hotel. She'll be fine. Besides, Yani has never been much of a drinker. She'd make it home either way."

There were all types of parties jumping off on South Beach. Some with who's-who rosters. Due to all of the reports of disasters, I didn't expect to see so many people out partying. I guess if it was the end of the world, they all decided to take

Prince's advice and party. That song, by the way, had clogged the airways all day and night.

We went back to Hayden's hotel and parked the car before we began our walk over to Washington where the real action was going on.

"Wouldn't you rather go sit on the beach and enjoy the sounds of the waves hitting the shore? I mean, make this a New Year's we both would remember?"

"Are you telling me that you'd rather sit and talk than go to a club with wall-to-wall people standing around, some getting their groove on of course, while others are trying to be seen?" He looked at me for a moment before answering.

"That's exactly what I'm telling you."

"Good. As much as I like to party, that sounds like a more enjoyable plan to me."

"Give me a minute; I have to get something from the car." He ran back to the hotel and returned shortly with a wicker picnic basket in his arms.

"Let's go." I hooked my arm through his as we waded our way through the non-stop convoy of cars on Ocean Drive and headed to the beachside.

I was amazed at the calmness of the beach. With all the blaring radios, honking cars, and music coming from the different dance spots across the street, it seemed like we'd stepped into the Twilight Zone or something.

There were a few people, who like us, opted to chill out and enjoy the nice breeze in the air. We walked a little further north until we found a perfect spot. Hayden opened the basket and retrieved a blanket and spread it out.

"What else do you have stashed in there?"

"Just a few things. Nothing much." He continued to pull out a pair of plates, forks, and plastic champagne flutes.

"Umm, I'm impressed. Anything in there to eat? I'm feeling a bit famished," I said in a mock English accent. My stomach growled at the thought of food. I'd only eaten a few finger foods at the party due to my permanent spot on the dance floor and then my quick getaway.

"Just relax, Baby. I've got everything covered." He kissed the back of my hand as he pulled it from prying in the basket.

Next he pulled a bottle of Cristal from his pickings and popped the cork on it.

"For you, my sweet."

"Why thank you."

He then retrieved a couple of Tupperware containers. One filled with jumbo shrimp, another with fruits and cheese. When he was finished arranging them in the center of the blanket where they would be easy to reach, there were three or four different types of cheese, crackers, and a fresh loaf of Italian bread with two different types of spreads.

"Where did all of this come from?"

"Thought we'd enjoy a midnight snack."

After eating shrimp until I thought I would burst, I crawled up close to Hayden.

"I don't remember you being this much of a romantic when we were together."

He smiled and wrapped his arms around me. "Back then, I didn't have time to be much of anything."

"So, you're reformed now?"

"I wouldn't call it that. I've always had it in me to be a romantic type of guy. I was just too busy trying to make my mark at the time." He kissed the top of my head.

"I need you to tell me something."

"What's that?"

"Where do we go from here?"

"Well, for starters..." He kissed me on my neck. "We're going to back to my hotel." He kissed the side of my neck. "Then I'm going to slowly undress you and..."

"That's not what I'm talking about and you know it." I pulled away and sat up before I was too far gone. Funny how you can lose contact with someone you were intimate with and they still remember what spots to touch to get you going.

"I'm talking about what happens when we leave here and get back on our home turf? Is this just one of those vacation flings?" We sat staring out at the waves crashing into the shore for a moment before he answered.

"Asia, I have nothing but the best intentions where you're concerned. Maybe we can just take things in stride and see where it takes us. Okay?"

"Take it in stride? You mind clarifying that for me? That could mean a lot of things and I just want to make sure I'm going into this on the same playing field as you."

He let out a nervous laugh. "Asia, Baby, I don't know. I mean…"

"Just what do you mean?" I cut him off.

"Look, can we talk about this when my head is a little clearer? I've had far too many glasses of champagne to discuss something this serious."

I had a familiar feeling bubble up inside me as my heart sank a little. Even though I wasn't expecting much in the beginning, he'd definitely hooked me again. Not to mention the sex was better than ever. My intention from the beginning was to keep it just about sex, but that strategy was out the window after the second night.

"You okay with that?" He pulled me into an embrace.

"I'm cool," I lied.

"Why don't we head to the room so I can finish what I started?" He scooped up the basket in one hand and gently lifted me to my feet with the other.

"And what would that be?"

"You have to ask?" He kissed me long and hard. He pulled me in close so I could feel just what his intentions were.

"Umm, not anymore." I moaned.

We couldn't get to the room fast enough. As soon as the door closed, we were out of our clothes. My dress fell to the floor like a puddle around my feet. I stood in front of him with nothing on but the invisible thong I wore under my dress and my stilettos.

"Damn, baby, you look so good."

I walked over to the desk and pulled the chair out and motioned for him to sit. I then threw my right foot up on the desk, giving him a bird's-eye view of his desire. I looked down at him as he began to please me with his skillful mouth.

"This what you want, Baby?" I asked.

"Umm hmm."

I grabbed the back of his head and pushed him back up in it. He continued to work me over until I was unable to stand. Then he scooped me up, carried me to the bed and gently laid me on my back.

I tried to kick off my shoes.

"No, leave them." He pushed the shoes back securely on my feet.

After strapping on his protective cover, he slowly slid my legs open and got into position. He looked down at me as he slowly entered me. My eyes did a quick dance to the back of my head as he shoved every inch deep inside of me. Without fail, he'd hit the spot that makes most women lose control. He was getting the exact reaction he wanted from me.

After a few more tease moves, he picked up the rhythm and began to put in some serious work. Sweat formed on his forehead and every other part of his body. Just as it was starting to get real good, he flipped me over on my side so I could feel him deeper.

"Feel good, Baby?"

"Yeah…Real good." He pumped and I pushed. Both working together to get to the climax we sought.

Just as I thought I was going to burst, he turned me again. This time I was up on all fours. He smacked me on my ass causing me to wince in pleasurable pain. This man was no joke! I could feel my juices as they ran down my leg.

He'd kicked into another gear as he teetered on the edge of his climax. Faster and faster he pumped.

"Smack!" I jumped slightly. He pulled my arms

behind me and then stretched them out to my sides. "Smack!" The sound of our skin making contact got louder as he picked up his pace. And just as suddenly as it started, it was over. Our sweat-covered bodies collapsed on the bed as he tried, to no avail, to keep the racking convulsions from overpowering him.

I struggled to move from under the weight of his spent body.

"Where are you going?" he asked breathlessly.

"Nowhere. You're heavy."

We laughed as I repositioned myself.

"Damn, you definitely have me whipped."

"Just like before," I said confidently. Truth be told, I was whipped my damn self.

# *Alex*

## CHAPTER 19

I opened my eyes and looked down at the beautiful woman who lay sleeping in my arms. We were both still fully clothed.

Her intention was to invite me in for a brief minute and then send me on my way. But we got to talking and the talking led to kissing. When things seemed like they were getting to a point where turning back couldn't be an option, we cooled off and went back to talking. Next thing I knew we were both sound asleep.

I glanced at the clock on the nightstand. It was after ten. Yani stirred.

"Umm. Hey," she said as she fluttered her eyes open to look up at me.

"Hey."

"You're staring at me. Am I drooling?" She swiped at the sides of her mouth.

I laughed. "I was just looking at you."

"What time is it?"

"Almost ten-thirty."

"Oh," she said as she snuggled deeper into my chest.

"What time do you guys usually get up?"

"Close to check out," she mumbled.

"What time is check out?"

"Eleven or twelve."

"Shouldn't we get up, then?"

"Um hmm."

I looked down at her. Her eyes were shut. Damn, she's beautiful! Bad as I wanted to get up and brush my teeth and shower, I didn't want her to move.

"Are you going to get up?" she asked.

"I didn't want to disturb you."

She opened her eyes and smiled at me. "Did you sleep well?"

"My arm is a little numb. Other than that, I slept fine."

She rolled off my arm. "All you had to do was move me."

I pulled her back into me and kissed her neck. "Maybe I didn't want to."

"Then don't complain about your arm." She tried to sit up but I held her down.

"Where are you going?"

"To the bathroom to freshen up. I'd like to kiss you good morning, but if I did right now, you'd probably never want to see me again."

"You are quite the comedian."

"Are you going to go to your room and get situated? Carmen will be here soon."

"And we wouldn't want her to find us like this." I looked at her dress and my suit. The wrinkles in it alone was a telltale that it'd been slept in.

"I'm not worried about that. Carmen is impatient and she's worse when she's hungry. It wouldn't be a good idea to make her wait to eat. It's not a pretty sight." She laughed and walked into the bathroom.

I sat up and looked around. My shoes were next to the bed and my jacket hung on the back of the chair. I stood and stretched before gathering my things. I walked to the bathroom door and knocked on it. Yani poked her head out.

"I'll be back, beautiful."

"Okay. Unlock the door so you can come back in without worrying about a key."

"No problem. I'm going to shower and change. I'll be back in about twenty, thirty minutes."

"I'll be waiting."

# Yani

## CHAPTER 20

I emerged from the shower. Towel wrapped securely in place, I ran to the phone that seemed to be ringing off the hook.

"Hello?"

"Good morning, sleeping beauty. It's almost time to check out."

"I'll have you know that I'm up and showered. All I have to do is put on my clothes. How long have you been up?"

"We've been up almost two hours now."

"So I know you're good and hungry."

"Yes, ma'am. How long will you be?"

"Twenty minutes."

"Leave the door cracked, I'll be down in five."

"All right." I hung up and went over to the door and placed the metal flap from the extra lock in the door jam to keep it open.

I went back into the bathroom to finish my morning facial and my hair. Since the formal festivities were over, I pulled my hair to the back into a ponytail. There was no way I was going to try and put the hairpins back into place in hopes of making the pinup look like something.

I heard a knock at the door.

"I'll be out in a minute." I rushed out with nothing on but my cranberry bra and matching thong.

"Girl, I'm sorry, but you know I have to do my ritual. I'll be dressed in one minute. Have you been outside yet? I brought two different outfits just in case it was cool today or a little more on the warm side. So which one should I go with?" I laid out both selections and waited for her response.

"I think you should go with the capris. It's sorta warm out today," said Alex.

I quickly turned around to face him. Dressed in khaki shorts and a multicolored polo shirt, he stood taking all of me in. At that instance, I remembered how exposed I was.

"I-I…thought you were Carmen. She should… be here any minute."

"I came to see if you were ready. I'll leave if you want…"

"No, no! That's okay. I'll be dressed in a minute." I grabbed the denim, stretch capri suit and back-pedaled into the bathroom.

I stood with my back against the door as I tried

to steady the rapid rate at which my heart had suddenly begun to beat.

"Let me hurry up." I rushed and put on my clothes and makeup.

As I opened the door, I could hear Carmen's over-exaggerated laugh.

"You're a fool, Alex."

"I forgot that you don't know the difference between one minute and ten," I joked with her as I placed my things back in my bag.

"Don't you look nice? Doesn't she look good, Alex?" Carmen said with a big grin on her face.

He smiled back while his eyes were glued to me.

"Yes, she does. I told you that was a good choice." He winked at me.

"Oh, so you helped her pick that outfit?" In pure Carmen fashion, she was putting the carriage before the horse.

"You know, I'm hungry. Can we check out of here so we can eat?" I strategically tried to change the subject. I slipped on my black platforms to match the black bag I was carrying.

"I bet you're hungry." She stood up from the bed and looked back at it like she could see the imprint of two bodies. She grinned from ear to ear.

I rolled my eyes at her. "Ready?" I asked Alex. He nodded and rose from the chair.

"You need help with anything?" he offered.

"No. This is it." I flung my bag over my shoulder and draped my dress from the night before over my arm.

"I guess we're off then. Bryce is already downstairs squaring up the bill." She slipped her red Dooney on her shoulder and led us down to the elevator.

"Let me get that for you." Alex gently pulled my bag from my shoulder.

"Thank you."

"Now isn't that better?" He softly placed his hand on my back as he guided me to the door.

I looked back at him and smiled. Carmen was already out the door and a few feet down the hall ahead of us.

"You have your things?"

"Right here." He picked up his overnight bag sitting at the door. I pulled the door in and turned around right into his chest.

"I was hoping to get that good morning kiss you promised me." I stared up at him. He leaned down and kissed me gently on the lips. I gave him a gracious response.

"So, what are your plans for us today?" he asked.

"For us? Did you have anything in particular that you wanted to see or do?"

"I'm looking at all I want to see and do."

Heat rose up and settled in my cheeks.

"I'm not going to touch that. We can do whatever you want. I mean…"

We both laughed.

"You're really leaving yourself open."

"I realize that."

The bell rang signaling the elevator had arrived.

"Are you two coming?" Carmen called. We picked up the pace in order to catch her. She looked at us and shook her head, then jabbed me in the side lightly. I jabbed back. Soon as we hit the lobby, she walked over to where Bryce stood waiting for us and whispered in his ear. He looked back at us and smiled.

"She knows," I said.

"They were gonna find out anyway." He grabbed my hand as we joined them and walked out to the valet area.

❤❤❤

"So, Yani, are you going to head home?" Carmen asked as we emerged from the restaurant headed to our cars.

"I think we're going to walk around down here for a little while and then maybe head north. Go check out Ft. Lauderdale beach and walk around out there for a little while. Take him to some of the hot spots. I'm not sure what we're doing tonight, but I'd like to go somewhere to eat."

"Maybe we could…Oww," Bryce called out after getting a sharp elbow in the side from Carmen.

"You two go ahead and have a good time. I have plans for my husband tonight, so don't worry about us." We hugged and said our goodbyes before heading off in different directions. Them toward the expressway and us closer to SoBe.

"So what would you like to do first?" I asked after parking on Ocean Drive.

"What do you usually do when you come down here?"

"Look in the different boutiques. I'm a shopaholic. My weaknesses are shoes and cute tops."

"If that's what you want to do, it's fine with me."

"I like a man that's easy to please."

We walked around for about an hour. Did the tourist stroll past Versace's compound. It had been a hotel once and the designer turned it into a grand palace.

"After his murder they stopped people from parking in front of here," I said. "Now everyone comes to have their picture taken in the spot where he was shot. Isn't that sick? It seemed like they showed that story non-stop."

"You know how the media is when they get a hot story. They juice it for all they can get."

"Sad thing is if it had been you or me it wouldn't have made a blip on the radar."

"Never know. Especially since they'd profiled the guy that killed him on *America's Most Wanted.*"

"That may have been the only reason and even then it would've only been mentioned and dropped like it had never happened. If you're not a 'who's who' no one cares."

"Ready?" Alex grabbed my hand.

"I'm sorry. Didn't mean to preach."

"You're not. I just don't want to ruin your day with bad thoughts."

"Okay, let's get out of here. Fort Lauderdale is just as pretty and almost as crowded." We walked back to the car and drove up A1A. I took the scenic route. I slowed down as we reached the posh Golden Isle Beach area. The mansions that lined the street on both sides were beautiful. Some of them were as big as hotels.

Once we got close enough, I rode back inland and rode up U.S.1 to Andrews and made a right.

"Things are really spread out here."

"I know, but you get used to it. My motto is, 'Have car, will travel.' I'll jump in my car and go anywhere." I turned right on Andrews.

"What's this place?" He pointed to the entertainment complex.

"That's the Riverfront."

"What's in there?"

"Restaurants, a few shops, bars, and a huge movie complex with twenty-three screens. Right in the movie theater, they have games and a few rides." I turned left on Los Olas.

"Really? Think we can check it out?"

"Maybe on our way back we'll park and get out for a minute."

"Where are we headed now?"

"This area is called Los Olas. It's a pretty ritzy part of Fort Lauderdale. There are shops, restaurants, and a few museums here." As we drove a little further down, we rode past the Intercoastal.

"Some of these houses are incredible."

"Damn, that's a big ass house," he said as we passed by what looked to be a library. I laughed and kept going until I crossed over the drawbridge to the beach side. We parked in the public parking and headed to the machine to pay.

"This is really nice, too."

"It's sorta a mixture of South Beach and Coco Walk down in the Grove. It's almost as busy as South Beach at times."

He grabbed my hand as we crossed one of the

many corners before reaching Beach Place, the open-air mall.

"You weren't kidding when you said you liked to shop," he said, smiling.

"It's not that. Here in South Florida, we have more malls than probably any other place. That's why you mainly see people from Florida on talk shows when they do a show on compulsive shoppers." We both laughed.

"I'm not going to see you on there one day, am I?"

"I do have my limits."

"So you're saying that you're a controlled buyer?"

"A sensible shopper. I have an allotted amount of money every month I spend on shopping for non-necessities."

We stopped in front of a group that was serenading the crowd with an uptempo salsa beat. I didn't take Alex as one to let go, but he grabbed my hand and began to work me out. There were a few other couples dancing, but everyone seemed to be watching us as Alex twirled me around and we stepped with rhythmical ease. Lost in the magic of dance, I didn't realize that people had gathered around to watch us until we finished to a loud applause. Alex gracefully bowed and held his hand out for me to do the same. I blushed and bowed and grabbed him to make a getaway.

"I can't believe I just did that." I was smiling from the inside out.

"You should do it more often. Where'd you learn to dance Salsa like that?"

"You do realize that I'm a Miami girl?" I wasn't about to tell him I'd had lessons at the gym as a workout class. He seemed to be impressed that I was a natural.

"My bad. This is the Latin capital," he said in a heavy Latin accent.

"Where'd that come from?"

"I have Puerto Rican roots."

"So that's where the curly hair and the golden tan are from. You lived there?"

"I told you, I'm a New Yorker through and through."

"So, you're fluent in Spanish?"

"Si."

"¿Usted está listo para comer? Acabo de se dio cuenta que nosotros Haven'T comida desde que más temprano."

"Whoa, where'd that come from?!"

"Four years of Spanish in high school and another four in college."

"You never cease to amaze me."

"So, are you hungry or not?"

"I guess these are hunger pangs that I'm feeling. What did you have in mind?"

"We have to go to Mangos. They have this dish I just love and I haven't had it for a while."

"And what's that?"

"Boston Lobster Pie."

"What?" He scrunched up his nose like he'd smelled something sour.

"Don't tell me you're one of those people who doesn't like something without trying it?"

"Of course not. I've just never heard of it before."

"Well, it's delicious. It has chunks of lobster meat in a creamy sauce with a Ritz Cracker topping. It comes with a side of pasta topped with crushed garlic in a marinara sauce that's also delicious. You can taste mine if you want."

"All right. Ready?" He lifted me slightly and spun me around. I squealed with delight.

"Let's go."

"You two make such a lovely couple. How long have you been married?" an elderly white couple standing next to us asked.

"Oh, we're..."

"We're newlyweds," Alex cut me off. He pulled me close and kissed me long and hard on the lips.

"Oh how adorable," she whined out in her nasal voice.

"Me and Stan here have been together for fifty years."

"Wow! Congratulations!" Alex said.

"Well, you kids keep doing what you were doing back there, and you'll be telling people about your fifty years together," Stan said.

"We'll keep that in mind."

"Well, me and my Margaret are going to leave you two alone. And congratulations to you, too." We bid Stan and Margaret farewell and walked off laughing.

"You are something else."

"What are you talking about?"

"Newlyweds?" I raised my eyebrow.

"Don't you feel like one?"

"Well…"

"I was just telling them what I felt like. Come on, let's go." He held my hand and talked non-stop as we walked back to the car.

We drove back up Los Olas and parked behind the restaurant. There was a forty-five minute wait, so we put our name on the list and walked down the street and browsed through the shops.

There happened to be a showing at the gallery a few doors down. So we walked in and mingled until the pager they gave us vibrated, indicating that our table was ready.

Just as we stepped out the door, in true South Florida style, it began to rain without warning. We had to make a run for it in order not to get soaked.

"Where did that come from?" Alex asked as we entered Mangos.

"Something you get used to here. The showers roll in off the water and make their way across one end to the other before you can find your umbrella."

The hostess seated us at a cozy little booth. A minute later our server came and took our drink orders. This time we were up for something a little harder than tea and soda. We enjoyed the music from the live band that was in full swing as we waited for our drinks from the bar.

We talked more about my business and kids.

"Do you think they'll like me?"

"I think you'll pass the test."

"And what test is that?"

"Honestly, I wouldn't know since you're the first man I've dated in more than a decade." I laughed.

He reached over and grabbed my hands. "I would gladly take any test for you."

I blushed and turned my head as the waitress returned with our drinks.

"So what's good, other than your favorite dish?"

"The Mahi-Mahi is delicious."

"I see someone is a regular," the waitress said.

"Not that regular, but I've been here enough to know."

"She's right. You can have it blackened or grilled."

"Blackened."

"Okay. I'll be back with your salads."

The other side erupted in applause as the band ended the first stretch of their set.

"This is really nice."

"We have our share of trendy spots. Maybe not as many as New York though."

"Do you like New York?"

"Like New York? I love New York."

"Really?"

"Oh, please. I always said if I hadn't married my husband…" I paused.

"Finish."

"If I hadn't gotten married, I would be living there now. A displaced New Yorker is what my sister calls me. She's tried numerous times to get me to move there."

"Would you consider that?"

"I don't know. I never had anything there worth moving for."

"Maybe that is about to change."

When our food arrived, he looked over at my plate to survey my dish. Needless to say, he loved it, which I enjoyed feeding to him in between bites of his Mahi-Mahi.

The waitress brought out the check. Alex reached in his back pocket and began to pat all of them frantically.

"Damn. I forgot my wallet in my clothes from last night."

"Don't worry. It was my idea to come here so it's on me."

"That's not how…"

"I'm not going to accuse you of being one of those guys who conveniently leaves his wallet so he doesn't have to pay." I laughed as I pulled out my Platinum American Express card.

"You don't know how embarrassed I am right now. I've never done this before."

"Why are you stressing? I said it was my treat. That was my initial plan anyway. I guess your reflexes made you reach for the check." The waitress took the bill and quickly brought it back with two peppermints.

"Have a nice night," she said as we prepared for our exit.

"Thank you, Yani, for dinner. I've never had a woman treat me before," he said as he grabbed my hand as we walked down the hall to the parking lot out back.

"You've just been dating the wrong women. There are some of us out here that are fine with picking up the bill sometimes."

He smiled. "Now I know."

"So, you ready to call it a night? I need to get home and see about my household." I grabbed my cell phone from my purse and punched in Natalia's personal line. No answer. I wondered if she'd been there today. I hung up and called the main number. No answer still. I began to wonder if Asia had found her way back today or was she still hemmed up with Hayden in his hotel room. One last place to try. I punched in Kelly's number where Natalia was supposed to be.

"Happy New Year!"

"Hi, Carol?"

"Hi, Yani! How's your first day of the new millennium going?" she cheerily asked.

"Just great. I was calling to check on my child. Is she still there?"

"Oh yes. The girls just left to go to the movies. So, you might as well let Natalia stay over again. It's perfectly fine with me."

"Okay, Carol. Thanks a lot. Just tell her to give me a call when she gets in. If I'm not at home, tell her to call me on my cell."

"I will. Talk to you later, Yani."

"Bye, Carol." I pushed the end button to hang up.

"No one home?"

"Nope." I was dialing the number to where Jay was staying. "I have to check on them though." I got the answering machine and left a message. I knew they both were in good hands.

"So, since you have no one to go home to, what

do you want to do?" He turned the radio down as Chante Moore bragged about the man she's got at home.

"I don't know. What would you like to do?"

"After our lil' salsa demonstration today, how about doing it in the club?" He winked and melted me with that infectious smile.

"I haven't been out dancing in years. I don't even think I know where to go."

"Oh."

"But I do know who to call to find out." I smiled at him with a devilish grin.

"Then make that call."

"We're going to have to change first, because we're definitely not dressed for it." I continued up U.S.1 to jump on 595 heading west.

"If it's going to be a hassle, we can take a raincheck and maybe go tomorrow night. That way we can just make one trip out. I don't want you driving all over everywhere for me."

"Believe me, I don't mind. Let me call my girlfriend, Haydee, and see if tonight is the best night to go or not."

"You sure?"

I was dialing her number. "Stop worrying so much. If I thought you were putting me out, I'd let you know."

Haydee told me that tomorrow night would be a

better bet and then proceeded to question me about why I wanted to know. I told her that we'd talk later and hung up before she could protest.

Alex and I settled on taking in a movie, which ended up being a trip to Hollywood Video where we picked up *Hav Plenty* and *Analyze This*. Both were movies I'd promised myself to see, but couldn't find the time.

❤❤❤

As we pulled up to the house, I was a little nervous about bringing him there. This would be the first time I'd ever shared company with a man other than Jarrin in my home.

"This is nice. How long have you been here?"

"A little over fourteen years." I opened the garage door leading into the house, clicked on the kitchen light, and tossed my purse on the counter.

"So you kept the house?"

"Yeah. We bought it after our daughter was born. When he disappeared, I decided to keep it since the payment was something that I could handle and I didn't want to uproot my children at the time."

"Can't say that I blame you. I lived in a rent-controlled apartment for years. It was hard for me to move out of it. I ended up subleasing it to my

cousin just so I could keep it in the family at least."
He followed me into the family room. I placed the
bag of movies on the coffee table.

"Pick out what you want to watch first. I'm going
to go put this stuff away. Make yourself at home." I
gave him the universal remote and turned on the
surround sound system. I grabbed my overnight bag
and dress from the night before and marched off to
my room.

I returned a few moments later catching the opening credits of *Hav Plenty*.

"I met the guy that did this film."

"Who?"

"Chris Cherot," Alex said as he pointed at the
screen.

"So he wrote it?"

"Wrote, directed, and starred in it."

"Good way to keep the budget under control." We
snuggled close as the movie started. I can't remember what happened beyond the point that all the
drama seemed to unfold. Somewhere around the
sister chasing him in the kitchen I looked and saw
that being up all day on four hours of sleep had
taken its toll on us.

# *Alex*

## CHAPTER 21

As I relaxed in the slightly oversized leather seat, I thought back to the terrific time I'd had on my brief, but enjoyable vacation. I'd spent almost every waking hour with Yani from New Year's on.

We went to the Salsa club her friend told us about that Sunday. Then we went to Coco Walk down in the Grove which consisted of restaurants, a movie theater, some novelty shops, and few spots to go dancing.

We dragged Carmen and Bryce out to dinner and dancing one night. Yani didn't want them to think that she was trying to monopolize my time, but I think that's what Carmen had in mind. She was pushing us to do something every night; not knowing that we'd already made plans. We decided to just let her think that she was orchestrating everything.

Last night she cooked me a going-away dinner, giving me a chance to meet her children. Not only was she a successful businesswoman and a great mother, but she was also an excellent cook.

After dinner, I helped her clear the table, then went in the playroom and got my butt whooped in *NFL Blitz 2000* by Jay. I think he enjoyed it just as much as I did.

Natalia and I had a long talk about New York. She told me of her plans to attend NYU film school. She was trying to talk her mom into letting her come up to spend a few weeks in the summer with her aunt. That way she'd get a feel for being in the city.

Yani smiled as she watched our interaction.

"Can I get you something to drink, sir?" the flight attendant asked as she stood over me.

"I'll have some water for right now." I looked out the window as the pilot announced that we were flying over Virginia.

I opened my laptop to check the endless list of emails that I knew were waiting for me. Especially since the last time I'd turned on my computer was New Year's Eve. How I dreaded the thought of what was awaiting me when I got back to the hustle bustle that was my life. But I had to suck it up. We were about to begin a huge project that would bring in the big bucks for sure.

The flight attendant returned with a bottle of spring water.

"Thank you."

I turned off my laptop and leaned back in the seat. Yani was heavy on my mind and all I could think about was seeing her again.

Wait until I get to the office on Monday. Ed's not going to believe me when I tell him I found her without even trying.

♥♥♥

As promised I pulled out my cell as I disembarked the plane and headed to baggage claim.

"Hey, lady."

"Hi. You're home already?"

"Just stepped off the plane."

"Oh." There was a pause. "Is it still cold there?"

"They say it's snowing."

"Really? I haven't seen snow in years."

"We need to do something about that then."

She laughed. "How long will it take you to get home from there?"

"No more than twenty, thirty minutes."

"That's not bad. Do you have a way home?"

"There should be a car waiting for me. If not, I'll just catch a cab."

"That's good." We were quiet for a moment.

"I miss you."

"I miss you, too. Remember, we promised to stay in touch."

"We'll talk at least once a day. If for no other reason than to say good morning, I'll call you."

"Have you ever done this long distance relationship thing?"

"Never."

"Think you're up for it?"

"For you, I can handle anything," I said.

"I guess we'll play it by ear and see what happens."

I spotted the driver we normally used and nodded my head toward him. He walked over and helped me with my bags.

"I won't keep you. Thanks for calling to let me know you made it home."

"Okay. I'll give you a call tomorrow as soon as I get a break."

"I'll be waiting."

# Asia

## CHAPTER 22

I finished packing up my things as Yani sat on the edge of the bed watching me. She'd been wearing a smile that seemed to have become a permanent part of her face since meeting this Alex guy. My quick departure from the party and Hayden's domination of my time interfered with me meeting him. Hayden had been gone for three days now. I told him I'd give him a call when I got back to town. We never got back around to that discussion about the future of our rekindled relationship before he left. He'd kept me so busy going and doing things that I decided to put it on the back-burner until the time was right to address it again.

"So, big sis, I take it that you've made plans to see him again?"

"I think it's in the cards."

"When?"

"I'd say in the near future. He called the other day and asked me what I thought about coming to New York for a visit."

"Is he paying?"

"Why does he have to pay? I'm the one going on the trip. Besides, I don't need anyone to pay for anything." A little pissed, she walked off into the bathroom.

"Damn, no need to get your panties in a bunch. You know I'm just messing with you. Anyway, I would love for you to come up. It's been a while since you've been up to visit. Besides, it'd be good for us to make some contacts and expand a bit. Maybe open up that office we've been talking about."

"That would be a good thing. New York is definitely a market I want us to dominate."

"Damn shame it took a man to get your ass to come and visit." I stood in the bathroom mirror behind her. Her face was glowing. All of sudden I grabbed her arm and turned her around. "Did you fuck him?!" I blurted out.

Shocked, she pulled my hand off her. "How could you even ask me some dumb shit like that?"

"Just like I did the first time. Did you fuck him?"

"Of all people, Asia, you should know me better than that."

"Bitch, please. Don't try to act like your ass is Ms. Goody Two Shoes. I know your ass is an under-cover slut." I playfully bumped her with my hip in an attempt to lighten her mood.

"Whatever. But, hell no. The most we did was kiss."

"Well you should've fucked him. I know your horny ass wanted to."

"Whatever." We laughed.

"What was it you said he did again? I'm trying to figure out if there's a possibility that I might know him."

"He works at a production company."

"What production company? You never know, I might just know him or know someone that knows someone that knows him. At least enough to get the lowdown on him." Yani looked at me with a confused look on her face. I could tell she was thinking about the question. I started humming the music to *Jeopardy* as I waited.

"You know something, I really can't remember. Now that I think of it, I don't even remember his frickin' last name." She looked over at me and burst into laughter.

"What's so funny, dodo head? You spent all that time with a man and you can't remember his last name? For all you know he can be married with a house full of children. You have been out of the game far too long. Help me with my bags." We each picked up a bag and walked downstairs.

"Married men don't give you their home telephone number. I even have the home address, so I'm not that stupid."

"How do you know if his information is legit? You're here and he's there…" Just then the doorbell rang.

"I hope that's your mother. I wanted to get to the damn airport early enough so I don't have to stand in line forever." When we rounded the corner we could hear Nat talking to Mama, who was dishing out kisses to the kids.

"Hey, girls. I know I'm running a little late, but I made it." We both gave her a hug.

"You're not late, you're right on time. I just finished packing," Hey, I wasn't about to tell her what I'd just said to Yani. A black mother will put fear in you that will last a lifetime.

"I had to drop your Aunt Kat off first. She had one of the boys drop her over earlier, and you know she didn't call. She's always been good at inconveniencing people." Mama walked into the kitchen and sat on one of the tan leather stools at the breakfast bar.

"Let me run in the room and grab my purse so we can get out of here," Yani said. "Nat, are you and Jay ready?" she called out. Natalia rolled her eyes as she looked up at the ceiling.

"Yes, Mommy. We've been ready. We were waiting on you two." She looked over at me.

"Then why don't you and your big-head brother take my bags and put them in the truck." I draped my arm around her neck. She was definitely going to be tall like her father, making her the tallest Fenton woman.

"Come on, Jay." She walked over and grabbed her mom's keys from the porcelain bowl and headed to the garage with her brother in tow.

Yani reappeared with a pair of cute red, strappy platform slingbacks that went perfectly with the mesh sarong skirt and matching halter she had on.

"Ma, what do you think about Yani? Doesn't she have a beautiful glow?" I winked at her as Mama gave her the once-over.

"Umm, she does sort of look like she's, ya know… more carefree. That can only mean one thing. She met a man." Yani's mouth popped open. Still couldn't pull one over on the old girl.

"Can we go now?" she asked in an attempt to switch to another subject.

"I guess that answered my question." Mama held her hand up so she could slap me a high-five. Not amused with our display of comradeship, Yani rolled her eyes and walked out the garage door.

"I thought you said you wanted to get there early."

I was appropriately dressed for the return to the cold weather. Blue jeans, deep red, fluffy turtleneck sweater, and a pair of square front, red leather boots that I'd picked up on sale at Sam & Libby's. My three-quarter length, black leather coat was draped across my bags as we waited at the boarding gate.

Once they began to board flight number 180, non-stop to LaGuardia, I hugged everyone and said my goodbyes.

"We're going to miss you, Auntie," the kids each said as they hugged me.

"Aw, I'm going to miss you guys, too."

Mama leaned in and gave me a long hug. "Oh, my baby. You know it breaks my heart every time you leave. You'd think I'd be used to it by now." She dabbed at her eyes.

"Oh, Ma. I love you, woman." I kissed her on the cheek. She didn't know how hard it was on me, too.

"I love you, too." She stepped back as I adjusted my bag on my shoulder and waited for Yani.

Yani pulled her shades up so they rested in her hair. She stood in front of me and wrapped her arms around me.

"Oh, Girl. I am going to miss you. Thank you for everything."

"I'll miss you, too. Think about making that trip up. We can go out and have a good time." We gave each other one last squeeze as they gave the call that anyone left could board. I rushed off toward the door.

"I'll call as soon as I get in. I love you guys." I waved as I handed the woman at the gate my ticket.

I placed my carry-on bag in the overhead and took my seat. I stared out the window in anticipation of takeoff.

I searched through my purse and ran across the paper Hayden had given to me with his information on it. All this time and he only lived a few blocks away from me. Funny how small a place could seem, but be so big. I began to wonder if he'd try to call me tonight. He definitely knew when I would be back. He'd asked me for the specific time and flight number yesterday.

I began to wonder how serious this relationship was going to be. Would it lead back to where it left off? Would we go through with it this time? I guess I'm rushing things. It's only been a couple of weeks and here I was thinking about marriage again. I better remember the reason we never made it to the altar before.

We were young and ambitious and neither wanted to give up anything. Back then it was if we were opera singers. Always thinking about me, me, me. After realizing there was never an us, I pulled out.

I felt that marriage should be a partnership, but Hayden didn't see it that way at the time.

❤❤❤

I pulled my bags from the turnstile and gathered up everything.

"How was your flight?" I turned around to the familiar voice.

"Hayden?"

"Couldn't let you stand out here waiting for a cab on a cold night like this one." I smiled as he hugged and kissed me.

"Got everything?"

"Now I do," I said as I leaned up for him to kiss me.

Maybe he was ready to become us with me. Time would definitely tell.

# *Alex*

## CHAPTER 23

"Things are pretty hectic in the office. What about you?"

"Business as usual. We have a pretty big event coming up in a few weeks. I'm tying everything up with that this week."

"What type of event?"

"An entertainment conference that the BBA has every year."

"BBA?"

"Black Business Association."

"I've heard about that. This is their second year doing it, right?"

"It did pretty well last year so, they're doing it again. We're also putting together a package for a huge wedding scheduled to happen in six months."

"You ladies are pretty busy."

"There's no other way to be."

Just as promised, Yani and I had talked on the phone every day, three and four times a day, since I'd stepped foot off the plane.

Everyone in the office commented on the difference in my mood after my vacation. This in turn had made the work on the project really flow. We would have it wrapped up sooner than we projected, which would open up the door for other upcoming projects.

"I miss you, Alex."

"Not more than I miss you."

"I guess we'll have to see about that."

"I'm having a hard enough time trying to make the rest of this month without seeing you, but I don't know." She laughed.

"It'll be three months next week."

"Three looong months."

"That's not that long."

"See, that statement right there lets me know that I miss you more, because that's long to me."

"You never know, you just may receive a FedEx package with a plane ticket inside. Then that would make me the winner."

"I like a woman with a competitive side." Just then I got an idea. "After you finish tying everything up with the BBA, do you think you'll have some free time?"

"Next week will be pretty open for me. Why?"

"I was just wondering."

"Just wondering?"

"That's all." Constance buzzed in. "Hold on, Sweetie."

"Yeah?"

"Your scheduled conference call is coming though. Everyone's waiting in the conference room."

"Okay, let them know I'm coming now."

"Tell Yani I said hello." I could hear the smile in her voice.

"Will do." I clicked the button for the line where Yani was waiting.

"Hey, I've got to go. Duty calls."

"Okay."

"Tonight?"

"Same time?"

"Same place. Bye, Sweetie."

"Bye."

"She's the sweetie already?" Ed said as he walked into my office. He had a big smile on his face.

"Stop standing in doors spying on a brotha."

"She's truly got to be something. She's got my boy sprung and he hasn't even touched her yet."

"Ready for the meeting?" I asked steering him away from the topic.

"I came to get you. You're the one that's caught up in something else."

"Let's roll then." I grabbed the files from my desk and walked out the door.

"Constance, I need you to work on something for me." I placed the note on her desk and kept walking.

"Have you told her anything about you yet?"

"Of course I have."

"I'm not talking about your name and where you live. I'm talking about what you do for a living. Have you given her a heads up on what she's getting into? Are you going to give her the option of whether or not this is something she wants to deal with?"

"Ed, I'd give this up for her."

He stopped in his tracks. "That serious?"

"Yes, that serious. So there's nothing for her to deal with. Besides, her business has had her involved in a few industry circles."

"That's what makes it hard to believe that she's never heard of you before."

"Well believe it. Ready?" I asked as I put my hand on the handle of the glass conference room door.

"Always." We walked into the room where the investor waited for us. Those that couldn't be there physically were being connected by conference call.

❤❤❤

"So, how'd your meeting go today?"

"Very well."

"What's this project you're working on? If you don't mind me asking."

"Now why would I mind?"

"Well, you know—some people don't like discussing business after hours."

"That's only with people we don't care that much for." We both laughed.

"We're producing a movie and soundtrack that's being directed by a new, up and coming, hotshot director. The cast consists of some of the hottest African American actors on the scene…"

She laughed.

"What's funny?"

"It sounds like you're pitching it to me." I thought about it and laughed too since that was exactly what I was doing. I'd said it so many times, that it'd come as the natural thing to say.

"Well, does it sound like something you'd put your money into if I was seeking you out to be an investor?"

"If it's something you're doing, without a second thought."

"Good. Did you get everything squared away for the event you're working on?"

"Signed the last contract today. I'm so exhausted, I don't think I'm even going to show up to the event."

"Why not?"

"It's not like they need me to be there."

"So that means you're going to have two free weeks coming up."

"Pretty much." *Good*, I thought, as I placed the glass on the kitchen counter.

"What'd you eat for dinner?"

"Nothing exciting. I grabbed a sandwich from the deli near the office. Did you cook?"

"Did I cook? Of course I cooked. I have to make sure the kids eat."

"I didn't mean it like that. It was more of a melancholy thought. You know, wish I could've had some type of thing."

She laughed.

I looked up at the ceiling above my bed. I had two days—actually one to get everything done so my plan would go off without a hitch. I'd check with Constance tomorrow and make sure she'd done her part. The only other person I needed to contact was Carmen and she was getting a call first thing tomorrow, or should I say today.

"You sleep?"

"Hmm?"

"You got all quiet on me."

"Oh, no. I was thinking about something."

"Was it a good thought?" she asked in a sexy tone.

"Very good."

"Kiss and tell?"

"You'll find out soon enough. Soon enough."

# *Asia*

## CHAPTER 24

I checked my watch again to determine how much more time I was going to wait before I chalked it up to being stood up. In five minutes he would be forty-five minutes late.

"That's all you're getting, Hayden, is five more minutes and then I'm out." Hell, normally I would've been gone after twenty minutes, but I'm trying to make changes. Trying to be a new Asia and give this relationship thing a chance to blossom into something. Lately Hayden has been making it hard though. I can understand he has to work late, but damn, he can be courteous and let a sistah know what's going on. I'm not one for being strung along. You'd think he knew this beforehand.

"Hey, Baby, I'm sorry. I had to wrap something up before I left the office and then traffic was…"

"Umm, hmm," I said nonchalantly. He lifted my chin and kissed me on the lips.

"But I'm here. That counts for something?"

"I guess."

"Asia…"

"Hayden, I'm hungry. Can we just eat? Maybe after I get something in my stomach besides these damn chips and salsa I'll feel better."

He signaled the waiter.

Our meeting place was Calientes in the Village. They had good drinks and even better food.

"What do you want?"

"I was thinking we'd get a Poo-Poo platter and split it. It's more than enough food for two."

"Sounds good." He gave the waiter our order. I asked for another Colada for me.

"How many of those have you had?"

"Two."

"I'm that late?"

"Yep," I said as I slurped down the remaining contents of the glass in front of me.

"Baby, look…"

"There's nothing to explain. You had to work a little late. I'm okay with that. Just next time, can you call me and let me know something? I think that's the main reason we have cell phones." He got up and slid into the booth next to me.

"Hey, I know it seems that I've been a lil' distant, but I'm working on something at work and I need to get it knocked out. You understand, don't you, baby?"

I sucked on the orange slice. "I do. All I'm saying is you can't just forget about me if something comes up."

He placed a soft kiss on my neck. He knew it was the one spot that made me melt. I smiled a little.

"I promise." The waiter returned with my drink and placed another platter of the red and regular chips in front of me.

"So what's on the agenda for this weekend?" he asked as he dipped the chip into the dish of salsa.

"Nothing exciting. Thought I'd find a good book and curl up with it."

"Interested in curling up with a good man?"

"Maybe."

"Maybe?"

"That's what I said. You do speak English?"

"What can a brotha do to turn that maybe into a bonafide yes?"

"Let me see…" I placed my finger on my chin as I pretended to be deep in thought.

"Can't be that hard to think of something?"

"Okay. If the brotha is willing to give this sistah a most satisfying massage—with scented oils of course—then I can see her curling up with that brotha over that book."

"I'll do one better. I'll give you a full spa. Mani-cure, pedicure, and a Swedish massage. Accom-panied by a nice lunch. How does that sound?"

"Sounds like it can definitely be a plan."

"How does curling up with me tonight sound?"

"Sounds like you're going to be doing a massive amount of sucking up for making me wait damn near an hour."

He kissed me. "You drive a hard bargain."

"Yeah, I bet."

The waiter walked over and placed the platter that had more than enough food for two in front of us. "Enjoy your meal," he said as he walked away.

I picked up the fried ravioli to take a bite of it, but Hayden stopped me before I got close to my opened mouth.

"What?"

"If I feed you, would that be considered part of my sucking up?"

I laughed. "Yes, Baby." I was softening already.

# *Alex*

## CHAPTER 25

"**S**ince everyone has been briefed and you all know what you have to do, I'll see you all bright and early Monday morning. We've got our work cut out for us. So, enjoy your weekend."

Everyone quickly filed out the conference room as they went back to their workstations to grab their belongings. I'd given the entire office a half-day, because we would be extremely busy in the coming weeks. I'm a firm believer in employee morale and give back to them as much as possible.

I walked past Constance's desk as she packed up her things.

"Were you able to get to that list I gave you?"

She handed me a printout. "Here's the itinerary for the flight. I arranged for the car to be there ten minutes before the flight lands and the gift box will be inside waiting. The tickets will be waiting for you to pick up at the will-call window and dinner reservations are all taken care of. Now all that's left for you to do is call her." She placed the last of her things in her bag and threw it on her shoulder.

I smiled. "Good, good. Thanks, Constance. I keep telling you, I don't know what I would do without you."

"I hope you remember that when I put in for my vacation time." She smiled and waved at me as I walked into my office to place a call.

I'd been hinting around to Yani about her making a trip up to visit me since a week after I'd left. She promised that she'd think about it, but was never able to give me a date or time. After her statement that she'd FedEx me a plane ticket I thought it was time for me to be my usual proactive self and do something about her coming to see me.

I picked up the phone and punched in the number that I'd learned by heart.

"Xposure, how may I direct your call?" the friendly-sounding receptionist answered.

"Yes, Ms. Miller, please."

"May I tell her who's calling?" Screening the boss' calls.

"Alex Chance."

"Oh, okay. One second please." A smooth jazz tune floated through the earpiece while I waited for Yani to pick up.

"Hello?"

"Hey, beautiful. How's your day going?"

"Hey, you. Pretty good so far. How about you?" Her voice was animated with a sense of pleasure.

"Mine is over."

"Over? Aren't you lucky?"

"Well, we got some very good news and the boss gave us the rest of the day off." I thought I'd keep the charade going and tell her the truth when she got here.

"That's great. So, what plans do you have for the rest of your day?"

"That's why I'm calling you. I remember you saying last night that you're going to have some free time. Have you made any plans for the weekend yet?"

"Not yet. Why?"

"Do you think you can manage to get a babysitter for the weekend?"

"I can probably get my mother to watch the kids. What does this have to do with the rest of your day? Are you coming to visit?"

"One of us is visiting, but it's not me."

"Me?"

"Look, you're the boss around there; why don't you call it a day and see about making the arrangements for the kids. I'll give you a call in an hour with more detailed instructions. Okay?"

"Alex..."

"No excuses. I told you I miss you more and I need to see you. An hour?"

"You're crazy."

"Talk to you in an hour."

"An hour."

I hung up the phone and dialed Carmen. In order to make this work I had to have her help. If I gave Yani an hour to think, she'd come up with one reason after the next why she couldn't come.

"Hello?"

"Hey, Mrs. Douglas, how are you?"

"Hey, Alex. You miss us?" Carmen asked.

"Of course I do. I need a favor from you though."

"What's that?" I went on to tell her the details of my plans as she squealed with delight.

"Okay. Where am I taking her?" she asked without hesitation.

I gave her all the information and thanked her before I hung up. Part one was taken care of. Now to handle the rest.

# *Yani*

## CHAPTER 26

I was shocked to see Carmen at my house when I pulled up.

"Hey, Chica. I've come to deliver you to the airport."

I laughed. "So he called out the Calvary."

"That goes to show you that he really wants to see you. I guess you've got his nose wide open." She winked at me.

"I was going to go inside and try to throw a bag together."

"We don't have time for that. I have to get you to the airport in forty-five minutes. So, park your car in the garage and let's go."

"Okay. Just give me a minute."

"Come on now, my car is running."

I pulled my car in the garage and walked back out to Carmen's truck.

"Ready?" she asked.

"Since I've been instructed not to bring anything, I guess so." She sped off toward the expressway.

Thirty minutes later we pulled up to a hangar that was on the service side of the airport.

"How am I going to get to the terminal from here?"

"This is the address he gave me and the name is on the building so, it's got to be the right place." We both climbed out and walked into the front office.

A guy followed us in from the hangar. "Hi. Can I help you ladies?"

"I hope so. I'm looking for Mark?" I asked as my brows knotted with confusion.

"I'm Mark, and you are?"

"Yaniece Miller."

"Oh, yes. The pilot just walked out to the plane. Do you have any bags?"

"No. Where exactly is the plane?" I asked hesitantly.

"Right back here in the hangar. I'll show you which one."

Carmen and I looked at each other in utter amazement.

"You mean one of those Learjets?" she asked him.

"Yes, ma'am. You'll have the plane to yourself. It's like being in your living room, so you'll be extremely comfortable." He walked over to the door and held it open.

"I want to come just so I can get a peep. Then I'll leave," Carmen said.

We both followed him out to a sleek plane. The

stairs were down for boarding and a few guys were doing last-minute checks on it.

"Oh my God! Girl, is this nice or what?" Carmen asked as we stepped on the plane.

He didn't lie about it looking like someone's living room. There was a couch, a dining area, and a television. I was totally speechless.

"We're ready to depart," Mark informed us.

"Well, that's my cue. You make sure you have a good time. I really think Alex went all out for you on this one." We hugged tightly.

"I'll call you when I get there."

"You better. I'll call and check on the kids for you. Maybe I'll get Jay so he can come over with the boys."

"Thanks, Girl. I really appreciate it." After another brief hug, Carmen smiled so hard, her slightly slanted eyes nearly closed. She waved goodbye as she walked off the plane.

I sat down in one of the comfortable chairs and put on my seatbelt. The pilot came back and introduced himself to me. Told me about all of the accommodations on the jet and our estimated flight arrival time.

I was on cloud nine as we whizzed down the runway and up into the air. I felt like I was part of the rich and famous. I expected Robin Leach to walk in at any moment.

We cruised all the way. It seemed less than two hours later the pilot announced we were cleared for landing at JFK. I'd just finished watching *The Best Man*, which happens to be one of my favorites. The pilot and crew of one flight attendant, who'd sat down and watched the movie with me, thanked me for flying and bid me farewell.

"I hope you have a good time while you're in New York," the bubbly attendant said as I prepared to step off the plane.

"Thanks." I adjusted my leather bag on my shoulder and descended the stairs. I spotted a guy in a dark suit holding up a card with my name on it.

"I'm Yaniece Miller," I said as I approached him.

"Hello, Ms. Miller. The car is waiting right outside the door. If you'll follow me." He led the way out to a long, sleek black stretch limo.

"Oh my God." I held my hand up to my mouth. The driver opened the door and waited for me to slide in. He then walked around to take his place in the driver's seat.

On the seat directly in front of me were three boxes. Each was wrapped with silver paper with a big red ribbon. On top of the smallest box was an envelope with my name beautifully scripted on it. I anxiously tore it open.

"I hope your flight was nothing but pure delight. Now open the boxes and I'll see you shortly. Alex."

I picked up the smaller box first and tore the paper off. Inside was a pair of sexy bare, asymmetrical, black slingbacks. They were beautiful. I quickly moved on to the next box, ripping the paper to shreds. I pulled the black sexy, open back, floor-length gown out of the box. The surprises just seemed unending. I reached for the last box. Inside it was a dozen beautiful red roses! *This is how it must feel to be a princess*, I thought.

Looking at the dress and shoes, I knew I needed to change before we got to wherever it was that we were going. I quickly slid off my shoes and undid my skirt. After checking to make sure that the driver wasn't getting his peep on, I slipped my shirt quickly over my head and replaced it with the dress. I undid my bra and slid it off, then stood as much as I could to pull the dress down. Next I slipped the shoes on and located a mirror to check my hair. Thank God I'd had it done that morning. I grabbed my bag to freshen up my makeup and sprayed a little Michael on my neck and wrists to make sure that I smelled good. I was ready. As if on cue, the car came to a stop.

*I'm going to freeze my ass off*, I thought as I waited for the driver to open the door.

"Good evening, Ms. Miller," another male voice said to me as he extended his hand to help me out of the car.

"Good evening," I responded. I glanced around taking in my surroundings in search of any signs of Alex. A guy from the restaurant walked me into the interior of Jezebel's and led me over to a secluded booth.

"How was your flight?" the smooth familiar male voice whispered close to my ear.

I turned around to find a tuxedo-clad Alex. I threw my arms around his neck before I had a chance to think where I was. He responded with a tight squeeze and a gentle kiss.

"Oh, Alex. Everything is just... I mean, the flight, the limo, the dress and shoes. I don't know how many more surprises I can take."

"Don't say that 'cause I'm just getting started." He kissed me again as he waited for me to take my seat.

After enjoying a delicious meal, we hopped into the limo and headed over to Broadway where we had balcony seats to see *Aida*. I was totally blown away. This man had planned the most unforgettable romantic evening of my life. I never wanted it to end.

As we exited the theater, I pulled my wrap closer around my shoulders and Alex held his elbow out awaiting my arm. As soon as we parted the door, a photographer stopped and asked if he could get a quick picture. Not thinking much of it, I stopped to pose and flash my vibrant smile.

"Thanks, Mr. Chance."

"No problem," Alex replied.

Alex opened the door and stepped to the side so that I could climb into the car first. As we pulled off, I started thinking about how everyone seemed to treat Alex as if he was royalty or something. A few people had come over to our table to shake his hand while we were in the restaurant.

"Maybe he's a…" I said in my head. "Naw." I shook my head to make the thoughts go away. He's lived here all his life, so quite naturally he would know lots of people. I was reading far too much into it.

As we rode through Times Square, Alex pulled me close to him. "Is there anything else you can think of that you might want to do? Tonight is all about pleasing you."

"Something to top that? I can't think of a thing."

Alex kissed me long and hard. "So you ready to call it a night?"

"That sounds good."

We pulled up in front of a huge building directly across the street from Central Park. A uniform-clad doorman opened the door for us.

"Hello, Mr. Chance. How are you this evening?"

"I'm good, Mike." Alex reached in to help me out of the car.

"Mike, this is Ms. Miller. A friend of mine from

Florida. She's going to be visiting with me for the weekend and hopefully into next week." He wrapped his arm around me and pulled me close to his side

My cheeks burned with embarrassment. I waved to Mike.

"How are you, ma'am? I hope you enjoy your stay in the city. If you need anything, just give me a call and I'll do my best to take care of it for you."

"Thank you, Mike, but I don't think that'll be necessary. I'm a little familiar with New York."

He held the door for us as we walked inside the lobby. I'd been in different hi-rises before back home, but this was just stunning. I almost forgot that we were in a place of residence and not some expensive hotel.

Alex was leading the way with the gift boxes from earlier in his arms. They now contained the clothing I'd changed out of earlier. We caught the elevator up to the penthouse and stepped out in front of his door.

He pulled his keys from his pocket and unlocked the door.

"Welcome to my abode," he said with an extended hand, bowing slightly as he allowed me access inside.

I slowly walked in taking in my surroundings. He had impeccable taste. The walls were painted one of those brown earth tone colors that everyone is into now. We walked down a few steps into the living room area. My heels made a clink-clink sound as I walked across the marble flooring. The beveled mirrors that spanned the living room wall made the room appear to be two times larger than it already was.

By the looks of things, he hadn't lied about not having any children. There wasn't one fingerprint on the mirrors, and nothing seemed to be out of place. An exquisite chandelier hung high above the dining room table that was made of a whitewashed-looking wood with a stainless steel top. The table was adorned with a colorful setting for four and fresh lilies in a crystal vase as the centerpiece.

Alex grabbed my hand and led me over to the butter-colored, extra-long, four-cushion sofa. Pillows in different shades of brown were thrown strategically on it. The room screamed, "I've been professionally decorated."

After seating me, he disappeared. I walked over to what looked to be a balcony. I looked out and noticed that he had a view of the park.

"Yani," Alex called from the room he'd gone in.

"Yes?"

"Come in here. I'm just putting your things in the room." I slowly made my way in the direction his voice had come from. I wondered how many rooms he had in this place. I knew it had to be more than one. I was curious to find out which one I was expected to occupy.

I walked into a large room with a huge flat-screen television mounted to the wall. A fireplace crackled in the corner as the fire danced around in it. In another corner was a floor-to-ceiling bookshelf that looked to be built into the wall. There was an oversized couch with extra-long cushions. The kind that when you sat on it your feet never touched the floor. It was great for lounging while watching movies on the television.

Alex drew open the heavy drapes revealing another balcony that looked over at the park. He opened the French doors and asked me to join him as he walked outside.

We stepped out into the frigid air. It was breathtaking. I didn't feel my lips part as my mouth hung slightly open. He pulled me in front of him and securely wrapped his arms around me. I could feel him rub slightly against my backside as he placed soft kisses on the nape of my neck.

"How long have you lived here?"

"About three years. Ever since I was kid, I knew I wanted to live in this building. I went to college, did all the right things so that I could. I made sure everything I did was legit. There was no way I was going to work hard and then lose everything because I decided to take the low easy road."

I snuggled closer to him. "This is so beautiful, Alex. I've always seen stuff like this in the movies or in a magazine, but seeing it with your own eyes is a whole different experience."

"I know. When the real estate agent opened the curtains, I was sold. I couldn't remember what the rest of the house looked like after that." We laughed.

"Now what is it you said you did again?"

# *Alex*

## CHAPTER 27

I t was time for me to come clean. I knew I probably should have told her during our initial meeting. Maybe even one of those nights we spent in each other's company, but for some reason it never seemed to be the right time.

She searched my face with those beautiful brown eyes that seemed to twinkle whenever she smiled and made me smile.

"Why are you looking at me like that? I just told you that I've never dealt in anything illicit or illegal," I protested.

Figuring it was probably better to show her, I grabbed her hand as I walked her back into the house and into my office.

The walls were covered with memorabilia from different projects I'd done, pictures of me with some of the biggest names in the game, and a plaque with an article about my company.

She looked at me after she finished reading it.

"So that explains it."

"Explains what?"

"Why people were treating you like that. I was trying to figure out why everyone was approaching you. I started to think that maybe you were a rapper or a singer. Something of the sort. Why didn't you tell me before now?"

"I'm so tired of women who only see *what* I am instead of *who* I am. With you, I was enjoying just being Alex."

"Did I make you feel that you couldn't tell me?"

"No. Never. I just..." I searched for just the right words. She placed a finger on my lips to silence me.

"I never really asked you either and that's because it never really mattered." She smiled.

I held her beautiful face in my hands and began to place soft kisses on her eyelids, her nose, then the corners of her mouth. I worked my way down each side of her neck. She graciously accepted my roaming tongue into her sweet mouth, sliding her arms up around my neck. I could feel the heat rising from our bodies. Her breathing became labored.

"Yani, I wanna make love to you. Will you let me love you, Baby?" I panted out in between kisses.

"Yes, Alex. I want you to love me."

I carried her down the hall into my bedroom and then into the bathroom. Hoping that she would accept, I'd taken the time to fill the tub with hot water and rose petals when we first arrived.

I sat her on the double sink and removed her shoes and gently kissed and massaged her feet. I kicked my shoes off and threw my socks on top of the hamper in the corner. Our shadows danced in the candlelight. Slowly I undid her dress and watched it drop to the floor. At first she held her arm over her swollen, exposed breasts, shielding them from my view. After a minute of kissing, teasing, and licking, she allowed me to shower some attention on them. She threw her head back, basking in the sensations my tongue was inflicting upon her.

She moaned a throaty sound as I made my way down to her bellybutton, stopping just short of the tip of her black thong. I carefully slid them down her well-toned legs. I slowly stood from my crouching position and guided her to my oversized, oval-shaped tub. I sat her on the edge while I quickly shed the rest of my clothing. Slinging everything behind me. She sat quietly as she enjoyed the fast forward strip show I was giving her. I pulled my black boxer briefs down and kicked them to the side. I observed her face to register her reaction as she tried not to stare at the part of me that was damn near in her face.

I put out my hand to pull her up to me and kissed

her, pressing her close into me. She wrapped her legs around my waist as I hoisted her up and stepped into the tub, submerging us in the hot, soothing water. I retrieved the condom that I'd put on the glass shelf up above our heads and armed my rigid manhood.

She positioned herself over me and with one fluid motion I was inside her warm, moist cavity. She moved in a slow, methodical rhythm. Each thrust deeper with each plunge. The water swished up and over the sides of the tub.

My toes curled up. I grabbed a handful of her ample butt as I pumped back to add more force to her thrusts. She threw her head back as she moaned out my name.

Wanting to take control, I stood her up, pressed her back against the wall as she wrapped her legs around me. I pushed my way deep inside her soft, wet flesh.

"Oh shit, Alex." She threw her head back.

"Yeah, Baby. I'm here." I pulled out and turned her around so I could enter her from the back. I bent her over slightly, propped one of her legs up on the tub. I could feel her body shiver as I filled her middle over and over again. Banging, shoving, and grinding my way deeper inside her, I felt the onset of her orgasm as she reached back for me. I quickly pulled out and dropped to my knees so I could savor her sweet juices. My tongue danced around her vagina.

Pulling me back up, she let me know that she wanted me inside of her. It was my turn to release the liquid that was building inside of me. After a few more minutes of back and forth motion, my body began to twitch. I could feel the onset of an explosion. I pulled her back against me and held on tight, as I expelled my warm and sticky contents into the condom.

Yani turned around and placed my head on her heaving chest as we both collapsed against the wall. Me leaning on her.

"Let's go to the bed," she whispered in my ear.

More than willing to oblige, I quickly recovered and made a water trail into the room. I sat her on the edge of the bed as I slid another prophylactic on. She lay back as I hovered over her. I placed a trail of kisses on her body as she guided me down to the spot she wanted me to kiss most.

"Wet me so you'll slide right in," she whispered in a raspy voice.

I eased down in the bed and stroked her skillfully with my tongue. Her sweet nectar secreted from her walls as if a magic button had been pushed.

"You taste so good," I said as I kissed the hairy outside.

She smiled sexily at me. A look of complete satisfaction was plastered on her face. She moved her finger in a curling motion, beckoning me to come inside her. I bent over her to claim her other lips in a passionate kiss. She whispered in my ear.

"I want you, Baby...now."

I smiled as I positioned myself between her legs, close enough to stroke her spot to prepare it for my entrance. I gently slipped inside initiating the second round of our dance.

Another side of Yani was unleashed. With every push I made, she met it with a thrust of her hips.

"Is it good to you, Baby?" she asked in a sexy whisper.

"Oh, yeah. Damn good." I pumped harder, faster.

"That's it, Baby. I want to feel all of you."

I pumped harder, faster.

"Harder, Baby... harder," she cried. Her hands were gripping my ass as she gave me an extra push, pulling me deeper and deeper into her. "Oh damn, Baby, right there...that's my spot...I'm coming, Baby! Don't stop! Please don't stop!"

I was working at top speed, panting, sweat rolling down my back. I was ready to fall off the edge with her. Every pore in my body seemed to come alive when I felt her love come down with mine following right behind it. I was trying hard to control my jerking.

She let out a sensuous cry of pleasure. She clung to me, tears rolling down her face.

"Hey," I stroked the wetness from her cheeks, "what's with the tears? Did I do something wrong?"

She shook her head back and forth as she tightened her grip. "No. You did everything perfectly."

We climbed up in the bed and lay in the spoon position. Our breathing and hearts were in rhythm as one. At that moment, I knew she was the one. She was my forever.

# *Asia*

## CHAPTER 28

My phone rang abruptly waking me from a semi-deep slumber. I glanced at the clock, which read 2:16 a.m.

"Who the hell is this calling me this time of morning?" I snatched the phone up. "Hello?!"

"Are you sleeping?" my sister's voice asked from the other side.

"Is something wrong?" I eased up on the pillows and propped myself up on my elbows trying to focus. A feeling of panic settled in my stomach.

"Just the opposite, sister dear."

"Have you been drinking?"

"I'm drunk, but not from alcohol," she said.

"What the hell are you talking about?"

"You wouldn't guess where I am right now?"

I looked over at my caller ID. It said private. "You're right, so why don't you just tell me?"

"You sure know how to spoil the fun."

"Damn it, Yani. It's after two in the morning and you call me wanting to play games? Could you please just tell me where you are so I can get some sleep?!"

"Pull your panties out your ass. That is, if you have any on. I know I don't right now."

She didn't have on any panties? What the hell is she talking about? "Yani…" Then it dawned on me.

She picked up on my hesitation. "Yes, I did. Numerous times tonight."

"Oh, shit, you got some!" I squealed at the top of my voice as I danced around in my bed. "With who? Alex? Was it good? Where are you?" I rapidly shot off each question without taking a break to breathe.

"Of course, with Alex. And, Girl…it was so, so, good. I'm still convulsing from the multiple orgasms. Girl, I found out those extra inches really do count."

We both laughed.

"Where are you? Did he come down for another visit?"

"I'm at his place. Stretched out in his big ol' bed waiting for him to finish in the kitchen. I'm breaking all kind of rules tonight."

I knew she was talking about the fact that she usually didn't eat after seven in the evening.

"How long have you been here? Why didn't you call and tell me you were coming?"

"I just got in this evening, and I didn't call because I didn't find out I was coming until an hour before the plane left. Alex made the arrangements and I decided to be spontaneous for once in my life. Guess what else?"

"What?" I sat up in the bed.

"He chartered me a private jet!" I squealed again.

"Damn, Girl. He must've really wanted that stank coochie of yours."

"I'd say so. I had a limo waiting for me, a bad ass dress, a sexy ass pair of shoes…"

"Not another pair of shoes." We both laughed. "This niggah sounds like a Prince Fucking Charming, if I ever heard of one. Do you know his last name, now that you've let him have some of your dusty cootie?"

"Of course, stupid."

"Well?"

"First let me finish telling you what else we did."

"What else? Damn, he really is a keeper."

"I know. He took me to eat at Jezebel's and then took me to see *Aida*!"

"Now you know you've got to tell me his last name and the name of the company he works for. By my calculations, this evening cost him a pretty penny. Where's his place?"

"On Park Place. Across from Central Park."

"Across from the park?! What's his name, Yani?"

"You probably don't know him, so what difference does it make?"

"You better tell me, or I'll find out exactly where you are and come and kick your ass."

She laughed. "You're too aggressive. Maybe if you had sex on a regular basis, you'd loosen up a bit."

"Fuck you. Just tell me his name. Please."

"I love you, too. Chance."

"What? Chance what?"

"That's his last name. Alex Chance."

"Alex Chance, Alex Chance." Why did this name sound familiar to me?

"I told you, you probably didn't know him. Look, take down the number so we can get together tomorrow for lunch or something. You know I can't come in town and not see my baby sis."

"Wait a second while I find a pen." I pulled the top drawer of my nightstand open and dug around until I found something to write with. "Okay, what is it?"

She gave me the number and I promised to give her a call so we could make plans to get together later that day. That is, if she was available. She laughed and said she was trying to make up for the five-year drought while she was here.

"Don't kill the man," I said as she told him who it was she was talking to.

"Well, I need to go. So, tomorrow okay?"

"Okay. Go enjoy your snacks," I teased.

"I love you."

"I love you, too, Girl."

After hanging up the phone, I lay back in the bed staring at the ceiling. Even my sister had found someone that made her feel special.

I thought about the brief conversation I'd had with Hayden a few days ago. He'd broken two dates last week. Claimed he was working late. I played it off. Told him I'd take a raincheck. Maybe I'd scared him off by asking for more than a fling. Seemed his sexual appetite had fallen off since his return.

I rolled over and looked at the clock. It was now 2:45 a.m. I got up and walked into my kitchen in search of something to quench all that was ailing me. I looked in the freezer and retrieved the pint of Edy's Dreamery New York Strawberry Cheesecake ice cream. Yani hipped me to it while I was there. We called it our Golden Girls thing. They ate cheesecake when they got the urge to talk with each other. Yani and I ate cheesecake ice cream.

I pulled a spoon from the dishwasher and shuffled back to my bedroom. I clicked on the TV and flipped through the channels until I found something halfway decent to watch.

The more I thought about how Hayden seemed to brush me off, the more I got the urge to call him and give him a piece of my mind.

After six spoons full of ice cream, I got up the nerve and punched in the numbers.

He answered groggily. "Yeah?"

"Hey." I didn't know what to say after that. Another moment to record as historical.

"Yeah?" he said again louder.

"Did I wake you?" I asked, knowing good and well I had.

"Who's this?"

"Oh, so you've forgotten my voice that quickly? Wonder if you still remember all the…"

He cut me off before I could finish. "Asia? What's wrong?" He sounded concerned.

"Nothing. I just felt the urge to hear your voice. Especially since I haven't heard from you in three days."

"Baby, I'm sorry for being so scarce, but I'm working on something that is monopolizing all my time. I didn't get home until late again tonight." He was throwing that lame ass excuse at me again.

"Do you have any plans for tomorrow? Or should I say today? My sister is in town and I thought it would be nice to do a double-date thing."

"A double date? She and the mystery man have gotten pretty close, huh?"

"Yeah. She just called me, bragging about her sexual escapades."

We both laughed. It was full of tension. We hadn't been together sexually in over three weeks.

"My schedule seems pretty clear for tomorrow."

"Okay. Then I'll give you a call once I find out what they want to do."

"All right then."

We both fell silent for a moment.

"Well, I won't keep you any longer. I guess I'll see you tonight."

"What about this morning?"

He caught me off guard.

"Wha...what?" I stammered.

"Can I come over?"

"You're turning my friendly call into a booty call?"

"If that's what you want to call it. I was thinking more of a 'Baby, I miss you and want to see you' thing."

A smile crept over my face. "I'm up. So, why not."

"See you in about...twenty minutes?"

"Damn, you're only three blocks away. Why so long?"

"Remember it's almost three in the morning and I was sleeping. I do need to freshen up."

"Okay then. Twenty minutes."

# *Yani*

## CHAPTER 29

**D**ressed in Alex's blue cotton pajama top, I walked into the bedroom holding a tray full of delicious breakfast foods, scrambled eggs, bacon, golden pancakes, sausage links, potatoes, and two glasses of orange juice. I paced myself to keep from dropping it and waking Alex.

I crept into the room and placed the tray on the nightstand and eased back into the bed. I kissed Alex seductively on the neck.

"Good morning, sleepyhead." He didn't budge.

I thought of what I could do to get him up. I pulled back the covers and eyed the semi-erect piece of flesh protruding from his middle. I held back all last night from forging an oral relationship with it, but this would be a hell of a way to wake him. After a few moments of debate, I decided to go for it. I leaned in and kissed the head of it, then took my tongue and traced around it; teasingly licking and sucking it as it began to stiffen and grow. I heard him moan and looked up to see if my efforts were working.

He slid his feet back and forth slowly against the sheet as his eyes fluttered. He moaned again. I took a little more into my mouth and worked my tongue around it in circles. His eyes were slits now. I went for the prize and took his entire shaft into my moist mouth. He made a hissing sound like a snake.

"Aww, Baby." He ran his hands wildly through my hair. Once I knew I had him fully awake, I pulled him out and eased up him so I could look into his face.

"Good morning, handsome. Your breakfast awaits you." I pointed to the tray on the nightstand.

"My breakfast is right here." He grabbed me and we tussled around briefly. I ended up on my back with him hovering over me, ready for entrance.

"Un-uh. You're forgetting something," I said. He reached for the box of condoms and pulled one out.

"Remind me to pick up three boxes of these today. Or should I try to find a case?"

"A case?! You want me to be raw by the time I leave here." I invitingly spread eagle, letting him invade my vaginal cavity.

He drove me wild. He'd managed to hit my G spot every single time. I can remember hearing my friends talk about what it felt like, how their eyes would roll in their heads. I could never imagine it, but after last night and right now, I knew that would be a common occurrence with Alex. His lovemaking was addictive.

"Yes, yes," I chanted. My hands were gripping the pillow next to me. I was about to explode. He threw my legs up damn near over my head and took me to another height as I could feel every stroke he made as he moved back and forth inside of me. My legs began to quiver. I could feel the trembles building in me.

"Ooh, shit," I said through gritted teeth.

"Yeah, Baby, come for me," he said as he kept banging away. A minute later, the quakes from the night before erupted from both of us as he collapsed on top of me. Grunting and moaning.

"Damn, Baby, what are you doing to me?" I smiled and wiggled myself free.

"The same thing you're doing to me," I said breathlessly. He finally glanced over at the breakfast I'd lovingly made for him. He rolled over and sat up. A smile curved at the corners of his mouth.

"Thank you, Baby."

I loved the way "Baby" rolled effortlessly off his tongue. "It's getting cold, so let's eat."

He jumped up and pecked me on my cheek. "Let me go freshen up first." He ran off to the bathroom.

"Hurry up, or I'm going to eat it all," I called behind him, knowing good and well that I wasn't going to eat more than a nibble.

He came back five minutes later and tongued me down.

"Better?" he asked.

"Umm," was all I could get out.

"Now," he rubbed his hands together, "this looks delicious," he said as he looked at the tray. He placed it on the bed between us. We fed each other, then kissed. Fed each other some more and then kissed some more until we had our fill of each one.

"I've got to call my sister before she gets the ass and leave. I told her to stay home and wait for my call so we could meet up later today." I reached for his sleek, state-of-the-art cordless phone that resembled a remote control.

"Okay cool. Am I invited? Or were you guys planning to sit around and talk girl talk?"

"You know I couldn't go longer than ten minutes without you," I playfully said as I slid my arms around his neck. I kissed him loudly on the neck.

"Whew, I'm glad to hear that. I would've felt you didn't want me to meet her." He smiled.

"It's a must that you meet Asia."

We finished breakfast and jumped into the shower where we went through another round of intense lovemaking.

He'd purchased an outfit for me to wear since I was instructed to bring nothing but myself. The blue, boot-cut jeans fit just the way he liked them. I pulled the beige, mock turtleneck on before putting on the tan leather boots with the squared-off toe.

"All that's missing is the hat," I teased as I gave him a quick fashion show. I sashayed across the floor in catwalk style, but with a little flavor.

He laughed. "Cute. Come here."

I stood in front of him while he turned me around so he could scope me out good. Once he saw everything he gave me his stamp of approval, a good slap on my butt.

"Damn, you look good." He pulled me down in his lap.

"If we don't leave now, we'll never leave and my sister is not one to be stood up."

He nuzzled my neck. "I have another surprise for you."

"What's that?"

"If I tell you, it wouldn't be a surprise. You'll see."

He kissed me and we got up.

"You know you're not right? Let's roll. Don't wanna keep your sister waiting."

I rolled my eyes at him playfully. I slipped on the matching leather coat to my boots and adjusted the collar.

"Did I tell you how beautiful you look today?" He bent to kiss me as we waited for the elevator to open.

"Yes, you did."

"Don't think I can tell you enough."

"I don't think I can hear it enough."

# *Asia*

## CHAPTER 30

Hayden and I sat in Chelsea Grill on Eighth Avenue between 16th and 17th streets, waiting for Yani and Alex to arrive.

"Hayden, do you know someone by the name of Alex Chance?"

He choked on his coffee and placed it back on the table in an effort not to spill it.

"Alex Chance? You mean Alex Chance of Chance Entertainment? Everyone knows Alex Chance."

"Evidently not everyone does," I said as I pointed to myself.

"Alex Chance is one of the top producers in the business. Word has it that his company is trying their hand at film distribution due to the lack of distribution available for black films. I heard that he's producing this film," he snapped his fingers as he attempted to remember the specific details. "Damn. I can't remember the name of it. All I know is that they're expecting it to be a blockbuster. Why'd you ask me about him?"

Before I could respond my mouth fell open as I looked up and spotted Yani heading our way. She looked radiant as she smiled at what obviously had to be a joke the gorgeous man she was holding hands with had just told her. Just by looking at her, I could tell my sister was falling hard for this man that looked to be doing the same thing for her.

I smiled and stretched out my arms as they approached our table. Yani and I hugged tightly.

"What do you think?" she whispered near my ear as she leaned in to kiss me on the cheek.

"He's definitely your type. Pretty as hell."

Hayden stood up and grabbed Alex's hand in a firm, vigorous handshake.

"What's up, man? Hayden Miles."

"What's up? Alex…"

"Chance, I know. It's a real pleasure."

"Thanks, man." Alex turned his attention to us.

"So I finally get to meet the mystery man." I reached out my hand to shake his.

"I wouldn't call me a mystery," he said as he ignored my hand and reeled me in for a hug instead. "You were the one that was always on the go."

I looked over at Hayden who seemed to be a slight bit starstruck.

"I guess you can say I was a bit preoccupied," I said as my eyes were still glued on Hayden.

"I'll carry that blame since I played a big part in it." Hayden winked at me.

As we sat back down, Alex held the chair for Yani.

*Damn, he's a gentleman, too,* I thought as I watched their interaction.

"So, I hear you're the New York connection for Xposure and special events," Alex said.

"Yes, I've been trying to talk her into opening an office here so we can blow up in this market."

"That sounds like a good idea." Alex looked at Yani.

"My sources tell me that you have a very successful business yourself."

He smiled. "I have a lil' company that's doing pretty good right now."

*He's humble, too,* I thought as I kept track of his personal points.

"A lil' company," Hayden said. "You're being way too modest, man. I heard Chance Productions occupies about four or five floors of the building that houses their midtown office alone."

Alex seemed to squirm in his chair a little. I took it as an indication that he wasn't too comfortable talking about his business, as much as Hayden seemed to enjoy it.

"Yani, have you talked to your mother and kids today?" I asked in an attempt to steer the conversation away from business.

"Of course. You know she asked me a million and one questions."

"You know she's the Worrywart Queen. Does she think you're at my house?"

She gave me a crazy look. "Asia, I'm thirty-five years old. I don't have to lie to my mother anymore."

"My bad. I just know how she is."

"She met Alex already. You're the only immediate family member that hadn't met him."

"She did?" I asked as I rose to excuse myself to go the ladies room and gestured for Yani to join me.

As soon as she stepped foot inside the bathroom she turned to me.

"So, what do you think? Is he fine or what? Girl, last night and this morning were like heaven."

"I see you are definitely making up for the drought."

"Girl…"

"So what did Mama think of him?" Mama was known to be an extreme critic about men. Especially the men I dated. Yani didn't have to go through it like I did. All she'd ever brought home was Jarrin.

"She loved him. The kids love him, now all I'm waiting on is your opinion." She stopped applying her lipstick and glanced at me in the mirror.

"I think he's wonderful, from the short time I've spent with him. He's very attentive to you and if Mama likes him, that means he's in like Flynn."

She smiled. "Thanks, Asia. You don't know how much your opinion means to me."

"If he's as prominent in the industry as Hayden told me, you can expect a lil' drama from these ruthless diggers out here."

"I'm not thinking about that. Right now I'm living in the moment."

"You saw *The Best Man* again?"

"All the way here."

"We better get back out there before Hayden tries to hem Alex up for a business deal."

She turned to head out the door, then stopped. She turned and wrapped her arms around me and gave me a big hug. "I love you, Asia. If you want to talk, I'm here for you, okay?"

Leave it to her to pick up on the vibes.

"I know and I love you, too. Now let's get our sentimental asses back out there to our men folk."

We finished our lunch and headed over to Fifth Avenue for a day of exclusive shopping. Since Alex told Yani not to pack anything, it was part of his surprise to give her carte blanche. Anything she wanted was hers for the asking.

Alex picked out a few fly outfits for her. They ranged from hip-hop gear to elegant and sexy. He took us over to the FUBU shop and told us to pick out anything we wanted. By this time, Hayden had departed our company. His pager went off and he muttered something about work and having to finish the project he was working on. He promised to call me later before walking off.

Whatever, I thought. I was going to enjoy spending the day watching a man dote on a woman. The fact that the woman happened to be my sister made it even more enjoyable.

I laughed as he had them bring one outfit after another out for us to try on. I walked out of the dressing room as he held her face in his hands before giving her a passionate kiss. I knew then that Yani had hooked a man that wanted more than a passing fling. From the few gestures I'd observed, I'd say that Alex was ready to invest some real time into it.

I guess she's always going to be the lucky in love one, while I continue to play hit and miss.

# Yani

J ust like the weekend to fly by when you're having fun. It's Sunday already and damn if I'm
ready to leave. I've been royally enjoying myself.
Anything I wanted to do, we did it. Anything I
wanted to see, we saw it. Anything I wanted to eat,
we ate it. I felt like a queen having her every fantasy
fulfilled.

When Asia left us she made me promise to call
her with my flight information so she could come
to the airport and see me off. I promised and hugged
her goodnight.

Alex and I had picked her up earlier before we
made our way out to Ellis Island to do the Statue of
Liberty tour thing. It was wonderful. He bought
me all kinds of junk to take back to the kids.

After a full day of fun and games, we came in and
Alex made the three of us a delicious dinner.

Asia joked about me keeping him. "And he cooks,
too? Girl, you slip if you want to. I'll be right here
picking up the pieces."

After Asia left for home with promises of coming

over the next day to see me off, Alex and I decided to stay in. I stared at Alex's bare chest as he lit the fireplace. After an erotic shower, we decided to kick back and watch a movie. He came out of the room with *Love Jones*, which happens to be another one of my all-time favorites. The love scene is so erotic. I shifted a bit just thinking about it.

"Comfortable?" He came and joined me on what I'd named the lounging sofa.

"Now I am," I said as I snuggled into his arms and laid my head on his chest. He pulled the afghan up over us.

By the time Nia Long threw her head back, we were in front of the fireplace, clothes scattered about the floor, creating our own sensual sex scene.

I straddled him as we rocked back and forth to our own rhythm. We were locked into our own space and time. The warmth of the fire meeting and mixing with the body heat we were generating.

After releasing our body fluids, we sat still for a moment. I held his head against my chest as I ran my fingers through his soft curls.

He broke our silence. "I wish we could stay like this forever." He kissed my breast.

I moaned. "Umm, me too."

"Then stay with me."

I pushed away and looked him in the eyes. "What

are you talking about? I just can't up and leave. I have a business to run…"

"You can think about what Asia said and open an office here."

"A house…"

"Sell it and I'll buy you a bigger one."

"And two children."

"They'll be here with us."

"I-I don't know, Alex. I need to think about this."

"What is there to think about? Yani," he lifted my chin with his finger. "Baby, this shit I'm feeling for you is real and I know this is how it's supposed to be. Me, you, Natalia, and Jay being a family. Baby, I've never felt this strong about anybody or anything in my life. I'm not about to let you slip away. I know what I'm asking you for is a major thing, but think about it before you say no. Okay?" His mesmerizing, gray eyes pleaded with me.

His strong arms were wrapped around my waist. I looked at him and wanted to throw caution to the wind, say yes and think about the rest later, but I knew I needed to think about this. Discuss it with the kids, Asia, my mom, and Carmen.

"I will."

I felt him exhale, releasing the air he'd held hostage while he waited for my answer. He hugged me tight, then looked into my eyes.

"I love you." Without any doubts, I let him know I felt the same.

"I love you, too," I said softly.

He showered me with soft kisses that turned into a deep passionate kiss. Our tongues danced round and round. Trying hard to hold on to this moment forever, never wanting it to end.

I pulled away. My breathing erratic and my love sopping wet again.

"So you're saying that you want me to live with you?"

## CHAPTER 32

That question came way from left field. I thought I'd made myself clear about wanting forever. I stared at her as I tried to compose my thoughts.

"I might as well let you know now that I have no plans to be roommates with a man ever again," she said.

She parted her lips to add something else, but I placed my finger on them to silence her.

"That's not my intentions. I'm asking you to give me forever."

She looked stunned and confused.

"Yani, this isn't how I wanted to do this, but..." I stood her up and walked her over to the sofa. I knelt down in front of her. "The best I can offer you is the man here before you." She let her eyes roam over my nakedness. "I've never been one to believe in love at first sight, but that was until I laid eyes on you. I want to wake up to you in the morning and go to sleep with you at night."

I swallowed hard. This was the first time these words had ever left my lips. "Yani, I want you to be my wife. Will you marry me?"

She sat motionless. Her eyes glistened from the onset of tears.

"I know I don't have a ring now, but if you want, we can go find one tomorrow."

She rose from the sofa and retrieved her satin wrap from the heap of clothes on the floor. She pulled it on slowly and securely tied it in place. She went over to the balcony door and walked out.

I jumped up and searched the floor for my pajama bottoms and ran out behind her.

"Baby, what's wrong? You're going to catch pneumonia out here," I said as I stood behind her. I wrapped my arms around her and kissed the back of her neck. She quietly stood there motionless as she stared out into the city night.

"Yani, talk to me." I spun her around to face me. Tears spilled from her eyes. "Baby, don't cry. I thought you'd be happy." I wiped at the tears streaming down her face.

"I am," she finally said in a little more than a whisper.

"Then talk to me. What's going on in that pretty head of yours?"

I felt her tremble. "I wasn't expecting you to—I

mean, I know I want to be with you and everything, but..."

"But what? What could possibly keep you from accepting my offer?"

"My situation with the first marriage," she blurted out.

I laughed. "Is that what's bothering you? Baby, he's dead. You have to come to terms with that and know that you can move on. Besides, since all of your paperwork is in to have him declared dead, I don't think we'll have a problem if we plan a June wedding."

She smiled through her veil of tears. "You're so wonderful."

"So does that mean that you're accepting my offer?"

She nodded her head up and down. "Yes. I will. I do."

I scooped her up in my arms and spun her around. "She said yes!" I yelled at the top of my lungs.

"Alex?"

"Yes, Baby?"

"Can we go inside now? I'm freezing."

"We can do anything you want." I laughed and carried her inside and deposited her on the afghan in front of the fire.

"Where's the phone?" I handed her the phone

from the table. She sat with it in her hand briefly as if she debated on who she was going to call first.

"I think your sister would be the best choice," I said as I bent down and kissed her on top of her head.

"Yeah, you're right."

I began to wonder what Asia's reaction was going to be. Would she tell her that we were rushing things? Would she think I had a hidden agenda? Whatever it was, I was about to find out soon as Yani punched in the numbers and waited for her answer.

# *Asia*

## CHAPTER 33

I pushed the pause button of my DVD player. "Hello?"

"What are you doing?" Yani said in a singsong voice.

"Watching *Soul Food* for the umpteenth time. Why? What's up?"

"I've got something to tell you, I've got something to tell you."

"What is it, what is it?" I sang back. "And why are you singing? Stop it and talk. I hope you're not calling me to brag about your multiple orgasms again. You sure are in a good mood, seeing that you're leaving tomorrow. I thought you'd be fucking his brains out right about now. Storing some up until next time."

"Will you shut up for one minute so I can tell you what I called for?"

"What?"

"I don't think I'm leaving tomorrow."

"Why not?"

"Because we've got to go find the rings."

"Girl, what the hell are you... Rings?! What type of rings?!"

"The kind you give to someone when you ask them to..."

"He asked you to marry him?!" I was up on my knees in the bed.

"Yes, Girl!"

We both began to scream with joy. I could hear Alex imitating us.

"And you said..."

"Yes! We're going ring shopping tomorrow."

"Oh, Yani, I'm so happy for you." I hugged the pillow close to my chest.

"Really, Asia? You know how much it means to me to have your blessings."

"Girl, please. Have you noticed that you're glowing lately? You actually have a reason to smile. If you can find a man that makes you smile just by the thought of him, I say he's a keeper. Besides, from what I observed, Alex really loves you."

"Thank you, sis. Now I have to call Mama and the kids. Then I'm going to wake Carmen up. You know the matchmaker deserves to be told."

"Let me speak to Alex right quick."

"Okay." I could hear her relaying the message. He picked up another extension. "Hello?"

"Well, hello, future brother-in-law."

He laughed. "What's up, future sister-in-law? So do I have your blessings? Or do I need to ask properly?"

"Evidently you've already asked properly. So if it's my blessings you want, you definitely have them. Gift-wrapped and hand delivered. Just promise me that you'll never hurt her, and we'll be friends for life."

"I could never intentionally hurt her."

"Not to bring up the past, but the last one told her that. So, I'm expecting you to live up to your word."

"No doubt. I've always been a man of my word."

"Good. Now, we have to get together and figure out where to hold the engagement party. You know, celebrity style. Have you set a date? Or is that still up for discussion?"

"We were thinking a June wedding," Yani chimed in.

"Oh, and don't worry, I plan to announce it to the world. I have a friend over at the *Times*. I'm going to give him the scoop," Alex said.

"You know you're going to be my maid of honor?" Yani yelled out.

"So you need to get started on the guest list for the engagement party, Asia. My secretary will put together a list of my friends and family and fax it over to you."

"Then we need to figure out the color scheme,

where I'm going to get my dress, and where we're going to have the ceremony."

"And…" They were throwing out demands at me faster than I could think.

"WAIT A MINUTE! You two need to take a breather and think for a minute. As much as I'd like to do all of this for you, my suggestion is that you may need to hire a wedding coordinator."

They both laughed.

"Isn't that some of what we do for a living?" Yani asked. "We're going to call Carmen, too. Between the three of us, it'll be the wedding of the century."

"The only thing I want a part of is the brides-maids' dresses. That way I'm guaranteed to get something that I like."

"Let me call Mama and the kids. Alex has to pro-pose to them, too. Let's do lunch tomorrow since I'm not leaving. I'll call you in the morning."

"Okay. Love you, Girl."

"Love you, too."

I hung up and sat still on the bed for a minute. The events for my sister over the past few months were unbelievable. Yani had gone from lady-in-waiting to bride-to-be. Here I was, in the same situation I was in last year. Maybe not as single, but definitely as lonely.

I hadn't talked to Hayden since the other day

when we all met up at the restaurant. If he couldn't
make time for me, then fine. I'd never been one to
run after a man and damn if I was about to start
now. If he wanted me, he had the number.

# Yani

## CHAPTER 34

"Be still, would you?"

"I'm sorry, but I'm nervous."

"I can't get your dress fastened if you keep running off every two seconds and what are you so nervous for?" Asia fastened the latch to secure my zipper in place.

"It's just that so many people are going to be there and I want everything to be perfect."

She placed her hand over my mouth to quiet me.

"Everything *is* perfect, Yani. So stop worrying. You have everyone that loves you here with you. The kids, Mama, Carmen, Bryce, and me."

"And Alex. We can't forget him." I fastened the two-carat, platinum diamond earring in my ear while Asia draped the matching pendant around my neck.

"He was a give-me, Yani."

I slipped on my Jimmy Choo slingbacks that Alex had given to me as a gift. Asia found an up-and-coming designer by the name of Jeanette to make my dress. She thought I should go with the Dorothy Dandridge style. Halter-like top, back out, with an elegant not-too-full skirt piece. Jeanette jazzed it up with jewel trimmings on the bodice around the cleavage area and the hem of the skirt. My curves were accentuated in modest taste.

"Ooh, look at you," Carmen sang as she walked into the room. "Girl, you're beautiful."

We hugged each other tightly. "I'm so glad you and Bryce came."

"Woman, wild dogs couldn't have kept me from being here tonight. Besides, without me, none of this would be happening. Can I get an amen?"

"Amen," Asia piped in.

"You may have brought us together, but we took care of the rest. Okay?"

"I hear ya now."

I strutted to the mirror and wiggled my hips for emphasis. We all burst into laughter.

"Now she wants to brag, Carmen. We better get out the way before the head explodes."

There was a light tap on the door. Asia walked over and opened it.

"Where's my beautiful fiancée?" Alex asked.

"In here bragging about how she worked her mojo on you."

"Yeah, Alex. Said you were screaming her name in three different languages," Carmen added.

"Baby, you know I don't kiss and tell. Forget these two. You ready?" I asked.

He walked over to me and kissed me firm on the lips.

"Now, I am. You look beautiful."

I blushed. "You do, too."

He was decked out in Calvin Klein. Black suit with a soft yellow shirt and a tie that matched the color of my dress.

"Well, that's our cue." Asia picked up her bag.

"See you out there, Sweetie." Carmen pecked me on the cheek before she and Asia left the room.

He held his arm out for me to hook mine through. "Our public awaits."

"You know I'm nervous, Baby?" I adjusted the huge diamond on my left hand.

"Stop worrying. Nothing is going to happen to mess up tonight. I promise." He kissed me again.

"Now I've got to retouch my lipstick."

"But it was worth it, right?"

I wrapped my arms around his waist and tipped my head up for another kiss. "Everything about you is worth it."

Just as Alex had promised, the night went off without a hitch. Good food, good music, and beautiful people everywhere.

Alex was well-connected in the industry. I thought I had an impressive roster of people that I'd worked with, but I was scraping the bottom of the barrel compared to the power players that had showed up in support of Alex. I would definitely have to get used to this scene. Some of the biggest names in the industry walked over to offer their congratulations to us.

Alex was by my side the entire night. My man looked handsome. His sister Lucia walked over and kissed me on the cheek.

"Wow, Mami, you look beautiful," she said in her beautiful Latin accent.

Alex took me home to meet his mother and sister the day after he proposed to me. His father, who had been deceased for some time now, was where his African roots came from. After listening to him carry on a conversation with his mother in Spanish, I started insisting he throw in a lil' Spanish whenever we made love. It turned me on something fierce.

"Hi, Lucia." I pecked her on the cheek. "Where's your mother?"

"She's over at the table with yours. Those two hit it off instantly. Where are the kids? I haven't seen them."

"Natalia's here, but Jay wouldn't be able to hang, so he's back at the hotel with his Godbrothers."

She hugged Alex and said something to him in Spanish. "English, speak English," I teased.

She playfully tapped me on the arm. "Don't worry, Mami, we're going to teach you to become fluent in Spanglish. You have to be able to communicate with the niece or nephew you're going to have for me."

Baby? I hadn't thought about the probability of him wanting me to have a baby. Jay was ten and Natalia fourteen. A newborn would be like a shock to my system.

"We'll cross that bridge when we get to it. Right now we have two beautiful children and they're more than enough," Alex said. It was as if he was in tune with my thoughts.

Alex and I continued to mingle with our guests. We approached a woman with a warm smile.

"There you are. I was wondering if you made it." Alex gave her a big hug.

"As much as I put into this, you really think I would not show? Hi, Yani, it's so nice to finally meet you." She gave me a big hug.

Alex looked at my face and started to smile. I had no idea who she was and why she was treating me so friendly.

"Honey, this is Constance."

"Oh! I'm so sorry. It is really a pleasure to meet you, too. I want to thank you for everything you've done to help us."

"If it'll keep him in good spirits, I'll help you with anything you need. You have made working for him much easier." She and Alex laughed.

"Then all the special women in his life must make him easier to deal with. He has nothing but praises about you," I told her.

"I try."

"I told you she was modest." Alex gave her another hug and we moved on.

After hours of nonstop congratulations, hugs, and kisses, it was time to call it a night. The writer and photographer for *Essence* were the last ones to leave. They made an appointment to come and take some pictures of us at his place tomorrow afternoon. They were considering us for a cover story.

"Did you enjoy yourself?" Alex asked as he pulled me between his legs where he sat on the bed.

"Umm," I moaned as he rubbed his hands up and down my bare back. "I had a great time, Baby. I felt like a princess in one of those fairytale stories I used to read."

"Now it's official. By tomorrow, the whole world will know that I am marrying the most beautiful woman in the world." He kissed my exposed cleavage.

"How could I turn you down?"

He gave me a long and passionate kiss. "Ready for another Spanish lesson?"

"Si, mi Amor."

# Asia

## CHAPTER 35

The news of Yani and Alex's engagement spread through the papers like wildfire. People were trying to find out as much as they could about this "mystery woman" that no one seemed to be able to link with anything.

The phones in the office we'd opened for our New York operations a month earlier were ringing off the hook. It was as if we were representing the next hottest artist on the charts.

My phone buzzed. "Yes?"

"Ms. Fenton, Hayden Miles is on line two."

"Thanks, Jennifer." I wondered what he wanted. He didn't show up to the engagement party. Another excuse about this project he's working on. Then he'd canceled three more dates on me. It prompted me to make a call giving him an ultimatum. I told him I couldn't go through this anymore and to give me a call when he finished with his project. Maybe I'd be available then or maybe not.

I decided to let him wait for a few minutes before

I picked up. He needed to see how it felt to be kept on hold. Then again, I wanted to know what his response was going to be to my message. I picked up.

"Ms. Fenton here."

"Good morning, Ms. Fenton."

"Good morning," I said impatiently.

"I, ah, got your message."

"I figured as much. I guess the only way I can get you to call me back is by making threats."

"That's not fair. You know I'm working hard and…"

"And did I not say that you should call me when you finish? I mean, I don't want to interfere."

"I know I've been a little scarce lately."

"Lately? Try ever since we got back. I should've given up on this months ago. I don't know why I've hung in there for this long."

"Come on, Asia, you don't mean that. Like I said, give me a little more time and…"

"And what? You'll have time then? Until the next project comes along."

"You know, you women kill me. You say you want a brother who's gainfully employed. One that can buy you anything you want, but when it comes down to it, you don't know what you want."

No he wasn't trying to flip the script on me? "Wait a minute. Don't you dare throw me in the barrel with every other woman. I understand that you're making career moves and things may be hectic, but not to the point where you can't return my phone calls, cancel dates at the last minute, or forget that I'm alive. You damn near sexed me to death while we were in Miami, then damn near cut me completely off once we got back." I was heated.

"I don't want to lose you again."

"You sure don't act like it. You make me feel like you're living a double life or something."

"Where did that come from?"

"Look, like I said before, give me a call when you're finished with this *project* and have more time to devote to building a relationship."

"You don't mean that."

"Like hell I don't."

"Just give me two more weeks, okay? I promise things will be better."

"Okay, the wedding is in two weeks. If I go to that by myself like I did the engagement party, then I suggest you lose my number."

# *Alex*

## CHAPTER 36

Five o'clock. I need to get out of here. I've got to meet the real estate agent over in Brooklyn Heights at six. Then get to the airport and on a flight by eight.

I shut down my computer and threw the folders in my briefcase. I'd been working nonstop all week. Making sure that everything major was done before I left for Miami.

Since we had the engagement party here, we decided to have the wedding there. This way we catered to both families.

My phone buzzed. "Yes, Constance."

"Marshall Banks on line one."

"Thanks."

"Alex Chance." I always answered business calls by saying my name.

"Hello, Mr. Chance. How are you?"

"I'm good. How's the editing coming along?"

"We're almost done. I can drop it by Monday."

"Bring it over and leave it with my secretary. You

know I'm getting married tomorrow so I won't be here."

"Oh yeah. Congratulations, man. I never thought you'd settle down."

"Well it was time, ya know? Can't run the streets forever."

We chatted for a few more minutes before I told him that I had to go. It was 5:15 and traffic going into Brooklyn was sure to be a mess.

I checked to make sure everything was in order before walking out the door.

"All right, Constance. I'm gone."

"Well, give me one last hug as a single man." She left her bag on her desk and embraced me. "Make sure to take lots of pictures."

"I will. Hold down the fort for me."

❤❤❤

At 6:05, I pulled up in front of the property. The agent was sitting in her car.

"Good evening, Mr. Chance."

"Hi, Gail. Sorry I'm a few minutes late."

"Oh please. Five minutes? I've had some people who showed up an hour later." She laughed. "Ready for the final walk-through?"

"Yeah. I wanna have everything done by the time we get back."

She opened the door of the five-story brownstone.

On a sightseeing ride with Yani, I rode her through here and she spotted it. I got the information and had the agent meet us so we could see the inside. It was in need of repairs, but the structure was pre-war and the rooms were huge.

I checked my watch. A quarter after six. "Well, I guess the only thing I need to do now is sign the papers."

Gail smiled and handed me a pen.

❤❤❤

I walked in my door at 7:00, grabbed the bags I had packed the night before and jetted out the door for the airport. I damn near had to jump in front of the cab to get him to stop. That black man in New York thing. By 7:45, I was running to the gate.

"Wait!" I yelled to the woman about to close the door. I had my ticket in my hand.

"Hurry up, sir. They're about to close the door to the plane." She took my ticket, scanned it and rushed me down the jetway.

The flight attendant held the door open for me. "You just made it."

"Thank you," I panted.

I sat in my seat and caught my breath. I was glad

to have the row to myself. Once we got in the air, I grabbed the phone behind the seat in front of me and called Yani. I wanted to know how things were going.

"Hey, Baby! Are you on your way?" she asked.

"I just made it. I had to run for the plane."

"Run? Why?"

"I had something to take care of at the last minute. Are you ready for tomorrow?"

"As ready as I can be. What about you? Getting cold feet yet?"

"Never. I don't know how I'm going to sleep tonight. Especially since I can't see you until tomorrow."

"I know. I hate that. Bryce picking you up?"

"Yeah. Did Asia get in?"

"She's been here since Wednesday. She and Mama are about to run me crazy. The kids can't wait to see you. You'll get to see Jay tonight. He's over at Carmen and Bryce's with the boys. The men are getting dressed over there so he wanted to stay."

"Oh, good. I know he's excited about giving you away. He and I had a long talk."

"About what?" She laughed.

"He just laid down the rules. Ya know, made me promise to take care of you and never break your heart, or leave you alone."

She was quiet for a moment.

"You still there?" I asked.

"I love you, Alex Chance." Her voice quivered.

"I love you, too, Yaniece Miller, soon to be Chance."

I heard a commotion in the background. "Who's that?"

"Some of the family. There's a shit load of food here. I'm going to send you a plate so you can eat when you get in."

"Thanks, Baby. I haven't eaten since this morning."

"And that airplane food can't compare to the home-cooked food here."

"Who brought food?"

"You know they're giving me a bridal shower tonight."

"Oh. They got you a stripper?"

"I hope not. I'm not crazy about a greasy man rubbing against me."

"Okay. Tell me anything. Don't have no niggah rubbing against my na'na," I playfully said.

"I told you…"

"The way you work me over—I don't know."

"Whatever."

"Who are you talking to?" I heard someone ask.

"Who else?" she answered.

"Hey, Alex."

"Who's that?"

"Asia. I told you she's about to work my last nerve."

"Tell her I said hey."

We talked the first half of the flight until Asia and Carmen dragged her off the phone. I decided to sit back and relax, because I was going to need it.

I walked to the bathroom at the rear of the plane since the one upfront was occupied. As I walked up the aisle to return to my seat, a hand grabbed me. I looked down in search of the body it belonged to.

"Well hello, Alex Chance. It's been a while."

Well, I'll be damned. Of all the flights I had to catch. "Taylor?"

# Alex

## CHAPTER 37

"Take it off!"

"Bring it over here!"

The room was filled with screams and laughter of grown women who were going berserk over two fine ass, damn near naked, good looking men.

Yani had made her way into the kitchen. I knew she wouldn't like the strippers, but the ladies were expecting them and you can't disappoint the mass majority. I went and stood next to her as she leaned on the island to watch from a safe distance.

"Sure you don't want a go?"

"No, thanks. I think they have their hands full already." She sipped on a glass of wine.

"Pass me a plate." I piled my plate with a few meatballs, shrimp, and hot wings.

"You eat something?"

"A little. I'm not that hungry."

"Jitters?"

"Not really. I'm more anxious than anything."

"Ready to get it over with?"

"Ready to see my man. I haven't seen him in two weeks and now he's here and I've got to wait until tomorrow."

"Well, just think, it's after midnight so you don't have to wait that much longer."

She smiled and took a shrimp from my plate. "I know."

"Go, Mae, go, Mae." We looked to find our aunt with her ass up, feet in the air, and one of the strippers pumping against her.

"Oh my Lord." We looked at each other unable to control the fits of laughter.

Carmen came over to us. Her face glistened with a light mist of sweat. "Why are you two hiding out in here?" She was shaking her hips to music.

"You know this isn't my thing," Yani said.

"I came in to get a quick bite. When I finish, I'm going to go and put his ass in the buck," I said as I popped a jumbo shrimp in my mouth.

"Okay? That's exactly what I was thinking."

"Aren't you married?" Yani asked her teasingly.

"This helps me to release some of the stress I was under today coming up with your menu."

Carmen grabbed a shrimp from my plate.

"Damn, I can't have nothing." I shoved the meatball into my mouth.

"Girl, quit whining. There's a platter full of them."

"Then you should get some of those."

"Later for you two. I'm going to get my hunch on."

"Hunch?" Yani and I said in unison.

"Country ass."

"Like you never said hunch before. Don't act like your ass isn't from here," Carmen said.

"I've been in New York almost as long as I lived here and I lived here as long as I did because I didn't have any choice in the matter." I popped the last shrimp in my mouth.

"Yeah, yeah, yeah," Carmen said as she walked back out into the family room where the action was.

I washed my hands and wiped them on the towel. "Well, I'm leaving you here on the sidelines. Got to get in on some of the fun. Especially since I'm paying for it."

"G'on with ya bad self."

I went in the family room where the women had a circle around the guys. I tapped the one decked out in a tan, leather-looking g-string on the shoulder. He turned to me and began to grind up against me.

"Yani, this is for you," I said as I got behind him and bent him over and started humping his ass.

"Go, Asia. Go, go. Go, Asia," the crowd sang.

"Let me get a piece of that." Carmen got in front of him and worked him that way.

"Work it, girls! Turn that man into a coochie sandwich," Aunt Mae yelled.

❤❤❤

After everyone had left, Yani was still downstairs putting away the dishes. "Damn, Girl, it's after two in the morning. You need to get some sleep." I scratched the back of my head as I came around the corner. My short do had now turned into a bob.

"I'm going in a minute. I didn't want to leave the kitchen a mess."

The kitchen? Huh, she'd cleaned the kitchen, the family room, and put away the load of gifts she'd gotten.

"Are you working off nervous energy?"

"I guess."

"Did Alex call when he got in?"

"Not that I know of. I did tell him that the shower would probably be in full swing by the time he got here. So, maybe he decided to just get some sleep."

"Well, you need to do the same thing. Can't have you carrying around an extra set of luggage tomorrow." She smiled.

"All right, all right. I'm going." She threw the towel up on the counter. "Asia?"

"Yeah?" My foot hovered over the bottom step.

"You feel like sleeping with me?"

"I thought you'd never ask." We had a house full of ladies. The bridal party decided to spend the night. "Let me go get my scarf."

"I've got an extra one. Come on."

She was stressing. I could tell.

Once we stepped inside her room, I asked, "What is it?"

"What?"

"Cut the dumb act. I can tell you're worried about something. If it's Alex, call him. I doubt very seriously if he's sleeping. He loves you, Yani. That I know. So stop worrying. He's going to show up tomorrow. Don't ever compare him to Jarrin. If you do, you'll lose him."

"I know that. Jarrin is dead. That check I got the other day confirmed that."

"I know that's right. Did you tell Alex about it? Don't start out with secrets."

"Of course I did."

"What did he say?"

"Nothing really. I told him that I was putting it in an account for the kids so they'll have it when they get older."

"What are you going to do about the house?"

She shrugged her shoulders. "I'm not sure. This

place has lots of memories. It's almost like a member of the family. Not to mention that it's paid for."

"But if you're going to be in New York with your *husband*, then what do you need to keep it for?"

"I don't know. When I come to visit?"

"How much visiting do you plan to do? Girl, you're going to be on the go so much that you won't have time to see about this place. I mean, I love it too. I've had some great times here as well, but you need to sell it. That's more money you can put into your bank account."

She threw the scarf in my lap. The phone rang. She looked over at me.

"Told you he wasn't asleep."

She smiled as she answered the phone.

I hope what I said didn't go in one ear and out the other. If she told Alex she was going to sell the house, she damn well better do it. Or it'll come back and haunt her in the long run.

# *Yani*

## CHAPTER 38

I slept all of three hours last night. At seven I jumped up and took a shower so I'd make my hair appointment. Asia was balled up on the other side of the bed.

I slipped on my simple olive-colored tank dress. "Hey." I shook her.

"What?" she groaned.

"Come on. If we don't leave in thirty minutes, we'll end up being at the beauty parlor all day. So let's get a move-on."

I dragged her legs off the bed.

"Okay, okay. Damn. I'm movin'." She dragged off to the bathroom, rubbing sleep from her eyes.

I went upstairs to wake the rest of the clan that was going with us.

"Carmen," I said as I tapped on the door.

"What?" I heard at my back.

"Ooh shit! Damn, Girl! You don't walk up on people like that! You almost gave me a heart attack!"

"Sorry. I was in the bathroom putting on my make-up. Ready to go?"

"Yeah. Asia should be finished in a minute. Where's Nat?"

"I've already gotten everyone else up."

"Good, 'cause we need to get out of here." I put on my lipstick and slid my feet into a pair of leather slip-ons.

❤❤❤

We got to the salon by eight and were out by eleven. Only three hours left to finish up everything else.

"Okay," I looked over my list.

"Girl, you need to pay attention to where you're going and put that damn list down," Asia said as she snatched the paper from me.

"Give it back. I need to have everything on that list done before I leave the house."

She looked over the list. "Give me something to write with."

"Look in my purse."

She reached in my bag and pulled out a pen. "Let me see. Pick up shoes. Did that. Get hair done. That's done. Take out dress, pantyhose, and other personals. It's waiting on the bed in a bag. Girl, everything on this list has been taken care of. So stop stressing."

"A-fucking-men. I thought I was the only one

whose nerves she was working," Carmen piped in from the backseat.

"I see. So it's gang up on Yani day?"

"You watch too many damn movies," Asia said. She knew that line was from *The Best Man*.

"Maybe being a married woman again will curve that," Carmen said.

"But look who she's marrying. I guess now she'll be quoting movies before they even come out."

"Whatever."

I pulled into the garage. "Now ladies, we have exactly," I checked my watch, "two hours to get dressed and situated before the limo gets here. Now, we all know that some of these drivers have the worst attitudes, so let's get a..."

"Move on," they all said in unison.

"Unlock the doors so we can get to movin' then," Carmen said as she sat there with her hand on the door ready to get out of the truck.

The house was as lively as the party from last night. The photographer arrived and started filming every move I made. I had to ask them to leave when I went into the bedroom to get dressed. This tape would be viewed by many people and I wasn't about to give anybody a peep show.

By 2:30, everyone was dressed and ready to load up the cars. Carmen and Asia helped me put on my veil.

"You look beautiful," Lucia said.

"Yes, you do," Asia said as she stepped back.

I stood in front of the mirror admiring myself. I was finally getting that fairytale wedding I'd dreamed about as a little girl. Since this was my second marriage, my dress was a light silver color that Jeanette called Platinum.

Asia stood behind me in her salmon-colored dress. She was absolutely beautiful. Her dress had spaghetti straps and it fit tight around the waist and filled out toward the bottom. Since Carmen was my matron-of-honor they both wore similar dresses in the same color.

Asia walked over to her bag and retrieved a small box. She walked back over to me and turned me to face her.

"We're going to check on everyone else and see if they're ready," Carmen said as she and Lucia left Asia and me alone.

"I know we tell each other this all the time, but I love you very much. I wanted to give you something that would help you remember this day forever." She handed the box to me. Inside was a diamond tennis bracelet.

"Asia! It's beautiful!" I handed it to her so she could fasten it on.

"Now you have something new."

I hugged her. "I love you so much. With me in New York, we're going to have a ball."

"I know. I'm looking forward to it."

"Can we get a move on?" Carmen called from the other room.

"Well, this is it."

"Yep. Ready?"

"As ready as I'll ever be."

# *Alex*

## CHAPTER 39

I stood in the mirror and adjusted my tie again.

"You okay?" Bryce asked.

"Yeah, Man. I'm trying to get this straight." I pulled at the collar.

"Need to talk about it?"

"Talk about what?"

"Look, we all get cold feet. I know I did. I was so stressed that I got a crook in my neck. After a long talk with my old man, the crook was gone, and I married the woman I was meant to spend the rest of my life with."

He had a point, but I couldn't stop thinking about what happened last night on the flight. Seeing Taylor was a big surprise.

"I heard you're about to get married. So much for the space thing."

I'd hoped in the seven months it had been since I'd last seen her that she'd have matured at least a little bit.

I swallowed hard. "Yeah. The wedding is tomorrow."

Her eyes widened. "So, just who is this 'mystery woman' as they're calling her?"

"Who is they?"

"You know, the media. I do read."

I shifted my weight from one leg to the other. "That's only because she's not the type of woman who wants to be in the limelight." I knew I'd hit home with that comment.

"So, why didn't I get an invite to the engagement party? I was told that it was a who's who list. Everyone who was someone was there." Unknowingly, she'd answered her own question.

"I need to take care of some work before the plane lands. It was nice seeing you. I hope you have a nice life." I headed back up the aisle to my seat thinking that it would be my last dealings with her, but no such luck.

Once the plane landed, she caught up with me outside of baggage claim as I waited for Bryce to pick me up. "What'd you'd do, run off the plane?"

"Nope. I have someone waiting to pick me up. That's all."

"So, where's the bachelor party being held?"

"I'm not having one." I leaned forward to look out at the cars pulling up, hoping Bryce was one of them.

"No bachelor party. I don't believe that."

"It was last night, okay? Wouldn't it make sense

for me to have it in New York since all of my peeps are there?" No matter how short I was with her, she wouldn't get the hint and just leave me alone.

She slipped her arm around my waist. "Since you're going to be off the market for good now, how's about giving me one last kiss. You know, one for the road." Before I could react, she'd planted her lips on mine.

Shocked, it took a minute before I pulled away. She stood with a smile on her face. I knew right then and there that I had to put her in her place.

"You just don't get it, do you? Taylor, tomorrow I'm marrying my soul mate. Something that I realized you weren't. So please do me a favor and get on with your life, because that's exactly what I've done."

"What makes you think you can talk to me any kind of way? All the shit I've done for you and you think you can just write me off like you did."

"Done for me? What the hell have you ever done for me? If anything, I'm the one that did all the doing in that thing we called a relationship."

"I decorated your place and office, I even…"

"And I paid you well for that. If you're worried about her enjoying the place that you help decorate, don't. I don't live there anymore. I bought her a new house that she's going to decorate however she wants."

"Whatever. Fuck you, then! You won't keep her long! Mark my words! You don't know how to treat a woman," she angrily shouted at my back as I started to walk away from her.

"Then why are you still talking to me? Like I said before, have a nice life, Taylor. I hope I never see you again."

Bryce pulled up next to me. I gave her one last look, shook my head and jumped in.

❤❤❤

"How long did you date her?" Bryce asked after I finished telling him what happened.

"A little over a year."

"Sounds like she's out of your system. What are you stressing for?"

I looked at him like he'd just cursed me. "I was over that relationship months before I told her."

"Then what's worrying you, homeboy? If it had been me, I would've thanked her."

I looked at him like he'd just slapped my mother. "Thanked her for what?"

"If it hadn't been for her jacked up ass attitude, you wouldn't have come here. Therefore, making it impossible for you to meet Yani."

"You've got a point."

"Ready to go jump this broom?" Bryce stood next

to me and patted me on the back. I looked in the mirror one last time and noticed that the tie was finally straight.

"Good and ready."

It turned out to be a beautiful day. Yani had been worried about the constant rain they'd had for the past few days, but God had answered our prayers.

We walked out the back door, past the pool to the beach area of the house we'd rented for the ceremony in the Golden Isle section. People had started to fill up the rows of chairs.

"How many people are going to be here today?" Bryce asked.

"Man, I don't know. I left all of that to Yani and the coordinator. All I had to do was show up today." We laughed.

I said hello to the few people I knew as I made my way upfront to take my place.

"It's nice to see you again, brother Chance."

"Same here, Reverend Daniels."

Sharla, the coordinator, started having everyone ushered to their seats. Bryce came and took his place next to me.

"The ladies are here."

My heart began to race. "Did you see Yani?"

"No. She's waiting in the car. Carmen said Sharla wants her entrance to be grand."

I couldn't wait to see her. I hadn't talked to her since

the brief phone call late last night, or early this morning. Either way it was late.

Just as promised, the music flowed from the speakers placed strategically around the area of the ceremony as the wedding party marched in.

I glanced down at my watch. Four on the dot. I straightened my jacket one last time.

Natalia smiled broadly as cameras went off everywhere. After Asia and Carmen made their way down the aisle, the music was changed to announce to everyone that the bride was coming. Everyone craned their necks to the spot where the bridal party had come from, only to be surprised as Yani pulled up around the rear of the house in a convertible Rolls Royce. It was a classic touch.

Two of Jay's friends rolled the carpet out for her as two flower girls sprinkled a mixture of different colored rose petals for her to walk on. Jay got out of the car first, did a gentleman's bow, and positioned his arm for his mother to hook it. He was dressed in the same suit as mine. She stepped out and you could hear a few oohs and ahhs from the spectators.

She was stunning. The jewels on her gown glistened in the sunlight. It fell off her shoulders with a long, slender dip in the front. The bodice was tight fitting while the bottom was straight with a full half skirt surrounding her sides. The train was almost halfway down the aisle when she reached the altar.

Our eyes were glued to each other as she turned to face me. Here was the most beautiful woman in the world, and she was marrying me.

Jay placed her hand in mine and stood back. We took the few extra steps to the altar. Jay announced to everyone that he was giving her hand in marriage to me. It was like a fairytale, and I was the prince.

After the exchange of vows and rings I was given permission to kiss my bride. I pulled the veil back slowly and tilted her chin up so I could look into her eyes. We shared a passionate kiss that lasted long enough to get cheers and thunderous applause as I pulled away.

Now it was time to party. We marched back down the aisle with the wedding party following on our heels.

We walked into the house to have a private moment alone before the photographers started with the pictures.

"I love you, Mrs. Chance."

"I love you, too, Mr. Chance," she said through a veil of tears.

"I promise to do my best to make you happy and love you forever." I helped her to wipe away her tears of joy.

"And I you." She leaned up for another kiss.

# *Yani*

## CHAPTER 40

Riding across the Brooklyn Bridge, I looked out the window at my surroundings. I noticed the people on the bikes and the others that walked across the bridge. This was not just a dream anymore, I was actually living in New York.

We had just gotten back from our honeymoon in the Cayman Islands. We didn't get out to do much sightseeing since we couldn't get out of the bed. The memory of the passionate love we'd made over the past two weeks made my middle tingle so much that I had to cross my legs.

"Are we going to get the kids?" They had come up with Asia after the wedding.

"Not yet. I need to stop somewhere right quick. It won't take long."

We rode until we got to an area where grand-style brownstones lined the street.

"Why does this street look familiar to me?"

"Because Brooklyn is full of brownstones?"

"Funny. No, that's not it."

He leaned over and kissed me. "Just enjoy the ride."

We pulled up in front of a huge brownstone with a grandiose set of steps in front of it. There was something familiar about this house.

"Give me a second to run in here. I'll be right back." He kissed me quickly and jumped out the car.

I looked out the window at the tree-lined street. The houses were beautiful and well-kept. "I know I've been on this street before." I kept looking around for something familiar that would jog my memory.

Alex opened the door for me.

"That was quick," I said.

"I need you to come inside for a minute." He reached for my hand.

"Whose house is this?"

"Someone very special to me."

I climbed the steps behind him. "Who?"

"Hurry up." He ran up the rest of the way, leaving me tagging behind.

I reached the top step and walked into the foyer area. The walls were painted a soft, relaxing, earthy tan color. Beautiful black art hung on the walls. A few looked like replicas of ones I'd seen at Alex's place. I walked down the hall area that led into a grand living room.

Alex turned around and kissed me.

"What's that for?"

"Damn, I can't kiss my wife just because?"

"Of course, Baby, but who are we here to see?"

Just then Asia and the kids ran out of what had to be the kitchen. "Surprise!"

My mouth fell open. "What are you doing here?"

"We live here, Mommy," Jay said.

"Live here?" I looked at Alex, then scanned the room we were standing in. Then it dawned on me... "Is this the one we looked at?"

He nodded his head and smiled. "How do you like your wedding gift?"

I clasped my hands together over my mouth. I could feel the onset of tears.

"Oh, Alex," I whispered full of emotions. He pulled me close to him and kissed me full on the lips.

"We couldn't have the kids growing up in a condo with no back yard. I wanted us to have a place we can call *ours*. You like it?"

I inspected every room on the first floor. He walked me into a kitchen that was the exact duplication of a kitchen I'd showed him in a magazine. Stainless steel appliances, bleached wood floors, mahogany cabinets, two huge ovens, and an eight-burner gas counter top stove.

"Like it? Baby, I love it."

He smiled. "Let's go look at the other four floors."

"Four?!"

"That's counting the basement. I turned it into a hangout for the kids."

"Mommy, you have to come see it." Jay grabbed me by the arm.

"Go ahead. I'll go get our things out the car and I'll be down in a minute." He kissed me on the forehead and slapped my rear as I turned around.

Jay gave me a grand tour of what was surely his favorite part of the house.

There was a huge screen TV on the wall and the sofa we'd lounged around on during my first visit sat in the middle of the room. A console housed a PlayStation, Dreamcast, and Nintendo 64. I could see that I was going to have to sit down and talk with Alex about him spoiling the kids.

"Mommy, look at the pool table."

I looked at Nat who sat patiently waiting for her turn to show me what she liked best. She pulled me up to the third floor where their bedrooms were housed. The rooms were huge. Each room had been nicely decorated and furnished with beautiful furniture.

"Look," she pointed to a bookshelf built into the wall. "Now I have enough room for all of my books and then some." She flopped down on the full-sized sleigh bed. The matching whitewashed armoire, desk, and dresser and mirror gave the room a sense of unity.

"Where's Jay's room?"

"At the other end of the hall." She jumped up to show me.

His room was done up in a subtle blue. A bunk bed was on one wall, the TV was on another, and a matching dresser sat on another.

"Who decorated your rooms?"

"We did." Asia stood in the doorway. "Alex took care of most the arrangements before he left for the wedding and I finished the rest. You don't like it?"

"Of course I like it. I was just wondering how everything ended up being so close to my taste."

"That's because I had a hand in it."

"Where's the master bedroom?"

"On the top floor. Wait till you see it."

"I think I'll wait for my husband for that one."

"Hey, if y'all want to break in that new bed, the kids are two floors down." We looked at Nat who was walking out the door to head back downstairs.

"The thought never crossed my mind."

"Right."

"So, what's going on with you? Has Hayden been over?"

"A few times, but he's still pretty much swamped with this *project* at work."

"Stop riding that man's back. At least he showed up to the wedding like you demanded."

"You damn right. 'Cause I told his ass if he didn't at least make it to that, I was dropping him like the theaters do movies that don't make any money."

"Then that alone should show you that he's interested."

"You know some of us aren't as lucky as you were to find Mr. Right after one date."

"Did I hear someone talking about me?" Alex came up behind me and wrapped his arms around my waist as he kissed the back of my neck.

"I was waiting for you."

"I was looking all over for you. I'm going to have to get an intercom system installed in here."

"So, are you going to show me the room we'll be sharing?"

He scooped me up in his arms. "Asia, we'll see you in about an hour or two." He winked at her.

"Damn, you just got back from your honeymoon and you're still at it?" She laughed.

He took off up the stairs with me in his arms.

"You better not drop me." I laughed.

"I got this. You just hold on."

We got to the landing and he stopped in front of the door. He kissed me.

"You love me?"

"More than anything."

He opened the door and carried me over the threshold. It was spectacular. Beautiful blond wood flooring with a throw rug in front of the fireplace. There was a sitting room near the window. A huge king-sized bed sat in the middle of the room. The sparse furniture gave it a cozy but comfortable feeling.

I walked back over to the door and locked it.

"What about the kids?"

"They're downstairs. W-a-a-y-y downstairs. And you might as well get used to having them in the house while we're having sex."

I lifted his shirt over his head and dropped it on the floor. I craved to feel him loving me. He sat on the edge of the bed and pulled me between his legs, then proceeded to invade my mouth with his warm thick tongue.

Piece by piece, our clothing was carelessly dropped on the floor. We christened the room, the chaise lounge in the sitting area, the sink, the tub, the shower, the closet, and the floor.

"You're tryin' to hurt me, huh?" Alex lay stretched out on the bed panting.

I threw my leg across him. "Don't tell me you're complaining already? We've only been married for what? Two weeks?"

"Oh, so now you're trying me? I know what to

do for that." He jumped up and flipped me on my back.

"Come on, Baby. We've been in here for almost two hours."

"Now who's complaining?" He was hovered over me in strike position.

"It's not a complaint, but I think I'm being rude to my sister."

"Oh damn! I almost forgot she was here. Hell, I forgot the kids were here, too." We laughed.

I leaned up and kissed him on his soft lips. "Can I give you a coochie coupon and let you collect it tonight?"

"Umm, that sounds good to me."

We got dressed and made our way downstairs to the basement. The three of them were laid out in the recliners as the TV watched them.

I grabbed Alex by the hand. "Ready to cash in that coupon?"

# *Asia*

## CHAPTER 41

I padded into the kitchen to get something to drink.

"Asia, can you bring me something to drink, Baby?" Hayden called behind me.

Bring him? Did I look like I was going for servant of the year? What was wrong with his legs that he couldn't get up? Hell, I was the one who had just spent the last thirty minutes having my legs pushed out, up, and over my head. He should be getting me something to drink.

"Okay. What do you want?"

"A glass of ice water is fine."

Okay, so I talk a good head game. After the lovin' he just laid on me, I would run outside in the snow butt naked with no shoes on to get him some water from the faucet outside.

I handed him his glass as I gulped down the last of mine. I slid back into the bed next to him.

"Umm, so what do we have planned for today?"

"How about staying inside," he kissed me, "cuddled up in the bed," he kissed me again, "and making love all day." This time he parted my lips and shoved his tongue in. I savored the feel of the softness of his lips.

"I thought we'd go over to Yani's house. She and Alex invited us to dinner," I said once he let me up for air.

"Aww, Baby, I was hoping to have you all to myself."

"Well, you can, but later. We'll only go for a few hours and then head straight back here." I climbed on top of him.

He was pouting like a baby. "What time are we supposed to be there?"

"In about two hours. So, that means we have time for, you know—"

"Yes, I do." He positioned me on top of him and commenced to take me to that realm once again.

❤❤❤

"Who made the gumbo?"

"Alex. Told you my man can cook." Yani leaned over and gave Alex a long kiss.

"All right, all right. Nobody wants to look at that," I teased.

"Aww. Hayden, give her a kiss so she won't feel left out." I gave Hayden a I-don't-think-so look.

"I think I'll pass right now." He shoved another fork of gumbo and rice in his mouth.

Yani had made a smooth transition to city life. It was fun having her so close to me now. We didn't spend every minute together, but we did interact with each other quite a bit since she'd opened the office here.

I observed my sister with her husband. They seemed to be in a state of euphoria. They couldn't seem to get enough of each other.

"So what's for dessert?" I asked.

"Mama's banana pudding?" My mouth instantly began to water. "No you didn't? You know I have to take some home." I raced into the kitchen.

Yani could lay down some cooking herself and Mama's banana pudding was one of the things she specialized in. I came back and sat at the table with a cup full of pudding.

"Umm, just like I like it. The cookies are soft."

"I made it last night so it would be ready." She squeezed my shoulder as she walked past me with plates in her hand.

"You want me to help you with the dishes, Baby?"

"I got it. Besides, Asia is going to help me out."

My eyes widened as I shoved a spoonful of pudding in my mouth. I didn't remember volunteering for kitchen duty. She looked at me as she stacked the last two plates on top of her pile. I knew that look meant she wanted to talk.

I slid out of my chair and followed behind her with my pudding still in my hand. I could hear Hayden and Alex talking shop. The only thing Hayden knows to do.

As soon as the door swung closed, I started in, "What's up?"

"I've got to go down to Florida for a few days. I finally decided to sell the house."

"Decided to? I thought you sold it months ago? Does Alex know about this?"

"Sorta. I mean, he knows the house is still there, but he doesn't know that I just put it on the market a few weeks ago."

"Why the hell are you holding on to a piece of your past? I mean, isn't Alex worth letting go of it? We've had this discussion before."

"That's why I'm getting rid of it. I love him and the last thing I want to do is put our relationship in jeopardy by keeping secrets. Besides, I have no intentions of going back there."

"So, what do you need me to do?"

"See about the kids for me. Alex is really putting in long hours at the office with the last-minute post-production on the project."

"Okay. Are you going to stay with Mama while you're there?"

"No, I'm staying at Carmen's."

"Does Mama know that you still have that house? You know girlfriend loves her some Alex and she'll bust you out." We both laughed.

Yani slipped the dirty dishes into the dishwasher and set it.

"So how did you like the story in *Essence, Ebony, Jet, Sister2Sister, Honey…*"

"And every other publication out there. Yes, you guys did make headlines around the globe. I loved the article in *Essence* though. That picture on the cover of the two of you is beautiful." I shoveled the last bit of pudding in my mouth.

"I know. I told Alex it was my favorite. I guess it helps to have friends in high places."

"I think it was more of who you married. I know our business has picked up big time since the articles."

"I know. Oh, and I have some more great news!"

"What?"

"Alex has helped us land the promotional campaign for the picture he's working on! We will be in charge of the premiere event!"

"Really?!"

"Yes, Girl. It does help to be married to a man with good connections." We both squealed with delight and jumped up and down.

Alex stuck his head in the door. "Everything okay in here?"

"I was just telling Asia how you hooked us up."

"Oh."

I walked over and wrapped my arms around his neck. "You are truly a Godsend. Thanks, brother-in-law."

He returned the hug. "Actually, I didn't really do anything. They were looking for someone and Constance suggested it. I wanted to talk with you guys about handling the whole ad campaign for it."

"Are you serious?!"

"I know it would be placing you in another field, but you do PR anyway. I mean, you put together all the advertising for the events you do."

"Oh, we can definitely handle it." Yani winked at me. I was finally getting a chance to put the other part of my degree to work.

Yani kissed him. He wrapped his arms around her and stared in her eyes.

I decided to slip back into the dining room to share the good news with Hayden. When I discovered he wasn't in there, I walked downstairs to the game room to see if he'd slipped off to challenge Jay to a rematch. Still no sign of Hayden.

"I know damn well he didn't leave me." I ran to the front door to check and make sure his car was still parked out front.

"I know, I know. Look, I'll be there. Don't do this.

Yes, I promise. I'll be there. As soon as I'm finished up with my work here."

I walked slowly back into the dining room in a trance-like state and sat at the table. *No, this is not happening. Hayden wouldn't do this to me.* I sat shaking my head.

"What's wrong, Asia?" I looked up into the prying eyes of my sister.

Hayden is out on your porch talking to another woman, is what I wanted to say. "Just thinking about something," is what came out.

"Ready to go, Baby?" Hayden asked.

I turned my head in his direction. He smiled and walked over and hugged Yani and thanked her and Alex for a wonderful dinner. I stared at him unable to make sense of what'd just happened. Or determine if it had happened at all. It had happened all right.

It amazed me how he was able to jump from the bumbling idiot he sounded like on the phone with *whomever* it was he was talking to, to this warm and inviting person he was now. But that's what wolves do. They put on sheep's clothing and get you to believe they're harmless until it's time to bare their teeth. This time I was going to handle this situation in a calm manner. I would make him show his hand to me instead of giving away my trump. I had to devise a plan to pull it off. And I would pull it off.

# Yani

## CHAPTER 42

"Hello?" I said groggily. All I could hear was something that seemed to sound like air.

"Hello?" I said louder this time.

When they didn't answer after the third attempt, I hung up. *If it was important they would've said something*, I thought as I rolled over to check the clock. It was well after one in the morning.

Alex rolled over and pulled me close to him.

"Who was that?" he whispered into the back of my neck.

"I guess they had the wrong number." I pushed my butt deeper into his middle until we fit together like a perfect set of spoons.

"I got one of those calls earlier tonight."

"Well if they call back, I'm taking this bad boy off the hook. I've got a busy day tomorrow."

After the short exchange, we fell back into a blissful sleep until the alarm went off at six. I hopped out of bed and started what had become our daily routine.

I woke the kids, went back to the room to get myself ready, and then back down to check on the kids. Jay has been known to lie back down, but he was up pulling his shirt over his head when I walked back in. I went downstairs to start breakfast, then came back up to wake Alex.

"Okay. Okay. I'm up," he moaned as I flung the covers off him.

"When are you coming back?" Natalia asked.

"I'll only be gone a few days. You make sure that you and Jay are good for Asia."

"I will, but, Mommy, I don't know why we couldn't stay here with Daddy. I'm old enough to be home by myself until he gets in," she whined.

"Yeah okay," I said sarcastically.

I smiled at how easily the kids and Alex had fallen into the family role.

"Mommy, I know how to get home by myself. Why do I have to wait for Asia to pick me up? When are you going to stop treating me like a baby?"

"When you stop acting like one. We haven't been here long enough for you to try and navigate your way home. Besides, Daddy is working hard trying to finish this project and has no idea what time he's going to be coming in from work. If he has to rush home to see about the two of you that would be an inconvenience to him."

Natalia rolled her eyes. "Okay."

"Thank you."

"Good morning, Mommy." Jay walked over and kissed me on the cheek.

"Good morning, son. We need to get a move on if I'm going to make my flight." They trailed me downstairs to the kitchen. I placed a bowl of hot oatmeal in front of him and walked over to the intercom.

"Alex, come on, Baby. I need you to drop me at the airport."

Alex descended the stairs. "I know." He placed his jacket over the back of the chair and sat down to the egg, bacon, and cheese bagel sandwich that I'd prepared for him.

I trotted up past him on my way to the stairs. He slapped me playfully on my backside. "Behave yourself," I scolded him as the kids snickered.

"Where you going?"

"To grab my bags."

He got up from the table. "Baby, I got it."

"Alex, sit down and eat so we can go. I'm not helpless."

"I know that, but can't a man help his wife?"

"Of course, Baby, but your wife needs you to finish eating," I called down. He pretended to pout as he walked back to the table.

When I got back down, everyone was finished and putting on their jackets.

"Here's your jacket. It's a lil' chilly out this morning." Alex handed me my black, wool pea coat. I quickly put it on and ushered everyone out the door.

After saying my goodbyes to the kids, we made our way over to the VanWyck heading to JFK.

"How long do you think you'll be gone?"

"For a few days. Why, are you going to miss me?" I grabbed his free hand dangling off the armrest.

"I'm gonna miss you so much, I'm debating on whether or not I should buy me a ticket and go with you." He kissed the back of my hand.

"But you can't do that. You have too much work and besides, I'll be back before you know it."

He pulled up in front of Delta's terminal.

"You want me to park and come inside?"

"You don't have to. My flight should be boarding by the time I get down to the gate." He got out and grabbed my bags and placed them on the curb for the skycap.

"You know something? This is the first time we've been apart since you became Mrs. Chance." He smiled nervously.

"Make sure you behave yourself until I get back, Mr. Chance." We hugged and kissed like we would never see each other again.

"You just get back here soon, or I'm coming to get you," he said as he looked down at me.

"Oh believe me, I will. I love you, honey," I said as I stared into his eyes.

"I love you more." He gave me one last long and passionate kiss, then jumped back in the car and drove off.

I stayed at the curb and watched until I couldn't see his car anymore before I headed into the terminal.

❤❤❤

A little less than three hours later the plane touched down in Fort Lauderdale. I picked up the rental car and jumped on I-595 west headed to my mother's house. I hadn't seen her since the wedding, although Asia and I had started a ritual of calling her every Sunday after church.

I stuck my key in the door.

"Ma?" I called out. I didn't want to scare her to death. I walked around the house and discovered she wasn't there. "Where could she be this time of morning?" Wanting to get on with my day, I left her a quick note telling her that I'd gotten in and I'd be back later to see her.

While in the car, I dialed Carmen.

"Hello?"

"Hey, Girl. Wanna go get some breakfast?"

"Hey! You just got in?"

"I'm on my way to your house, so get dressed."

"I'll be ready when you get here."

"That'll be the day. We can go to the Waffle House near you on Griffin. I'll be there in ten minutes."

"Watch, I'll be ready. Bye."

I hung up and turned up the radio; 99 Jamz was playing their "Eat to the Beat" mix. "Firecracker" was pumping through the speakers as I sped down Miramar Parkway to I-75.

I looked around amazed at how quickly they were building up the area. I remembered when there was nothing out here and now there were signs of suburban life everywhere. The cow pastures, which once dominated the area, were now few and far between.

I pulled up at the gate of Windmill Estates in Weston and waited as the guard signed me in and handed me a gate pass. I rode through the neighborhood of exclusive homes and lush palm trees until I got to Carmen's.

Wanting to prove me wrong, she was waiting at the door. Fully dressed, keys in hand, purse on her shoulders. She jumped into the car.

"Told you that I was going to be ready." She gave me a victorious smirk.

"I guess that was one of your New Year's resolutions." I reached over and gave her a hug and a sisterly peck on the cheek.

"Not really. I decided to get dressed when it got close to time for your flight to get in. Speaking of which, how was your flight?"

"It was good. You know how nervous I get every time I get on a plane."

I traveled southbound to the Waffle House that was five minutes away.

"I know. You talked to the realtor yet?"

"Not yet. I need to get something into my stomach before I talk any kind of business. I only had a cup of coffee this morning."

"You're not dieting again?"

"Hell no. Even though I think my appetite has changed a bit in the past few weeks."

"Maybe it's the change in climate or something."

"I know one thing, I'm starving." We both laughed as I pulled into the parking lot.

We grabbed a booth in the back and ordered our usual—waffles with ham. She ordered a cup of coffee while I opted for a glass of water.

"You know I framed my copy of *Essence*?" she said as she stirred in an ample amount of sugar and cream.

"They gave us a framed poster-size copy of it. It's so beautiful. I was floored when I saw Susan Taylor walk in. After all these years, I finally got to meet her and tell her how much of an impact she has had on my life. And she was *so* nice."

The waitress came over with her arms crammed with plates.

"Girl, you really are hungry. There's no way you're going to be able to eat all of that," Carmen said as she looked at the plates spread out on the table.

I'd called the waitress' attention two different times after we initially placed our order. I added an order of hash browns that were covered and chunked (cheese and ham), a bowl of grits, and a side of scrambled eggs.

"I know, but the longer I looked at the menu, the more I wanted it." I situated the plates in front of me.

"All right now, you know what they say about your eyes being bigger than your stomach…your ass is gonna blow up big as a house."

"Girl, please. I still work out every single day. I guess I'm just hungry 'cause I'm excited about selling the house."

"Or maybe because you're missing your man."

"I almost cried as I watched him drive away this morning."

"How is married life?" she asked as she shoved a piece of syrup-drenched waffle into her mouth.

"It's pure heaven. I'm truly in love with a wonderful man, and the kids love him, too. Did I tell you they've gotten into the habit of calling him Daddy?"

"Alex mentioned it to Bryce. Said it made him feel special. He said he feels truly blessed to have you and them in his life. So is what they say true?"

"And what's that?" I asked through a mouthful of waffles.

"About it being better the second time around."

"Girl, let me tell you. Alex has treated me like a queen. I wake every morning thanking God for the wonderful man He sent me. Alex has been working pretty hard though. I've surprised him at the office a few times with dinner. Damn if I'm going to let someone else feed my man. I cook and drive into the city and stay with him until he finishes up. He's even teaching me a few things about his business. Said we can turn it into a family business."

"I'm so happy for you. You guys are so good for each other."

"I know. And yes, I know we have *you* to thank for it."

"No need to toot the horn too many times."

After eating a good portion of my breakfast, we left. I dropped Carmen, along with my things, back at her house, then headed over to my former place of residence for what I hoped would be the last time.

I opened the door and walked into the kitchen and placed my purse on the counter. I continued to walk around inspecting everything. It was still the same except for the missing pieces of furniture.

I had a garage sale after the wedding and left Carmen and Bryce in charge. I walked upstairs and checked the second floor. The cleaning company had done a wonderful job. The carpets looked new and the fresh coats of paint gave the rooms the look of a new model home.

I made my way back downstairs into the room that had been my bedroom for close to fourteen years. I checked in the closet and then in the bathroom. I was shocked to see the bed made up with a fresh set of sheets.

"I could've sworn Terry asked for it." I wonder why she didn't take the mattress and box spring. I made a mental note to ask Carmen about it.

I looked out the window at my old neighborhood. I thought coming back here would make me homesick, but the homesick I was feeling wasn't for here. I knew that selling this was the best thing to do.

I pulled my cell phone from my purse and called the agent. We made plans to meet in an hour.

I decided to walk over and say goodbye to my old neighbor, Isis for what would probably be the last time. Isis was an older white woman who had been like a grandmother to me and my children.

I pressed the button for the doorbell and waited

for someone to answer. A minute later a short Hispanic woman answered the door. Her face lit up when she saw me.

"Senora Mee-ller." Millie threw her hands to her mouth, then reached to embrace me in a warm hug.

"Hi Millie. Is Isis home?"

"Si. Come, come. I go get her." She led me into the house and went off to the back of the house as I waited in the living room.

"Yani?! Oh my goodness! When did you get here?" she asked as she hugged me.

"A short while ago."

"What are you doing here? Don't tell me you're tired of New York already?"

"Oh no. I love New York. I'm only here for a few days. I came to sell the house."

She had a puzzled look on her face.

"I thought you sold the house already?"

"No. I gave it to an agent a few weeks ago and she has a buyer already. So, I came back for the closing. I also needed to check on a few other things."

"Oh, okay. That explains it then."

"Explains what?"

"Why that car has been there for the past couple of nights. I guess the people buying it wanted to make sure the neighborhood is nice even in the nighttime."

"That's probably it. I know Jarrin and I looked at the house for weeks once we decided to buy it."

I spent enough time to fill her in about the kids, Alex, and the beautiful brownstone we lived in before excusing myself so I could head back next door to wait for the real estate agent.

"Make sure to keep in touch. At least send me pictures of my precious babies from time to time."

"I will." I gave her a hug goodbye and walked down the walkway.

As soon as I reached the front door, Angela pulled up in a black C class Mercedes. In typical realtor mode, her cell phone was glued to her ear as she adjusted her jacket and grabbed a folder from the seat. She snapped her phone shut and greeted me.

"Hi, Mrs. Chance. I have all the paperwork for you to sign and there are a few work requests from the buyers that they want done before they take possession of the house." Without missing a beat, she handed over the manila folder.

"I'll look them over then drop off the signed copies to your office later."

"That'll be fine. The buyers want to do a final walk-through tomorrow so, that gives you almost twenty-four hours. I'll be looking for you later today then. If I'm not there, just leave them with my assistant or the receptionist." She stuck out a well-manicured hand and shook mine.

"Good doing business with you." We bid each other farewell and she jumped back in her car and left.

I walked inside the house and did one last sentimental walk through. After today this part of my life would be gone forever.

As I walked through the master bedroom, I thought about all the memories that were made in it. How I had once shared it with a man who'd meant the world to me. It was the place where my son was conceived. But that life was over with. It was my past. My future was in Brooklyn now, with a man who loved me more than Jarrin ever could. I smiled at the thought of Alex. I pulled my cell phone from my purse to call him.

"I hope thinking of me is the reason for that smile on your face."

I stiffened at the familiar voice. My finger hovered over the keypad of my phone. Slowly I turned to look into the face of the man that almost a year ago I would've given anything to have him return to my life, but at this particular moment in time he was the last person I expected or even wanted to see.

"I see I still have the ability to render you speechless."

"Jarrin?"

# Asia

**CHAPTER 43**

I made my way through downtown Brooklyn to pick the kids up from school. Before heading to Canarsie, I made a quick stop at Junior's on Flatbush to pick up a cheesecake for dessert.

"Have you heard from my mom?" Natalia asked.

"No, not yet."

"What about my dad?"

"Haven't talked to him either."

"Can I call him?"

"Once we get to my place you can."

"Can we stop by our house for a quick minute? I have to get something that I need for school." Natalia looked at me with pleading eyes.

"Okay, but hurry up. I need to get dinner started and help you guys with whatever homework you have."

I drove through the quiet streets past rows of residences that rivaled the mansions on Manhattan's Fifth Avenue and parked in front of their house.

Natalia ran up the stairs to the front door while Jay
and I waited in the car. Jay-Z's new song was thump-
ing on the radio. I turned it up. The kids loved riding
in my VW Beetle, or Punch Buggy as most people
referred to it. Its sporty, fun look was the main reason
I bought one.

"*I'm a hustler baby…*" I sang as we waited for
Natalia to come back. I glanced down at my watch.
Four-thirty. I blew the horn. I needed to get home
and get things started. I promised Hayden a home-
cooked meal he was never going to forget. My initial
plan was to feed him and then put it on him something fierce. The *it* being some hard down sex he
wouldn't forget as long as he lived. After draining
him of all his energy, I would set him up. Ask him
a few questions and then get around to the phone
call I overheard at Yani's the other night.

Natalia came dashing down the stairs. I rolled
down the window. "Did you lock the doors good?"

She ran back up to check both sets of doors. She
climbed in the car. She had a bag in her hand with
books in it.

"What's that for?"

"Homework. I have a project that I need to get
to work on."

My sister had them trained well. They were not
allowed to slack off.

"What about you, Jay? You have any homework?"

"Yes, but I'm almost finished with it." He kept bopping his head as he looked out the window.

We headed to my place in the suburban area called Canarsie. I rented the upper part of a two-family home. My two-bedroom, one-bath has plenty of room for me.

Knowing how much Hayden loves seafood, I was treating him to some lemon pepper shrimp with seasoned rice.

I got dinner going and helped the kids get situated in the spare bedroom that doubled as an office.

"You're sleeping on the pullout bed in the living room, Jay," Natalia said as she plopped down on the daybed.

"I don't care." They placed their bags in the closet.

"Finish up your homework while I finish dinner. Hayden should be here soon."

"Hayden's coming over? You sure you don't want me to call Daddy to pick us up?" Natalia teased.

While I had thought about doing that, I didn't want Yani to be upset.

"Are you telling me that you don't want to stay at my house?" I thought I'd put the idea out there and see what their response would be.

"It's not that, I just like being at home in my room." Natalia shrugged her shoulders as she fumbled around in her book bag.

"Yeah right. She likes the boy that lives down the street," Jay said teasingly.

"Shut up, twerp."

"Nat and what's his face, sitting in a tree, k-i-s-s-i-n-g."

She jumped up and pushed him over. "All right, stop it. Jay, don't be a brat."

"If you want to call Alex and see if he feels like picking you up, I don't care. I'm not driving you back home."

"Oh, thank you, Auntie." Natalia jumped up and wrapped her arms around my neck.

Besides, if he said yes, I could go ahead with my original plans for tonight.

# Alex

## CHAPTER 44

I'd been so busy today that I was shocked to see it was after four when I looked at my watch. I stopped off at Constance's desk before going into my office.

"Did I get any messages today?"

"Just a few," she said as she handed me the pink *"while you were out"* slips. I flipped through and noticed none of them were from Yani.

"Did my wife call me at all today?"

"Now that's one call that I would've found you for."

I knotted my brows as I tried to think of what would keep her from calling me. She had to know that I would be worried about her. Not to mention that I was missing her and needed to hear her voice.

I went into my office and dialed my mother-in-law's number. She picked up after three rings.

"Hello?" she said in her easygoing manner.

"Hi, Mom, it's Alex."

"Alex, how's my one and only son-in-law?"

"I'm fine and yourself?"

"I couldn't be better."

"I called to find out if you've seen my wife?"

"Not yet. She left me a note though saying that she'd be back by later. So, she's here. Is there something wrong?"

"No, I mean…" I paused for a brief moment. "She hasn't called and I was wondering if everything was okay."

"Have you tried Carmen's? Since that's where she's staying, she might be there."

"She said she was coming to your place first, so that's why I called you first. I'm going to call Carmen's. So everything okay with you?"

"Oh, more than okay."

"And what does that mean, young lady?"

"Just that things are good for me right now."

"In other words, none of my business."

"Now that's not what I said."

"Okay, I'll let you off the hook this time. Let me call and find out where this woman of mine is. Talk with you later."

"Bye, Alex."

Mrs. Fenton had informed us all a few months ago that she'd been seeing an old love from high school. Yani and Asia had to get used to the idea of another man being in their mother's life that wasn't their father. But she reminded them that their father had been dead for quite some time. She had been a good wife to him while he was there, but she was lonely. I reminded Yani that basically we were in the same situation. That seemed to change their perspective.

I quickly punched in Carmen's number and waited for an answer. Four rings later one of the kids picked up the phone.

"Hel-lo?"

"Hi, is your mommy there?"

"Yes. Who's calling?"

"Alex."

"Okay." Before I could ask for Yani I heard him toss the phone on the counter and run off yelling for his mom.

"Hello?"

"Hey, Carmen. It's me, Alex. I was calling to see if my wife was there. I haven't heard from her today and I wanted to make sure everything is okay."

"I haven't talked to her since she dropped me off after breakfast. She had to meet with the agent."

"I wanted to know how everything went."

"Aww, that's so sweet. Him missing his wifey," she said in baby talk.

I laughed a little.

"Hey, I'm just making sure that everything is okay. She told me she'd call once she got in."

"Maybe something came up with the house."

"Maybe."

"Did you try her cell phone?"

"Yeah. I thought she'd be there with you since she didn't answer it and she wasn't at her mom's."

"I'll tell her to give you a call when she gets here. That is, if you haven't found her by then."

"Thanks, Carmen. Bryce still at the office?"

"Yep. I'm preparing dinner now. What are you going to do about dinner while Yani's gone?"

"I'm very capable of taking care of myself," I teased.

"That's not what I was saying…"

"I'm messing with you. Get back to your dinner. I'm going to try her cell again."

"Okay, Alex. Talk at you later."

"Bye." Just as I hung up, Constance buzzed me.

"Yes?"

"You have a call on line one."

Hoping it was Yani, I hurriedly picked up.

"Alex Chance."

"Hi, Daddy."

"Hi, Nat."

"I was just calling to see what time you're gonna leave work."

"In a few, why? You want me to pick you guys up on my way home?"

"Thank you, Daddy!"

"That is, if it's okay with Asia." I knew that was the reason for her call.

"It's okay with her!"

"I should be there in about forty-five minutes or so."

She'd already succeeded in wrapping me around her finger. I loved them both as if they were mine.

"No problem. Bye, Daddy." She hung up the phone.

I pushed the button for a free line and dialed Yani's cell phone. Her voicemail picked up after the first ring.

"Hey, Babe, it's me. Wanted to know how your day went. I'm about to leave the office and swing by and get the kids from Asia. Give me a call when you get this message. I miss you and you know I love you. Bye."

"Where the hell is she?" I wondered aloud.

# Yani

## CHAPTER 45

Jarrin walked closer to me and reached out to stroke the side of my face.

"Damn, Baby, you look good. I almost didn't recognize you when I saw you in those magazines."

"What are you doing here?" I said almost in a whisper, still reeling from the shock of seeing him.

"I came to see my wife."

I shivered at the words. His wife? I wasn't his wife anymore. I'm married to Alex now.

"How did you know I was going to be here?"

He had an evil grin on his face.

"After reading about your recent nuptials, I had a realtor look into the house for me. I asked him to do a little research and give me a call when it was put up for sale and let me know when it was about to go through."

I couldn't believe that he was standing here in front of me as if him being here was the most natural thing in the world. I had so many questions I wanted to ask but didn't know where to begin. So, I let the first thing that came to mind roll out of my mouth.

"Where in the hell have you been?"

He laughed. "I had to get lost for a little while. Take a lil' vacation."

"A vacation that lasts for five years? That's a little excessive, don't you think?"

"Depends on who you ask." His hazel eyes shone. "If it makes you feel any better, I thought about you and the kids every day."

"You thought about us? You could've fooled me. I guess that explains the phone calls. Oh, and let's not forget about the shit load of postcards you managed to send. The kids were excited every time they got those birthday cards," I said in a mocking voice. "Niggah, do I look that stupid to you?"

He smiled. "Haven't we become quite the aggressor? Anyway, it's a long story."

"I have the time." I placed my hand on my hip. I'd waited five years for this story. I took a seat on the bed as I waited for Jarrin to tell me what would cause him to walk out on his wife and children and not make any kind of attempt to contact us in over five years.

Jarrin took a squat next to me on the floor. He let out a long sigh and massaged the back of his neck briefly.

"Look, I was involved in some heavy shit and had to get out of town fast."

"What are you talking about? Why didn't you have the decency to at least call me?"

"That would've tipped them off to my whereabouts and I didn't want to pull you into this."

"Into what?"

He rested his face in his hands for a moment, then looked back up and took a deep breath.

"I was about to be indicted on money laundering charges."

"What?!"

"A few of my clients were heavily involved in the dope game and I sorta got caught up in it."

"Caught up in it? How?"

"I would, you know...get things for them. Help them find ways to clean their money."

"Why would you do some stupid shit like that? The law firm was doing well enough that you didn't have to do anything like that."

"Yani, do you actually think that a new firm would be able to pull in the kind of money I was bringing home in less than a year of opening its doors?"

"Jarrin, you had built your clientele up before you left..."

"And who do you think my clientele was?"

"I don't know. Especially since you and I never really

talked about your business dealings. Now I know why."

"I got caught up in the whole scene. The money, the cars…the women." He looked at me sheepishly to check my reaction.

It was a slight blow, learning about his infidelities. I always thought that I had been all he needed and wanted. I shook my head slowly and tried to laugh the situation away, but the laughter never came.

"Look, Baby, I'm not proud of the things I've done, but I did them for you and the kids. I wanted to make sure that your futures were secure."

It irritated me that he could so easily still call me baby.

"That explains why you left us damn near penniless and close to being homeless."

"What are you talking about? I left you secure."

"Jarrin, please. You cleaned out the bank account and the box."

"What about the bag in the attic?" We both diverted our eyes toward the closet.

"What bag in the attic?"

He got up and walked in the closet and pulled on the latch causing the attic door to snap open. He pulled down the stairs and disappeared in the opening in the ceiling. I stood watching him as he disappeared and came back with a huge, black duffel bag. He threw it in the middle the floor and opened it.

Inside were stacks and stacks of hundred dollar bills banded together in stacks of ten thousand dollars.

"This is what I left you."

I was stunned. "Why would you put it up there? You know damn well that I would never set foot in the attic."

"When I left, I figured that you would search the house from top to bottom for anything that would give you a clue to my whereabouts." He retrieved an envelope from the bag and handed it to me.

"How much is in there?!" I leaned in for a closer inspection.

"Three million." He smiled as he scooped his hand into the bag and removed a few stacks. He moved a few more stacks around. Searched through the bag thoroughly, then placed the money back in and zipped it closed. He stood and hoisted the bag up on his shoulder.

"Why do I have the feeling that this is the real reason you came back?" I pointed to the bag.

"I told you I came back to see you, Baby."

"Then that means you wouldn't mind if I take the bag, would you? Seeing that you left it here for me in the first place." I reached out my hand to retrieve the bag and he stepped out of my reach.

"From what I read, you've married Mr. Moneybags himself. So, you don't need it."

"Yeah right. You didn't leave that money for me. You hid it in the attic because you thought I would never give up hope on you being alive and it would be here whenever you decided to pop back in. Once you found out I was selling the house, you hightailed it back here to get it. It just so happened that I actually flew in for the closing. You're a lawyer, or *were* one. You knew there was a possibility that I could've handled everything via express mail. The scenario you would've preferred. All this bullshit about wanting to see me is just that, bullshit." I stared him down.

"How can you say that to me? I love you, Yani. I took a real chance coming back here. And besides, I know you. There's no way you would take a chance on anything going wrong with such a big transaction. I knew for a fact you would be here." He reached for me. I took a step backward. Confusion took over my thinking process.

"Why are you doing this to me? Why couldn't you just stay gone?"

"After I saw you with him, it made me remember how much I loved you. How wrong I had been for leaving the way I did."

I shook my head. "Don't. I can't do this, Jarrin. I love Alex."

"Just answer one question for me then." He grabbed

my hand and looked into my eyes. I was surprised at the slight feel of butterflies floating in my stomach as I stared into the eyes of the man I had loved more than life itself at one time. Those unforgettable eyes that used to melt my heart.

"Can you honestly say that you no longer love me, Yani?"

I bit down on my bottom lip and searched for an appropriate response. Up until that moment, I thought Jarrin was completely out of my system. I don't know if it was from the sight of him or hearing his voice, but for some reason I felt as if something had begun to rekindle that feeling that I thought was long gone when I said yes to Alex.

"Look, you don't have to answer that right now and as an act of good faith, I'm going to leave the bag with you." He placed the duffel bag at my feet.

I looked down at it. "Jarrin, I..." He placed his finger to my lips to quiet me.

"I know this is an awkward situation for you. So, think about it hard. If you let me, I want to make everything up to you. How long are you going to be in town?"

"I wasn't planning on being here that long. Maybe a few days."

"I'll see you tomorrow." He kissed me softly on my forehead and headed for the door.

"Jarrin, wait!" He stopped and turned around. "How do I get in contact with you?"

"Just wait for my call. You're going to be at Carmen's or your mom's?"

"Carmen's," I stated a little too quickly.

"I'll give you a call tomorrow morning. Oh, and I expect an answer to my question then." He smirked as he walked off, proving that he was still cocky as hell.

❤❤❤

As I drove to Carmen's house, a constant flow of thoughts ran through my mind. How could he do this to me? I'm happy with my life. I thought about Alex and how much I loved him. I knew that Jarrin being alive would mean trouble for our marriage. Did Jarrin's reappearance make me a bigamist? What was I going to tell Alex?

"Oh my God!" I just remembered that I hadn't called Alex all day. I looked at the last remaining streaks of orange that scattered across the sky indicating the sun's departure was almost final.

Hot tears slowly streaked down my cheeks. I gripped the steering wheel tight as my frustration seeped out. What am I going to do? Things felt as if they were falling apart, just when they were starting to go so right.

## Alex

## CHAPTER 46

When I got to Asia's to scoop up the kids, it seemed she was just as happy to see me as they were.

"What do you guys want to eat tonight? Is pizza cool?" It was too late to cook and I wanted to be home just in case Yani tried to call.

"That sounds good to me," Natalia said.

"What about you, Jay? Up for some pizza, lil' man?"

"Okay." His head was bowed as he concentrated on the Gameboy in his hand.

"Then pizza it is." We ordered two pies when we got home and waited for them to be delivered. It was after eight by the time we ate and cleaned our mess. I sent Jay off to get ready for bed while Natalia talked on the phone.

I went in my office to try and do some work. Soon as I sat down to my desk, my phone rang. Hoping it was Yani, I snatched the phone up.

"Hello?"

"Alex?"

"Hey Ma', que' pasa?"

"Where's Yani?"

"She's in Florida. She finally sold the house." I turned on my computer screen.

"Dios mios."

Knowing that phrase was connected to some type of bad news, I began to question her. "What's wrong, Ma'?"

"I dreamt about her. She was in Florida and she was in danger."

"Danger? What kind of danger?"

"I saw a man with her. He was threatening her." She continued to roll out her story.

"Ma', it's just a dream."

"Just a dream?! You call and make sure she's okay."

"As soon as I hear from her, I'll call you and let you know."

"Don't be a smart ass, Alex. I'm telling you, something is wrong with her!" She mumbled a few choice words in Spanish as she hung up the phone in my ear.

I laughed as I thought about her and those crazy dreams she was always making a big deal about. I typed in my password to access the Internet. As I checked my emails, my mother's words stuck in my head. Unable to fully concentrate, I clicked off the computer and picked up the phone.

"Hello?" I heard another voice on the other end say.

"Hello?" I answered back.

"Who were you about to call?" Yani asked.

"Oh, just this woman I'm married to that hasn't called me all day." I came across with a little more attitude than I'd intended.

"I miss you, too."

"Really? Then I'd hate to see what would happen if you didn't."

"Is this going to be our first fight?"

The thought made me smile. "I was worried about you."

"I know, Baby, and I'm sorry. I just got busy with the house thing and lost track of time, and I know that you're pretty busy now, so I didn't want to bother you at work."

"Bother me? Don't use that as an excuse. Everyone in that building knows to find me if you call. No matter what."

"I'm sorry," she whined.

She was breaking down my defenses. "I know you're sorry. You said that already."

"Do you forgive me?"

"I'll think about it," I teased. "My mother just called here asking about you."

"Really? How is she?"

"Oh, she's fine. She actually called because she'd had some kind of dream about you."

"A dream? Dream about what?"

"Something about you being in trouble. A man was giving you trouble." I laughed as I finished explaining it to her. "Is that crazy or what?" The line was dead silent. "Yani? You okay, Baby?" It sounded as if she was sniffling.

"I'm okay."

"You don't sound like it."

She exhaled loudly. "I don't know how to tell you this…"

"Just say it. That seems to work most times," I said, trying to lighten the moment.

"I saw him."

"Him who?"

"Jarrin. Today," she blurted out.

It was my turn to be stunned into silence.

"Did you hear me?" She sounded as if she was on the verge of tears.

"Yeah, I heard you. What did he want?"

"I'm not sure. Alex, you know that I love you, right?"

"Yeah, of course." I waited to find out where this questioning was leading.

"No matter what happens, I want you to know that I love you."

I closed my eyes and shook my head. I couldn't believe this. "He didn't tell you what the occasion was after all these years?"

"No. He mentioned something about seeing the stories about us getting married and how he saw the wedding in the different magazines."

"And?!"

"I don't know. He didn't really go into specifics. He just mentioned that he wanted to meet with me tomorrow."

"Well, are you?"

"Do I have a choice?"

The idea of her being alone with him unnerved me. What could he possibly want after all of this time?

"You want me to fly there?"

"No. I'll be fine. Jarrin has never raised his hand to hurt me in any kind of way."

"Did he ever show any signs that he would up and leave either?"

"That hurt."

"Well, think about it."

"How are things coming along at the office?" she asked in an attempt to steer me away from the subject.

"Everything is almost ready for the premiere next week."

Silence. "That's good. I really like the trailers. Did I tell you that?"

"Yeah, we talked about it last week when we saw one while watching *For Your Love*."

"Someone in the office said they saw the print advertisement while she was on the train. We've got everything set up as far as the event. We've got the leads booked to do all the nighttime circuits and a couple of the daytime. You know, *Oprah*, *The View*, and *Regis*."

"Oh. That's good." Silence again.

"Yani?"

"Yeah?" she said, sounding like she was thinking about something else.

"Baby, you need me?" I wanted her to say yes. Hoped she'd tell me to jump on a flight and get there as soon as I could. But my hopes were dashed out like a fire that never got a chance to rage.

"Don't worry, Baby. I can handle Jarrin. I'm going to go down to the kitchen to get a bite to eat. I'm feeling a little famished."

"All right." I couldn't think of anything else to say to her.

"Alex?"

"Yeah?"

"I love you."

"I love you, too, Baby."

"Call you back a little later?"

"Yeah, do that."

We professed our love to each other again and hung up. As soon as I laid the phone on my desk, my mother's words came back to me. "She's in danger. A man is threatening her."

I would let her try and take care of it first but, if need be, I'd be on the first thing smoking to Florida and give his ass a New York beat down he'd never forget.

# Asia

## CHAPTER 47

I placed the last piece of silverware on the table as the doorbell rang. On my way to answer it, I stopped and took one last look in the mirror. Every hair was in place. My DKNY was permeating the air. It was Hayden's favorite scent. Tonight I was going straight for the jugular.

I paused at the door before opening it. Made sure to put my emotional state in check as I adjusted my dress a bit. Making sure the split in the front showed an ample amount of cleavage. The bell rang once more and I reached for the knob.

Hayden stood on the other side with a bouquet of flowers in one hand and a bottle of wine in the other. Damn, why does he have to look so good?!

His chocolate colored skin was shaven smoothly clean and had a slight shine from his moisturizer.

"These are for you, beautiful lady." He handed the flowers to me.

I put up a shy front. "Why, thank you, Mr. Miles.

Won't you please come in?" I stepped back allowing him just enough room to pass.

His persona filled the foyer. The manly scent of his cologne filtered through my nostrils.

"Umm, something smells good in here."

"I made your favorite, Lemon Pepper Shrimp."

"To what do I owe the honor?"

"I hope there's nothing wrong with a woman cooking for her man? That is, if you *are* my man?" I watched his face to see what his reaction would be.

"Then let's eat because I'm starving. Where's your opener so I can remove the cork?" He headed over to the kitchen.

"In the drawer next to the refrigerator." I grabbed the lighter from the curio behind me and lit the candles. I dimmed the lights just enough to give the room a romantic glow. Like I said, I was going all out. Before tonight is over, not only am I going to know who the hell it was he was talking to on the phone the other night, but I'm going to know what he's done for the past two years when we weren't together.

Hayden walked over and filled the glasses with wine. He pulled out the chair for me. "I'll be right back." I slipped into the kitchen to get the food. I placed the main dish in the center of the table and went back for the salads.

"Umm. I must've done something real good to deserve this." He got up and waited for me to take my seat.

"That remains to be seen." I waited for him to return to his seat before making another move.

He grabbed his fork and knife and was about to dig in. I looked at him like he'd lost his mind. "What?"

I reached for his hands. He looked at my out-stretched palms and then placed his in them and waited for me to finish blessing the food. As soon as the amens were said, he eagerly dug into everything.

"Slow down, Baby. There's plenty left." I daintily picked at my salad.

"Am I pigging out?"

I nodded my head yes. "There's no one here but us, so you can have all you want."

"You always could burn in the kitchen."

"My mother always told me that the best way to a man's heart is through his stomach. I now know that's not the case all the time though."

He looked up at me with knowing eyes, a forkful of shrimp causing the sides of his mouth to bulge slightly. He smiled.

"So, how does it taste?"

"Delicious," he said between chomps.

"Good. Make sure to leave room for dessert."

"Dessert?"

"Cheesecake."

"Oh Lawd. From Jr.'s?"

"You know it."

He placed his fork on his plate, wiped his mouth and sat back. "Is it good or bad news?"

I gave him a puzzled look. "What news?"

"First you cook me the best meal I've had in God knows when. Then you make a special trip to Jr.'s for the best damn cheesecake in all of New York?! Something is definitely up."

"See, there you go thinking a sistah is up to something. Maybe I was just in the mood to enjoy your company. I happen to like, if not love, everything I cooked. And we don't have to go there with the cheesecake. If I could forget the lasting effects it would have on my figure, I would probably eat it every day. So the trip to Jr.'s was not as though I was going out of the way." I smiled. "My only intention tonight is to enjoy an evening with a handsome, *single* man."

He grabbed my hand and kissed it. "And that's exactly what you shall do."

After dinner had been devoured and half of the cheesecake consumed, Hayden wanted to go straight to the bedroom. "Relax for a minute. You act like you're in some kind of rush. Like you've got another hot date or something." I looked at him to see if that lil' comment had any effect on his demeanor.

I sauntered sexily over to the stereo and turned it on. It was pre-programmed to the jazz station. The sound of a sultry sax floated through the speakers.

"Can I refill your glass?"

"That's cool."

I grabbed the wine bottle from the table. "This is a nice cut," I said as I poured the clear liquid into his glass; making sure to bend low enough to expose a good glimpse of my braless breast.

"Umm, hmm" he said, letting me know my mission had been accomplished. When I stood back up, I noticed his eyes were definitely on target.

I placed the half-empty wine bottle on the coffee table in front of us. "So, how was your week?" Small talk is always a good way to get things going.

"Busy."

"Still working on that project?"

"Yeah. It's almost wrapped up though. Maybe another week." He patted the spot next to him on the leather sofa.

"Give me one minute." I got up to light the cast iron sconces hanging on my walls. The magnifying glass gave the room a romantic glow. I killed the other lights.

"You trying to seduce me?"

I feigned a look of innocence. "Me?"

"Well, it's working." He stood and extended a hand to me. "Would you like to dance?"

I placed my hand in his and he pulled me in close to him. Slowly we rocked back and forth to the poignant rhythm flowing from the speaker as our shadows bounced off my faint yellow walls.

Hayden's breathing got heavy as he slowly began to grind his midsection into me. His movements intensified, as his erection through his slacks became more evident. Ten minutes later, we'd kissed our way down the hall into my bedroom. Red satin sheets awaited our arrival. I'd sprayed my scent on them so that he would feel like he was surrounded by me. Ten candles at staggered heights were on the dresser with a few more strategically placed around the room.

Hayden's eyes glowed with desire. He picked me up and gently sat me on the wide footboard. I kicked my heels off and they landed on the floor with a hard thud as Hayden untied the wrap dress I sported. The front flopped open, exposing my hardened nipples, which Hayden consumed equally. Playfully flicking his tongue across each nipple.

"Umm," I moaned.

He slid the dress down my shoulders as I slowly removed each arm and let it fall behind me. I slid down from my position and flipped the script on him. I pinned him against the footboard and began to undress him. He tried to help me.

"No. This is my show." I moved his hand from the tie and loosened it. I slowly and deliberately unbuttoned his shirt. Exposing the fine hairs on his chest. Next, I undid his belt and his pants and slid them slowly down his legs. They fell to the floor to rest in a pile around his ankles. He furiously kicked at his shoes in an attempt to remove them. His white, Calvin boxer briefs were barely holding back the bulge that had grown in his midsection.

I leaned into his chest and licked each of his nipples as I stroked his erection through the cloth that separated it from my grasp. He hoisted me up and I wrapped my legs around his waist. He walked to the side of the bed and deposited me on the edge. I scooted to the center and rolled over on my stomach, revealing my exposed rear. I slid my thong down slightly like an exotic dancer does when they tease their patrons. I gave a slight roll of my hips and turned back over. Hayden eyed me like I was the second coming of the dinner he'd devoured earlier.

"You ready for this?" I asked as I slid my finger slowly between my breasts, down to my moist middle.

He readily joined me on the bed. He quickly stripped himself of his last piece of clothing and looked down at what was about to give me pleasure. "What do you think?"

I tried to screw his brains out. I worked him from one end of the bed to the next. He hovered over me on the edge of his climax. "Oh, Asia," he called out as he released himself into the condom.

I collapsed as my cream seeped out against my thighs. Moans of pleasure escaped my slightly parted lips.

Hayden cradled me against his chest while I tried to gain control of my breathing. I propped up on my elbow and looked down in his face. He opened his eyes.

"Umm." He stroked up and down my back with his finger. "You really put it on me tonight."

"You liked?"

"I loved."

Perfect answer. "I aim to please." The sex was incredible. That was the one thing I would miss, but I'm not about to knowingly share with anyone.

Waiting for the right moment to strike, I rolled over and lay in the crook of his arm. Slowly, I stroked my fingers through the fine hairs on his chest.

"Can I ask you something?"

His eyes were almost slits. "Shoot."

"Who were you talking to the other night?"

"When?"

"When we were at my sister's."

He slowly opened his eyes fully. "What are you talking about?"

"Hayden, don't play games with me."

"I'm serious, Baby. I don't know what you're talking about." He slid up and leaned his back against the headboard.

I tried to roll out of the bed but he caught me by the arm.

"Where you going?"

"I'm getting dressed. Is that a problem?" I shot at him nastily.

"Damn. How'd we go from one realm to the next so quickly?"

"'Cause your ass is a liar and I can't deal." I tried to free my arm from his grip.

"What makes me a liar?"

So he wanted to go there. "Because you can't be honest with me. You do know what a liar is?"

"Asia, Baby, I don't think we're on the same page. Tell me what's going on and when I *supposedly* was talking to someone." He had pulled me down on top of him. I stared directly into his eyes.

"You remember the other night when we were at Yani's?"

"Of course I do."

"Well, do you remember when I went into the kitchen with Yani? I was supposed to be helping her clean the kitchen." He nodded his head, indicating that he did in fact remember.

"I came out maybe five minutes later and couldn't

find you. I wondered where you'd disappeared to and went off to look for you. When I finally found you, you were on the porch talking on your cell. And from what I got of the conversation, you weren't talking to a client. So, that rules out that lie."

"Baby, I don't know what you're talking about." He pulled the sheet up to cover his nudeness.

"Oh you don't, do you? You know what? Do me a favor. Let go of me, get up, put on your clothes, and get the fuck outta my house," I said in a slow and even tone.

A look of surprise registered on his face. "You know, I don't understand you!"

"I can tell since you haven't moved yet."

"I was on the phone with a client."

"What?!"

"I was talking to one of my clients," he said again.

"Did you not just hear me tell you that I know that wasn't the case and you're still going to try me with that bold-faced lie?"

"I'm telling you the truth, damn it!" He jumped up from the bed.

I looked at him and shook my head and strode into the bathroom. "Just be gone when I come out." I slammed the door.

Once inside the bathroom, I sat on the toilet to regain my composure. I turned on the shower and jumped in, in an attempt to wash this evening away.

Thirty minutes later I emerged to find Hayden fully dressed, sitting on the bed with his head in his hands.

"I thought I asked you to leave?" I pulled the belt on my wrap tighter.

"I was about to when I realized that I would be making the same mistake as last time."

I leaned against the door so I could hear what bullshit he had thought of while I was gone.

"I know I've been a little distant since we got back. When I saw you and all the time we spent together in Florida, it brought back a rush of feelings that I thought I had buried deep inside me. When you asked me that night on the beach where did I want this to go, I'll be honest, I hadn't given it much thought up until that point. I looked at you that night and could see myself spending the rest of my life with you. I felt this the first time also, but I was too young, too stupid, and too scared to go through with it then."

"Hayden, all I ask is that you be honest with me. If you can't do that, then what do we have? Nothing. I can't commit myself to a relationship that I feel I can't trust the other person in it with me."

"I know this." He inhaled loudly as he tried to figure an easy way to put this. "Could you come over here and sit next to me?" he asked.

I slowly walked over and climbed on the bed. Not

wanting to look at him, I stared straight ahead in the mirror. As I looked at our reflections I started to remember how I once felt about this picture. Hayden and I together. I silently waited for him to tell me what I knew I didn't want to hear.

"Asia, I love you. I really do. I would never do anything to hurt you. Not purposely."

I braced myself for that "but" that was sure to follow. But always has its ass up in there screwing things up.

"But..."

See.

He grabbed my hand. I could feel a slight tremble in his. My focus still on the picture in the mirror, I silently waited.

"I was seeing someone before Linda called me about the flight. I hadn't planned on us clicking like we did. I honestly thought you wouldn't want more than casual conversation. But once I saw you... and you..."

"Oh, Hayden," I cried. "Why couldn't you have been straight with me? I asked you more than once, if you were seeing someone." My heart rate quickened.

"I wanted to be straightforward, but I didn't feel that the other relationship was that serious. I'd only been seeing her for a month."

"So why didn't you end it? You could've called her while you were in Florida, or once you got here. If it wasn't that serious, it shouldn't have been a problem."

"I tried to, but..."

"But what? I'm sick of hearing *but*!"

"I found out she was pregnant," he said almost in a whisper.

Feeling immobile, I sat with my mouth open. I wanted to say something. Needed to say something, but my voice was unattainable. Hayden waited for my response. For five minutes we sat in total silence looking at each other through the mirror. I slowly processed the information over and over in my mind.

"Pregnant?" I was finally able to mumble. "Pregnant..." I blinked my eyes a few times, then stretched them wide. I nervously played with the hair at the nape of my neck.

"I wanted to tell you. I just didn't know how. Asia, I want to be with you, but I want to be there for my child, too."

"All those times you were telling me that you were working on a project. Boy, were you ever." A low laugh danced in my throat to cover up the wail that wanted to escape in its place.

"Asia..."

"Look, you just said yourself what your choice

is." I walked out the bedroom down the hall to the front door and opened it.

Hayden slowly walked toward me. "I'll give you a call in a few days. Give you enough time to…"

"I don't think so."

He reached for the door and turned to look at me. "Goodbye, Hayden."

He tried to kiss me. I turned my head.

After I heard his car start up, I closed the front door that I was holding on to. With my back against the door, I slowly sank to the floor and cried.

# *Yani*

## CHAPTER 48

I'd tossed and turned all night. Unable to clear my head of the events from the day before. I called Alex back before calling it a night, only to partake in a limited conversation.

I sat in Carmen's family room trying to focus on the people dancing across the television. Music videos seem to be more T&A (tits and ass) than anything else nowadays.

"Here's a cup of my famous coffee." Carmen handed the tangerine-colored mug to me and sat down next to me.

I took a quick, cautious sip. "I think I need something a little stronger, if you ask me."

"It's a little too early in the day to be hitting a bottle. Besides, you need all your wits about you right now."

"I'm so nervous."

"I know. I'm nervous for you. But you've got to deal with him so you can get past this nightmare."

"That's exactly what it is. A damn nightmare." I

took another sip. "You know, a year ago I would've given anything for this moment. For him to walk back into my life. I mean, just to know that he wasn't dead would've been a good thing for me. But now…"

"That's because you've put him and that life behind you."

"Have I really, Carmen? When I looked at Jarrin yesterday, it confused me. Don't get me wrong, I love Alex. He's been the best thing to happen to me in a long time…"

"And he's going to keep being that. Stop thinking the worst."

"Thinking? Girl, the worst has happened and I don't know what to do."

"No, it hasn't. The worst would be you losing Alex and that hasn't happened."

"Hmm, not yet."

"What do you mean, not yet?" She looked at me like I'd cursed her.

"I don't know what to say to him. He's about to experience a very important event in his career, and where am I? Stuck in Florida trying to figure out what I'm going to do about my *other* husband who was supposedly dead. Can you imagine if the press was to get a hold of this story? It would make Alex a great big joke."

"Now you're trippin'. Who would tell them?"

"I don't know. Maybe Jarrin."

"Think about it, Jarrin is still running from who-ever and whatever it was that made him leave in the first place. So, I don't think he wants to call any attention to himself."

The room did a slight dance and I shook my head. "You sure you didn't spike this coffee with anything?"

"Not a thing."

"Maybe I'm stressing a lil' too hard." I lay my head back on the couch in an attempt to relax.

"Don't let this mess and stress make you sick. You should just…" The phone rang. We both looked at each other. Carmen answered it. After a few curt words she handed it to me.

I nervously took it and placed it slowly to my ear. "Hello?"

"Were you expecting my call?" Jarrin said in a cocky voice.

I released the breath that I'd been holding since the phone rang. "I guess you can say that."

"How's everyone?"

"They're fine."

"That's good." He paused for a moment. I patiently waited for his next words. "So, have you thought about what we talked about yesterday?"

"I know you can't expect me to just give you an answer like that?"

"You have a point. But I was hoping it would be a no-brainer."

"Well, that's not the case."

"Did you put the bag up?"

"Yeah."

"Good. How about you join me for breakfast?"

"Carmen cooked."

"So you've eaten already."

"Yeah."

It seemed as if he was looking for something else to say. "So, what's a good time for us to get together?"

"Right now I'm waiting on this agent to call me. The closing is today." The conversation was starting to feel like the first time we talked to each other on the phone as teenagers.

"Oh yeah. I forgot about that. Is everything okay with that? Do you need me to look over any paperwork?"

"Everything is fine," I quickly intervened.

"Remember when we found that house?" He gave off a soft laugh. "You wouldn't look at anything else. You were so headstrong then. Are you still that way?"

"Even more so now." I smiled. Carmen got up and went into the kitchen.

"Look, why don't we get together for dinner tonight? I'd like to spend a little quality time with you. We can go anywhere you want. Just name it."

"I think I can handle that." My stomach was doing flips.

"Well, I won't keep you any longer. See you tonight?"

"Okay."

"I love you, Yani."

"Bye, Jarrin."

"You can't give me a little love back?"

"Good-bye, Jarrin."

"Okay. I'll let you off this time. I still love you though."

I hung up the phone. Carmen stood staring at me. I could feel my face turning red as I realized I was smiling.

"What did he want?" She sat back down in her spot.

"Nothing much. He just wants to go out for a bite to eat tonight."

She choked on her coffee. "Go out tonight?! Girl, are you crazy?! I know you said no?!"

"Not exactly." I picked up my coffee and took a sip.

"Not exactly? What the hell does that mean? I hope you're not having a lapse in memory. This is the same man that walked away and left you and two kids with nothing."

"I think it's pretty hard to forget that. But what's wrong with having dinner with him?"

"Duh. Hello? You have a husband. One that really loves you and your kids. One that is going to be there for you no matter what."

"Technically, Jarrin is my husband also."

"Girl, I can't believe you let that niggah get to you. Just like he's always been able to do, and I hope you realize that he knows it. Damn, Yani. I thought you were going to be stronger this time. You have too much on the line for you to be acting like some silly ass schoolgirl!"

"I'm not acting that way," I said defensively.

"Whatever. I'm just telling you what I see and I've known you much too long not to know what's going on."

"You don't understand."

"Understand? All I know is this, if Bryce's ass was to ever pull the shit Jarrin did, there's no way in hell he could ever get the time of day from me *or* my children."

I got up and went in the kitchen with my mug.

"And speaking of children, did he even ask about them? Ask to see them?"

"Of course he did," I lied.

She walked over and placed her hand on my shoulder. "Yani, listen to me. I know this is confusing as hell for you and I know how old feelings have a way of coming back into play, but be smart about this. Why did he wait until now to come back? I'm only saying this because I'm looking out for you and my God-babies. Don't forget that old saying…'Fool me once, shame on you. Fool me twice, shame on me.' Don't let Jarrin get away with it twice, you hear me?"

"I hear you. So stop worrying. I'm not thinking about being with Jarrin. I love Alex."

I was trying my best to convince her of something I was unsure of myself. My feelings for Jarrin had been jumpstarted from the first look. No matter how hard I was trying to act unaffected.

# *Alex*

## CHAPTER 49

I was in a foul mood at the office today and decided that it was in my best interest to leave early. I jumped in my car and headed Uptown to ride through the old neighborhood. I couldn't get over all of the renovations that were going on. Magic Johnson's multiplex and BET were a few of the new tenants. There was also the strong presence of whites that had started to move into Harlem. Growing up here, I would have never believed it if someone had told me yuppies would start running to the ghetto. At least that's what most people thought of when they thought of Harlem. Now there is those couple of blocks called Strivers Row. They'd managed to feign off the poverty that seemed to fall all around them.

After riding around taking in the sights, I realized it was getting close to time for me to pick up the kids. I jumped on the FDR headed south to the Brooklyn Bridge. All the way there I thought about the conversation I'd had with Yani. The more I mulled it over in my mind, the angrier I became.

"Get it together, Alex," I said as I tightened my grip on the steering wheel.

I sat in front of Jay's school for about five minutes before I saw him and a group of boys headed toward me. He waved goodbye and made his way over to the car. As I watched him walk toward the car, I wondered if Yani would tell them that he was back. I wondered if they would want to see their dad. Would they still love me after they find out that he's back?

"Hey, Dad!" Jay said as he climbed in.

"Hey, lil' man. How was school today?"

"It was cool."

"Anything exciting happen today?"

"Nope, not a thing. What about you?"

"Nope. Just another day."

"Are we picking up Nat?"

"She should be home already." I put the car in gear and pulled away.

"Are we going to do anything exciting this weekend? When is Mommy coming back?"

My heart quickened at that question. "I'm not sure about Mommy but Saturday is the premiere, but that's at night. Did you have something in mind that you'd like to do?" I turned down our block.

"Not really. Maybe I'll think of something by tomorrow."

"Tell you what, let's find out if your sister wants to do anything before we start making plans. Okay?"

"Okay." As soon as I put the car in park he jumped out and ran to the front door taking the steps two at a time. I sat in the car and watched him. What would I do if I had to give them up? I shook the thought out of my head and grabbed my briefcase out the back.

Natalia stood at the door as I made my way up the stairs.

"Hey, Daddy. How was work?"

"It was okay." I hugged her.

"So what's for dinner tonight? Are we going out, or shall I cook us something?"

"You cook?! Girl, please. We're not ready to die," said Jay.

"No one was talking to you, little boy."

"You get a cookbook and now you think you're a great chef. I'm not being your guinea pig. No way, Jose." I laughed as they went back and forth for a minute longer.

"How about I cook us something?" They both turned and stared at me. "What? I can cook."

"Cook what?" they said in unison.

"Oh, so now you wanna try me like that? Okay, I'll show you." I walked into the kitchen and opened the cabinets to search for ingredients to prepare a meal they would never forget. After deciding on making my famous lasagna, I shooed them off downstairs.

"So what did you think?"

They both sat back and patted their stomachs.

"Who taught you to cook like that? Can you teach me? Or better yet, teach Nat?"

"You know, I'm too full to argue with you. That was really good, Daddy." Nat pushed her chair back and began to gather the dishes.

"Jay, help your sister and then go up and get ready for bed."

"Okay, Dad." He slowly pushed his chair back and staggered off to the kitchen with his dishes.

"Since homework is checked, if you hurry up, we can see what's coming on tonight and watch a lil' TV until your bedtime." I rubbed his head as I sat my plate on the counter.

"Ooh, can we watch *Spawn*?"

"That movie is so gross."

"Then don't watch it. I wasn't asking you anyway."

"Okay, you two. We'll see, Jay. Right now, just get your bath."

The phone rang. Nat almost broke the glass as she sat it down a bit too hard on the counter and ran to answer.

I wondered if it was Yani calling to check up on us.

"Daddy, it's Auntie," Nat said as she handed the phone to me.

"Hello?"

"I'm just calling to check on you guys. How are the kids? Did you guys eat? Are they giving you a hard time?"

"Everyone is fine. I cooked dinner. And I'm pretty sure I'm capable of keeping things under control."

"I didn't mean anything by it."

"I know that. You're just concerned."

"Have you talked to Yani today?"

"No, we talked late last night."

"Did everything go well with the closing?"

"Yep." There was a pause.

"So, what did she say? When is she coming home?"

"Your guess is as good as mine right about now."

"What does that mean?"

"Look, I can't really talk right now. Let me get the kids situated and I'll try to give you a call you back."

"Oh, don't worry about it. I'll just call Yani on her cell. You know if you need anything all you have to do is just call."

"I know and I will. Good night, Asia." I hung up the phone and climbed the stairs for the sanctuary that was our room. I lay across the bed and wondered if this day would come to a close without me hearing from my wife.

# *Yani*

## CHAPTER 50

I sat in PF Chang's across from Jarrin, enjoying an order of lettuce wraps while we waited for our entrees.

"I can't get over how good you look. Yellow is very becoming on you," he complimented about the yellow linen pants with a matching yellow, sleeveless, mock turtleneck sweater I was wearing.

"You don't look so bad yourself," I said as I checked him out. Other than a few gray hairs that had started to invade the soft curls at his temples, he seemed almost as fit as the day we got married. His dark gray slacks coordinated well with the black, short-sleeve cotton shirt.

Before I got too caught up in admiring Jarrin, the waitress with the 100-watt smile approached our table with a tray of plates. "Okay, lemon pepper shrimp, Chang's spicy chicken, shrimp fried rice, and Chinese vegetables. Can I get you anything else?" she asked as she finished placing everything on the table.

"I think we're fine for now, Noel," Jarrin said. Noel flashed her smile once more and left us to our meal.

"How long has this place been here?" Jarrin asked as he took a helping from each dish and piled it on his plate.

"For a little while now, I think. I've only been here once though." I thought of the night that Carmen recommended Alex and I go. I'd been dying to come back ever since then. Never in a million years would I have imagined that my return visit would be with Jarrin.

"The food is delicious!" I shook my head in agreement.

I began to think about Alex. I wondered what he was doing at that very moment. Suddenly I was filled with guilt as I thought about what I was doing. I mean, how would I feel if I got back to New York and found out that he'd taken Taylor out to dinner? The food in my mouth seemed to feel as though it were expanding with every chomp from my teeth. Making it hard to swallow.

"So, how long are you going to be here?" I blurted out in an attempt to take my mind off Alex.

"Not long. There's a few things that I need to take care of and then I'm out."

"And just where is it that you're *out* to?" I took a sip of my tea.

"That I haven't decided on yet."

Seeing that I wasn't getting anywhere with my line of questioning, I decided to drop it until we were in a place with a little more privacy. The rest of dinner was eaten with small talk sprinkled in here and there.

As we stood at the valet stand waiting for the car, he grabbed my hand. My mind reprimanded me. Screamed that I should remove my hand from his, but those familiar feelings made it hard to do.

"How are the kids, Yani?" I tried to control myself from bucking my eyes open in surprise. This was the first time that he'd actually asked about them.

"They're fine now. Honestly, I thought you had forgotten about them."

"Forgotten them? How could I forget them?"

"You really don't want me to answer that."

"You know I miss them, don't you?"

"Jarrin, I really don't know anything about you anymore."

The valet pulled up and held the door for me to get in. He walked over to Jarrin's side and thanked him for the ten-dollar tip he'd handed him. He always was a good tipper. That showed me that some things were still the same.

We pulled out the parking lot and headed south on U.S. 1. I was totally shocked when he got in the turning lane on 163rd Street en route to the beach. I couldn't help but smile as I thought about the many times we'd traveled this same road before. Sensing my melancholy feelings, Jarrin reached over and squeezed my hand in a gesture that let me know that he too remembered.

We rode silently until we got to the docks at Hallover Beach. We parked and found an empty bench near the water.

"I thought this would be a better place to talk."

I stared out at the water as a boat glided by causing the water to lap against the rocks in front of us.

"So, Mr. Miller, now can you be more specific and clear on what your plans are from this point on?"

"Baby, if I could take back the hurt and pain I must have caused you, I would in a heartbeat..."

"But you can't, so that brings us back to my question. What do you plan to do from this point on?"

"It's obvious that I can't stay here, Yani."

"That it is."

"I have a few more things to do and then I'm out of here."

"You said that before. So I'll ask you again, where is it that you're headed out to?"

"I never know until I get there. But I was hoping that this time you'd come with me."

I silently stared at the water as I played what he'd just said over in mind. He slid close to me and wrapped his arm around my shoulders.

"You know that I can't do that."

"Well, technically, you can."

"Do you realize that I've moved on? That I have another life that doesn't involve you?" I turned to face him.

"Of course I do, but I was hoping the love that we once shared is strong enough to make you overlook that. Enough to make you realize that we belong together."

"We belong together? Jarrin, it's not that simple."

"Yes, it is. I don't know if you've thought about it yet, but legally, you're still my wife. And I think being the first husband would make our marriage the legal one."

"Don't you dare go there, okay? 'Cause as far as everybody knows, you're dead and I'm thinking that's the way you'd prefer to keep it."

"You're right," he said as he smiled his overly-cocky smile. "You were always a smart one. Never could pull anything over on you."

"But you still managed to leave and keep me hanging for five years. So, I guess you can."

He turned my face so that he could look into my eyes. "I'm sorry, Yani. Before that day, leaving seemed to be unthinkable. I've loved you so long that I don't know how not to. As incomprehensible as this may sound, I don't think I can just sit by and let another man have you. I've dreamed about the day that we would make love again. When I would be able to kiss you again." He moved his face closer to mine.

His cinnamon-flavored breath invaded my nostrils as he placed a feathery kiss on the tip of my nose.

My mind was flashing red lights and warning signs, but my lips were thinking something else as he continued to place random kisses on my face.

As I parted my lips to return the kiss, my mind screamed out, "Yani, what are you doing?!"

"Not this time. I can't." I jumped up from the bench and walked closer to the rocks where the water slapped against them.

"Yani…"

"Jarrin, do you know how long I've waited for this moment? Just to know that you were okay at one point would've been all I needed. You're the one who doesn't comprehend what your leaving did. How I sat up at night and cried and prayed until my body ached." I could feel the heavy tears as they pooled in the bottom of my eyes. He walked up behind me.

"Baby, I thought about you night and day. It just wasn't safe for me to make any contact with you."

"So you feel it's safe now?"

He picked up a rock from the ground and flung it into the water.

"I'll be honest, when I saw those pictures of you and him, it bothered me. You were to supposed to love me and only me."

"How can you love someone that's not there?"

"But I'm here now." He reached out for me.

I sidestepped and walked down a bit further.

"That's beside the point. Right now my life is content. Whether you believe it or not, Jarrin, I love Alex. Very much."

"More than you love me?"

"Love you? You ought to be glad that I don't hate you right now. The love I had for you isn't the same as my love for Alex."

"Prove it."

"What?"

"Prove it. If you feel that there's nothing between us, kiss me. If you still don't feel anything after kissing me, I'll walk away and never bother you again."

"What would that prove? Kissing you has nothing to do with anything."

"My dear, a kiss has everything to do with it. Kisses don't lie." He walked closer to me again and placed his finger under my chin. He stared at me and I felt my defenses weaken.

What should I do? If I kissed him, would I be cheating on Alex? I closed my eyes and let my human instincts take over. I prayed that God would help me make the right choice. But either way I chose, it would have a profound impact on my life in one way or another I thought as I closed my eyes and puckered up.

# *Asia*

## CHAPTER 51

My cell phone seemed to ring nonstop for the first two days. Hayden had to have called every hour on the hour. I wish he'd have shown the same determination when it came to being with me in the first place.

Tiring of the constant ring, I answered.

"Hell-O!"

"Damn, Girl! Where the hell have you been?"

"Oh it's you."

"What's that supposed to mean?"

"Nothing. I just thought you were someone else. Just forget about it. What's up? Where are you?"

"I'm still in Florida."

"Still in Florida? I thought you were closing on the house and then coming right back."

"There was a slight change in plans. I had an unexpected occurrence happen."

"What the hell are you talking about?"

"You will never guess who I went to dinner with tonight."

"You are so right, so cut the bullshit and just tell me what's going on."

"I know you're going to say I'm crazy, but I just got in from a night out with Jarrin."

"With Jarrin?!"

"Yes, Jarrin."

"Yani, I hope you haven't done anything stupid. Have you forgotten about your husband here? You know, Alex?"

"Technically, Jarrin is my husband, too."

"Technically? Technically, Jarrin is an asshole who decided, for whatever reason or another, that he didn't want to be a husband and a father anymore and walked the hell away."

"That's not the reason he left."

"So says Jarrin, right? Yani, for what it's worth, I love you and I know how you felt about Jarrin, but I'm begging you...please, please think this over. Alex is a good man, and those are hard to come by these days. Believe me, I know. You have too much at stake here. What happens if Jarrin decides to pull another disappearing act? Have you thought about that?"

"I haven't made any decisions. All we did was talk."

"And what about the kids? How do you think this is going to sit with them? I don't think they're going to be as forgiving as you seem to be about this situation. They love Alex, Yani, and he loves them. And let's not forget how much he loves you, crazy ass girl. Why the fuck would you even entertain the thought of Jarrin?" I was vexed with her.

"Who said I was entertaining anything with Jarrin?"

"Uhh, hello…Did you not just say that you had dinner with him?"

I knew Yani was getting pissed with me, but I had to make her come to her senses.

"Girl, what are you thinking? Here you have a man that's ready to give you the world on a platter if you so desired and I can't find a man who's willing to give me just a lil' bit of his time. You want to throw that away on a selfish, insensitive asshole?! Who, when he was married to you, gave you nothing but grief. And what the hell was his excuse for leaving anyway? It has to be a doozy, because he's definitely fooled your ass with it."

"It's a long story."

"I hope so. I mean, five years? Lots of things happen in five years. Did you ever think to ask him who's been keeping him company during that time? You know there's no way that he's been practicing the same celibate lifestyle you were before Alex came along."

"I'm not that damn stupid, Asia."

"If he told you he's been celibate all this time and you believed him, then you are that stupid."

"Look, I need to call Alex and check on the kids. I just wanted to tell you what was going on."

"Thanks for sharing." I was so upset with her, I

hung up the phone on her. I can't believe she's that damn gullible. I snatched the phone up and dialed my mother.

"Hello?"

"Hey Ma, it's Asia."

"So Yani called you?"

"You know about this?"

"Of course I do. Have you forgotten that I raised you girls to talk to me about any and everything."

"Ma, please tell me that she's not seriously thinking about going back to that asshole?"

"They went out to eat and talk is all I got from it."

"Have you seen him?"

"Now you know he's not gonna show his face around here until he's smoothed everything over with her."

"Ma, don't let him come there. Make her ass keep meeting him in the damn street somewhere." I was livid.

"Don't worry, she'll come to her senses. I know I didn't raise either one of my girls to be fools."

"Remember this is Jarrin we're talking about. If he isn't a snake, my name isn't Asia Fenton."

"Well, it's up to Yani to make the right decision, Baby. Jarrin can't make her do anything she doesn't want to do. Let's just pray she has all her senses about her when she's dealing with him."

"Oh, I'll not only be praying, I'll be begging, too. If that fails, I'll be on the next plane to come down there and kick some sense into her ass."

"Calm down now." She laughed.

"Sorry, Ma."

We talked a few more minutes and then said good night.

Later as I prepared to climb into bed, I did something I hadn't done in years. I kneeled down on the side of my bed and prayed.

"Lord, please give my sister the hindsight to see that if she leaves Alex for Jarrin that she'll be making the biggest mistake of her life. Please bring her back *here* where she belongs. To the man that really loves her. And while you're at it, please help me sort out this mess of a life that I'm living. Amen."

# *Alex*

## CHAPTER 52

"Hello?"

"Hi."

"Yani?" I sat up and looked over at the clock on the nightstand. It was two in the morning. This was the first time we'd talked all day.

"I'm sorry to wake you. I…"

"It's okay, Baby. I wasn't really sleeping. How did things go today?"

"What things?"

"Didn't you close on the house?"

"Oh that. Yeah. Everything is taken care of."

"That's good." I skirted around the question that I really wanted an answer to. I would give her a chance to bring it up.

"How are the kids?"

"They're fine. Sleeping of course."

"What did you guys do today?"

"Nothing really. I cooked dinner and then we played a couple of board games."

"What did you cook?" She perked up a little.

"My famous lasagna."

"Really? Did you eat it all?"

"I had to tell them to slow down so we could save you some."

"That was sweet of you." I could hear the smile in her voice.

"So, when are you coming home?"

She paused for a second. "Right now I don't know."

"And why is that? You said you closed on the house. What else is there for you to do there?" I could feel my anger begin to surface.

"I was thinking about spending the weekend here."

We were both silent for a moment. I had to process the information before I said the wrong thing.

"So, you've forgotten all about the event this weekend?"

"What event?"

"What event? One of the most important events of my life, besides the day we got married, and you ask what event? The premiere, Yani. It's this Saturday. I would like to have *my wife* on my arm when I walk down the red carpet. I mean, it's only right, don't you think?"

"Oh, Baby. I totally forgot."

"So I see. Are you okay?"

"Of course, I'm okay. Why wouldn't I be?"

"I don't know. Why don't you tell me?"

"There's nothing to tell, Baby. I'm fine."

"So why does it feel like this conversation is strained?"

"Strained how?"

"I feel like you're not telling me something."

"You know what? I'm tired and I don't feel like going through this. I'll call tomorrow to try and get a flight back so I can be there for your premiere, okay?"

"Hey, don't do me any favors. If you want to spend the weekend there, go right ahead."

"So now you're telling me what to do?"

Just that quick we'd gone from lovey-dovey to on the brink of yelling.

"No, I'm not telling you what to do, Yani, but it seems to me that you have a lot on your mind and if you need time to think things out, I'm willing to give you that. Just remember one thing…"

"What's that?"

"I love you, but I'm not willing to be on standby forever while you try to figure out who you want the most."

"Can we talk tomorrow?"

"No problem."

"I love you, Alex. You do know that?" she pleaded.

"Of course I do, Baby. The question is how much?"

I hung up the phone and sat up straight and stared into the darkness.

I got up and looked out the window at the deserted street. The first signs of fall were becoming evident in the trees as the green leaves started to change colors.

"Damn it, Yani! What am I going to do?" I ran my fingers front to back through my hair.

I needed to talk to someone and find out what rights I had. Find out if I had married another man's wife.

❤❤❤❤

"So you're telling me that the husband that she thought was dead has now returned?"

"That's exactly what I'm telling you."

"Has he told her what he wants? I mean, for a man to be gone the amount of time he has, there has to be a reason for him to come back all of a sudden."

"I'm not sure if he's told her or not. She hasn't told me."

"You want me to check him out? You know I've got a few connections down at the bureau." Ed stood up and walked over to the phone on my desk.

"Thanks for the offer, but the ball is completely in her court. Whichever way she chooses, I'll respect that."

"That's bullshit, man. You know that if she dumps you for him, there's going to be hell to pay." Ed sat back down.

"I'm telling you it's not like that. I'm willing to bow out gracefully if she decides that she wants to be with him. I may not like it and yes, my ego may be a lil' bruised, but I'll respect her choice."

"That makes you a better man than me. Cause a niggah like me would want to kill both of their asses. No questions asked."

"Now if I was to kill him, I'd always know that it was him that she wanted."

"I don't give a damn. Man, I've never seen you as happy as you've been with Yani. That is, before the *other husband* showed back up. So there's no way that I see you just walking away without any kind of fight."

I twirled the pen through my fingers as I thought about what he was saying. Would it come down to being a fight?

I let out a breath. "I don't know, man. I never thought I'd be married to another man's wife. This is some type of shit you either read about or see in the movies."

"You always were a drama magnet. I never thought you'd top the drama queen, though." Ed laughed. I tossed the pen in his direction.

"Please don't even mention her name. She just may show up." We both laughed this time.

Ed stood to leave. "Well, man, whatever happens, you know I've got your back."

"Oh, for sure." We gave each other a brotherly hug before he walked out of my office. I closed the door and sat back down and thought about the dilemma that had become my life. What would I do if she chose to stay with him?

# Yani

## CHAPTER 53

A gainst the judgment of all involved, I called the airline and changed my departure date. If anything, I needed to take some time and sort things out. I wasn't about to go back to New York with this monkey on my back.

Jarrin had been calling constantly, while Alex seemed to avoid me all together. Whenever I called, he was always out or too busy to talk.

"Hi, Mommy!"

"Hi, Baby. You miss me?"

"Of course I do. When are you coming home?"

"I'll be home Sunday. Where's Daddy?"

"He's not here. You wanna' speak to Nat?"

"Yeah, put her on the phone. I love you, Jay."

"Love you, too, Mommy." He dropped the phone on the counter and screamed for Natalia. A few seconds later she picked up.

"Hi, Mommy," she said breathless. She was more than likely downstairs glued to the television.

"Hey, Sweetie. How's everything?"

"Everything is fine. So when are you coming home? You know we all miss you?"

"Who is we? You and Jay?"

"Me, Jay, and Daddy. Remember that he has his big event this Saturday so that's the only reason he's been busy. Have you decided what you're going to wear Saturday?"

"I don't think I'll be home in time to go."

"What are you talking about?"

"I probably won't be back until Sunday."

"Mommy, you have to go. What's it gonna look like if he shows up alone?"

"I can't get a flight back until Sunday." I felt horrible for telling that lie.

"Now, Mommy, you know Daddy'll charter a plane for you, if that's the only thing that's keeping you from getting here."

"It's a little more complicated than that. I have something that I really need to do here."

"Aiight then," she said in the best New York accent she could muster up. I laughed. In an attempt to fit in, she stood in the mirror and practiced every day.

"Natalia, I need to talk to you about something."

"Sure, Mommy. What's up?"

"What would you think if I were to tell you that your dad has come back? Would you want to see him?"

"What are you talking about? Daddy isn't gone anywhere."

"I'm not talking about Alex." The line went silent. So silent that I thought she'd hung up for a moment.

"Nat?"

"I don't know, Mommy. I'm happy with the way things are. We love Alex and as far as I'm concerned, he *is* my dad and I'm sure I can guarantee you that Jay feels the same."

"Okay, sweetie."

"He's there, isn't he?"

"Who's where?" I leaned back on the sofa.

"Come on, Mommy. You know who I'm talking about. Is he there in Florida?" It was my turn to hesitate. I stared out my reflection as I thought about whether or not I should tell my child the truth.

"Mommy?"

"Yes, he's here."

"Is that why you're not back?"

"It's difficult, Nat. I mean he is your father."

"Maybe to you, but not to me. In my mind, he's dead. He's been dead. The only thing he did for me and Jay was donate the sperm."

"Natalia Miller! When did you start talking that way?"

"Oh please. I'll be fifteen soon, Mommy. I do know how babies are made." No matter how I tried to fight it, my baby was growing up.

"Mommy, I remember what it was like before Daddy came into our lives and I don't ever want it to be like that again."

"Me either, sweetie. Look, I'll talk to you later. Tell your daddy I called and I'll try him later tonight."

"Mommy?"

"Yes, Nat?"

"In order to move forward you have to stop looking back. I read that in one of Iyanla Vanzant's books."

"What am I going to do with you?" I laughed.

"Just come home. We really need you."

"Okay, Baby."

❤❤❤❤

As I walked through the lobby of the Radisson Bahia Mar in Fort Lauderdale, the words my daughter had said to me before we hung up played over and over in my mind. I realized that once I'd let go of the idea of Jarrin coming back to us, I'd made room so that my blessings could come in. And that blessing had been Alex. Now, due to poor judgment and mixed emotions I was about to lose that blessing. I knew what I had to do.

I smiled as the bellhop greeted me. I kept walking until I reached the elevators. I pushed the button for the third floor and stared at the doors as I thought

of what I was going to say to Jarrin. I knew nothing
would ever be the same again. I just prayed that he
would realize it, too. The bell sounded my arrival.
I pulled my purse up on my shoulder and fixed my
shirt. I looked at the numbers on the wall that
would lead me in the right direction. The closer I
got to the room, the larger the knot in my stomach
got. At one point I was almost tempted to run back
to the elevator and just ride back down to the lobby
and leave, but I had to do this. I refused to live the
rest of my life with regrets. I'd done that long enough.

I stood in front of the door that displayed the
same number that I'd seen on the slip of paper I'd
found in the car. I took a deep breath and then
knocked. After a few seconds, clad only in a white
standard hotel towel, Jarrin answered. His eyes
displayed his surprise to find me standing on the
other side.

"Yani? Wha-what are you doing here?"

I smiled. "I thought I'd surprise you. Surprise!"
He stood there with his mouth open as I fought
back my nerves.

"Aren't you going to invite me in? I really feel
that we need to talk." As I stepped forward in an
attempt to enter the room, a little boy walked up
behind Jarrin and wrapped his arms around his
legs. He peeked around to get a better look at me.

"Daddy, who's that?" he asked. I looked up as Jarrin closed his eyes and said what must have been a silent prayer.

"Daddy?" Oh, now you know my black ass was about to raise pure hell up in here.

"**Y**ou could've at least read the card before you chucked them," Angie said as she walked in on me throwing out a box of Godiva chocolates.

"For what? It only says what I already know. How sorry his ass is."

"Girl, you're cruel." She laughed.

"I like to think of it as being smart. What are you doing here anyway? I thought you were meeting with a client this morning?"

"They canceled, but I'm going to leave early so I can find something to wear for tomorrow night. You got your dress?"

"I've been so preoccupied with other things that I haven't had time to look for one." I went though the messages on my desk.

Angie sat in the chair across from my desk and crossed her legs. Her bob swayed as she cocked her head to the side. An indication that she wanted detailed information as to what was going on.

I looked up at her. "I don't have the time, Angie. Maybe later."

"Okay." She threw her hands in the air and stood up.

"Thank you," I said. Avoiding eye contact with her, I dug around in my bag for nothing. As much as I loved Angie, she was a gossip tree. If you wanted to know the dirt on anyone, she was the woman for the job.

"I guess I'll come back when you're in a better mood."

"Umm hmm. I think that would be best." I sat at my desk and opened my email. I had twenty-four emails in my inbox waiting for my attention.

"Asia…" Betty buzzed in.

"Yes?"

"Your brother-in-law is on line one."

I almost made the mistake and asked which one, but I knew there was no way in hell Jarrin would even think to call me. I pressed the button next to the flashing light.

"Hey, Alex."

"So you knew it was me?"

"What other brother-in-law do I have?"

"After what your sister is pulling, I think the count is up to two. As you probably already know, the dead one has come back to life."

"Please, don't remind me. I think I've had a migraine ever since we had that conversation. Have you talked to her?"

"I haven't talked to her in a couple of days."

"So, what are you gonna do about this?"

"Do about what?"

"Shit, about this whole situation."

"What can I do?"

"You can get off your ass and go and get your wife and bring her back here where she belongs." I couldn't believe how nonchalant he was being about this.

"Asia, this is a decision that Yani has to make. Of course I could fly down and drag her back here, but I would forever wonder if she was here because she loved me more than him and wanted to be here, or was she here because I gave her no choice."

"My stupid-ass sister has to be the luckiest woman alive. She has a man that loves her enough to give her space to be with a man that she once gave up a part of her life for. You do know that other than you, he's the only other man Yani has ever been with?"

"Yeah, I know. So what's up with Hayden?"

"Don't try and jump to another issue. And for the record, I guess you can say Hayden is history."

"What happened?"

"I think a man should be able to tell you when he's involved with another woman and especially when that woman is pregnant with his child."

"Damn, that's serious."

"You just don't know."

"I guess I should stop my pity party then."

"Oh, yours is a little more involved than mine and you definitely deserve to have one. So I ain't mad at you."

"So what's your point of view on this bullshit?" I knew it had to be hurting him.

"Honestly, I don't understand why Yani would ever talk to him again, let alone entertain anything he's suggested, but that's just me. I hold grudges." I sat back in my chair.

"I love her, Asia," he said in a most humble tone.

"I know you do. And believe me, she loves you."

"But what am I supposed to do? Sit back and let her play me like a fool? Next to our wedding, Saturday is one of the most important events of my life and she's not sure she's going to make it? What kind of shit is that?"

"Bullshit." We both laughed.

"What kind of relationship did they have? Was he abusive to her? Did he have some kind of hold over her?"

"He'd never been physically abusive that I know of. If he was, she never told me. And you know we talk about *everything*. But he had a way of getting her to believe anything he told her. I think that's the problem. She didn't really go into detail, but he's told her some cockamamie-ass story about why he left and I think he's working overtime trying to get her to buy into it."

"You know she told Natalia that he's in Florida?"

"No?!"

"Yes. She mentioned it to me, but reassured me that I was the only daddy she ever needs."

"See, that right there should be encouragement enough."

"It could be either or. I mean, for Yani to mention it to Natalia means that she's contemplating about letting him see them."

"Stop worrying. My sister is crazy sometimes, but she's never been stupid. My mother didn't allow it in her house. Now you make sure that your shit is tight for Saturday night. Yani'll be back here and everything will be okay."

"I sure hope you're right."

"Believe me if anybody knows my sister, it's me. I promise you that everything will be fine."

After hanging up with Alex, I dialed Carmen's number to see if I could talk some sense into my sister's head. I couldn't just stand by and let Jarrin ruin her life a second time.

"Hey, Carmen. How are things down there?"

"Asia? Hey, Girl. Things are pretty much the same.

And if you're looking for Yani, which I know you are, she's out."

"With him?"

"Maybe. I'm pretty sure she is."

"We've got to talk some sense into her head. She's about to mess up big time and we can't let her do it."

"I've talked to her up one way and down another. She keeps promising me that everything will be okay and that I just have to trust that she'll make the right decision."

"Right decision? What decision is there to make? You need to tell her to bring her ass home!" I began to worry.

"Asia, you weren't here with Yani as she damn near drove herself crazy worrying and wondering about Jarrin. I feel that she needs this time if for nothing else to bring some closure to this whole fiasco."

"I may not have been there physically, but I did my share of late-night phone calls and crying sessions. Just give her this message for me—while she's down there looking for closure, she's about to get some up here." I angrily slammed the phone down. As I sat there and fumed, I realized that I had taken my anger out on the wrong person. I picked up the phone and hit the redial button.

"Yes, Asia."

"I'm sorry. It's just…"

"Believe me, I know. I've been there and back, but we just have to realize that Yani is the one that has to live with this. Bryce and I have called and talked with Alex to reassure him that things would be okay. And I'm telling you like I told him, things have a way of working themselves out for the better. So, just believe that she will make the right choice."

"If you say so. Just make sure to tell her that I called."

"I will."

I hung up and sat back and stared at my computer screen. I hoped like hell that Carmen was right. I'd hate to see my sister ruin her life a second time behind Jarrin.

# Yani

## CHAPTER 55

"Daddy? He did just say Daddy?" I asked again.

"Let me explain."

"I'm listening." Arms crossed over my chest, I leaned back slightly and gave him a look that said in more ways than one that I was beyond pissed. Before he could open his mouth a little girl who looked to be a few years older came to the door.

"Jay, Mommy wants you." She pried his hands from around Jarrin's legs.

"Stop, Nya!"

"Jay and Nya?" I asked as I looked down at the butterscotch-colored children.

The kids looked up at me. I began to laugh as I stood in front of his attempt to duplicate our family.

"Who is that, Daddy?" Nya asked this time. I bent down and stared into two sets of questioning eyes.

"Hi, Nya and Jay. I'm Yani."

"Hi, Yani," they both said.

"Nya, how old are you?"

"I'm five, almost six," the little girl said as she smiled displaying the missing space that once housed her two front teeth.

"I'm three years old!" Jay said in what was unmistakably a baby's voice as he held up two fingers on one hand and one on the other.

"Three? Wow, you're a big boy. You know, I have a son and it just so happens that I call him Jay."

"Really?" they both asked.

"I sure do." This time I looked up at Jarrin who seemed to be at a temporary loss for words.

"Jay has the same name as Daddy. Isn't that right, Daddy?" I stood back up and looked at Jarrin.

"What's taking you two…" The voice was attached to a face that seemed familiar. The jacked weave do was a telltale sign that I didn't know her from any of the circles that he and I once hung in. The women I knew would never walk around with their tracks showing like hers. Her dark eyes registered that she knew exactly who I was. I wasn't quite able to place a name to it.

"Mommy, this is Yani and she has a son name Jay, too! Just like me," he excitedly told his mother.

Feeling that I was going to go ballistic or something, she protectively scooped little Jay up in her arms and swiftly grabbed Nya by the hand as she kept her eyes on me.

"Come on, guys. Daddy needs to talk to Ms. Yani." She eased her way back into the room out of sight.

"Yani, let me put something on and we can go someplace and talk about this," Jarrin said, bringing me out the trance I had temporarily slipped into.

"Talk about what? There's really nothing to talk about. Actually, I came to tell you goodbye. A wise little birdie said something to me today and made me see things ever so clearly. That when it comes to you and me, there is no us. Those days are long gone. And this little thing here," I waved my index finger in a back and forth motion, "this was just the icing on the cake."

"Look, I…" I threw my hand up to stop him.

"Save it for someone who cares. I've heard enough of your lies. Damn, I'll just duplicate my family; that way I won't miss them!" I said in a mocking voice. "Oh, and don't think I missed the fact that your little girl said she'd be six soon. That means that your lil' girlfriend was pregnant before you skipped town. You were in such a rush to leave that you left your wife and children without saying goodbye. But yet you had time enough to pick up your pregnant girlfriend." I laughed at the irony.

"Yani, I need…" He reached out and grabbed for me. I sidestepped him.

"Need what?"

"The bag with…"

"Oh please. You can't possibly think I'm that damn gullible. Give it to you so you, your bitch and your lil' bastards can live high off the hog on money you made while putting me and my kids' lives in jeopardy? I don't think so. I guess the fugitive life was a little harder than you expected it to be."

"But you don't need it." I could see the frustration in his hazel eyes.

"Fuck what I need! It's not about that anymore! Now it's about what you owe me, niggah. And unless you've got a time machine stashed somewhere, I suggest you shut the hell up. Now if you wanna call my bluff on it, I guarantee you'll be sacrificing a lot more than money in the long run. Hmm, I wonder who wants you more…the Feds, or the niggahs that went to jail after you left them high and dry? I'm thinking the latter would pay a much bigger price." I looked at my hands as I pretended they were scales.

"You wouldn't?"

"Muthafucka, try me," I said through gritted teeth. Sensing the reality of my threat, he reached for me, but I sidestepped him. He looked at me as if he wanted to say something, but abandoned the thought after he observed the look on my face. My lip curled up at the corner, giving an indication of my disgust with him.

"For years I almost killed myself wondering whether or not you were dead. Now, I know you are. At least to me and the children we had together, you are." As I turned to leave, the woman came back to the door and stood at his side. I stopped and looked at her long and hard as my memory kicked in and I finally remembered where I'd seen her before.

"I guess this means that you'll be back giving lap dances. I hope you can still do that trick you used to do with the champagne bottle, 'cause you're going to need those extra tips." She rolled her eyes as I turned and walked off and left them standing in the doorway.

The elevator doors opened as soon as I pressed the button. As I looked back down the hall I could see Jarrin rush inside the room. I guess he was going to put something on and meet me downstairs before I left. I pressed the button to close the doors and pulled my keys out of my purse as I waited to reach the lobby. I was happy to see that my car was still parked at the curb when I got outside. I gave the valet a hefty tip and jumped in and sped off.

As I sat at the light waiting for the traffic to ease up enough to allow me a chance to jump in, I glanced out my rearview mirror and saw what looked to be Jarrin talking to the valet. The guy pointed in my direction and Jarrin took off in a slight jog.

"Good-bye, Jarrin," I mouthed as I pulled into traffic and sped away down the SE 17th Street Causeway away from my past.

# *Asia*

## CHAPTER 56

"Are you serious?"

"As a heart attack, Girl."

"What I wouldn't have given to be a fly on the wall," Carmen said as she laughed loudly.

"You and me both. They probably would've swallowed me as close as I would've been." We all laughed.

"And you're sure it's the girl that danced at Wallace's party?" I asked.

"Damn sure."

"Which one?" Carmen asked.

"The one that picked the bottle up and drained it. You know, the one we said had a tipsy pussy. I guess when he couldn't get me to try it, he went and got the original."

"He wanted you to do that?!" Carmen asked.

"Your ass is crazy, Yani," I said.

"She had me scared there for a minute though, Asia. She was acting like a teenager around here," Carmen said.

"That makes two of us, Carmen. Shit, three actually. Alex was calling me for advice."

"All right, you two. I feel bad enough about the situation. I thought you knew me better than that. I'm not that stupid."

"You were teetering the stupid scale kinda hard there."

"Damn near tipping it over, you mean," Carmen chimed in.

We laughed a little more and then calmed down.

"What time does your flight get in?"

"Tomorrow evening. I'll have just enough time to hit the red carpet."

"Have you called Alex yet?"

"No. I want to surprise him."

"What about a dress?"

"Everything is already taken care of. I'm going to Nita to get my hair done early tomorrow morning before I leave. Then I'm gonna run over to this boutique over on South Beach that carries designer dresses and get something to wear."

"Then I'll just send a car to pick you up and drop you off at the theater."

"Oh, I wish I could be there," Carmen said.

"Why don't you fly with Yani? I don't think Bryce would mind."

"Matter of fact, why don't both of you come?

Alex would love to see you guys. And you haven't made a trip to our place yet," Yani said.

"We can't. It's too last-minute. We would need to find someone to stay with the kids and…"

"Now you know Mama will watch them."

"I'd love to jump at the chance, but the baby would give her a hard time. Besides, you haven't seen Alex in five days. You're going to be too busy having make-up sex that you're not going to want us tagging along."

"Look, I gotta go. Carmen, if you guys do decide to come up you can stay with me. Yani, I'll see you tomorrow night. I love you guys."

"Love you, too," they both said.

"Asia, I'm sorry for not being there when you needed someone to talk to, but I promise I'll make it up to you when I get back."

"Hey, I understand. I'll see you when you get here tomorrow."

I thanked the Lord that He'd heard at least one of my prayers as I hung up the phone.

❤❤❤

I dug my cell phone out my bag to call Linda to see what time she would be ready.

"So are we still on for tonight?" I asked.

"I'll meet you outside the theater."

"That'll work."

"So how's everything else going?"

I knew she wanted to talk about what happened with Hayden.

"Look, it's not your fault, Linda. How would you have known that things would've progressed as rapidly as they did?"

"I know, but I do feel like I'm somewhat at fault. If I had only kept my nose out of it."

"But that's not in your nature. Besides, for a short time, I enjoyed some of the best sex I've had in a long time." We both laughed.

"You are so crazy, Girl."

"I'll see you tonight."

"All right. Thanks for inviting me."

"Now how could I go to something as important as this and not invite my ace?"

After saying goodbye one last time, I hit the end button on my cell and walked into the building on Madison Avenue that housed Gazelle's. I got in the elevator and instructed the attendant that I wanted to go to the fourteenth floor.

The young receptionist buzzed me in and greeted me with her warm smile.

"Hi, Asia. Cynthia is waiting for you. Why don't you go in and get undressed and she'll be right in to get you."

Familiar with the layout, I walked over to the ladies room so that I could slip into my bathing suit and the complimentary robe they provided. I walked a short distance to another room to wait for Cynthia. I poured myself a glass of water and dropped a slice of lemon in to freshen the taste.

I was surprised to find that I was the only one there on a Saturday morning. *Better for me*, I thought as I sat down in the reclining chair.

I was scheduled to have the works done today. I was getting a full body massage, a facial, a manicure, a pedicure, and my hair and makeup done.

Since I would be going solo tonight, I had to make sure I looked my best. With the press that we'd set up for this thing, the paparazzi would be out in force. I'd rather have my name mentioned for how stunning I looked instead of how I showed up alone.

We'd all agreed to wear something in the silver family. I picked up a sultry strapless dress by Vera Wang. The gem-encrusted top had rows of rhinestones that went around it in a horizontal pattern, while the satin bottom half-flared at the hip and draped to the floor. I even had a matching wrap in case it got a little chilly.

I'd found a perfect pair of square diamond earrings that complemented the medium-length flip style I'd chosen to wear. My hair was at that in-between stage after wearing a short cut for a couple of years. So this style was the safest way to go.

Just as I'd predicted, two hours later, I was back on Madison flagging down a cab.

I pulled my jacket closer around me as the cab stopped in front of me. I climbed in the back and told him my destination. As he pulled away from the curb, I sat back and inspected my nails. Usually I wear a French manicure, but I went with a nice soft shade of silver today. Everything was about coordination.

I carefully pulled my Palm Pilot out so I could check my "To Do List" as I headed back to Brooklyn. I checked off the spa and the car. I called the company first thing this morning. I'd laid out what I was wearing before I left out. So, that was something else I could check off my list. I'd made all the last-minute phone calls on my list, too. I placed the pencil back in place and slipped my Palm Pilot back into my bag. I smiled as I realized I was ahead of the game. Hopefully the day would continue like this and the night would go off without a hitch.

I thought about Hayden and the last conversation we had. I wondered if he was telling the truth about his situation. God, I missed him. Things seemed to be going so perfect for us. I'd planned to have him at my side tonight. I even thought about calling him later to still invite him, but the possibility of her answering his phone caused me to push it out of my mind.

He'd made things more difficult than they had to be. All he had to do was be honest with me. But what if he had told me everything? Would I have been willing to deal with it?

I guess I'll wonder about that for years to come. Just like I wondered for years how things would've been if we had gotten married.

I don't know. Maybe I wouldn't hold this grudge forever. Life is definitely too short to walk around being mad about something you had no control over to begin with.

I picked up my cell and punched in his number. I held my breath as I waited for someone to pick up. Be it him or her. His answering service kicked in. I was about to hang up, but decided not to.

As his sexy outgoing message ended, I cleared my throat.

"Hi, Hayden. It's Asia. I just wanted to let you know that..." I paused for a moment. "That I'm sorry things went the way they did. Hopefully you'll find a woman that deserves your love. One that you'll be willing to give your undivided attention to. Especially since I couldn't get it either time. Know that I don't hate you. Maybe one day our paths may cross again. Even though I don't think it'll be anytime soon. Just know that I loved you. Maybe I always will in some sort of way." I smiled as I hung up.

"I guess this is what closure feels like."

# Alex

## CHAPTER 57

I came downstairs to an awaiting audience. Natalia and Jay clapped and whistled as I spun around and modeled for them.

"Wow! You look smooth," Jay said.

"I knew this was going to be tight," Natalia beamed as she checked out the ensemble she helped put together. The black Armani suit was accented with a metallic silver shirt and tie.

"I think you seriously have a career opportunity in the fashion industry, young lady." I kissed her on the forehead.

I searched my pockets and made sure I had everything I would need tonight. A car horn honked outside. Jay ran over to the window and peeked out.

"Whoa! A stretch limo!" He ran to the door and opened it.

"If you guys need me just call my cell. Just remember to give me a few minutes to call back."

"Don't worry about us. We're old enough, and

smart enough to fend for ourselves for a few hours or more. You go and have a good time," Natalia said as she pushed me toward the door.

"Okay, just make sure…"

"Not to open the door for anyone, don't tell anyone that we're home alone, and no company," they chimed in.

I smiled and kissed them goodbye. "See you guys later."

"Bye." They stood on the porch and waited for me to climb in the limo and pull away before they walked back into the house.

As we sat at a light, I watched a couple cross in front of the car. From the smiles on their faces and the way they hugged and kissed, it was obvious that they were in love. I really began to miss Yani. Even though I had missed her calls on purpose, I prayed every night that whatever choice she made, it would be the life she had with me.

We pulled up to the Ziegfeld and joined the line of other cars that were unloading passengers. I adjusted my tie one last time, knowing that I would exit the car to a barrage of flashes and the prying eyes of onlookers out to get a glimpse of a star. Even though to them I was going to be a nobody compared to the list of who's who that was going to be there.

Before my car reached the red carpet, I decided

to get out and walk down. Just as my foot touched the red carpet, a slender arm entwined with mine. I looked to find Taylor at my side; all smiles for the camera.

Not wanting to draw more attention than necessary, I plastered on a smile and escorted Taylor quietly inside the theater. The last thing I needed was a picture of me and my ex engaged in what would look to be a lover's quarrel.

"So where's the wifey? Don't tell me there's trouble in paradise already," Taylor asked sarcastically.

"I hope you enjoy the movie," I said as I released myself from her grip.

"Oh, Alex, come on now. What harm is there in two old friends enjoying each other's company?"

"I didn't know we were friends. Last time I saw you, you were calling me everything but a child of God."

She smirked. "I'll admit that my behavior was a bit childish, but come on—I was upset and jealous when I found out you were marrying someone else. But, I'm over that now." She smiled brightly.

"That's good to hear, I guess." Not that it made any difference to me one way or another.

I glanced around at the other couples and thought about Yani. I wondered if she was thinking about me or was she out with Jarrin trying to rekindle what they once shared.

"Earth to Alex." Taylor waved her hand in front of my eyes.

I looked at her and smiled. At that moment, being with her didn't feel as bad as it did initially. The guilt slid out of mind with the thought of Yani being with Jarrin while I was here in limbo. She had let me down in a serious way when she refused to return for this. An old saying ran through my mind as I looked at Taylor.

*If you can't be with the one you love, then love the one you're with.*

"Are you okay?"

"I'm cool. Ready to go in?"

Shocked, Taylor asked, "Are you inviting me to sit with you?"

"What happened to you and I being old friends?"

"Lead us to our seats."

# *Asia*

## CHAPTER 58

I stood at the gate awaiting Yani's arrival. Her flight had been delayed. I knew I should've let her catch a cab like she'd offered, but being the dutiful sister that I am, I opted to pick her up so she would have someone there waiting for her. I called Linda and told her that I would meet her at the theater.

I don't know why Yani didn't just call Alex and have him charter a plane. As much as he wanted her to be with him tonight, he probably would've flown the plane himself. But there I stood, four hours later as my sister tramped down the ramp looking exhausted and worn out.

"Hey, Asia. I'm so sorry about this." She shifted the garment bag she was carrying to her other arm as she leaned in to hug me.

"It's nothing. There'll be other premieres to go to."

"I just want to get my luggage so I can get home to my husband and children." She swung her carry-on bag high up on her shoulder.

We went down to baggage claim and grabbed her luggage and headed home to Brooklyn from JFK.

"I'm stopping by my place first so I can change. I'm gonna hit Metro Nome tonight."

Yani laid her head back on the headrest and looked out the window. Her disappointment at missing the event showed on her face.

"I changed into my jeans once they announced the delay. I got plenty of compliments on my dress though. Too bad my baby didn't get to see me."

"Don't worry. Alex didn't know you were coming anyway, so he'll still be excited about seeing you when he gets home."

"I know, but I feel like I let him down."

A song by a new artist was playing on the radio. She sung a song about falling in love with another man. Yani sat up and turned the volume up.

"Who is this?"

"I think her name is Michelle Valentine. She's been hitting rotation pretty hard for the past week."

"No wonder why. How many women have been in a bullshit relationship only to start getting attention from another man and find herself in the situation she's singing about?" Yani rocked her head back and forth to the slow tantalizing beat.

"You've been in love with three men in your life and one of them was Daddy, so what are you talking about?" I teased her.

"I didn't necessarily say myself. But this lil' incident I just went through was almost what she's singing about. I mean, I fell in love with Alex after Jarrin was lacking."

"Lacking? Girl, he was doing a lot more than lacking." We both laughed.

"But I really think she's singing about something altogether different from your situation."

"I'm going to buy this tomorrow," she said as she closed her eyes and swayed her head to the song.

I exited on Rockaway and made my way over to Seaview past Canarsie Park. A few minutes later we pulled in front of my place. Unbelievably, I found a spot to park almost in front of my door.

"Come on. I won't take long."

Yani climbed out my car and followed me up the mountain of stairs that led to my front door.

"This is why your ass is in such good shape. I know it's a bitch bringing in groceries."

"Girl, stop complaining and bring your ass on."

"I'm coming."

She plopped down on the sofa while I walked back to my bedroom to find something to wear.

"Who're you going with?" she yelled.

"Brina, Cheryl and maybe Linda. I've got to call her so she can meet us. Brina and Cheryl called and said they're going to Justin's to eat and after, they'll just walk down to the club." I unhooked the gown and stepped out of it. Unlike my usual routine of placing everything on the chair, I hung it up and placed it in the garment bag. I paid too much money for this.

"If I wasn't desperate to get home to see my man, I'd come with you. I really had a good time when we went the last time." She smiled.

"You should come. It's not like Alex is at home waiting for you. More than likely, he's going to go to one of the many after-parties they've got planned."

"Why are you trying to corrupt me? Thanks but I'll pass tonight. I really want to get home. Hell, I'm about to call a cab if you don't hurry up."

I walked out of my room and into the bathroom. "I know you're not tripping after I waited for damn near forever on your ass to get here tonight."

"Hey, that wasn't my fault. You have to take that up with the airline. And you know it's never their fault. It'll be blamed on the weather or something."

I stood in the mirror and applied a fresh coat of makeup. I lined my eyes with silver and touched up my MAC lipstick. I puckered and smacked for the finishing touch. I walked over to the closet and pulled out my sexy, silver, spaghetti-strap slip dress. I stepped in it and walked into the living room where Yani was watching television.

"Ready?"

454

"I was born ready," she said as she bolted up from the couch.

I followed her out the door and locked up behind us.

"How can you stand sitting this low to the ground all the time?" she asked as she climbed into my car.

"Well, since I can't afford a big SUV or a fat ass Mercedes, I have to drive what my money can afford, so leave my Bug alone. Besides I love my car and so do your kids."

"You can afford to drive whatever you want. And I didn't say I didn't like it. I just feel like I'm sitting on the ground." She strapped herself in.

"Let me hurry and get your complaining ass outta my shit."

I flew over to Brooklyn Heights and dumped her in front of her stoop.

"You're not going to get out?"

"Nope. I'll see you tomorrow." I waited for her to drag her bags to the door and drove off when she stepped inside.

I turned up the music and dialed my girl Cheryl.

"Hello?"

"What's up, Girl? It's Asia."

"Hey. How'd the thing go tonight?"

"I wouldn't know. I didn't quite make it."

"Why?"

"Long story. Tell ya later. Where are you?"

"We're just leaving Justin's. Are you meeting us at Metro Nome?"

"Yep. I'm on the bridge now. I should be there in a few."

"We'll wait for you outside then. I'm parked right across from the club. So we'll be sitting in my car."

"All right then, Girl." I hung up and continued across the Brooklyn Bridge and made my way over to Broadway. Once I reached the general area of the club, I was lucky enough to find a pretty close spot to park around the corner.

As promised, Cheryl and Brina were waiting for me in her car. I tapped on the driver's window. Cheryl opened the door.

"Damn, Girl! What'd you do—fly a jet here?"

"Close to it. Ready?"

"Come on."

Cheryl and Brina got out of her Honda Accord and we all walked across the street to get in line.

"Is it still early enough for us to get in free?" Brina asked.

"Well, if it's not, I'll pay your way since you missed it waiting on me."

"Okay," she said with a big smile.

Cheryl turned and looked at me and gave me the eye. Signaling our inside joke about Brina. While she was cool and all, she seemed to be broke all the damn time. I've never seen somebody that works all week and never has any money. And it's not like she has any astronomical bills. She still lives at home with her parents, doesn't have a car, or any children. If she could keep her ass out of the mall trying to buy designer this and designer that, she'd be able to treat us for a damn change.

When we got to the door, we were in luck. Cheryl, like always, knew one of the guys at the door and he told them we were on the list. They hadn't opened up the other part of the club yet. It was a telltale sign that the usual crowd had yet to arrive.

"Let's go upstairs so we can scope from up there," Brina suggested.

We found a booth where we could look over the balcony at the people downstairs. We sat and laughed at those who were brave enough to wear ridiculous hairstyles and those who were brave enough to wear clothing that made it look like their extra flesh was oozing out.

"Ooh, damn. What the hell was she thinking?" Brina stared at a sistah whose clothing was so tight, you could see every hump and roll on her body. Her large breasts were smashed so tight against her that they were somewhere between mid-stomach and her chin.

"Damn. Did she look in the mirror before she walked out the door?"

Her friend walked up and handed her a drink.

They laughed as they walked down the stairs heading for the dance floor.

"Now you know that ain't right," said Brina.

"What?" Cheryl asked.

"I hope she doesn't think that she's her friend."

"Why you say that?"

"If she was really her friend, she would've told her not to come out looking like that." Cheryl and I laughed.

"I'm serious. If either one of you would've attempted some shit like that, I would let you know."

"While I'm glad to hear that, I don't think you'll ever have that problem with either one of us," Cheryl said.

"I know…"

"Asia! Look who's walking this way." Cheryl pointed to a body that was moving through the crowd on the stairs.

Headed straight toward us was none other than Hayden. Dressed to the nines, he confidently strolled up to our table and stopped. I turned my attention back to the crowd that had gathered on the dance floor.

"Good evening, ladies," he said as he flashed us his best smile.

"Hey," Cheryl and Brina replied in a lackluster tone.

I'd mentioned to them about the breakup, but didn't go into details.

Noticing that I wasn't giving him the time of day, Cheryl tapped my leg with hers. I looked up at Hayden.

"Can I talk with you for a minute?"

"You can sit here. Brina and I were about to go downstairs to dance." Cheryl motioned to Brina who was openly staring.

"Oh...Yeah, that's my cut there." Brina rose out of the seat dancing.

Hayden slid into the seat that Brina had just abandoned across from me. We watched as Cheryl and Brina headed down the stairs to the dance floor. I kept my eye on them until they became one of the many in the sea of moving bodies.

"Why haven't you returned any of my calls?"

"I've been busy."

"Asia, we need to talk."

"About what? Your baby's mama? I don't think so."

"Look, I know that I should've gone about things differently, but I love you. And being faced with the possibility of losing you a second time—I don't think that's something I want to go through again."

"The possibility? I hate to break it to you, but you've already *lost* me. Hayden..."

He cut me off. "Listen to me for one minute. If

what I say doesn't change your mind, I promise that I'll never bother you again."

"I can't think of anything you can say to make me change my mind, but I'll give you the benefit of the doubt right now. Speak your peace so we both can move on." I sat up and pretended that I was totally enthralled in what he was about to say.

He took a deep breath and looked into my eyes. From the look in his, I could tell he'd been having his share of sleepless nights.

"After leaving your place that night, I went by to see her to let her know what happened. Whatever the reason, she confessed to me that she wasn't really pregnant. That she'd only used it in hopes of deterring me from being with you. I guess I was such a pitiful sight that she felt bad for me and decided to fess up. Although I was hurt by her deception, I felt relieved. So the problem doesn't exist anymore."

"And?" He reached for my hands and held them.

"Asia, I'm not expecting you to just instantly forgive me. I mean, I know I fucked up big time, but I want the chance to make it up to you and prove to you what you mean to me. I feel that we were brought back together for a reason."

"You know, Hayden, that's all fine and good, but like you just said, I can't see myself forgiving you right now. If it's my forgiveness you want, I'm telling you now, you will have to work hard for it. You would have to help me to trust you again. But since I'm not big on forgiving, I don't know if you should waste your time." I removed my hands from his and slid out of the booth. He stood up quickly and grabbed my arm.

"Would you just think about it at least? That's all I'm asking." He gave me the look that used to melt my heart, but this time I was protecting my heart.

"I'll think about thinking about it. That's the most I can promise you." I took his hand off my arm and went to join Cheryl and Brina.

Hayden stood glued in the same spot as he watched me sway and wiggle to the non-stop beat as I maneuvered through the crowd on the stairs.

*Next time, if there is a next time, you'll think twice about fucking up*, I thought as I glanced up at him when I reached Brina and Cheryl.

# *Yani*

## CHAPTER 59

**M**y eyes fluttered open to the glaring light of the sun. It was around four in the morning when I lost the battle to sleep. I waited as long as I could for Alex to come in.

I looked over to the spot where he should've been to find it still empty. I instinctively began to worry.

I jumped out of bed and went to the bathroom. After freshening up, I went downstairs to prepare breakfast. I peeped out the front door to check if his car was still there.

A copy of the Post lay on the porch, so I grabbed it and tucked it under my arm. I continued my journey to the kitchen where I prepared a breakfast consisting of eggs, bacon, pancakes, and home fries.

On instinct, the kids appeared.

"Mommy?!" Jay ran over and hugged me.

Natalia was right behind him, giving me a tight squeeze.

"When did you get in?"

"I got in late last night and didn't want to wake you guys. Are you ready to eat?"

"Um-hmm. Everything smells delicious."

The three of us sat down for breakfast and they told me about all the events of their lives that I had missed in my absence. I told them what I did in Florida, but omitted the part about their father.

"Is Daddy still sleeping?" Jay asked.

Not knowing what to say, I jumped on something else.

"Finish up so you can clean your room and maybe we can go into the city once we get dressed." I took my plate to the sink and washed it. I heard the sound of keys being inserted into the lock. I quickly glanced at the clock on the microwave, which read 9:30.

Alex strode into the kitchen. His clothes looked disheveled, like he'd slept in them. A look of shock was on his face when he saw me standing there.

"Surprise," I calmly said.

"When did you get in?"

"Late last night. I take it that the premiere went well."

He looked down at his clothing.

"Oh, yeah. Everyone loved it."

A moment passed before another word was said.

"I'm going to go upstairs and take a shower and get dressed."

"Don't you want something to eat?"

"That's okay. I'm fine."

"Okay. I'll be down here a few more minutes and then I'll be up and you can tell me all about last night." I tried to sound upbeat, but there was something hanging in the air. I knew it had to do with me and the mess with Jarrin, but I would tell him that he would never have to worry about that again.

"Okay," he mumbled as he turned and walked out. No hug? No kiss?

I looked over at the kids who seemed a bit confused at what had just transpired. I gave them a reassuring smile as I loaded the last dishes into the dishwasher.

"When you guys finish, rinse your plates and put them in."

"Okay, Mommy."

I hugged and kissed them again, then grabbed the newspaper and walked upstairs. When I walked in the room, I could hear Alex in the shower. I contemplated stripping down and joining him, but after the cold reception I'd just received, I decided it was best just to wait for him.

I unfolded the paper and searched through it for an article about last night. I knew there had to be something after the press junket we'd put together. We had touted it as if it was the event of the year.

I turned to the second page of the entertainment

section and what I saw floored me. My heart sank as I looked in horror at a picture of my husband arm in arm with another woman. Tears instantly sprang into my eyes as I scanned through the article for information about the woman who stood in the spot I should've been in. At the sight of her name a sob caught in my throat.

I never heard the water being shut off or the door being opened. Through a blur of tears, I looked up at Alex as he stood in the doorway of the bathroom. Towel wrapped around his waist, he vigorously rubbed his hair dry with another one as he walked over to me.

"What is it?" he asked with concern in his voice.

I looked at him and watched as the color drained from his face as he watched the paper fall to the bed. He looked at me with eyes that were apologizing before he ever opened his mouth.

"Yani, Baby...I can explain."

"I think I'm gonna be sick!" I jumped off the bed and ran past him to the bathroom and locked the door. He knocked furiously.

"Open the door, Yani. Let me explain."

Over and over I heaved until the contents of my stomach would no longer come up. It fell into the toilet making a splashing sound as it made contact with the water.

"Baby, open the door so I can help you. Please," Alex begged.

I sat on the floor clutching the rim of the toilet tightly. After I caught my breath, I stood and walked to the sink to rinse my mouth and splash my face with water. After holding my head over the sink for a minute, I looked up at the reflection in the mirror.

*How did I get here again?* I wondered. How had my life taken such a drastic change in such a short time? It was if some sort of curse was bestowed upon me.

Could it be possible to lose two husbands in the span of a few days?

# *Alex*

## CHAPTER 60

"Yani, Baby, open the door!" I pleaded.

The standoff had been going on for almost twenty minutes. I heard water running again, then another wave of crying.

"Damn it!" I paced the floor as I rubbed my hand back and forth through my hair. Trying to figure out what I was going to do.

I'd brought this pain into our home. Pain I promised I'd never give her.

The knob turned and slowly Yani emerged from the bathroom. Her red swollen eyes hauntingly passed over me. I had never felt so low in my life.

"I'll be packed and out by the end of the week at the latest," she said in a monotone voice as she brushed past me.

"What are you talking about? No one asked you to leave."

"You know, Alex, I call to talk to you and you're never available to take my calls. When I really needed you, you turned your back on me."

"That's not true. I was just giving you what you asked for."

"What I asked for?!" She stared at me in disbelief. "What I asked for was your understanding! For you to be there to help me get through the situation! For you to realize that our happily-ever-after was in jeopardy at the time!"

"No, you were the one who got confused when you saw the man you had basically devoted your life to loving and it caused you to doubt your love for me!"

"No! That's not true! I told you from jump that I loved you! That I would always love you no matter what!"

"I guess you couldn't figure out who you loved more. Or better yet, who loved you more."

"Then why in the hell am I back here?!"

"But where were you last night?! Huh? The one night *I* needed you."

"I was stuck in an airport trying to get here!" She pushed by me and sat on the bed. "I wanted to surprise you. You were going to walk in and I would be there. But my flight got delayed and I ended up being stuck in the airport for four hours." A new onslaught of tears filled the corners of her eyes.

My chest felt hollow as I watched the first tear slide down her face and settle under her chin. I slowly approached the side of the bed where she sat.

"You know, Alex, I may have talked with Jarrin, and that should've been understandable considering the situation. But I didn't sleep with him. Nor did I make it publicly known that I was with him. So what's your excuse?"

"Excuse for what?"

"For this!" I caught the paper as she flung it in my face.

"I didn't sleep with her."

"Alex, you don't have to…"

I sat on the bed next to her. "Look…" She swiped at the tears. "I did *not* sleep with her. After the screening, I went my way and she went hers. I'll admit that I was hurt by all of this shit with Jarrin, but I would never stoop that low. Especially not with Taylor."

"But why her, Alex?! Out of all the millions of women in New York City who showed up last night, how did you end up with her on your arm? It was a known fact that people were going to question my absence, but this will speak volumes."

"Taylor and I are nothing but friends."

"Oh, so now you're friends? A minute ago she was stooping low. I mean, damn, I need you to help me understand this."

I was getting frustrated. It seemed the more I talked, the deeper the hole I dug was beginning to get.

"Yani, Baby… Listen to me. The photographer snapped that picture before I knew what was going on. Believe me when I tell you that *nothing happened* between Taylor and me."

"Then if nothing happened, where were you all night? Why is it that you're just rolling in here? And the first thing you did was jump into the shower?"

Unsure of how to answer that question, I just stared at her.

"I thought so."

"Why don't you believe me?"

"Why should I?"

"Why wouldn't you?"

"You know, I'm not sure what to believe right now."

"So, what are you saying?"

"What I'm saying is, maybe we should step back and reevaluate this whole thing."

"Reevaluate? There's nothing to reevaluate. Yani… I love you." I reached out for her. She placed her hand to stop me.

"And I love you, but we need to get our heads straight."

"There's nothing wrong with my head. But you know what, that's cool. You do what you have to do, because I'm going to do the same."

I grabbed my clothing and walked in the bathroom to get dressed. After I finished, I walked out the room without looking at Yani.

As I reached the front door, Natalia and Jay stood back and stared at me. I felt like hell as I walked out the door and jumped into my car. I'd promised them that I wouldn't hurt her and here I was hurting them all. And as for last night, I couldn't remember one way or the other what happened. All I know is that when I woke up on the couch at Taylor's, without looking for her, I hurriedly dressed and left.

"So what are you gonna do?"

"What do you mean, what am *I* gonna do?"

"Yani, it's been two weeks. You need to do something."

Yani sat on the floor Indian-style as I brushed her hair. She took another spoonful of the Edy's Dreamery New York Strawberry Cheesecake ice cream. She had been in blue funk since Alex drove off.

"I will."

"You will? Girl, you need to quit being petty and go and get your man. If you really sit down and think about it, you're the cause for all this shit. If you had brought your hot ass back here, instead of chasing fucking pink elephants…"

"Pink elephants?"

"Yes. That's what Jarrin is, a fucking pink elephant. And you and I both know they don't exist. Him wanting you back shouldn't have ever been an issue for you. Now what has it gotten you? Not a damn thing. Now things are screwed-up between you and Alex."

"Well, at least pictures of me and Jarrin weren't pasted in all the newspapers and how ever many magazines that have gotten a boost in sales from the infamous 'Honeymoon's Over' picture. Look at Alex Chance and his ex."

"You knew to expect your life to be under a microscope. It's not like Alex didn't let you know who he was and what he did before you said 'I do.'"

"Wait a minute, whose side are you on?"

"Neither. I'm just telling you like it is. And frankly, you're a bigger fool for proving them right. If you're so worried about what they're writing, take your ass and find your husband and make shit right."

"Well, little sister, tell me something…"

"What?"

"Why aren't you following your own advice?"

"What are you talking about?"

"Why haven't you made more efforts to make up with Hayden? I mean, he only omitted to tell you about a woman who tricked him into believing that she was pregnant so that he would stay with her. You and I both know that's the oldest trick in the book."

"See now your ass is reaching. My situation with

Hayden is w-a-a-y-y-y different than what's going on with you and Alex. And besides, you're married. Hayden and I weren't even close to making the trek down that road."

"Are you finished?"

"Hell no! And I'm not going to be finished until you straighten this shit out."

"Let's talk about something else."

"Something else? Like what?"

"Well...this morning, I found out that I'm pregnant." She shoved another spoonful of ice cream in her mouth. The brush slipped from my hand and hit the floor.

"You're what?"

"I went to the doctor and what I thought was a case of lovesickness turns out to be actual morning sickness. I'm ten weeks pregnant."

"Yani, you have to call Alex." I jumped and grabbed the phone and handed it to her.

"I can't," she said, pushing it away. The ice cream on her spoon trickled down the front of her over-sized T-shirt and fell onto the wood floor.

"Why not?" I asked baffled.

"I'm not ready to tell him yet."

"It is *his* baby?"

"I can't believe you asked me that dumb shit. Of course it's his."

"Well, I do remember how Jarrin used to have the ability to push those certain buttons."

"I said I'm ten weeks; not three. And I told you that nothing happened between us. A little kiss and that was it."

"Don't get an attitude with me 'cause your shit's a lil' raggedy."

"I don't have an attitude."

"Look, what are you gonna do?" I reached down and picked the brush up and continued to brush her hair.

"I don't know." She stared blankly into the nearly empty container.

"Yani, you need to call Alex. This is something that the two of you should be celebrating. You still love him?"

"Of course I do. More than anything," she almost whined. I could see the pain on her face.

"Are you gonna have this baby?"

"Yes!"

"Then you need to talk to your baby's daddy."

"I am. I promise."

Right then my cell phone rang.

"Hello?"

"Hey, Lady. Can you talk?"

"Not right now. Can I give you a call back?"

"Sure. Just hit me on the cell."

"Okay, bye." I hung up the phone.

Yani looked at me puzzled. "What was that all about?"

"That's not important. What's important is that you call your husband and make things right. Have the kids discussed with you how they feel?" I quickly jumped to another subject. I'd been secretly talking to Hayden, but I was unsure of where the relationship was going to go, so I decided to not tell anyone yet.

"Not in so many words, but they've been moping around the house. So I know they miss him, too."

"Now don't you think you owe it to them?"

"Asia, I asked him a simple question and he couldn't answer it. Now you tell me, what would make a man stay out all night? Remember what Daddy used to say? If a man is out past eleven o'clock at night, he's out looking for a woman. I know he had the after-party to go to, but it did end."

"I know, Yani, but you have to put everything in perspective. He was hurt. Here it was a very important moment in his life and the one person who should've been there with him was somewhere else and as far as he knew, she was with a man she had once loved almost more than life itself."

A tear slid down Yani's cheek.

"I know, Girl, I know. But…"

"Leave the buts out of it this time." I reached down and pulled her chin up so she was looking at me. "This is the man you should be fighting for. He loves you, Yani. I only hope and pray that one day I find a man who can give me half the love that Alex has for you."

"And how do you know this?"

"Because I see the way he looks at you. The way he touches you. And because he told me so."

"You talked to him?" She turned her body around to face me.

"Hey, just because you're mad with him doesn't mean the whole family has to cut him off. He calls me to see how you're doing. He picks the kids up after school sometimes."

"So you're all abandoning me?" she cried.

"We're not abandoning you. We're trying to help you realize that you need to get it together. Besides, we are not *Soul Food*," I joked with her as I made a comment about our favorite TV show.

She smiled and shook her head.

"You're right. If I was willing to entertain the thought of taking Jarrin back, mending things with Alex is definitely a no-brainer."

"Now that's my sister talking." I got up and hugged her.

She went to the kitchen and threw the empty

container in the garbage and dropped the spoon in the sink. She went over to the shoe graveyard at the door to put her sneakers on.

"You're leaving?"

"Yes, Girl. Like you said, I need to talk to my baby's daddy. And now is as good a time as ever."

"Well, I think it would be a good idea to make yourself a little more presentable." I pointed toward her hair. She reached up and ran her hand through it.

"I forgot you were doing my hair!" We both burst into laughter.

"Get your butt back over here. Matter of fact, I have a great idea of what you can do." I excitedly jumped up and ran to my room. I'd been cooking this plan up ever since I went to her house and found her balled in a fetal position on her bed.

All I had to do now was make the appropriate calls and everything would be ready.

# *Alex*

## CHAPTER 62

I sat staring out the window of my office watching the traffic go by. I never heard Ed come in.

"Hey, man. How you holding up?" He took a seat on the leather couch.

Startled I turned around.

"Holding up what?"

"You don't have to play tough man with me. Remember, I've known you much too long and I've been married longer than you. Need an ear?"

"Nah, man. I'm fine."

"You're lying through your teeth."

I smiled and exhaled the air from my lungs.

"Why don't you make the first move?"

"I don't know. I guess 'cause I feel I haven't done anything wrong. If she hadn't been in Florida weighing her options none of this would've happened."

"You know, sometimes you have to put your pride aside and do what's right. No matter whose fault it is or was, it wouldn't kill you to say I'm sorry."

"But it's not that easy."

"Why not? All you have to do is make your mouth say the words."

"Man, I've picked up the phone to call, but hung up before I dialed the last number. I miss her, but I want to give her time."

"Give her time? Man, please. Is that what she asked for?"

"Not in so many words. But…"

"But hell! Man, have you seen how miserable your ass is? And I know I speak for everyone in the office when I say this…Go home and make up with your wife! I've been married for umpteen years and the one thing I can guarantee you is that there will be ups and downs. But…" He raised his hand to silence the response that was on the tip of my tongue. "Like with anything in life worth having, it's going to take time and effort to maintain. Now, take that food for thought and as Spike told us, 'do the right thing.'"

As I toyed with the platinum diamond wedding band on my finger, I started to think of what its significance meant. Was this marriage a whirlwind affair? Did I rush into it with my eyes closed? Is the love of my wife worth fighting for?

I walked over and gave Ed a brotherly hug.

"Thanks, man."

"Sometimes we need someone else to open our

eyes to what's really going on in our lives." Before he turned to walk out of my office he smiled.

"And besides…" I was shocked to hear him burst into the chorus of Dionne Warwick's collaboration with Stevie, Gladys, and Elton. "That's what friends are for."

"Don't quit your day job," I jokingly replied.

I picked up the phone to call the house, but got the answering machine. Undeterred, I cleared the line and was about to call Yani's cell when Constance buzzed in.

"Mr. Chance, your sister-in-law is on line one."

I clicked over.

"Asia?"

"Hey. I've got a courier delivering something to you. Don't ask any questions, just follow the instructions. I'll talk to you later."

She hung up before I could utter a response.

I buzzed Constance to let her know that I was expecting a package from Asia and to bring it in right away.

*I wonder what she's up to*, I thought as I sat back and waited.

# Yani

## CHAPTER 63

E verything was in motion. Asia had sent him instructions to meet me at Jezebel's at eight o'clock tonight. I didn't know if it was my nerves or sickness that had sent me running to the bathroom. I hadn't been this nervous on our first date. I splashed cold water on my face in an attempt to get my bearings together.

"You can do this," I said to my reflection.

There was a soft tap on the door.

"Yes?"

"Come on out of there. You need to start getting ready," Asia yelled through the door.

"I'm coming." I took one last deep breath and slowly emerged into the bedroom.

Asia was fast at work picking the perfect outfit and the right accessories as I sat on the bed and watched.

"Girl, I think you're pretty in pink, so we're going to go with this." She laid the ensemble on the bed. Boot-cut slacks with the matching three-quarter-length jacket and a shirt in a softer shade of pink.

"Jezebel's is a pretty classy place. Shouldn't I wear something else?"

"Classy is what you make it. Believe me, when I finish, you'll be the classiest thing that comes through the door tonight." She went on about her business as I went over to my lingerie drawer and pulled out a pink bra and panty set. I'm a firm believer that what you have on under your clothes also plays an important part. I slipped into them. I dabbed on an ample amount of Michael. The same scent I had on when he first took me to Jezebel's.

Asia came up behind me.

"Umm, good choice." She laced my diamond pendant around my neck. A gift from Alex, of course. I fingered it and thought about the night he'd given it to me. A smile flirted at the corners of my mouth.

"Here. This bracelet is excellent." She fastened the diamond bracelet she'd given me on my wedding day on my wrist. "Now get dressed. The car will be here shortly." She ran off downstairs while I threw on my clothes.

Just as she'd said, I looked like I'd stepped off the pages of a fashion magazine. My hair hung in big, beautiful, bouncy curls and my makeup was done in a tasteful manner. I hadn't felt this beautiful in weeks.

The kids came over and gave me a hug. Even Natalia, who had become a little distant over the course of the events, walked over and hugged me tightly.

"I guess this is my stamp of approval." I smiled at my daughter who was growing into a lovely young lady.

"You look great, Mommy." A car horn blew outside.

"I don't know why I couldn't drive myself over there."

"Stop complaining and get your butt out of here. And don't worry, we won't wait up," Asia jokingly said as she pecked me on the cheek.

I opened the door and climbed into the back of the black Lincoln Town Car and waved goodbye to them as the car pulled off. I stared out the window thinking about seeing Alex for the first time in weeks. I made a promise to myself right then and there, that I would never let things progress to this point ever again.

The driver jumped on the highway heading in the wrong direction. "Excuse me, I think...No. I know you're going the wrong way. We're headed to..." I was cut off by a familiar voice.

"Just sit back and relax. We have some unfinished business to take care of."

"Jarrin?" I asked in shock.

This could not be happening. Not now.

# Alex

## CHAPTER 64

I sat at the bar scanning the room every time the door opened.

"Where could she be?"

I checked my watch. Yani was well over an hour late. I picked up my cell and punched in the house number this time after trying unsuccessfully to reach her on her cell. Two rings later Natalia answered.

"Nat, it's Daddy. Did Mommy leave yet?"

"Hi, Daddy. She left here a long time ago to meet you at the restaurant. Where are you?"

"Who's there with you?"

"Auntie's here."

"Let me speak to her," I abruptly said. Natalia called for Asia to pick up the phone.

"Alex?"

"How long ago did Yani leave?"

"A while ago. She should've been there and you guys should be at the hotel by now."

"She's not here, Asia. Has she called since she left?"

"No. The kids and I have been here the entire time. The phone hasn't rung once."

"Was she driving?"

"No. I had a car service pick her up."

"Which company? Do you have the number?"

"Wait a second. I'll click over and call them on the other line."

I sat and waited for her to return. She clicked back over as the phone rang. The service informed us that someone called and cancelled the pickup.

"Alex, something's wrong. I saw the car when it came. I was standing at the door when she climbed in."

"Did anything seem out of the ordinary? Was it a normal car?"

"Yes. A Town Car. The ones they always send."

"Did you see the driver?"

"I-I can't remember now."

"Think, damn it! Did the driver get out of the car? Did he open the door? Did he say anything?" My heart was racing.

"No. She opened the door and climbed in."

"Do you remember seeing the driver at all? Was he black, white, what?!" I settled up my tab and rushed out to the valet area to retrieve my car.

"Look, Alex, I'm just as worried as you, but I use the car service so much that I didn't pay attention to the driver. I only look at them if I'm riding with them and that's usually once I'm sitting in the back seat and I catch a glimpse of him in the mirror."

"Look, call every car service and see if they had a pickup scheduled for our address. I'm going to call and see if there were any accidents reported in the area."

"Alex, she's got to be okay. We've got to find her, Alex!" Asia sounded as if she was on the verge of crying.

"Get yourself together. You've got to keep your head so the kids won't know something's wrong. We'll find her. I promise. If I find out anything I'll call you and you do the same."

"Okay," she sniffled.

*What could've happened?* I thought as I got into my car. I began to say a silent prayer.

*God, please let me find her and she's okay. Please let it be that she's stuck in traffic or the driver got lost. I promise if you bring her back to me I'll never let her away from my side again.*

❤❤❤❤

I gripped the steering wheel tightly as I drove back to my office.

"Damn it!" I banged my fist on the wheel in frustration at the amount of traffic. As I pulled up to the building, I double-parked on the side street around the back and ran through the doors. Once up in my office, I picked up the Yellow Pages and turned to the section for hospitals. One after another, I called each and every one to no avail. I called Asia to see if she'd had any luck.

"Nothing yet. I have a few more companies to call."

"I'm gonna call a friend of mine who's a police officer and see if he can tell me if anyone has reported a stolen car that fits the description."

"Call me back."

"Bye." I pulled my Rolodex out and punched in Johnny's number.

"Detective Johnson here," he bellowed into the phone.

"Hey, JJ, it's Alex. Man, I need a favor."

"Hey, Alex. What's going on?"

"I need a huge favor from you. My wife was supposed to meet me for dinner tonight and she never showed up. I know a person has to be missing for more than twenty-four hours, but her sister had a car pick her up and no one has seen or heard from her since. I was wondering if you could check and see if there's been a report of a car being stolen in any of the boroughs. You know I wouldn't bother you if it wasn't an emergency."

"I understand. Give me a minute." He placed me on

hold. I sat tapping my fingers on the desk. It seemed as if I'd been on hold forever when he returned five minutes later.

"Alex?"

"I'm here."

"Yo, man, we did have a driver call in and say that his car had been stolen and the perp tied him up and left him in the bathroom at a gas station. The guy took his jacket and hat, after asking him directions for an address in Brooklyn."

"Does he know where about in Brooklyn?"

"Yeah. Over in the Brooklyn Heights area."

My heart dropped as Johnny repeated my address to me.

"Did he get a good look at the guy? Did the guy say anything else to him?"

"The description he gave was sort of iffy on the race. But, the guy has light-colored eyes. Oh, he said something about surprising his wife."

"His wife?" Right then a light went on in my head. But why would Jarrin come all the way to New York to see Yani?

"Do you think this has something to do with your wife?"

"It's her ex-husband. And if he's come this far to see her, I suspect that he's dangerous." I sat staring out the window.

"Look, don't worry. I'll put out an APB. Especially

SHONDA CHEEKES

since this has stepped up from a carjacking to a kid-
napping. Can you get a picture of her and possibly
him over to me ASAP?"

*A picture of him? Yeah, in the kids' baby books.*

"I've got to go home and get it."

"I'll meet you there."

I hung up the phone and rushed out to my car. I
felt as if I was racing against time as I sped toward
home. I pulled up to the curve in front of the house
and ran up the steps. I fumbled with my keys as I
searched for the one to open the front door. Asia
heard me and rushed and opened the door.

"What's the matter?" Her face registered the panic
I felt.

"It's Jarrin. He's got her. I need to find a picture
of him to give to the police." I ran past her to the
upstairs closet where Yani had stored her old photo
albums.

Asia called Natalia. She came out her room and
looked at me curiously.

"Nat, I need a big favor, okay?" She shook her head
as she listened for Asia's request.

"Do you happen to have a picture of your dad?"
She looked over at me.

"No, not Alex—Jarrin."

Natalia slowly nodded her head yes as tears began
to fill her eyes. I stopped my frantic search.

"Where?!" Asia and I both blurted out.

"In my room. I-I just had it so that I…" she whispered.

"No, Baby. No one is mad with you about it. Could you get it for me?" She shook her head and walked to her room with Asia and me in tow.

With shaking hands, she went into a box that sat on her dresser and retrieved the picture. She looked at me as she handed it to me. Her eyes were saying that she was sorry. As if she'd committed a crime against me by having it in her possession. I knelt down in front of her.

"Sweetie, I'm not mad with you for this. He is your father and I expect you to love him." I kissed her forehead and hugged her tightly.

"Has he done something to Mommy?"

"We don't know, but he has her and we need this picture so that the police can find him." I looked to see if she understood me. She nodded her head. I stood and wrapped my arm around her shoulder.

"Asia, can you go and get the picture of Yani off our dresser?" She hurried off as I walked downstairs with Natalia to wait for Johnny.

"Daddy, are you coming home?" I looked down at her and wiped the tear from her cheek.

"Yes, I am, Sweetie. And I promise I'll never leave again." She smiled and hugged me.

"Do me a favor. Go downstairs with your brother. Don't let him know what's going on, okay? Make sure to keep him down there until either Asia or I come and get you. He doesn't need to know what's going on."

"Okay. Find my mommy, Daddy. Please?"

"Don't worry, I will."

# *Yani*

## CHAPTER 65

I silently looked out the window as Jarrin drove toward Connecticut. He'd demanded I give him my bag earlier after hearing my cell phone ring. I slipped my two-way out before I passed my purse up to him. I turned it on silent and slipped it down the front of my pants and fastened my jacket to keep the slight bulge from showing.

He began to slow the car down as he looked at the paper in his hand. I craned my neck in an attempt to get the street name. He drove a little further down the street and took what looked to be a remote of some kind out of his pocket and pulled into the driveway of a house that seemed to be abandoned. The garage opened wide enough for us to pull inside and then closed behind us.

Totally pissed at the situation, I sat with my arms folded across my chest as I recited the street name over and over in my head. Jarrin opened the back door for me to get out. I didn't budge.

"Get out, Yani."

"No," I said. Drawing my arms tighter around me, I gave him a hateful look and rolled my eyes, then I continued to look straight ahead.

He grabbed my upper arm and yanked me out.

"Look, you *will* do what I say and *give* me what I want. Or you will see a side of me that…"

"That what? I've already seen that." I placed my hand on my hip and took a stance of defiance.

He grinned at me. "I forgot you've got a lil' backbone now. I wonder if this will change your tune." He pulled a gun from his waistband and stuck it in my face. My eyes opened wide in disbelief. My hand fell off my hip and hung at my side. "Yeah, I thought so. Now, let's go." He shoved the gun in my side and instinctively my hands went up to signal my defeat.

We walked into a door that led into the house. He motioned with the gun for me to keep going. I carefully walked through the kitchen and into another room that, if furnished, would have been the living room. A table with a light on it and two chairs sat in the corner. He pulled out a chair and told me sit. I frantically looked around the room for any other signs of life.

He pulled a bag that was sitting on the floor over to him and reached in and pulled out some twine. I couldn't believe that he was going to tie me up?

Knowing that I had to think fast, I made a request.

"Jarrin. Before you do that, can I please go to the bathroom? We've been riding for a while and this whole situation really has my stomach in knots. I wouldn't want to, you know…"

He smiled.

"Okay. There's one down the hall." I stood and slowly made my way down to it.

"Oh, and if you're thinking about slipping out the window, forget about it. It's boarded up." He smiled and blew me a kiss.

I continued down the hall until I found the bathroom. I clicked on the light. I was surprised to find that it was cleaned and stocked with toilet paper, a toothbrush, and any other necessity Jarrin might have needed. I suspected that he'd been here for quite some time. I locked the door behind me and pulled out my two-way. Frantically I punched in the address and a quick message to Alex. I prayed he got it. For insurance, I sent a message to Asia, and then one to the kids' email accounts. Someone was bound to get my message. When I finished, I stuffed it in the inside pocket of my jacket. I flushed the toilet and ran the water pretending to wash my hands. I looked in the mirror to straighten myself out. I fluffed my hair out and took a deep breath before I stepped out into the hall.

"I was starting to think you fell in for minute. Feel better?" Jarrin asked.

"Not exactly. I'll feel better if you stop this madness and let me leave."

"If you play your cards right, that can be arranged." He motioned for me to sit in the chair.

"You don't have to do this, Jarrin. I'm not going anywhere—nor am I going to try anything. We can sit here and talk about whatever it is that you want." I smiled at him sincerely.

"Oh so you're ready to talk now? Well, let me see what subject do I want to talk about?" He placed his free hand under his chin. "I think I'd like to talk about my money." He looked at me harshly.

"Your money? You mean the money in the bag from the house? I don't have it."

"But you're going to get it."

"No, you don't understand. I never brought it with me to New York."

"What are you talking about?"

"Don't you understand? I couldn't justify why I was traveling with that much money in a duffel bag. So I left it in Florida." I tried to remain cool and calm.

"You left it in Florida? Where in Florida?"

"In a safe deposit box."

"And where is the key for this alleged box?"

"It's at home with all my important papers. It's not

like I would carry something like that around on my keychain with my house keys."

"Damn! Damn!" he said as he punched his clenched fist against the wall. Each hit sent a shudder through me.

"What am I going to do?" He sank to the floor with his hands on the side of his head.

Trying to think fast, I made a suggestion.

"What if I could help you with a little something?"

"What's a little something?"

"Around a hundred and fifty thousand?"

He started to laugh as he slid back up to standing position.

"Still the same old Yani. Always trying to fix it. A hundred and fifty thou? You're nowhere in the ball-park with that figure, but I just got a better plan. That husband of yours, he's probably got what? A few million stuffed securely away somewhere. I wonder how much you're worth to him?" He walked over and shoved the gun in my face. His eyes shimmered as he desperately looked at me. He grabbed my bag off the table and searched through it for my phone.

"Why are you doing this?"

"Because I'm in sort of a desperate situation." He pulled out my cell phone. "Here. Call him." He placed the phone in my trembling hands and watched as I dialed the number.

# Asia

## CHAPTER 66

The house was bustling with movement after it was invaded by police officers. Alex's friend Johnny was the epitome of tall, dark and handsome. His smile would melt butter in sub-zero weather. If he had been here under different circumstances, I would've been probing Alex for more details about his status, but right now, my mind was on my sister.

I prayed that Jarrin wouldn't do anything stupid. Or his days on earth would definitely be numbered.

Alex listened as Johnny gave the other officers instructions. Suddenly, his two-way pager went off. He opted to ignore it, trying to make sure that he didn't miss anything that was being said. Then a few minutes later, mine went off. Alex glanced at me as I went to retrieve it from my bag. I flipped it open.

From the number on the screen, I knew it was Yani. I ran out of the room calling Alex.

"Alex! Alex! Check yours! It's Yani!" Every head

in the room turned in my direction. Johnny walked over and looked at my screen.

"They're in Connecticut!" Everyone ran to grab their coats.

"Asia, stay here with the kids. I'll call as soon as we know anything."

"Stay here?! NO! I'm going. She's my sister!"

"Look, we don't know right now what his mind-set is. So it would be best if you remained here with the children. I wouldn't want you to get hurt." Johnny placed his hand on my shoulder in a reassuring gesture. I shook my head in agreement.

Alex walked over and hugged me.

"Keep the kids off the phones. She may try to call."

"Be careful, Alex."

"I'll try." I grabbed his hand tightly as he got ready to walk out the door. He spun around.

"Bring my sister back safe," I pleaded through tears.

"Don't worry. I'm not coming back here without her," he assured me.

I stood in the door and watched as the three-car caravan sped off down the street. The fall chill wrapped itself around me as I blankly stared at the spot where I'd last seen my sister. All I could do was hope and pray that she'd be okay.

I felt a hand on my shoulder. Natalia had heard everyone leave and came upstairs to investigate.

"Did they find her?"

"I think so, Baby. She's going to be okay." I hugged her and walked back into the house. At least I was praying she would be.

I thought about calling Hayden, but opted not to. Talking to him wouldn't do anything but bring me down more. It seemed to me that he was trying too hard and I wasn't trying hard enough.

*I could call Linda*, I thought as I picked up the phone. As I began to dial her number, I thought of exactly who I needed to call.

"Hello, Mama?"

"Asia? Is everything okay? You sound like something is wrong."

No one could accuse Janice of not knowing her children.

"It's Yani, Mama." I sobbed out the story to her.

"Don't worry, Baby. She's going to be just fine. We just have to have faith that God will step in and take care of this. Where are the kids?"

"They're downstairs in the basement." I wiped my nose with the balled-up piece of tissue I had in my hand.

"Good. They don't need to be in the middle of this." We were quiet for a few seconds.

"Do you think I should call Carmen?"

"I'm not sure if you should. There's really nothing she can do from down here. But if you just need to talk to her, yes—call her."

"Mama, I'm just so scared. How did he find out where she lived? Do you know any reason he would have to want to hurt her? From what she told us, he's got another family and didn't give any indication that he was that interested in getting back together with her. So why?"

"Maybe we *should* call Carmen. You know they talk about everything. She just might know what brought him that far. Hold on." She clicked over and dialed her number.

"Asia?"

"I'm here." The phone was ringing.

"Hello?"

"Carmen? It's Janice and Asia."

"Hey, ladies!"

"I wish I could say that this was a friendly call, but something has gone terribly wrong in New York."

"What's wrong with Yani?!"

"It's Jarrin. He's kidnapped her and took her somewhere in Connecticut. Alex and the police are on their way up there, but we're trying to figure out why he would do this? Did Yani tell you anything?" I waited for her answer.

"It's got to be the money." She sighed.

"What money?"

"That's what the whole charade was about. He pretended that he wanted them to get back together so he could get the money."

"But what money?!"

"Money he had stashed in the attic of the house. That was the whole reason for him showing up to the house. It was over three million dollars. He told Yani that he'd left it for her and the kids, but we all know that Yani wasn't going to step foot one into that attic."

I tried to remember the conversations I'd had with Yani to remember if she'd mentioned any of this.

"So where is the money now?"

"It's here at my house. She couldn't travel with it and she wanted to make sure that he was gone before she tried to wire any of it."

"In other words, he's broke?"

"That sums it up. I didn't think it was that serious though. I know she said that it seemed like he was going to follow her when she left the hotel, but he doesn't know where we live now. And with the tight security we have, there was no way he was going to get in here."

"Do you think I should call and let Alex know?"

"I don't know."

"Maybe you should just sit tight and let the police handle it from here. If Yani wants Alex to know about the money, she'll tell him," Mama said. "Asia, you go and see about the kids and give us a call as soon as you hear something."

"I will, Mama." I said my goodbyes and walked to the basement.

So that's what it was all about. Jarrin had become a really desperate man to pull this. I began to worry what the outcome of it would be when he found out that she didn't have the money.

*Alex*

## CHAPTER 67

We raced up I-95 with the lights and sirens blaring. Johnny had put in a call to the local police in Bridgeport and had them on alert to our arrival. They gave us in-structions where to meet them so they could assist us in finding the address.

I sat in the backseat praying. Asking God to forgive me for being such a fool. Begging Him for Yani's safe return.

We exited the highway and pulled into the Barnum Museum where we were greeted by the local sheriff. He informed us that he had a man at each end of the block watching the activity of the house to make sure they didn't slip out before we could get there.

We followed him a few miles before turning into a neighborhood near a lake. We parked across the street from a house that seemed to be abandoned. The neighborhood seemed to be well-to-do, other than the abandoned two-story dwelling that was boarded-up. For some reason it seemed to stand out to me. I thought I saw a light shining through one of the slats in the boarded-up front window.

Johnny turned and addressed me from across the seat.

"Stay here. We don't know if he's armed or not. No need for you trying to be a hero." Everyone exited the car as I sat and looked out the window at the abandoned house across the street. There was something that was pulling me to it. Although I'd been informed to stay put, something in my heart told me to go to that house.

I slowly exited out of the car once the officers had entered the other house and walked casually across the street. I crept around to the side of the house where I found an unlocked door that led into the garage. I pulled out the penlight I carried on my key ring to give me a little light. Inside the garage was the black Lincoln that he'd used to bring them there. I glanced around and found the door that led into the house. Before my sensible mind could kick in and remind me that this wasn't a plot in a movie, I grabbed the handle and went in as quietly as possible. I placed my penlight back in my pocket.

"Call him again!" I heard a man's angry voice yell.

"I've called him how many times? I'm telling you,

he doesn't have his phone on him," I heard Yani desperately trying to convince him. I patted my pockets and realized that I didn't have my phone so, it had to be me that they're talking about.

My heart was banging rapidly against my ribcage as I tried to figure out my next move.

"You better hope for your sake that he answers soon." I peeked around the corner and spotted him pointing a gun in her face. Right then and there I knew I had to do something and fast.

I knew I should've run across the street and got Johnny and the other officers, but I didn't know if I had enough time for that.

Yani sat in a chair. Her eyes were red from crying. Since his back was to me, I slowly crept up. Yani looked up and spotted me. I signaled her to remain quiet and prayed that he didn't register the look in her eyes. She quickly cast her eyes down toward the floor.

"Why are you risking everything for this? What happens when I do contact Alex? You know he's going to contact the police. And then what? If you get caught, you're going to jail and the people who were looking for you will…"

"Shut up! I don't want to hear that shit! You know damn well why I'm doing this!"

"And what about Dede and the kids? Have you

stopped to think about them? Oh, I forgot—family isn't that big up on your list of priorities. If it was, we wouldn't be here, now would we?"

"I guess we wouldn't." He smirked. Yani quickly glanced up at me as she signaled me with her hands to wait.

"Did our time together mean anything to you?" she asked with as much emotion as she could evoke.

He softened. "Of course it did. I loved you, but sometimes in life you have to do things that you're not proud of. This being one of them," he jokingly said.

"So why did you feed me all of that garbage about wanting to be with me and seeing the kids?"

"Yani, you know why. Honestly, I thought you would've moved on with your life much sooner than you did. I mean that's a long ass time to wait for someone you didn't know what happened to. Me, I probably would've waited a month or two before I would've had someone else up in there taking your place." He laughed.

My stomach turned at the way he talked to her as if she was nothing but gum under his shoe. I couldn't understand how he could be so cruel to the woman who had given him his first-born. The woman who had devoted her life to him. My next reaction shocked me. I charged at him and before I knew it, he and I were rolling on the floor. In all the commotion, Yani scrambled to get out of the way.

I kicked him as he tried to aim the gun at me. His arm jerked back and suddenly the gun went off. Everything seemed to move in slow motion as I watched my wife's eyes grow wide and her body sink to the floor.

"Nooooooo," I cried out in pain.

Jarrin looked at her in disbelief. Just then the door burst open. Johnny and the other officers came in with their guns drawn. Jarrin turned, still blazing his gun.

"Drop your weapon!" Johnny yelled.

Jarrin looked over at Yani as I cradled her in my arms.

"I'm sorry, Baby," he said with tears in his eyes. "I never meant for things to turn out this way."

Suddenly, he held his gun up as if he was going to fire it, but before he could get a good aim, the shots rang out. He crumbled to the floor as he took his last breath. All I could do was rock Yani and plead with her to hold on.

"Come on, Baby! You can't leave me! Not now!"

Johnny came over to me as the sheriff called for an ambulance. He knelt down and looked at Yani.

"Alex, let me see where she's been hit." He tried to remove my arms from her.

"No! Leave her!"

"Alex, please, man. The paramedics will be here soon. If you don't let go, they can't help her." He pulled me up as we heard the paramedics run into the house. They went to work attending to her. I looked at where she lay and saw the pool of blood. My knees went weak. Johnny held me up.

"Come on, Man. Let's go." As we walked out, I overheard the sheriff tell one of the paramedics that they needed a body bag for Jarrin. I glanced down at his crumpled body one last time. His face bore a smile. It was as if he welcomed his death.

Johnny led me out the door and over to the ambulance that waited to carry Yani to the hospital.

"We'll follow them to the hospital. They're going to be working on her and you may be in the way." I shook my head as I watched them run from the house with her on a stretcher.

I thought to myself, *I never got a chance to tell her that I loved her. I never got to tell her that I was sorry.*

# Asia

## CHAPTER 68

ere we are on the verge of another year. I looked in the mirror making the last adjustments to my dress. There was a knock on the door. I flipped the light off and opened the door. Johnny stood on the other side. Roses in hand.

"Hello, beautiful," he beamed at me.

"Hello yourself, handsome. Ready?"

"Of course." He extended his arm as I hooked mine through it and walked out the room. We took the elevator downstairs and walked over to the ballroom.

"Hey, Asia!" Carmen said as she made her way over to hug me.

"Hey, Lady."

"I'm so glad you could make it again this year. And who is this handsome hunk of a man?" She held out her hand for Johnny. He graciously shook it.

"Carmen, this is Johnny Johnson. Johnny, this is our gracious hostess, Carmen, and her handsome husband, Bryce, is around here somewhere I'm sure."

"You know he is."

"It's nice to meet you, Carmen. This seems to be the happening spot tonight." Johnny glanced around the room.

"We do this every year and it seems like each time is better than the last."

"We're not going to keep you. I know you have other guests to attend to."

"I'm glad that you guys could come. Make sure not to leave this time without saying goodnight, Miss." Carmen gave me the eye.

"I promise." I smiled as I grabbed a hold of Johnny and led him deeper into the room.

"She's a ball of energy and damn, is she tall!"

"She used to be a model, but now she's the proud mother of three and part-owner of one of the most successful event planning businesses in the area."

"I like hearing that. There's nothing like doing your own thing."

I searched the room for an empty table. Spotting one in the back near the corner.

*Is this the same spot?* I thought. It was damn near the same table I had sat at last year snuggled up with Hayden. How time changes things.

Hayden would still call from time to time. That is, until he saw me out one night with Johnny. How ironic that it was our first date? The last I heard, the girl who supposedly was having his baby but wasn't, is now *really* having his baby. I guess she wasn't as bad as he said.

Brina had once challenged me, saying that I was anti-men after we'd had a lengthy discussion about all the reasons I would not see Hayden anymore. I told her, "I'm not anti-men, just anti-game."

Johnny and I had a seat. "Would you like something to drink?"

"Sure." I smiled at him as he made his way through the crowd that seemed to grow by the minute, over to the bar. I felt truly blessed to have Johnny in my life. While I wish the circumstances that led to our meeting were different, I thank God for answering all my prayers. Even the one about sending a good man my way.

Johnny came back to the table and sat my apple martini in front of me.

"Thanks, JJ."

"You're welcome." He placed the drink on the table and reached for me.

"Can I have this dance?"

I blushed. "Why, you most certainly can."

He slid my chair out for me and waited for me to get up. Mystikal's "Shake Ya Ass" was pumping strong through the speakers. I broke it down and did as Mystikal asked. Johnny was right on me. Carmen and Bryce came and took the space next to us.

After the tragedy that had happened with my sister,

I promised to live my life to the fullest, because no one is promised tomorrow.

As far as me and Johnny, where will things go from here? Who knows? I just want to enjoy the ride while I can.

Three months later and we're still trying to put the horrible event out of our minds.

"Are you ready, Baby?"

"In a minute," she called out through the bathroom door.

"Come on now. It's a quarter till."

"I'm coming!"

The lock clicked and Yani walked into the room.

"What do you think?" She spun around.

I walked over to her and kissed her passionately. "I think you need to redo your lipstick." We laughed.

She playfully popped me on the arm. "And you're complaining about me taking too long."

"Baby, you're going to be the most beautiful woman in the room tonight." Her lavender dress fit her curves stunningly as it took a slight plunge in the back.

I wrapped my arms around her and rubbed the spot that had once held a piece of me and her.

After being shot in the stomach, she lost the baby. The doctor told us that there was a possibility that she would never be able to conceive again. I assured her that the two we had were more than enough for me.

"We'd better get going before Carmen comes up here looking for us."

"I know. She's already called five times." She laughed.

I handed her patent leather handbag to her as I ushered her out the door. We stood embracing, as we waited for the elevator.

After standing in the emergency room that night, not knowing whether or not my wife was going to make it, I promised God that if He spared her life, I would make sure to show her how much she was loved every day. I'd never take her for granted again.

After three hours of not knowing, the doctor came out to give us the good and bad news.

"You wife has lost a lot of blood, but she seems to be strong-willed and I think she's going to be just fine. But the baby..."

"Baby?" I asked as I looked at the scrawny doctor with wire spectacles.

"Yes, Mr. Chance. Your wife was almost four months' pregnant. Didn't you know that?"

"No. She... hadn't told me yet." I started to really feel like a jerk.

"I'm sorry, Mr. Chance. There was nothing we could do."

"Can I see her now?" I followed him to her room where she was hooked up to a monitor.

"Would you like to see the baby? It was a girl."

"How about my wife? Is she okay? When is she going to be able to leave?" I hit him with a barrage of questions in an effort to forget the one he'd asked me.

"We won't know anything until tomorrow."

"Thank you, doctor," I said as I eagerly shook his hand.

"I'll leave you alone now. If you decide that you do want to see the baby, just let us know." He smiled and backed out of the room.

I walked over closer to the bed and grabbed Yani's hand and kissed it. Yani's eyes fluttered open. I bent down and kissed her on the lips.

"I love you, Mrs. Chance."

She smiled. In a whisper through dry, chapped lips, she responded, "I love you, too, Mr. Chance."

"Have you talked to the doctor at all?"

Tears spilled out her eyes. "I was going to tell you tonight. Alex, I'm..."

"Don't." I placed my fingers on her lips to silence her. "I'm the one that's sorry. Things should've been handled differently, but we can't worry about that now. The best thing we can do is make everything from this point on count."

She closed her eyes and another tear squeezed out and rolled down her cheek.

"Did you see her?" she asked as I wiped the tear.

"No. You?"

"Yes. She's beautiful. See her, Alex. At least say goodbye."

"Shhh. Don't start worrying. You just lie here and relax so I can take you home."

"A piece of me—a piece of you," she whispered as her eyes fluttered closed.

I looked at the peaceful look on her face. I kissed her again and walked out to the nurse's station. I took a big gulp and asked them about the Chance baby.

The nurse looked at me with sympathetic eyes and told me to wait a moment. She picked up the phone and called someone, then looked up at me. She gave me directions and I headed off.

The doctor that had taken me in to see Yani was waiting for me.

"You've made the right decision."

He took me to a room and I was instantly filled with grief as the nurse rolled in a tiny bed. While she was barely bigger than the palm of my hand, she had developed into a baby. They had wrapped her in a hospital blanket. She looked so peaceful. I would never forget the tragedy that caused me to lose her.

At that moment I thought of the perfect name for her. I picked her up and held her close to me.

"Goodbye, Angel," I said as I placed a kiss on her little hand.

Even though we would never get to know her, I felt that God had sent us this little Angel to remind us of what we had.

❤❤❤

The incident made the news and when we got home, there was a slew of flowers and get-well cards at the house and both of our offices.

When I went back to work the next week, I found an envelope on my desk with my name on it. Inside was a letter from Taylor. With all the madness that had happened, I'd completely forgotten all about my incident with her. I opened the envelope and pulled out the folded paper.

"Alex, I just wanted to let you know that nothing happened that night. You were gone when I woke up and I never got a chance to tell you. While I do admit that my intentions were anything but respectable, after going on and on about how much you loved Yani, you passed out. I merely covered you up and went in my room to sleep. So, if you've been beating yourself up about cheating on your wife, you didn't. I

SHONDA CHEEKES

hope she has a speedy recovery. I have to admit, she is the woman for you."

I smiled as I tore the letter up and placed it in the wastebasket.

❤❤❤

"Earth to Alex," Yani said loudly. I jumped. She was standing in the elevator holding the door open for me. "You coming?"

I smiled. "I wouldn't be anywhere else."

She smiled and pulled me into the elevator with her. We got to the lobby and made our way over to the ballroom.

Carmen must have smelled us walk in. She hurried over to us; with Bryce in tow as usual.

"Well it's about time. I thought you guys were going to miss the countdown. Here…" She handed us hats and party horns.

"Hey, Man," Bryce said as we embraced in our sacred brotherly hug.

"Yani, you work it, Girl. That dress is gorgeous." Carmen inspected Yani.

"Thanks, Girl. You're looking good yourself. As usual."

"It's time to start the countdown. Everyone grab a glass of champagne," the DJ called out over the microphone.

"Well, I've got to do my thing. Come on, guys," Carmen said. We followed her to the middle of the room and took our place next to her and Bryce in front of the big-screen television as we watched the ball in Times Square once again make its journey down the pole.

"Wow, can you believe that just last year, you two kissed for the very first time in this very room?"

"Time seems to fly when you're having fun," I said as I kissed Yani softly on the lips.

❤❤❤

"Ten, nine, eight..." Asia and Johnny came and stood next to us.

"Five, four, three..." I looked over at Yani who seemed to be glowing.

"I love you, Mr. Chance."

"I love you, Mrs. Chance." As everyone blew their horns indicating that we had made it into yet another year, I gave my wife a passionate kiss.

"Maybe we'll work on those odds tonight." She looked up at me and smiled.

"What odds?" I asked.

"You know, the ones against us conceiving." She winked at me.

"So that means that I don't have to be a gentleman this time?"

"You didn't have to be one last year."

"I didn't?"

"No. I just thought you were scared."

"Scared? If you say so."

"I'm serious."

"You mean to tell me that if I had tried hard enough, I would've…"

"Umm hmm."

She gave me a wicked smile as we stood in the middle of the room embracing.

I pulled her in closer and gave her another kiss.

This symbolic event would become a yearly ritual in our lives as I silently vowed to love her for the rest of my life.

# ABOUT THE AUTHOR

SHONDA CHEEKES resides in Pembroke Pines, Florida with her husband and kids. In addition to *Another Man's Wife*, she also penned one of the five novellas in *Blackgentlemen.com* entitled "Lessons Learned," and has recently published her newest novel, *In The Midst of It All*. She can be reached via email at PubliSista@aol.com.